IRRESISTIBLE PRAISE FOR THE AUTHORS OF *IRRESISTIBLE FORCES*

Jo Beverley
"Arguably today's most skillful writer of
intelligent historical romance."
—*Publishers Weekly*

Lois McMaster Bujold
"Bujold continues to prove what marvels genius
can create out of basic space operatics."
—*Booklist*

Mary Jo Putney
"It's no wonder that bestseller Putney is a favorite
of romance fans. . . . A master storyteller."
—*Booklist*

Jennifer Roberson
"Sensitive readers of both sexes should appreciate how
Roberson rises above the usual genre clichés."
—*Publishers Weekly*

Deb Stover
"Clever, original, and quick-witted."
—*Publishers Weekly*

Catherine Asaro
"Catherine Asaro continues to dazzle us with brilliance
in combining science, romance, and adventure. . . ."
—*Romantic Times*

Irresistible Forces

Edited by
CATHERINE ASARO

A SIGNET BOOK

SIGNET

Published by New American Library, a division of
Penguin Group (USA) Inc., 375 Hudson Street,
New York, New York 10014, USA
Penguin Group (Canada), 90 Eglinton Avenue East, Suite 700, Toronto,
Ontario M4P 2Y3, Canada (a division of Pearson Penguin Canada Inc.)
Penguin Books Ltd., 80 Strand, London WC2R 0RL, England
Penguin Ireland, 25 St. Stephen's Green, Dublin 2,
Ireland (a division of Penguin Books Ltd.)
Penguin Group (Australia), 250 Camberwell Road, Camberwell, Victoria 3124,
Australia (a division of Pearson Australia Group Pty. Ltd.)
Penguin Books India Pvt. Ltd., 11 Community Centre, Panchsheel Park,
New Delhi - 110 017, India
Penguin Group (NZ), cnr Airborne and Rosedale Roads, Albany,
Auckland 1310, New Zealand (a division of Pearson New Zealand Ltd.)
Penguin Books (South Africa) (Pty.) Ltd., 24 Sturdee Avenue,
Rosebank, Johannesburg 2196, South Africa

Penguin Books Ltd., Registered Offices:
80 Strand, London WC2R 0RL, England

Published by Signet, an imprint of New American Library, a division of Penguin
Group (USA) Inc. Previously published in a New American Library trade
paperback edition.

First Signet Printing, January 2006
10 9 8 7 6 5 4 3 2 1

 REGISTERED TRADEMARK—MARCA REGISTRADA

Printed in the United States of America

To the dancers and teachers of

The Ballet Theatre of Maryland

for their expertise, kindness, insights
and most of all
for helping a starry-eyed young girl
reach for her dreams.

ACKNOWLEDGMENTS

I would like to thank the people who made this book possible. To Denise Little, who listened to my dreams of such an anthology and led the way; to Laura Anne Gilman, our much appreciated editor at Roc; to our agent, Lucienne Diver, who worked wonders for us; to Marty Greenberg, for his help and support; to my assistant editors, Jeri Smith-Ready and Tricia Schwaab, for their thoughtful input; to the publisher and all the fine people at NAL who put out this book; to publicist Binnie Syril Braunstein, for her enthusiasm on our behalf; and to the authors, who were a joy to work with.

—Catherine Asaro

CONTENTS

INTRODUCTION

Writers are fond of two adages: Write what you like to read, and write what you know. I've always enjoyed love stories and I'm a scientist, so I naturally write science fiction romance. When I first started, I had no idea it was an unusual combination. I didn't know optimistic stories of courtship and love had an entire genre called romance or that science fiction with a strong scientific basis was called hard science fiction. I just knew I enjoyed both.

I never expected my work to stir controversy. So I was startled by the commotion my first book caused. Commentators remarked with surprise on how I blended strong romance with strong science fiction. Yet to me, both romance and science are integral aspects of life. I have always thought that the sharp distinction we make between our emotions and intellects arises more out of cultural expectations than an intrinsic quality of the human mind.

Some of the best authors in both romance and the genres of science fiction and fantasy have blended these aspects of our humanity to beautiful effect, as in Ursula Le Guin's classic science fiction romance, "Forgiveness Day." In fact, the seeds of speculative romance are as old as storytelling itself, such as in the Greek myths, when our ancestors tried to understand both the human heart and the universe they lived in by invoking a pantheon of gods and goddesses with the power to alter nature.

Today, what characterizes a speculative romance?

I've often thought of romance as the figure skating of literature. Skaters constantly seek to perfect their performance, to go for the 10. Romance seeks to tell the ultimate story of romantic relationship, including such classics as a Regency tale of a rake falling for a vicar's daughter, or a time-travel adventure with a modern-day woman stranded in the past. We watch figure skating or read romances for the sheer pleasure of seeing it done well. And just as ice-skaters push the boundaries of their sport with innovative movements, so romance authors push the boundaries of their genre with innovative ideas. As a literary movement, romance is an art with many and diverse forms.

With science fiction and fantasy, my thoughts turn to rock music. It may be wild or lyrical, rough or gentle, based on classical technique or it may challenge accepted forms, but it always pushes the envelope, trying something new. It's no wonder that such music has become inextricably linked with youthful rebellion: It's about breaking rules. So it is with speculative fiction. It wants to be different. The stories may be exhilarating, dark, optimistic, dire, humorous, gritty, beautiful, in-your-face, or sedate. But they always push boundaries. Extrapolate into the unknown. The story must differ in some basic way from our normal lives. It asks the question "What if?"

So how do we mix the genres? It doesn't surprise me that science fiction romance became popular in hard science fiction. Such works are about science, and science is about solving problems. Science seeks to better understand the universe, to extend our knowledge and discover new insights. That worldview—or perhaps I should say universeview—is why hard science fiction is often referred to as an optimistic subgenre; inherent in many of its works is the assumption that whatever intellectual problem drives the plot will be solved. Not all my works or those of other speculative romance authors fit into the hard science fiction subgenre, but they do share that optimism.

Romance is the emotional equivalent of hard science fiction; fundamental to its many forms is the assumption that no matter how great the problems of the heart, we can solve them and achieve emotional fulfillment. Underlying romance literature is an intrinsic faith in the human spirit—a belief in the strength of love, honor, and loyalty.

In my more mischievous moments, I think of science fiction as a strapping young fellow showing off for his ladylove, romance. Intrigued, she comes closer, deciding that maybe this handsome stranger isn't so strange after all. Science fiction romance is their marriage. As in any marriage, it succeeds best when the two partners love and respect each other. A fantasy or science fiction romance will work if the author enjoys both genres and translates that into her or his fiction.

In this anthology, I have the pleasure of bringing you stories by many accomplished writers in both speculative and romance fiction. They offer a cornucopia of romantic adventures that take the best of these genres and meld them into a marriage of heart and mind.

Best regards,
Catherine Asaro
www.sff.net/people/asaro/

Winterfair Gifts

by Lois McMaster Bujold

From Armsman Roic's wrist com the gate guard's voice reported laconically, "They're in. Gate's locked."

"Right," Roic returned. "Dropping the house shields." He turned to the discreet security control panel beside the carved double doors of Vorkosigan House's main entry hall, pressed his palm to the read-pad, and entered a short code. The faint hum of the force shield protecting the great house faded.

Roic stared anxiously out one of the tall, narrow windows flanking the portal, ready to throw the doors wide when m'lord's groundcar pulled into the porte cochere. He glanced no less anxiously down the considerable length of his athletic body, checking his House uniform: half-boots polished to mirrors, trousers knife-creased, silver embroidery gleaming, dark brown fabric spotless.

His face heated in mortified memory of a less expected arrival in this very hall—also of Lord Vorkosigan with honored company in tow—and the unholy tableau m'lord had surprised with the Escobaran bounty hunters and the gooey debacle of the bug butter. Roic had looked an utter fool in that moment, nearly naked except for a liberal coating of sticky slime. He could still hear Lord Vorkosigan's austere, amused voice, as cutting as a razor-slash across his ears: *Armsman Roic, you're out of uniform.*

He thinks I'm an idiot. Worse, the Escobarans' invasion had been a security breach, and while he'd not, technically, been on duty—he'd been *asleep,* dammit—he'd been present in the house and therefore on call for emergencies. The mess had been in his lap, literally. M'lord had dismissed him from the scene with no more than an exasperated *Roic . . . get a bath*, somehow more keenly excoriating than any bellowed dressing-down.

Roic checked his uniform again.

The long silvery groundcar pulled up and sighed to the pavement. The front canopy rose on the driver, the senior and dauntingly competent Armsman Pym. He released the rear canopy and hurried around the car to assist m'lord and his party. The senior armsman spared a glance through the narrow window as he strode by, his eye passing coolly over Roic and scanning the hall beyond to make sure it contained no unforeseen drama this time. These were Very Important Off-World Wedding Guests, Pym had impressed upon Roic. Which Roic might have been left to deduce by m'lord going personally to the shuttleport to greet their descent from orbit—but then, Pym had walked in on the bug butter disaster, too. Since that day, his directives to Roic had tended to be couched in words of one syllable, with no contingency left to chance.

A short figure in a well-tailored gray tunic and trousers hopped out of the car first: Lord Vorkosigan, gesturing expansively at the great stone mansion, talking nonstop over his shoulder, smiling in proud welcome. As the carved doors swung wide, admitting a blast of Vorbarr Sultana winter night air and a few glittering snow crystals, Roic stood to attention and mentally matched the other people exiting the groundcar with the security list he'd been given. A tall woman held a baby bundled in blankets; a lean, smiling fellow hovered by her side. They had to be the Bothari-Jeseks. Madame Elena Bothari-Jesek was the daughter of the late, legendary Armsman Bothari; her right of entrée into Vorkosigan House, where she had grown up with m'lord, was absolute, Pym had made sure Roic understood. It scarcely needed the silver circles of a jump pilot's neural leads on midforehead and temples to identify the shorter middle-aged fellow as the Betan jump pilot, Arde Mayhew—should a jump pilot look so jump-lagged? Well, m'lord's mother, Countess Vorkosigan, was Betan, too; and the pilot's blinking, shivering stance was among the most physically unthreatening Roic had ever seen. Not so the final guest. Roic's eyes widened.

The hulking figure unfolded from the groundcar and stood up, and up. Pym, who was almost as tall as Roic, did not come quite up to its shoulder. It shook out the swirling folds of a gray-and-white greatcoat of military cut and threw back its head. The light from overhead caught the face and gleamed off ... were those *fangs* hooked over the outslung lower jaw?

Sergeant Taura was the name that went with it, by process of elimination. One of m'lord's old military buddies, Pym had given Roic to understand, and—don't be fooled by the rank—of some *particular* importance (if rather mysterious, as was everything connected with Lord Miles Vorkosigan's late career in Imperial Security). Pym was former ImpSec himself. Roic was not, as he was reminded, oh, three times a day on average.

At Lord Vorkosigan's urging, the whole party poured into the entry hall, shaking off snow-spotted garments, talking, laughing. The greatcoat was swung from those high shoulders like a billowing sail, its owner turning neatly on one foot, folding the garment ready to hand over. Roic jerked back to avoid being clipped by a heavy, mahogany-colored braid of hair as it swept past, and rocked forward to find himself face to ... nose to ... staring directly into an entirely unexpected cleavage. It was framed by pink silk in a plunging vee. He glanced up. The outslung jaw was smooth and beardless. The curious pale amber eyes, irises circled with sleek black lines, looked back down at him with, he instantly feared, some amusement. *Her* fang-framed smile was deeply alarming.

Pym was efficiently organizing servants and luggage. Lord Vorkosigan's voice yanked Roic back to focus. "Roic, did the count and countess get back in from their dinner engagement yet?"

"About twenty minutes ago, m'lord. They went upstairs to their suite to change."

Lord Vorkosigan addressed the woman with the baby, who was attracting cooing maids. "My parents would skin me if I didn't take *you* up to them instantly. Come on. Mother's pretty eager to meet her namesake. I predict

Baby Cordelia will have Countess Cordelia wrapped around her pudgy little fingers in about, oh, three and a half seconds. At the outside."

He turned and started up the curve of the great staircase, shepherding the Bothari-Jeseks and calling over his shoulder, "Roic, show Arde and Taura to their assigned rooms, make sure they have everything they want. We'll meet back in the library when you all are freshened up or whatever. Drinks and snacks will be laid on there."

So, it was a *lady* sergeant. Galactics had those; m'lord's mother had been a famous Betan officer in her day. *But this one's a bloody giant mutant lady sergeant* was a thought Roic suppressed more firmly. Such backcountry prejudices had no place in *this* household. Though she was clearly bio-engineered, had to be. He recovered himself enough to say, "May I take your bag, um . . . Sergeant?"

"Oh, all right." With a dubious look down at him, she handed him the satchel she'd had slung over one arm. The pink enamel on her fingernails did not quite camouflage their shape as claws, heavy and efficient as a leopard's. The bag's descending weight nearly jerked Roic's arm out of its socket. He managed a desperate smile and began lugging it two-handed up the staircase in m'lord's wake.

He deposited the tired-looking pilot first. Sergeant Taura's second-floor guest room was one of the renovated ones, with its own bath, around the corridor's corner from m'lord's own suite. She reached up and trailed a claw along the ceiling and smiled in evident approval of Vorkosigan House's three-meter headspace.

"So," she said, turning to Roic, "is a Winterfair wedding considered especially auspicious, in Barrayaran custom?"

"They're not so common as in summer. Mostly I think it's now because m'lord's fiancée is between semesters at university."

Her thick brows rose in surprise. "She's a student?"

"Yes, ma'am." He had a notion one addressed female sergeants as *ma'am.* Pym would have known.

"I didn't realize she was such a *young* lady."

"No, ma'am. Madame Vorsoisson's a widow—she has a little boy, Nikki—nine years old. Mad about jumpships. Do you happen t' know—does that pilot fellow like children?" Mayhew was bound to be a magnet for Nikki.

"Why . . . I don't know. I don't think Arde knows either. He hardly ever meets any in a free mercenary fleet."

He would have to watch, then, to be sure little Nikki didn't set himself up for a painful rebuff. M'lord and m'lady-to-be might not be paying their usual attention to him, under the circumstances.

Sergeant Taura circled the room, gazing with what Roic hoped was approval at its comfortable appointments, and glanced out the window at the back garden, shrouded in winter white, the snow luminous in the security lighting. "I suppose it makes sense that he'd have to wed one of his own Vor kind, in the end." Her nose wrinkled. "So, are the Vor a social class, a warrior caste, or what? I never could quite figure it out from Miles. The way he talks about them you'd half think they were a religion. Or at any rate, *his* religion."

Roic blinked in bafflement. "Well, no. And yes. All of that. The Vor are . . . well, Vor."

"Now that Barrayar has modernized, isn't a hereditary aristocracy resented by the rest of your classes?"

"But they're *our* Vor."

"Says the Barrayaran. Hmm. So, *you* can criticize them, but heaven help any outsider who dares to?"

"Yes," he said, relieved that she seemed to have grasped it despite his stumbling tongue.

"A family matter. *I* see." Her grin faded into a frown that was actually less alarming—not so much fang. Her fingers clenching the curtain inadvertently poked claws through the expensive fabric; wincing, she shook her hand free and tucked it behind her back. Her voice lowered. "So she's Vor, well and good. But does she *love* him?"

Roic heard the odd emphasis in her voice but was unclear how to interpret it. "I'm very sure of it, ma'am," he avowed loyally. M'lady-to-be's frowns, her darkening mood, were surely just prewedding nerves piled atop examination stress on the substrate of her not-so-distant bereavement.

"Of course." Her smile flicked back in a perfunctory sort of way. "Have you served Lord Vorkosigan long, Armsman Roic?"

"Since last winter, ma'am, when a space fell vacant in the Vorkosigans' armsmen's score. I was sent up on recommendation from the Hassadar Municipal Guard," he added a bit truculently, challenging her to sneer at his humble, nonmilitary origins. "A count's twenty armsmen are always from his own district, y'see."

She did not react; the Hassadar Municipal Guard evidently meant nothing to her.

He asked in return, "Did you . . . serve him very long? Out there?" In the galactic backbeyond where m'lord had acquired such exotic friends.

Her face softened, the fanged smile reappearing. "In a sense, all my life. Since my real life began, ten years ago, anyway. He is a great man." This last was delivered with unself-conscious conviction.

Well, he was a great man's *son*, certainly. Count Aral Vorkosigan was a colossus bestriding the last half century of Barrayaran history. Lord Miles had led a less public career. Which no one would tell Roic anything about, the most junior armsman not being ex-ImpSec like m'lord and most of the rest of the armsmen, eh.

Still, Roic *liked* the little lord. What with the birth injuries and all—Roic shied away from the pejorative *mutations*— he'd had a rough ride all his life despite his high blood. Hard enough for him to just achieve normal things, like . . . like getting married. Although m'lord had brains enough, belike, in compensation for his stunted body. Roic just wished he didn't think his newest armsman a dolt.

"The library is to the right of the stairs as you go down, through the first room." He touched his hand to his forehead in a farewell salute, by way of paving his escape from this unnerving giant female. "The dining's to be casual tonight; you don't need t' dress." He added, as she glanced down in bewilderment at her travel-rumpled loose pink jacket and trousers, "Dress up, that is. Fancy. What you're wearing is fine."

"Oh," she replied with evident relief. "That makes more sense. Thank you."

Having made his routine security circuit of the house, Roic arrived back at the antechamber just outside the library to find the huge woman and the pilot fellow examining the array of wedding presents temporarily staged there. The growing assortment of objects had been arriving for weeks. Each had been handed in to Pym to be unwrapped and to undergo a security check, rewrapped, and as the affianced couple's time permitted, unwrapped again and displayed with its card.

"Look, here's yours, Arde," said Sergeant Taura. "And here's Elli's."

"Oh, what did she finally decide on?" asked the pilot. "At one point she told me she was thinking of sending the bride a barbed-wire choke chain for Miles, but was afraid it might be misinterpreted."

"No . . ." Taura held up a thick fall of shimmering black stuff as long as she was tall. "It seems to be some sort of fur coat. No, wait—it's a blanket. Beautiful! You should feel this, Arde. It's incredibly soft. And warm." She held a supple fold up to the side of her head, and a delighted laugh broke from her long lips. "It's purring!"

Mayhew's eyebrows climbed halfway to his receding hairline. "Good God! *Did* she . . . ? Now, *that's* a bit edgy."

Taura stared down at him in puzzled inquiry. "Edgy? Why?"

Mayhew made an uncertain gesture. "It's a live fur—a genetic construct. It looks just like one Miles once gave to *Elli*. If she's recycling his gifts, that's a pretty pointed message." He hesitated. "Though I suppose if she bought a fresh new one for the happy couple, that's a different message."

"Ouch." Taura tilted her head to one side and frowned at the fur. "My life's too short for arcane mind games, Arde. Which is it?"

"Search me. In the dark, all cat blankets are . . . well, black, in this case. I wonder if it's intended as an editorial?"

"Well, if it is, don't you *dare* let on to the poor bride, or I swear I'll turn both your ears into doilies." She held up her clawed fingers and wriggled them. "By hand."

Judging by the pilot's brief grin, the threat was a jest, but by his little bow of compliance, not an entirely empty one. Taura observed Roic just then, refolded the live fur into its box, and tucked her hands discreetly behind her back.

The door to the library swung open, and Lord Vorkosigan stuck his head out. "Ah, there you two are." He strolled into the antechamber. "Elena and Baz will be down in a little—she's feeding Baby Cordelia. You must be starving by now, Taura. Come on in and try the hors d'oeuvres. My cook has outdone herself."

He smiled up affectionately at the enormous sergeant. While the top of Roic's head barely came up to her shoulder, m'lord just about faced her belt buckle. It occurred to Roic that Taura towered over himself in almost exactly the same proportions that ladies of average height towered over Lord Vorkosigan. This must be what women looked like to m'lord *all the time*.

Oh.

M'lord waved his guests through to the library but, instead of following them, shut the door and motioned Roic to his side. He looked thoughtfully up at his tallest armsman and lowered his voice.

"Tomorrow morning, I want you to drive Sergeant Taura to the Old Town. I've prevailed upon Aunt Alys to present Taura to her modiste and fix her up with a Barrayaran lady's wardrobe suitable for the upcoming bash. Figure to hold yourself at their disposal for the day."

Roic gulped. M'lord's aunt, Lady Alys Vorpatril, was in her own way more terrifying than any woman Roic had ever encountered, regardless of height. She was the acknowledged social arbiter of the high Vor in the capital, the last word in fashion, taste, and etiquette, the official hostess for Emperor Gregor *himself*. And her tongue could slice a fellow to ribbons and tie up the remains in a bowknot before they hit the ground.

"How t' *devil* did you—" Roic began, then cut himself off.

M'lord smirked. "I was very persuasive. Besides, Lady Alys relishes a challenge. With luck, she may even be able to part Taura from that shocking pink she favors. Some damned fool once told her it was a nonthreatening color, and now she uses it in the most unsuitable garments—and quantities. It's *so* wrong on her. Well, Aunt Alys will be able to handle it. If anyone asks for your opinion—not that they're likely to—vote for whatever Alys picks."

I shouldn't dare do otherwise, Roic managed not to blurt

aloud. He stood to attention and tried to look as though he were listening intelligently.

Lord Vorkosigan tapped his fingers on his trouser seam, his smile fading. "I'm also relying on you to see that Taura is not, um, offered insult, or made uncomfortable, or . . . well, you know. Not that you can keep people from staring, I don't suppose. But be her outrider in any public venue, and be alert to steer her away from any problems. I wish I had time to squire her myself, but this wedding prep has gone into high gear. Not much longer now, thank God."

"How is Madame Vorsoisson holding up?" Roic inquired diffidently. He had been wondering for two days if he ought to report the crying jag to someone, but m'lady-to-be had surely not realized her muffled breakdown in one of Vorkosigan House's back corridors had included a hastily retreating witness.

Judging by m'lord's suddenly guarded expression, perhaps he knew. "She has . . . extra stresses just now. I've tried to take as much of the organizing off her shoulders as possible." His shrug was not as reassuring as it might be, Roic felt.

M'lord brightened. "Anyway, I want Sergeant Taura to have a great time on her visit to Barrayar, a fabulous Winterfair season. It's probably the only chance she'll ever have to see the place. I want her to look back on this week like, like . . . dammit, I want her to feel like Cinderella magicked off to the ball. She's earned it, God knows. Midnight tolls too damned soon."

Roic tried to wrap his mind around the concept of Lord Vorkosigan as the enormous woman's fairy godfather. "So . . . who's t' handsome prince?"

M'lord's smile went crooked; something almost like pain sounded in his indrawn breath. "Ah. Yes. That would be the central problem, now. Wouldn't it."

He dismissed Roic with his usual casual half-salute, a vague wave of his hand in the vicinity of his forehead, and joined his guests in the library.

Roic had never in his whole career as a Hassadar municipal guardsman been in a clothing store resembling that of Lady Vorpatril's modiste. Nothing betrayed its location in the

Vorbarr Sultana thoroughfare but a discreet brass plaque, labeled simply ESTELLE. Cautiously, he mounted to the second floor, Sergeant Taura's massive footsteps creaking on the carpeted stairs behind him, and poked his head into a hushed chamber that might have been a Vor lady's drawing room. There was not a garment rack nor even a mannequin in sight, just a thick carpet, soft lighting, and tables and chairs that looked suitable for offering high tea at the Imperial Residence. To his relief Lady Vorpatril had arrived before them and was standing chatting with another woman in a dark dress.

The two women turned as Taura ducked her head under the lintel behind Roic and straightened up again. Roic nodded a polite greeting. He couldn't imagine what m'lord had said to his aunt, but her eyes widened only slightly, looking up at Taura. The second woman didn't quail at the fangs, claws, or height either, but when her glance swept down the pink trouser outfit, she winced.

There was a brief pause; Lady Alys shot Roic an inquiring look, and he realized it must be his job to do the announcing, as when he brought a visitor into Vorkosigan House. "Sergeant Taura, my lady," he said loudly, then stopped, hoping for more cues.

After another moment, Lady Alys abandoned further hope of him and came forward, smiling, her hands held out. "Sergeant Taura. I am Miles Vorkosigan's aunt, Alys Vorpatril. Permit me to welcome you to Barrayar. My nephew has told me something about you."

Uncertainly, Taura stuck out one huge hand, engulfing Lady Alys's slender fingers, and shook with care. "I'm afraid he hasn't told me too much about you," she said. Shyness made her voice a gruff rumble. "I don't know many aunts. I somehow thought you would be older. And . . . and not so beautiful."

Lady Vorpatril smiled, not without approval. Only a few streaks of silver in her dark coiffure and a slight softening of her skin betrayed her age to Roic's eyes; she was trim and elegant and utterly self-possessed, as always. She introduced the other woman, Madame Somebody—not Estelle, though Roic promptly dubbed her that in his mind—apparently the senior modiste.

"I'm very happy to have a chance to visit Miles's—Lord Vorkosigan's homeworld," Taura told them. "Although, when he invited me to come for the Winterfair season, I wasn't sure if it was hunting or social, and whether I should pack weapons or dresses."

Lady Vorpatril's smile sharpened. "Dresses *are* weapons, my dear, in sufficiently skilled hands. Permit us to introduce you to the rest of our ordnance team." She gestured toward a door at the far end of the room, through which presumably lay more utilitarian workrooms, full of laser scanners and design consoles and bolts of exotic fabrics and expert seamstresses. Or magic wands, for all Roic knew.

The other woman nodded. "Do please come this way, Sergeant Taura. We have a great deal to accomplish today, Lady Alys tells me . . ."

"My lady?" Roic called in faint panic to their disappearing forms. "What should I do?"

"Wait here a few moments, Armsman," Lady Alys murmured over her shoulder to him. "I'll be back."

Taura, too, glanced back at him, just before the door eased silently closed behind her, the expression flitting over her odd features seeming for a moment almost beseeching—*Don't abandon me.*

Did he dare sit on one of the chairs? He decided not. He stood for a few moments, walked around the chamber, and finally took up a guardsman's stance, which by dint of much recent practice he could hold for an hour at a stretch, his back to one delicately decorated wall.

In a while Lady Vorpatril returned, a pile of bright pink cloth folded over her arm. She shoved it at Roic.

"Take these back to my nephew and tell him to hide them. Or better, burn them. Or anything, but do not under any circumstances allow them to fall into that young woman's hands again. Come back in about, oh, four hours. You are by far the most ornamental of Miles's armsmen, but there's no need to have you lurking about cluttering up Estelle's reception room till then. Run along."

He looked down on the top of her perfectly groomed head and wondered how she could *always* make him feel four years old, or as though he wanted to hide in a large bag. For his consolation, Roic reflected as he made his way out, she seemed to have the same effect on her nephew, who was thirty-one and ought to be immune by now.

He reported again for duty at the appointed time, only to cool his heels for another twenty minutes or so. A sub-modiste of some sort offered him a choice of tea or wines while he waited, which he politely declined. At last, the door opened; voices drifted through.

Taura's vibrant baritone was unmistakable. "I'm not so sure, Lady Alys. I've never worn a skirt like this in my life."

"We'll have you practice for a few minutes, sitting and standing and walking. Oh, here's Roic back, good."

Lady Alys stepped through first, folded her arms, and looked, oddly enough, at Roic.

A stunning vision in hunter green stepped through behind her.

Oh, it was still Taura, certainly, but . . . the skin that had been sallow and dull against the pink was now revealed as a glowing ivory. The green jacket fit very trimly about the waist. Above, her pale shoulders and long neck seemed to bloom from a white linen collar; below, the jacket skirt skimmed out briefly around the upper hips. A narrow skirt continued the long green fall to her firm calves. Wide linen cuffs decorated with subtle white braid made her hands look, if not small, well-proportioned. The pink nail polish was gone, replaced by a dark mahogany shade. The heavy braid hanging down her back had been transformed into a mysteriously knotted arrangement, clinging close to her head and set off with a green . . . hat? feather? anyway, a neat little accent tilted to the other side. The odd shape of her face seemed suddenly artistic and sophisticated rather than distorted.

"Ye-es," said Lady Vorpatril. "That will do."

Roic closed his mouth.

With a lopsided smile, Taura stepped carefully forward. "I am a bodyguard by trade," she said, evidently continuing a conversation with Lady Vorpatril. "How can I kick someone's teeth in wearing this?"

"A woman wearing *that* suit, my dear, will have volunteers to kick in annoying persons' teeth for her," said Lady Alys. "Is that not so, Roic?"

"If they don't trample each other in the rush," gulped Roic and turned red.

One corner of that wide mouth lifted; the golden eyes seemed to sparkle like champagne. She caught sight of a long mirror on a carved stand in one corner and walked over to it to stare somewhat uncertainly at the portion of her it reflected. "It's effective, then?"

"Downright terrifying," Roic averred.

Roic intercepted a furious glower from Lady Alys behind Taura's back. Her lips formed the words *No, you idiot!* He shrank into cowed silence.

"Oh." Taura's fanged smile fled. "But I already terrify people. Human beings are so fragile. If you get a good grip, you can pull their heads right off. I want to *attract* . . . somebody. For a change. Maybe I should have that pink dress with the bows after all."

Lady Alys said smoothly, "We agreed that the ingenue look is for much younger girls."

"Smaller ones, you mean."

"There is more than one kind of beauty. Yours needs dignity. *I* would never deck myself in pink bows," she threw in, a little desperately it seemed to Roic.

Taura eyed her, seeming struck by this. "No . . . I suppose not."

"You will simply attract braver men."

"Oh, I know *that*." Taura shrugged. "I was just . . . hoping for a larger selection, for once." She added under her breath, "Anyway, he's taken now."

What he? Roic couldn't help wondering. She sounded rather sad about it. Some very tall admirer, now out of the picture? Larger than Roic? There weren't too many men of that description around.

Lady Alys rounded out the afternoon by guiding her new protégée to an exclusive tearoom, much frequented by high Vor matrons. This proved to be partly for the purposes of tutorial, party to refuel Taura's ferocious metabolism. While the server brought dish after dish, Lady Alys offered a brisk stream of advice on everything from gracefully exiting a groundcar in restrictive clothing to posture to table manners to the intricacies of Vor social rank. Despite her outsized scale, Taura was naturally athletic and coordinated, seeming to improve almost as Roic watched.

Drafted as practice gentleman, Roic found himself coming in for a few sharp corrections, too. He felt very conspicuous and clumsy at first, until he realized that, next to Taura, he might as well be invisible. If they drew sidelong looks from other diners, at least the comments were low-voiced or far enough away that he was not compelled to take notice; besides, Taura's attention was entirely upon her mentor. Unlike Roic, she never needed the same instruction twice.

When Lady Vorpatril removed herself to consult with the head server about some fine point, Taura leaned over to whisper, "She's *very* good at this, isn't she?"

"Yes. The best."

She sat back with a smile of satisfaction. "Miles's people generally are." She regarded Roic appraisingly.

A server guided a well-dressed Vor matron shepherding a girl-child about Nikki's age past their table toward their own seating. The girl stopped short and stared at Taura. Her hand lifted, pointing in astonishment. "Mama, look at that gigantic—"

The mother captured the hand, shot an alarmed glance at them, and began some hushed admonishment about it not being polite to point. Taura essayed a big friendly smile at the girl. A mistake . . .

The girl screamed and buried her face in her mother's skirts, hands frantically clutching. The woman shot Taura a furious, frightened glower and hustled the little girl away, not toward their table but to the exit. Across the tearoom, Lady Alys's head swiveled around.

Roic looked back at Taura, then wished he hadn't. Her face froze, appalled, then crumpled in distress; she seemed about to burst into tears but caught herself with a long indrawn breath, held for a moment.

Tensed to spring—where?—Roic instead eased back helplessly in his chair. Hadn't m'lord *specifically* detailed him to prevent this sort of thing?

With a gulp, Taura brought her breathing back under control. She looked as wan as though she'd been wounded by a knife thrust. Yet what could he have done? He couldn't very well draw his stunner and pot some Vor lady's terrified kid . . .

Lady Alys, taking in the incident, returned quickly. With a special frown at Roic, she slid back into her seat. She smoothed over the moment with some light comment, but the outing did not recover its cheerful tone; Taura kept trying to shrink down and sit smaller, a futile exercise, and whenever she began to smile, stopped and tried to hold her hand over her mouth.

Roic wished he were back patrolling Hassadar alleys.

Roic arrived with his charges at Vorkosigan House feeling as though he'd been run through a wringer. Backward. Several times. He peered around the tower of garment boxes he carried—the rest, Madame Estelle had assured Taura, would be delivered—and managed not to drop them getting through the carved doors. Under Lady Vorpatril's direction, he handed off the boxes to a pair of maidservants, who whisked them away.

M'lord's voice wafted from the antechamber to the library. "Is that you, Aunt Alys? We're in here."

Roic trod belatedly after the two disparate women just in time to see m'lord introduce Sergeant Taura to his fiancée, Madame Ekaterin Vorsoisson. Like, it seemed, everyone but Roic, she had apparently been warned in advance; she didn't even blink, holding out one hand to the huge galactic woman and offering her an impeccably polite welcome. M'lady-to-be looked fatigued this evening, although that might be partially the effect of the drab gray half-mourning she still wore, her dark hair drawn back in a severe knot. The garb went with the gray civilian suits m'lord favored, though, giving the effect of two players on the same team.

M'lord regarded the new green outfit with unfeigned enthusiasm. "Splendid work, Aunt Alys! I knew I could rely on you. That's a stunning look with the hair, Taura." He peered upward. "Are the fleet medicos making some new headway with the extension treatments? I don't see any gray at all. Great!"

She hesitated, then replied, "No, I just got some customized dye to match it."

"Ah." He made an apologetic motion, as if brushing away his last words. "Well, it looks lovely."

New voices sounded from the entry hall, Armsman Pym admitting a visitor.

"No need to announce me, Pym."

"He's right in there, then, sir. Lady Alys just arrived."

"Better still."

Simon Illyan (ImpSec, retired) entered upon these words, bent to kiss Lady Alys's hand, then tucked it through one arm as he straightened. She smiled fondly at him, and he snugged her in close to his side. He, too, absorbed his introduction to the towering Sergeant Taura with unruffled calm, bowing over her hand and saying, "I am so pleased to have a chance to meet you at last, Sergeant. I hope your visit to Barrayar has been pleasant so far?"

"Yes, sir," she rumbled back, apparently controlling an impulse to salute the man only because he still held her hand. Roic didn't blame her; he was taller than Illyan, too, but the formidable former Chief of Imperial Security made *him* want to salute, and he'd never even been *in* the military. "Lady Alys has been wonderful." No one, it seemed, was going to mention the unfortunate incident in the tearoom.

"I'm not surprised. Oh, Miles," Illyan continued, "I've just come from the Imperial Residence. Some good news came in when I was saying good-bye to Gregor. Lord Vorbataille was arrested this afternoon at the Vorbarr Sultana shuttleport, trying to leave the planet in disguise."

M'lord blew out his breath. "That's going to put *that* ugly little case to bed, then. Good. I was afraid it was going to drag on over Winterfair."

Illyan smiled. "I wondered if that might have had something to do with the energy with which you tackled it."

"Heh. I shall give dear Gregor the benefit of the doubt and assume he did not have my personal deadline in mind when he assigned me to it. The mess did proliferate unexpectedly."

"Case?" Sergeant Taura inquired.

"My new job as one of the nine Imperial Auditors for Emperor Gregor took an odd and unexpected turn into criminal investigation a month or so back," m'lord explained. "We found that Lord Vorbataille, who is a count's heir—like me—from one of our southern districts, had involved himself with a Jacksonian smuggling ring. Or, possibly, been suborned by it. Anyway, by the time his sins caught up with him he was up to his eyebrows in illicit traffic, hijacking, and murder. Very bad company, now wholly out of business, I'm pleased to report. Gregor is considering sending the Jacksonians home in a box, suitably frozen; let their backers decide if they are worth the expense of reviving. If everything is finally proved on Vorbataille that I think will be . . . for his father's sake, he may be allowed to suicide in his cell." M'lord grimaced. "If not, the Council of Counts will have to be persuaded to endorse a more direct redemption of the honor of the Vor. Corruption on this level can't be allowed to slop over and give us all a bad name."

"Gregor is very pleased with your work on this one," Illyan remarked.

"I'll bet. He was livid about the *Princess Olivia* hijacking, in his own understated way. An unarmed ship, all those poor dead passengers—God, what a nightmare."

Roic listened a bit wistfully to all this. He thought he might have done more this past month when m'lord was buzzing in and out on the high-profile case, but Pym hadn't assigned him to the duty. Granted, someone had to stand night guard for Vorkosigan House. Week after week . . .

"But enough of this nasty business"—m'lord caught Madame Vorsoisson's grateful glance—"let's turn to more cheerful affairs. Why don't you finish opening that next package, love?"

Madame Vorsoisson turned back to the crowded table and the task everyone's arrival had interrupted. "Here's the card. Oh. Admiral Quinn, again?"

M'lord took it, brows rising. "What, no limerick this time? How disappointing."

"Perhaps this one is to make up for— Oh, my. I imagine so. And all the way from Earth!" From a small box, she drew a short, triple strand of matched pearls and held them up to her throat. "Choker-style . . . oh, how pretty." Momentarily, she let the iridescent spheres line up upon her neck, touching the two ends of the clasp in back.

"Would you like me to fasten it?" her bridegroom offered.

"Just for a moment . . ." She bent her head, and m'lord reached up and fiddled with the catch at her nape. She walked to the mirror over the room's unlit fireplace, turning to watch the exquisite ornament catch the light, and gave m'lord a quizzical smile. "I believe they would go perfectly with what I'm wearing the day after tomorrow. Don't you think, Lady Alys?"

Lady Alys tilted her head in sartorial judgment. "Why, yes, indeed."

M'lord bowed at this endorsement by the highest authority. The look he exchanged with his bride was less decipherable to Roic, but he seemed very pleased, even relieved. Sergeant Taura, watching the byplay, frowned in unease.

Madame Vorsoisson removed the strands and laid them back in their velvet-lined box, where they glowed softly. "I believe we should let your guests freshen up before dinner, Miles."

"Oh, yes. Except I need to borrow Simon for a moment. Will you excuse us? There will be drinks in the library again when you are all ready. Someone let Arde know. Where is Arde?"

"Nikki captured him and carried him off," said Madame Vorsoisson. "I should probably go rescue the poor man."

M'lord and Illyan withdrew to the library. Lady Alys escorted Taura away, presumably for one last tutorial on Barrayaran etiquette before the impending formal dinner with Count and Countess Vorkosigan. Taura glanced back at the bride, still frowning. Roic watched the giant woman out with some regret, distracted by the sudden speculation of what it would be like to patrol a Hassadar alley *with* her.

"M'lady—Madame Vorsoisson, that is," Roic began as she started to turn away.

"Not for much longer." She smiled, turning back.

"What's with . . . that is, how old is Sergeant Taura? Do you know?"

"Around twenty-six standard, I believe."

A little younger than Roic, actually. It felt unfair that the galactic woman should seem so much more . . . complicated. "Then why is her hair turning gray? If she's bioengineered, I wouldn't have thought they'd muff up such details."

Madame Vorsoisson made a little gesture of apology. "I believe that is a private matter for her, which is not mine to discuss."

"Oh." Roic's brow wrinkled in bafflement. "Where'd she come from? Where did m'lord meet her?"

"On one of his old covert ops missions, he tells me. He rescued her from a particularly vile bioengineering facility on the planet of Jackson's Whole. They were trying to develop a super-soldier. Having escaped enslavement, she became an especially valued colleague on his ops team." She added after a contemplative moment, "And sometime-lover. Also especially valued, I understand."

Roic felt suddenly very . . . rural. Backcountry. Not up to speed on the sophisticated, galactic-tinged Vor life of the capital. "Er . . . he *told* you? And—and you're all right with that?" He wondered if meeting Sergeant Taura had rattled her more than she'd let on.

"It was before my time, Roic." Her smile crimped a little. "I actually wasn't sure if he was confessing or bragging, but now that I've seen her, I rather think he was bragging."

"But—but how would . . . I mean, she's so tall, and he's, um . . ."

Now her eyes narrowed with laughter at him, although her lips remained demure. "He didn't supply me with *that* much detail, Roic. It wouldn't have been gentlemanly."

"To you? No, I guess not."

"To her."

"Oh. Oh. Um, yeah."

"For what it's worth, I have heard him remark that a height differential matters much less when two people are lying down. I find I must agree." With a smile he *really* didn't dare try to interpret, she moved off in search of Nikki.

A scant hour later, Roic was surprised when Pym gave him a heads-up on his wrist com to bring m'lord's groundcar around. He parked it under the porte cochere and entered the black-and-white paved hall to find m'lord assisting Madame Vorsoisson on with her wraps.

"Are you sure you don't want me to go with you?" m'lord asked her anxiously. "I'd like to go with you, see you get home and in all right."

Madame Vorsoisson pressed a hand to her forehead. Her face was pale and damp, almost greenish. "No. No. Roic will get me there. Go back to your guests. They've come so far, and you'll only be getting to see them for such a short time. I'm sorry to be such a drip. Give my abject apologies to the count and countess."

"If you don't feel well, you don't feel well. Don't apologize. Do you think you're coming down with something? I could send our personal physician round."

"I don't know. I hope not, not now! It mostly seems to be a headache." She bit her lip. "I don't think I have a fever."

He reached up to touch her brow; she winced. "No, you're not hot. But you're all clammy." He hesitated, then asked more quietly, "Nerves, d'you think?"

She hesitated, too. "I don't know."

"I have all the wedding logistics under control, you know. All you have to do is show up."

Her smile was pained. "And not fall over."

He was silent a little longer this time. "You know, if you decide that you really can't go through with it, you can call a halt. Any time. Right up to the last. Hope you won't, of course. But I need you to know you could."

"What, with everyone from the emperor and the empress on down coming? I think not."

"I'd cover it, if I had to." He swallowed. "I know you said you wanted a small wedding, but I didn't realize you meant *tiny*. I'm sorry."

She blew out her breath in something like exasperation. "Miles, I love you dearly, but if I'm going to start throwing up, I'd really prefer to be home first."

"Oh. Yes. Roic, if you please?" He motioned to his armsman.

Roic took Madame Vorsoisson's arm, which was trembling.

"I'll send Nikki home safely with one of the armsmen after dessert, or after he wears Arde out. I'll call your house and let them know you're coming," m'lord called after her.

She waved in acknowledgment; Roic helped her into the rear compartment and closed the canopy. Her shadowed form sat bent, head clutched in her hands.

M'lord chewed on his knuckle and stared in distress as the house doors swung shut upon him.

Roic's night shift was cut short at dawn the next morning when the count's guard commander called him on his wrist com and told him to report to the front hall in running gear; one of m'lord's guests wanted to go out to take some exercise.

He arrived, shrugging on his jacket, to find Taura bending and stretching in a vigorous series of warm-ups under Pym's bemused eye. Lady Alys's modiste hadn't gotten around to providing active wear, it appeared, because the huge woman wore a plain set of well-worn ship knits, although in neutral gray rather than blinding pink. The fabric hugged the smooth curves of a lean musculature that, without being bulky, gave an unmistakable impression of coiled power. The braid down her back looked cheery and sporting in this comfortable context.

"Oh, Armsman Roic, good morning," she said, started to smile, then lifted her hand to her mouth.

"You don't—" Roic motioned inarticulately. "You don't have to do that for me. I like your smile." It wasn't, he realized, altogether a polite lie. *Now that I'm getting used to it.*

Her fangs glinted. "I hope they didn't drag you out of bed. Miles said his people just used the sidewalk around this block for their running track, since it was about a kilometer. I don't think I can go astray."

Roic intercepted a Look from Pym. Roic hadn't been called out to keep m'lord's galactic guest from getting lost; he was there to deal with any altercations that might result from startled Vorbarr Sultana drivers crashing their vehicles into the sidewalk or each other at the sight of her.

"No problem," said Roic promptly. "We usually use the ballroom for a sort of gymnasium in weather like this, but it's being all decorated for the reception. So I'm behind on my fitness training for the month. It'll be a nice change to do my laps with someone who's not so much older, um, that is, so much shorter than me." He sneaked a glance at Pym.

Pym's wintry smile promised retribution for that dig as he coded open the doors for them. "Enjoy yourselves, children."

The biting air blew away Roic's night-fatigue. He guided Taura out past the guard at the main gate and turned right along the high gray wall. After a few steps, she extended herself and began an easy lope. Within a very few minutes, Roic was regretting his cheap shot at the middle-aged Pym; Taura's long legs ate the distance. Roic kept half an eye on the early morning traffic, fortunately still light, and concentrated the rest of his attention on not disgracing House Vorkosigan by collapsing in a gasping heap. Taura's eyes grew brilliant with exhilaration as she ran, as if her spirit expanded into her body as her body stretched out to make room.

Half a dozen laps barely winded her, but she slowed at last to a walk, perhaps out of pity for her guide. "Let's circle through the garden to cool down," Roic wheezed. Madame Vorsoisson's garden, which occupied a third of the block and was her bride-gift to m'lord, was among other things sheltered from view of the cross streets by walls and banks. They dodged around the barricades temporarily barring public access till after the wedding.

"Oh, my," said Taura as they turned down the winding walk descending between curving snow hillocks. The chilly brook, its water running black and silky between feathery fingers of ice, snaked gracefully from one corner to the other. The peach-colored dawn light glimmered off the ice on the young trees and shrubs in the blue shadows. "Why, it's beautiful. I didn't expect a garden to be so pretty in winter. What are those men doing?"

A crew was unloading some float pallets piled high with boxes of all sizes, marked FRAGILE. Another pair was going around with water hoses, misting selected branches marked with yellow tags to create yet more delicate, shimmering icicles. The shapes of the native Barrayaran vegetation grew luminous and exotic with this silver-gilding.

"They're putting out all the ice sculptures. M'lord ordered ice flowers and sculptured creatures and things to fill up the garden, since all the real plants are under the snow, pretty much. And fresh snow to be added, too, if there isn't enough. They can't put out t' real live flowers for the ceremony till the very last gasp, late tomorrow morning."

"Good grief, he's having an outdoor garden wedding in *this* weather? Is that—a Barrayaran thing, is it?"

"Um, no. Not exactly. I believe m'lord originally was shooting for fall, but Madame Vorsoisson wasn't ready yet. But he'd got his heart set on getting married in the garden, because it was hers, y'see. So he is, by damn, going to have the wedding in the garden. The idea is people will assemble in Vorkosigan House, then troop out here for the vows, then scurry back into the ballroom for the reception and the food and dancing and all." *And the frostbite and hypothermia treatments.* "It'll be all right if the weather stays clear, I guess." The backstairs commentary on the potential disasters inherent in this scenario, Roic decided to keep to himself. Vorkosigan House's staff seemed united in their determination to make the eccentric scheme work for m'lord, anyway.

Taura's eyes glinted in the level dawn light now filtering between the buildings of the surrounding cityscape. "I can hardly wait to try out the dress Lady Alys got up for me to wear to the ceremony. Barrayaran ladies' clothes are so interesting. But complicated. In a way, I suppose they're another kind of uniform, but I don't know whether I feel like a recruit or an enemy spy in them. Well, I don't suppose the real ladies will shoot me in any case. So much to learn about how to go on—though I suppose it all seems ridiculously easy to you. You grew up with it."

"I didn't grow up with *this*." Roic waved a hand toward the imposing stone pile of Vorkosigan House rising above the high, bare trees on its grounds. "My father is just a construction hand in Hassadar—that's the Vorkosigan's District capital city, just this side of the Dendarii Mountains, a few hundred kilometers south of here. Lots of building going on there. He offered to apprentice me to the trade, but I got the chance to become a street guard, and I took it—sort of an impulse, truth to tell. I was eighteen, didn't know up from down. Sure learned a lot after that."

"What does a street guard guard? Streets?"

"Among other things. The whole city, really. You do what needs done. Sort out traffic, before or after it's a big bent pile. Deal with upset people's problems, try to keep 'em from murdering their relatives, or clean up the mess after if you can't. Trace stolen property, if you get lucky. I did a lot of night foot patrol. You learn a lot about a place on foot, up close. I learned how to handle stunners and shock-sticks and big, hostile drunks. I was getting pretty good at it, I thought, after a few years."

"How did you end up here?"

"Oh . . . there was a little incident . . ." He gave an embarrassed shrug. "Some crazed loon tried to shoot up Hassadar Square at rush hour with an auto-needler. I, um, took it away from him."

Her brows went up. "With a stunner?"

"No, unfortunately, I was off duty at the time. Had to do it by hand."

"A little hard to get up close and personal with someone firing a needler."

"That was a problem, yeah."

Her lips curved up, or at least the ivory hooks lengthened.

"It seemed to make perfect sense at the moment, though later I wondered what t' hell I'd been thinking. I don't think I was thinking. At any rate, he only killed five and not fifty-five. People seemed to think it was a big deal, but I'm sure it's nothing compared to what you've seen out there." His glance upward was meant to indicate the distant stars, though the sky was now a paling blue.

"Hey, I may be big, but I'm not needler-proof. I hate the shrieky sound when the razor-strands unwind and whiz around, even though I know in my head that those are the ones that *missed*."

"Yeah," Roic said in heartfelt agreement. "Anyways, after that there was a stupid fuss, and someone recommended me to m'lord's own armsman commander, Pym, and here I am." He glanced around the sparkling fairy garden. "I think I was a better fit in the Hassadar alleys."

"Naw, Miles always did like having big backup. Saves a lot of small-scale grief. Though the large-scale grief we still had to take as it came."

He asked after a moment, "How did you bodyguard, um, m'lord?"

"Such a funny way of thinking of him. To me, he'll always be the little admiral. Mostly, I just loomed at people. If I had to, I smiled."

"But your smile's really kind of nice," he protested, and managed not to add the *once you get used to it* out loud. He'd get the hang of this savoir faire thing yet.

"Oh, no. The *other* smile." She demonstrated, her lips wrinkling back, her jaw thrusting out. Roic had to admit, it was a much *wider* smile. And, um, *sharper*. They were just treading past a workman on the rising path; he gasped and fell backward into a snowbank. With lightning reflexes, Taura reached past Roic and caught the heavy, life-size ice sculpture of a crouching fox before it hit the pavement and shattered into shards. Roic lifted the gibbering man to his feet and dusted snow off his parka, and Taura handed back the elegant ornament with a compliment upon its artistry.

Roic managed not to choke with muffled laughter till they both had their backs to the fellow, heading away. "See what you mean. Did it ever not work?"

"Occasionally. Next step was to pick up the recalcitrant one by the neck. Since my arms were invariably longer than theirs, they'd swing like mad but couldn't connect. Very frustrating for them."

"And after that?"

She grinned. "Stunner, by preference."

"Heh. Yep."

They'd fallen unconsciously into an easy side-by-side pace, tracing loops around the garden paths. Talking shop, Roic thought. "What mass d'you lift?"

"With or without adrenaline?"

"Oh, without, say."

"Two hundred fifty kilos, with a good grip and a good angle."

He emitted a respectful whistle. "If you ever want to give up mercenary-ing, I can think of a fire fighting cadre might could welcome you. M'brother's in one, down Hassadar way. Though come to think of it, m'lord'd be a more powerful reference."

"Now, there's an idea I'd never thought of." She pursed her long lips, and her brows bent in a quizzical curve. "But, no. I expect I'll be, as you say, mercenary-ing till . . . for the rest of my life. I like seeing new planets. I like seeing this one. I could never have imagined it."

"How many have you seen?"

"I think I've lost count. I used to know. Dozens. How many have you seen?"

"Just t' one," he admitted. "Though hanging around m'lord, this one keeps getting wider till I'm almost dizzy. More complicated. Does that make sense?"

She threw back her head and laughed. "That's our Miles. Admiral Quinn always said she'd follow him halfway to hell just to find out what happened next."

"Wait—this Quinn you all keep talking about is a *lady* admiral?"

"She was a lady commander when I first met her. Second-sharpest tactical brain it's ever been my privilege to know. Things may get tight, following Elli Quinn, but you know they won't get *stupid*. She didn't sleep her way to the top by a long shot, and they're half-wits who say so." She grinned briefly. "*That* was just a *perk*. Some might say his, but *I'd* say hers."

Roic's eyes crossed, trying to unravel this. "Y'mean m'lord was lovers with *her*, t—" He cut off the *too* not quite in time, and flushed. It seemed m'lord's covert ops career was even more . . . *complicated* than he'd ever imagined.

Taura cocked her head and regarded him with crinkling eyes. "That's my favorite shade of pink, Roic. You *are* a country boy, aren't you? Life's uncertain out there. Things can go down bad, fast, anytime. People learn to grab what they can, when they can. For a time. We all just get a time, in our different ways." She sighed. "Their ways diverged when he took those horrible injuries that bounced him out of ImpSec. He couldn't go back up, and she wouldn't come down here. Elli Quinn's got no one but herself to blame for any chances she threw away. Though some people are born with more chances to waste than others, I'll admit. I say, grab the ones you're issued, run with them, and don't look back."

"Something might be gaining on you?"

"I know perfectly well what's gaining on me." Her grin flashed, oddly tilted this time. "Anyway, Quinn might be more beautiful, but *I* was always taller." She gave a satisfied nod. Glancing at him, she added, "I guarantee Miles likes *your* height. It's sort of an issue with him. I know recruiting officers in three genders who would swoon for your shoulders, as well."

He hadn't the least idea how to respond to *that*. He hoped she was enjoying the pink. "M'lord thinks I'm a fool," he said glumly.

Her brows shot up. "Surely not."

"Oh, yeah. You have no idea how I screwed up."

"I've seen him forgive screwups that put *his* guts on the bloody ceiling. Literally. You'd have to go some to top that. How many people died?"

If you put it in *that* perspective . . . "No one," he admitted. "I just wished *I* could have."

She grinned in sympathy. "Ah, one of *those* kinds of screwups. Oh, c'mon, tell."

He hesitated. "Y'know those nightmares where you find yourself walking around naked in the town square, or in front of your schoolteachers, or something?"

"My nightmares tend to be a bit more exotic, but yeah?"

"So, no lie, there I was . . . Last summer, m'lord's brother Mark brought home this damned Escobaran biologist, Dr. Borgos, that he'd picked up somewheres, and put him up in the basement of Vorkosigan House. An investment scheme. The biologist made bugs. And the bugs made bug butter. Tons of it. Slimy white stuff, edible, sort of. We found out the biologist had jumped bail back on Escobar—for fraud, no surprise—when t' skip-tracers they'd sent to arrest him showed up and talked their way into Vorkosigan House. Naturally, they picked a time when almost everyone had gone out. Lord Mark and the Koudelka sisters, who were in on the bug butter scheme, got in a fight with them when they tried to carry off Borgos, and the house staff waked me up to go sort it out. All in a tearing panic—wouldn't even let me grab my uniform trousers. I'd *just* got to sleep . . . Martya Koudelka claims it was friendly fire, but I dunno. I'd just about pushed the whole mess of 'em out the front door when in walks m'lord with Madame Vor-

soisson and all her relatives. He'd just got engaged and
wanted to make a good impression on 'em all . . . It was an
unforgettable one, I guarantee. I was wearing briefs, boots,
and about five kilos of bug butter, trying to deal wit' all
these screaming, sticky maniacs . . ."

A muffled sound escaped from Taura. She had her hand
over her mouth, but it wasn't helping; little squeaks still
leaked out. Her eyes were alight.

"I swear it wouldn't a' been half so bad if I'd not had my
briefs on backwards and my stunner holster on frontways.
I can still hear Pym's voice . . ." He mimicked the senior
armsman's driest tones: " 'Your weapon is worn on the
right, Armsman.' "

She laughed out loud then, and looked him up and down
in somewhat unsettling appreciation. "That's a pretty
amazing word picture, Roic."

Despite himself, he smiled a little. "I guess so. I dunno if
m'lord's forgiven me, but I'm right sure Pym hasn't." He
sighed. "If you see one of those damned vomit bugs still
around, squash it on sight. Hideous bioengineered mutant
things, kill 'em all before they multiply."

Her laughter stopped cold.

Roic reran his last sentence in his head and made the unpleasant discovery that one could do far worse things to
oneself with words than with dubious food products, or
possibly even with needlers. He hardly dared look up to
see her face. He forced his eyes right.

Her face was perfectly still, perfectly pale, perfectly
blank. Perfectly appalling.

I meant those devil-bugs, not you! He managed to stop
that idiocy on his lips before it escaped to do even more
damage, but only just. He couldn't think of any way to
apologize that wouldn't make it worse.

"Ah, yes," she said at last. "Miles did warn me that Barrayarans had some pretty ugly issues about gene manipu-
lation. I just forgot."

And I reminded you. "We're getting better," he tried.

"Good for you." She inhaled, a long breath. "Let's go in.
I'm getting cold."

Roic was frozen straight through. "Um. Yeah."

They walked back to the gate in silence

*   *   *

Roic slept the day around, trying to force his body back onto the boring night shift cycle that by the duty roster was to be his junior armsman's fate this Winterfair. He was quite sorry to thus miss seeing m'lord take his galactic guests and a selection of his in-laws-to-be on a tour of Vorbarr Sultana. He'd have been fascinated by what the two disparate parties made of each other. Madame Vorsoisson's family, the Vorvaynes, were solid provincial Vor types of the sort Roic had always regarded as normal to the class, before he'd taken up his duties in Vorkosigan House's high Vor milieu. M'lord, well . . . m'lord wasn't standard by anybody's standard. The four Vorvayne brothers, though dutifully pleased with their widowed sister's upward social leap, plainly found m'lord an unnerving catch. Roic wished he could see what they would make of Taura. He melted into sleep with a vague scenario drifting through his reeling brain of somehow imposing his body between her and some undefined social insult. Maybe then she would see that he hadn't meant anything by his awful gaffe . . .

He woke at sunset and made a foray down to Vorkosigan House's huge kitchen, belowstairs. Usually m'lord's genius cook, Ma Kosti, left delectable surprises in the staff refrigerator and was always looking for a good gossip, but tonight the pickings were slim and the personal attention nonexistent. The place was plunged into final preparations for tomorrow's great event, and Ma Kosti, driving her harried scullions before her, made it plain that anyone below the rank of count, or perhaps emperor, was very much in the way just now. Roic fueled up and retreated.

At least the kitchen did not have to deal with a formal dinner atop all the rest. M'lord, the count and countess, and all the guests were off to the Imperial Residence for the Winterfair Ball and midnight bonfire, the heart of the festivities marking solstice night and the turning of the season. When they all decamped from Vorkosigan House, Roic had the vast place to himself, but for the rumble from the kitchen and the servants rushing about completing the last-minute decorations and arrangements in the public rooms, the great dining room, and the seldom-used ballroom.

He was therefore surprised, about an hour before midnight, when the gate guard called him to code open the front door. He was even more surprised when a small car with government markings pulled up under the porte cochere and m'lord and Sergeant Taura climbed out. The car buzzed off, and its passengers entered the hall, shaking the cold air out of their outer garments and handing them off to Roic.

M'lord was dressed in the most elaborate version of the brown and silver Vorkosigan House uniform, befitting a count's heir attending upon the emperor, complete with custom-fitted polished riding boots to his knees. Taura wore a close-fitting, embroidered russet jacket, made high to the neck where a bit of lace showed, and a matching skirt sweeping to ankles clad in soft, russet-colored leather boots. A graceful spray of cream-and-rust colored orchids was wound into her braided-up hair. Roic wished he could have seen her entrance into the Imperial Winterfair Ball, and heard what the emperor and empress had said upon meeting her . . .

"No, I'm all right," Taura was saying to m'lord. "I saw the palace and the ball—they were beautiful—but I've had enough. It's just that I was up at dawn, and to tell the truth, I think I'm still a little jump-lagged. Go see to your bride. Is she still sick?"

"I wish I knew." M'lord paused on the steps, three up, and leaned on the banister to speak face-to-face with Taura, who was watching him in concern. "She wasn't sure even last week about attending the emperor's bonfire tonight, though I thought it would be a valuable distraction. She insisted she was all right when I talked to her earlier. But her aunt Helen says she's all to pieces, hiding in her room and crying. This is just not like her. I thought she was tough as anything. Oh, God, Taura. I think I've screwed up this whole wedding thing so badly . . . I rushed her into it, and now it's all coming apart. I can't imagine how bad the stress must be to make *her* physically ill."

"Slow down, dammit, Miles. Look. You said her first marriage was dire, yes?"

"Not bruises and black eyes bad, no. Draining the blood

of your spirit out drop by drop for years bad, maybe. I only saw the very end of it. It was pretty gruesome by then."

"Words can cut worse than knives. The wounds take longer to heal, too."

She didn't look at Roic. Roic didn't look back.

"Isn't that the truth," said m'lord, who wasn't looking at either of them. "Damn! Should I go over there or not? They say it's bad luck to see the bride before the wedding. Or was that the wedding dress? I can't remember."

Taura made a face. "And you accuse *her* of having wedding heebie-jeebies! Miles, listen. You know how the recruits got precombat nerves before they went out on a mission the first time?"

"Oh, yes."

"Now. Do you remember how they got precombat nerves before they had to go out on a big drop for the *second* time?"

After a long pause, m'lord said, "Oh." Another silence. "I hadn't thought of it like that. I thought it was *me*."

"That's because you're an egotist. I only met the woman for one hour, but even I could see that you're the delight of her eyes. At least consider, for five consecutive seconds, the possibility that it might be *him*. The late Vorsoisson, whoever he was."

"Oh, he was something else, all right. I've cursed him before for the scars he left on her soul."

"I don't think you have to say anything much. Just *be* there. And be not him."

M'lord drummed his fingers on the banister. "Yes. Maybe. God. Pray God. Dammit . . ." He glanced across at Roic, ignored as if he were Vorkosigan House furniture, a rack to hold coats. A dummy. "Roic, scrape up a vehicle; meet me back here in a few minutes. I want you to drive me over to Ekaterin's aunt and uncle's house. I'm going to run up and change out of this armor-plating first, though." He ran his fingers across the elaborate silver embroidery upon his sleeve. He turned away, and his bootsteps scuffed up the stairs.

This was way too alarming. "What in t' world's going on?" Roic dared to ask Taura.

"Ekaterin's aunt called him. I gather Ekaterin lives at her house—"

"With Lord Auditor and Professora Vorthys, yes. She's been going to University from there."

"Anyway, the bride-to-be seems to be having some sort of awful nervous breakdown or something." She frowned. "Or something . . . Miles isn't sure if he should go over and sit with her or not. I think he should."

That didn't sound good. In fact, it sounded about as not-good as it could be.

"Roic . . ." Taura's brows knotted. "Do you happen to know if I could find any commercial pharmaceutical laboratories open at this time of night in Vorbarr Sultana?"

"Pharmaceutical labs?" Roic repeated blankly. "Why, do you feel sick, too? I can call out the Vorkosigans' personal physician for you, or one of the medtechs who ride herd on the count and countess . . ." Would she need some kind of off-world specialist? No matter, the Vorkosigan name could access one, he was sure. Even on Bonfire Night.

"No, no, I feel fine. I was just wondering."

"Nothing much is open tonight. It's a holiday. Everyone's out to the parties and bonfires and the fireworks. Tomorrow, too. It'll be the first day of the new year here, by the Barrayaran calendar."

She smiled briefly. "It would be. A new start all round; I'll bet he liked the symbolism of that."

"I suppose hospital labs are open all night. Their emergency treatment intakes will be. Busy as hell, too. We used to bring the ones in Hassadar all kinds of customers on Bonfire Night."

"Hospitals, yes, of course! I should have thought of them at once."

"Why do you want one?" he asked again.

She hesitated. "I'm not sure that I do. It was just a train of thought I had earlier this evening, when that aunt-lady called Miles. Not sure I like its destination, though . . ." She turned away and swung up the stairs, taking them two at a time without effort. Roic frowned, then went off to scare up a vehicle from whatever remained in the sub-basement garage. With so many signed out to transport the household and its guests already, this might take some rapid extemporizing.

But Taura had spoken to him, almost normally.

Maybe . . . maybe there were such things as second chances.
If a fellow was brave enough to take them.

Lord Auditor and Professora Vorthys's home was a tall,
old, colorfully tiled structure close to the District University. The street was quiet when Roic pulled the car—
borrowed without notification, ultimately, from one of the
armsmen off with the count at the Residence—up to the
front. From a distance, mainly in the direction of the university, drifted the sharp crackle of fireworks, harmonious
singing, and blurred drunken singing. A rich, heady scent
of wood smoke and black powder permeated the frosty
night air.

The porch light was on. The Professora, an aging, smiling, neat Vor lady who intimidated Roic only slightly less
than did Lady Alys, let them in herself. Her soft round face
was tense with worry.

"Did you tell her I was coming?" m'lord asked in a low
tone as he shed his coat. He stared anxiously up the stairs
leading from the narrow, wood-paneled hallway.

"I didn't dare."

"Helen . . . what should I do?" M'lord looked suddenly
smaller, and scared, and younger and older all at the same
time.

"Just go up, I think. This isn't something that's about
talking, or words, or reason. I've run through all those."

He buttoned then unbuttoned the gray tunic he'd
thrown on over an old white shirt, pulled down his sleeves,
took a deep breath, mounted the stairs, and turned out of
sight. After a minute or two, the Professora stopped picking nervously at her hands, gestured Roic to a straight
chair beside a small table piled with books and flimsies,
and tiptoed up after him.

Roic sat in the hall and listened to the old house creak.
From the sitting room, visible through one archway, a glow
from a fireplace gilded the air. Through the opposite archway, the Professora's study lay, lined with books; the light
from the hall picked out an occasional bit of gold lettering
on an ancient spine in the gloom. Roic wasn't bookish himself, but he liked the comfortable academic smell of this
place. It occurred to him that back when he was a Hassadar

guard, he'd never once gone into a house to clean up a bad
scene, blood on the walls and evil smells in the air, where
there were books like this.

After a long time, the Professora came back down to
the hall.

Roic ducked his head respectfully. "Is she sick, ma'am?"

The tired-looking woman pursed her lips and let her
breath run out. "She certainly was last night. Terrible
headache, so bad she was crying and almost vomiting. But
she thought she was much better this morning. Or she said
she was. She wanted to be better. Maybe she was trying too
hard."

Roic peered anxiously up the staircase. "Would she
see him?"

The tension in her face eased a little. "Yes."

"Is it going to be all right?"

"I think so, now." Her lips sought a smile. "Anyway,
Miles says you are to go on home. That he expects to be a
while, and that he'll call if he needs anything."

"Yes, ma'am." He rose, gave her a kind of vague salute
copied from m'lord's own style, and let himself out.

The night duty guard at the gate kiosk reported no entries
since Roic had left. The festivities at the Imperial Residence would go on till dawn, although Roic didn't expect
Vorkosigan House's attendees to stay that late, not with
the grand party planned here for tomorrow afternoon and
evening. He put the borrowed car away in the sub-
basement garage, relieved that it hadn't acquired any hard-
to-explain dings in its passage back through some of the
rowdier crowds between here and the university.

He made his way softly up through the mostly darkened great house. All was quiet now. The kitchen crew
had at last retreated till tomorrow's onslaught. The
maids and menservants had gone to roost. For all that he
complained about missing the daytime excitements,
Roic usually enjoyed these quiet night hours when the
whole world seemed his personal property. Granted, by
three hours before dawn, coffee would be a necessity little less urgent than oxygen. But by two hours before
dawn, life would start trickling back, as those with early

duties roused themselves and padded down to start
work. He checked the security monitors in the basement
HQ and started his physical rounds. Floor by floor, window and door, never in quite the same order or at quite
the same hour.

As he crossed the great entry hall, a creak and a clink
sounded from the half-lit antechamber to the library. He
paused for a moment, frowned, and rose on his toes, moving his feet as gently as possible across the marble pavement, breathing through his open mouth for silence. His
shadow wavered, passed along from dim wall sconce to
dim wall sconce. He made sure it was not thrown before
him as he moved to the archway. Easing up beside the door
frame, he stared into the half-gloom.

Taura stood with her back to him, sorting through the
gifts displayed upon the long table by the far wall. Her
head bent over something in her hands. She shook out a
cloth and upended a small box. The elegant triple strand of
pearls slithered from their velvet backing into the cloth,
which she wrapped around them. She clicked the box
closed, set it back on the table, and slipped the folded cloth
into a side pocket of her russet jacket.

Shock held Roic paralyzed for a moment longer.
M'lord's honored guest, rifling the gifts?

But I liked her. I really liked her. Only now, in this moment of hideous revelation, did he realize just how much
he'd come to . . . to *admire* her in their brief time together.
Brief, but so damned awkward. She was really beautiful in
her own unique way, if only you looked at her right. For a
moment it had seemed as though far suns and strange adventures had beckoned to him from her gold eyes; just possibly, more intimate and exotic adventures than a shy
backcountry boy from Hassadar had ever dared to imagine.
If only he were a braver man. A handsome prince. Not a
fool. But Cinderella was a thief, and the fairy tale was gone
suddenly sour.

Sick dismay flooded him as he imagined the altera-
tion, the shame, the wounded friendship and shattered
trust that must follow this discovery—he almost turned
away. He didn't know the value of the pearls, but even if
it were a city's ransom he was certain m'lord would trade

them in a heartbeat for the ease of spirit he'd had with his old followers.

It was no good. They'd be missed first thing tomorrow in any case. He drew a breath and touched the light pad.

Taura spun like a huge cat at the flare of the overhead lights. After a moment, she let out her breath in a huff, visibly powering down. "Oh. It's you. You startled me."

Roic moistened his lips. Could he patch up this shattered fantasy? "Put them back, Taura. Please."

She stood still, looking back at him, tawny eyes wide; a grimace crossed her odd features. She seemed to coil, tension flowing back into her long body.

"Put them back now," Roic tried again, "and I won't tell." He bore a stunner. Could he draw it in time? He'd seen how fast she moved . . .

"I can't."

He stared at her without comprehension.

"I don't *dare*." Her voice grew edgy. "Please, Roic. Let me go now, and I promise I'll bring them back again tomorrow."

Huh? What? "I . . . can't. All the gifts have to go through a security check."

"Did this?" Her hand twitched by her pocket full of spoils.

"Yes, certainly."

"What kind? What did you check it for?"

"Everything is scanned for devices and explosives. All food and drink and their containers are tested for chemicals and biologicals."

"Only the food and drink?" She straightened, eyes glinting in rapid thought. "Anyway, I wasn't stealing it."

Maybe it was the covert ops training that enabled her to stand there and utter bald-faced . . . what? Counter-factual statements? *Complicated things?* "Well . . . then what *were* you doing?"

Again, a kind of frozen misery stiffened her features. She looked down, away, into the distance. "Borrowing it," she said in a gruff voice. She glanced across at him, as if to check his reaction to this feeble statement.

But Taura wasn't feeble, not by any definition. He felt out of his depth, flailing for firm footing and not finding it. He dared to move closer, to hold out his hand. "Give them to me."

"You mustn't touch them!" Her voice went frantic. "No one must touch them."

Lies and treachery? Trust and truth? What was he seeing here? Suddenly, he wasn't sure. *Back up, guardsman.* "Why not?"

She glowered at him narrow-eyed, as if trying to see through to the back of his head. "Do you care about Miles? Or is he just your employer?"

Roic blinked in increasing confusion. He considered his armsman's oath, its high honor and weight. "A Vorkosigan armsman isn't just what I am; it's *who* I am. He's not my *employer* at all. He's my liege lord."

She made a frustrated gesture. "If you knew a secret that would hurt him to the heart—would you, could you, keep it from him even if *he* asked?"

What secret? This? That his ex-lover was a thief? It didn't seem as though that could be what she was talking about—around. *Think, man.*

"I . . . can't pass a judgment without knowledge." Knowledge. What did she know that he didn't? A million things, he was sure. He'd glimpsed some of them, dizzying vistas. But she didn't know *him*, now, did she? Not the way she evidently knew, say, m'lord. To her, he was a blank in a brown-and-silver uniform. With his mirror-polished boot stuck in his mouth, eh. He hesitated, then countered, "M'lord can requisition my life with a word. I gave him that right on my name and breath. Can you trust *me* to hold his best interests to heart?"

Stare met stare, and no one blinked.

"Trust for trust," Roic breathed at last. "Trade, Taura."

Slowly, not dropping her intent, searching gaze from his face, she drew the cloth from her pocket. She shook it gently, spilling the pearls back into their velvet box. She held the box out. "What do you see?"

Roic frowned. "Pearls. Pretty. White and shiny."

She shook her head. "I have a host of genetic modifications. Hideous bioengineered mutant or no—"

He flinched, his mouth opening and shutting.

"—among other things I can see slightly farther into the ultraviolet, and quite a bit farther into the infrared, than a normal person. *I* see dirty pearls. Strangely dirty pearls. And that's not what I usually see when I look at pearls. And then Miles's bride touched them, and an hour later was so sick she could hardly stand up."

An unpleasant tremor coursed down Roic's body. And why the devil hadn't *he* noticed that progression of events? "Yes. That's so. They'll have to be checked."

"Maybe I'm wrong. I could be wrong. Maybe I'm just being horrible and paranoid and—and jealous. If they were proved clean, that would be the end of it. But, Roic—*Quinn*. You don't have any idea how much he loved Quinn. And vice versa. I've been going half-mad all evening, ever since it all clicked in, wondering if Quinn really sent these. It would about slay him, if it were so."

"Wasn't him these are meant to slay." It seemed his liege lord's love life was as deceptively complicated as his intelligence, both camouflaged by his crippled body. Or by the assumptions people made about his crippled body. Roic considered the ambiguous message Arde Mayhew had evidently seen in the live fur blanket. *Had* this Quinn woman, the other ex-lover—and how many more of them were going to turn up at this wedding, anyway? And in what frame of mind? How many *were* there, altogether? And what t' *hell* did the little guy do to have acquired what was beginning to seem far more than his fair share, when Roic didn't even have— He cut off the gyrating digression. "Or—is this necklace lethal, or not? Could it be some nasty practical joke, to just make the bride sick on her wedding night?"

"Ekaterin barely touched them. I don't know what this horrible goo may be, but I wouldn't lay those pearls against my skin for Betan dollars." Her face twisted up. "I want it to not be true. Or I want it to not be Quinn!"

Her dismay, Roic was increasingly convinced, was unfeigned, a cry from her heart. "Taura, think. You know this Quinn woman. I don't. But you said she was smart. D'you think she'd be plain stupid enough to sign her own name to murder?"

Taura looked taken aback, but then shook her head in renewed doubt. "Maybe. If it were done for rage or revenge, maybe."

"What if her name was stolen by another? If she didn't send these, she deserves to be cleared. And if she did . . . she doesn't deserve anything."

What was Taura going to do? He hadn't the least doubt she could kill him with one clawed hand before he could fumble his stunner out. The box was still tightly clutched in her great hand. Her body radiated tension the way a bonfire radiated heat.

"It seems almost unimaginable," she said. "Almost. But people mad in love do the wildest things. Sometimes things they regret forever afterward. But then it's too late. That's why I wanted to sneak the pearls away and check them in secret. I was praying I'd be proved wrong." Tears stood in her eyes now.

Roic swallowed and stood straighter. "Look, I can call ImpSec. They can have those—whatever they are—on the best forensics lab bench on the planet inside half an hour. They can check the wrappings, check the origin—everything. If *another* person stole your friend Quinn's name to cloak their crime . . ." He shuddered as his imagination sketched that crime in elaborating and grotesque detail: m'lady dying at m'lord's feet in the snow while her vows were still frost in the air; m'lord's shock, disbelief, howling anguish— "Then they should be hunted down without mercy. ImpSec can do that, too."

She still stood poised in doubt, on the balls of her feet. "They would hunt *her* down with the same . . . un-mercy. What if they got it wrong, made a mistake?"

"ImpSec is competent."

"Roic, *I'm* an ImpSec employee. I can absolutely *guarantee* you, they are *not* infallible."

He ran his gaze down the crowded table. "Look. There's that other wedding gift." He pointed to the folds of shimmering black blanket, still piled in the box. The room was so quiet he could hear the live fur's gentle rumble from here. "Why would she send two? The blanket even came with a dirty limerick, handwritten on a card." Not presently on display, true. "Madame Vorsoisson laughed out loud when m'lord read it to her."

A reluctant smile twitched Taura's mouth for a moment. "Oh, *that's* Quinn, all right."

"If *that's* truly Quinn, then this"—he pointed at the pearls—"can't be. Eh? Trust me. Trust your own judgment."

Slowly, with the deepest distress in her strange gold eyes, Taura wrapped the box in the cloth and handed it to him.

Then Roic found himself facing the task, all by himself, of stirring up ImpSec supreme headquarters in the middle of the night. He almost wanted to wait for Pym's return. But he *was* a Vorkosigan armsman: senior man present, even if merely because sole man present. It was his duty, it was his right, and time was of the essence, if only to relieve Taura's troubled mind at the earliest possible instant. She hovered, bleak and worried, as he gulped for nerve and fired up the secured comconsole in the nearby library.

A serious-looking ImpSec captain reported to the front hall in less than thirty minutes. He recorded everything, including Roic's verbal report, Taura's description of what the pearls had looked like to her, both their accounts of Madame Vorsoisson's witnessed symptoms, and a copy of Pym's original security check records. Roic tried to be straightforward, as he'd often wished witnesses would have been to him back in Hassadar, although in this version the fraught confrontation in the antechamber became merely *Sergeant Taura voiced a suspicion to me*. Well, it was *true*.

For Taura's sake, Roic made sure to mention the possibility that the pearls had not been sent by Quinn at all and pointed out the other gift certainly known to be from her. The captain frowned and bundled up the live fur as well, and looked as though he wanted to bundle up Taura along with it. He carried off the pearls, the still-purring blanket, and all related packaging in a series of sealed and labeled plastic bags. All this chill efficiency took a bare half hour more.

"Do you want to go to bed?" Roic asked Taura when the doors closed behind the ImpSec captain. *She looks so tired.* "I have to stay up anyway. I can give you a call to your room when there's any news. If there's any news."

She shook her head. "I couldn't sleep. Maybe they'll have something soon."

"There's no telling, but I hope so."

They settled down to wait together on a sturdy-looking sofa in the antechamber opposite the one displaying the gifts. The noises of the night—odd squeaks of the house settling against the winter cold, the faint whir or hum of distant automated machinery—were very noticeable in the stillness. Taura stretched what Roic suspected were knotted shoulders, and he was briefly inspired to offer a back rub, but he wasn't sure how she'd take it. The impulse dissolved in cowardice.

"Quiet around here at night," she said after a moment.

She was speaking to him again. *Please, don't stop.* "Yeah. I sort of like it, though."

"Oh, you, too? The night watch is a philosophical kind of time. Its own world. Nothing moving out there but maybe people being born or people dying, necessity, and us."

"Eh, and the bad night people we're put on watch against."

She glanced through the archway into the great hall and beyond. "Apparently so. What an evil trick . . ." She trailed off in a grimace.

"This Quinn, you've known her a long time?"

"She was in the Dendarii mercenaries at the time I joined the fleet—'original equipment,' as she says. A good leader, a friend by many shared disasters. And victories, sometimes. Ten years adds up to some weight, even if you're not watching. Especially if you're not watching, I suppose."

He followed the thought spoken by her glance, as well as her words. "Eh, yeah. God spare me from ever facing such a puzzle. It would be as bad as having your count revolt against the emperor, I suppose. Or like finding m'lord in on some insane plot to murder Empress Laisa. Shouldn't wonder that you've been running around in circles in your head all night."

"Tighter and tighter, yes. I couldn't enjoy the emperor's party from the moment I thought of it, and I know Miles so wanted me to. And I couldn't tell him why—I'm afraid he thought I was feeling out of place. Well, I was, but it wasn't a problem, exactly. I'm usually out of place." She blinked tawny eyes gone dark and wide in the half-light. "What would you do? If you discovered or suspected such a horror?"

His lips twisted. "That's a tough one. A higher honor must underlie ours, the count says. We can't ever obey unthinkingly."

"Huh. That's what Miles says, too. Is that where he got it, from his father?"

"I shouldn't be surprised. M'lord's brother Mark says integrity is a disease, and you can only catch it from someone who has it."

A little laugh sounded in her throat. "That sounds like Mark, all right."

He considered her question with the seriousness it merited. "I'd have to turn him in, I guess. I hope I'd have the courage, anyways. Nobody would win, in the end. Least of all me."

"Oh, yeah. I can see that."

Her hand lay on the sofa fabric between them, clawed fingers tapping. He wanted to take it and squeeze it for comfort—hers, or his? But he didn't dare. *Dammit, try, can't you?*

His argument with himself was interrupted when his wrist com sounded. The gate guard reported the return of the Vorkosigan House party from the Imperial Residence. Roic coded down the house shields and stood aside as the crowd disembarked from a small fleet of groundcars. Pym was in close attendance upon the countess, smiling at something she was saying over her shoulder to him. The guests, variously cheerful, drowsy, or drunk, streamed past chatting and laughing.

"Anything to report?" Pym inquired perfunctorily. He glanced in curiosity past Roic at Taura, looming over his shoulder.

"Yes, sir. See me in private as soon as you can, please."

The benign sleepy look evaporated from Pym's features. "Oh?" He glanced back at the mob now divesting wraps and streaming up the stairs. "Right."

Low-voiced as Roic had been, the countess had caught the exchange. A wave of her finger dismissed Pym from her side. "Although, if this is of moment, Pym, I'll take a report before bed," she murmured.

"Yes, my lady."

Roic jerked his head toward the antechamber of the library, and Pym followed him and Taura through the arch-way. The moment the guests had cleared the next room, Roic decanted a short précis of the night's adventure, self-plagiarized from the one he'd given to the ImpSec foren-sics captain. Omitting, again, the part about Taura's attempted theft. He hoped like hell that it wasn't going to turn out to be horribly pertinent later. He would submit the full account to m'lord's judgment, he decided. When the devil was m'lord going to return?

Pym grew rigid as he took in the report. "I checked that necklace myself, Roic. Scanned it clear of devices—the chemical sniffer didn't pick up anything either."

"Did you touch it?" asked Taura.

Pym's eyes narrowed in memory. "I mainly handled it by the clasp. Well . . . well, ImpSec will run it through the wringer. M'lord always claims they can use the exercise. It can't hurt. You acted correctly, Armsman Roic. You can continue about your duties now. I'll follow it up with ImpSec."

With this tepid praise, he moved off, frowning.

"Is that all we get?" Taura whispered as Pym's ascending footsteps faded on the winding staircase.

Roic glanced at his chrono. "Till ImpSec reports back, I guess. It depends on how hard that dirty stuff you saw"—he didn't insult her by phrasing it as *you claimed you saw*—"is to identify."

She scrubbed tired-looking eyes with the back of her hand. "Can I, uh, can I stay with you till they call?"

"Sure."

In a moment of true inspiration, he led her down to the kitchen and introduced her to the staff refrigerator. He'd been correct; her extraordinary metabolism was in need of fuel again. Ruthlessly, he cleared out everything on the shelves and laid it in front of her. The early morning crew could fend for themselves. There was no shame here in offer-ing up servants' food to a guest; *everyone* ate well from Ma Kosti's kitchen. He dialed up coffee for himself and tea for her, and they perched together on two stools at the counter.

Pym found them there as they were finishing eating. The senior armsman's face was so drained of blood as to be nearly green.

"Well done, Roic, Sergeant Taura," he began in a stiff voice. "Very well done. I just now spoke with ImpSec headquarters. The pearls *were* doctored—with a designer neurotoxin. ImpSec thinks it's of Jacksonian origin, but they're still cross-checking. The dose was sealed under a chemically neutral transparent lacquer that dissolves with body heat. Casual handling wouldn't release it, but if someone put the necklace on and wore it for a time . . . half an hour or so . . ."

"Enough to kill someone?" Taura's tone was tense.

"Enough to kill a bloody elephant, the lab boys say." Pym moistened dry lips. "And I checked it myself. I bloody *passed* it." His teeth clenched. "She was going to wear them to— M'lord would have—" He choked himself off and ran a hand over his face, hard.

"Does ImpSec know who really sent them?" asked Taura.

"Not yet. But they're all over it, you can believe."

A vision of the deadly pale spheres lying on m'lady-to-be's warm throat flashed through Roic's memory. "Madame Vorsoisson touched the pearls last night— night before last, that is now," said Roic urgently. "She had them on for at least five minutes. Is she going to be all right?"

"ImpSec is dispatching a physician to Lord Auditor Vorthys's to check her—one of their toxins experts. If she'd taken in enough to kill her, she'd have died right then, so *that's* not going to happen, but I don't know what other . . . I have to go now and call m'lord there and warn him to expect a visitor. And—and tell him why. Well done, Roic. Did I say well done? Well done." Pym drew a shaken, unhappy breath and strode back out.

Taura, her chin in her hand as she drooped over her plate, scowled after him. "Jacksonian neurotoxin, eh? That doesn't prove much. The Jacksonians will sell anything to anyone. Miles made enough enemies there in some of our old sorties—if they knew it was intended for him, they'd probably offer a deep discount."

"Yeah, I imagine tracing the source is going to take a little longer. Even for ImpSec." He hesitated. "Although, wouldn't they know him on Jackson's Whole only under his old covert ops identity? Your little admiral?"

"That cover's been well-blown for a couple of years, he tells me. Partly as a result of the mess his last mission there produced, partly from some other things. Over my head." She yawned, hugely. It was . . . impressive. She'd been up since dawn, Roic was reminded, and hadn't slept through the afternoon as he had. Stranded in what must seem to her an alien place and wrestling terrible fears. All by herself. For the first time, he wondered if she was lonely. One of a kind, the last of her kind if he understood correctly, without home or kin except for that chancy wandering mercenary fleet. And then he wondered why he hadn't noticed her essential aloneness sooner. Armsmen were supposed to be observant. *Yeah?*

"If I promise to come by and tell you if I get any news, d'you suppose you could try to sleep?"

She rubbed the back of her neck. "Would you? Then I think I could. Try, that is."

He escorted her to her door, past m'lord's dark and empty suite. When he clasped her hand briefly, she clasped back. He swallowed, for courage.

"Dirty pearls, eh?" he said, still holding her hand. "Y'know . . . I can't speak for any other Barrayarans . . . but *I* think your genetic modifications are beautiful."

Her lips curved up, he hoped not altogether bleakly. "You *are* getting better."

When she let go and turned in, a claw trailing lightly over the skin of his palm made his body shudder in involuntary, sensual surprise. He stared at the closing door and swallowed a perfectly foolish urge to call her back. Or follow her inside . . . He was still on duty, he reminded himself. The next monitors check was overdue. He forced himself to turn away.

The sky outside was shifting from the amber night of the city to a chill blue dawn when the gate guard called Roic to code down the house shields for m'lord's return. As the armsman who'd been called out to chauffeur drove the big car off to put away, Roic opened one door to admit the hunched, frowning figure. M'lord looked up to recognize Roic, and a rather ghastly smile lightened his furrowed features.

Roic had seen m'lord looking strung-out before, but never so alarmingly as this, not even after one of his bad seizures or when he'd had that spectacular hangover after the disastrous butter bug banquet. His eyes stared out from gray circles like feral animals from their dens. His skin was pale, and lines of tension mapped the anxiety across his face. His movements were simultaneously tired and stiff, and jerky and nervous, a spinning exhaustion that could find no place of rest.

"Roic. Thank you. Bless you," m'lord began in a voice that sounded as though it were coming from the bottom of a well.

"Is m'lady-to-be all right?" Roic asked in some apprehension.

M'lord nodded. "Yes, now. She fell asleep in my arms, finally, after the ImpSec doctor left. God, Roic! I can't believe I missed the signs. Poisoning! And I fastened that death around her neck with my own hands! It's a damned metaphor for this whole thing, that's what it is. She thought it was just her. *I* thought it was just her. How little faith in herself, or me in her, to misidentify dying of poison for dying of self-doubt!"

"She's *not* dying, is she?" Roic asked again, to be sure. In this spate of dramatic angst, it was a little hard to tell. "T' bit of exposure she got isn't going to have any permanent effects, is it?"

M'lord began to pace in circles around the entry hall, while Roic followed vainly trying to take his coat. "The doctor said not, not once the headaches pass off, which they seem to have done now. She was so relieved to find out what it really was she burst into tears. Go figure *that* one out, eh?"

"Yeah, except that—" Roic began, then bit his tongue. Except that the crying jag he'd inadvertently witnessed had occurred well before the poisoning.

"What?"

"Nothing, m'lord."

Lord Vorkosigan paused at the archway to the antechamber. "ImpSec. We must call ImpSec to take away all those gifts and recheck them for—"

"They already came and collected them, m'lord," Roic soothed him, or tried to. "An hour ago. They say they'll try t' get as many as possible cleared and back before the wedding guests start arriving come midafternoon."

"Oh. Good." M'lord stood still a moment, staring into nothing, and Roic finally managed to get his coat away from him.

"M'lord . . . *you* don't think your Admiral Quinn sent that necklace, do you?"

"Oh, good heavens, no. Of course not." M'lord dismissed this fear with a startlingly casual wave of his hand. "Not her style at all. If she were ever that mad at me, she'd kick me downstairs personally. Great woman, Quinn."

"Sergeant Taura was worried. I think she thought this Quinn might a' been, um, jealous."

M'lord blinked. "Why? I mean, yes, it's almost exactly a year since Elli and I parted company, but Ekaterin had nothing to do with *that*. Didn't even meet her till a couple of months later. The timing's pure coincidence, you can assure her. Yeah, so Elli turned down the wedding invitation—she has responsibilities. She got the fleet, after all." A small sigh escaped him. His lips screwed up in further thought. "I'd sure like to know who knew enough to steal Quinn's name to smuggle that hellish package in here, though. *That's* the real puzzle. Quinn's connected to Admiral Naismith, not to Lord Vorkosigan. Which was the sticking point in the first place, but never mind now. I want ImpSec to put every available resource on to tearing *that* one apart."

"I believe they already are, m'lord."

"Oh. Good." He looked up, and his face grew, if possible, more serious. "You saved my House last night, you know. Eleven generations of Vorkosigans have narrowed down to the choke point of me, this generation, this marriage. I'd have been the last, but for that chance—no, not chance— that moment of shrewd observation."

Roic waved an embarrassed hand. "Wasn't me who spotted it, m'lord. It was Sergeant Taura. She'd have reported it herself earlier, if she hadn't been half taken in by t' bad guy's nasty camouflage with your, um, friend Admiral Quinn's name."

M'lord took up his taut orbit of the hall again. "Bless Taura, then. A woman beyond price. Which I already knew, but anyway. I could kiss her feet, by God. I could kiss her all over!"

Roic was beginning to think that line about the barbed-wire choke chain wasn't such a joke after all. All this frenetic tension was, if not precisely infectious, starting to get on what was left of his nerves. He remarked dryly, in Pym-like periods, "I was given to understand you already had, m'lord."

M'lord jerked to a halt again. "Who told you that?"

Under the circumstances, Roic decided not to mention Madame Vorsoisson. "Taura."

"Eh, maybe it's the women's secret code. I don't have the key, though. You're on your own there, boy." He snorted a trifle hysterically. "But if you ever *do* win an invitation from her, beware—it's like being mugged in a dark alley by a goddess. You're not the same man after. Not to mention critical feminine body parts on a scale you can actually *find,* and as for the fangs, there's no thrill quite like—"

"Miles," a bemused voice interrupted from overhead. Roic glanced up to see the countess, wrapped in a robe, leaning over the balcony railing and observing her son. How long had she been standing there? She was Betan; maybe m'lord's last remarks wouldn't discombobulate her as much as they did Roic. In fact, he reflected, he was certain they couldn't.

"Good morning, Mother," m'lord managed. "Some bastard tried to poison Ekaterin, did you hear? When I catch up with him, I swear I'm going to make the Dismemberment of Mad Emperor Yuri look like a house party—"

"Yes, ImpSec has kept your father and me fully apprised during the night, and I just spoke with Helen. Everything seems under control for the moment, except for persuading Pym not to throw himself off the Star Bridge in expiation. He's pretty distraught over this slipup. For pity's sake, come up and take a sleeptimer and lie down for a while."

"I don't want a pill. I have to check the garden. I have to check everything—"

"The garden is fine. Everything is fine. As you have just discovered in Armsman Roic here, your staff is more than competent." She started down the stairs, a distinctly steely look in her eye. "It's either a sleeptimer or a sledgehammer for you, son. I am *not* handing you off to your blameless bride in the state you're in, or the worse one it'll be if you don't get some real sleep before this afternoon. It's not fair to her."

"Nothing about this marriage is fair to her," m'lord muttered, bleak. "She was afraid it would be the nightmare of her old marriage all over again. No! It's going to be a completely *different* nightmare—much *worse*. How can I ask her to step into my line of fire if—"

"As I recall, she asked *you*. I was there, remember? Stop gibbering." The countess took his arm, and began more or less frog-marching him upstairs. Roic made a mental note of her technique for future reference. She glanced over her shoulder and gave Roic a reassuring, if rather unexpected, wink.

The brief remainder of the most memorable night shift of his career passed, to Roic's relief, without further incident of note. He dodged excited maidservants hurrying to the big day's tasks and mounted the stairs to his tiny fourth-floor bedroom thinking that m'lord wasn't the only one who should get some sleep before the afternoon's more public duties. M'lord's last, decidedly free-floating comments kept him awake for some time, though, beguiling him with visions of somewhat shocking charm. Such as he'd never dreamed of back in Hassadar. He fell asleep with his lips curling up.

A few minutes before his alarm was set to go off, Roic was awakened by Armsman Jankowski tapping at his bedroom door.

"Pym says you're to report to m'lord's suite right away. Some kind of briefing—you don't have to be in your uniform yet."

"Right."

Dress uniform, Jankowski meant, although Jankowski

was already sharp in his own. Roic slipped on last night's wear and ran a comb through his hair, frowned in frustration at his beard shadow—*right away* presumably meant just that—and hurried downstairs.

Roic found m'lord in his suite's sitting room, halfway dressed in a silk shirt, the brown trousers with silver side-piping and the silver-embroidered suspenders that went with, and slippers. He was attended by his cousin Ivan Vorpatril, resplendent in his own House's blue-and-gold uniform. As m'lord's Second and chief witness in the imminent ceremony, Lord Ivan was also playing groom's batman as well as general supporter.

One of Roic's fonder secret memories from the past weeks was of witnessing, in his role as disregarded coatrack, the great Viceroy Count Vorkosigan himself taking his handsome nephew aside and promising, in a voice so low as to be almost a whisper, to have Ivan's hide for a drumskin if he allowed his misplaced sense of fun to do *anything at all* to screw up the impending ceremony for m'lord. Ivan had been humorless as a judge all week; side bets were being taken belowstairs for how long it would last. Remembering that deeply ominous voice, Roic had selected the longest shot in the pool—and thought himself likely to win.

Taura, also in last night's gear of skirt and lacy blouse, lounged on one of the small sofas in the bay window, apparently offering bracing advice. M'lord had evidently taken the sleeptimer, for he looked vastly better: clean, shaved, clear-eyed, and very nearly calm.

"Ekaterin's here," he told Roic, in the awed tone of a besieged garrison commander describing the unexpected relieving force. "The bride's party is using my mother's suite for their staging area. Mother's going to bring her down in a moment. She needs to be in on this."

In on what? was answered before Roic could voice the question by the entry of ImpSec chief General Allegre himself, in dress greens, escorted by the count, also already in his best House uniform. Allegre was a wedding guest in his own right, but it clearly wasn't for social reasons that he'd arrived an hour early.

The countess and Ekaterin followed on their heels, the

countess graceful in something sparkling and green, m'lady-to-be still in her drab dress but with her hair already braided up and thickly entwined with tiny roses and other exquisite little scented flowers that Roic could not name. Both women looked grave, but a smile like a fugitive gleam from paradise lit Ekaterin's eyes as they met m'lord's. Roic found he had to look away from that brief intensity, feeling a clumsy intruder. He thus surprised Taura's expression: shrewdly approving, but more than a little wistful.

Ivan drew up extra chairs, and all disposed themselves around the small table near the window. Madame Vorsoisson took a seat beside m'lord, decorously but with no wasted centimeters between. He gripped her hand. Roic managed to slip in next to Taura; she smiled down at him. These chambers had once belonged to the late great General Piotr Vorkosigan, before they'd been claimed by his grandson, the rising young Lord Auditor. This spot, not the grand public rooms downstairs, was the site of more military, political, and secret conferences of historic import to Barrayar than Roic could readily imagine.

"I dropped by early to give you ImpSec's latest report in person, Miles, Madame Vorsoisson, Count, Countess." Allegre, half leaning on a sofa arm, nodded around. He reached into his tunic and withdrew a plastic bag in which something white glimmered and gleamed. "And to return these. I had my forensics people clean them after collecting and recording the evidence. They're safe now."

Gingerly, m'lord took the pearls from his hand and set them down on the table. "And do you know yet who gets the thank-you note for this gift? I'm rather hoping to deliver it in person." Ill-concealed menace vibrated beneath his light tone.

"That has actually broken open much faster than I was expecting," said Allegre. "It was a *very* nice forgery job on the date stamps from Escobar on the outer packaging, but the inner decorative wrapping checked out under analysis as of Barrayaran origin. Once we knew which planet to look on, the item was sufficiently unique—the necklace *is* of Earth origin, by the way—we were able to trace it by jeweler's import records almost at once. It was purchased two weeks ago in Vorbarr Sultana for a large sum of cash, and the store security vids for the month hadn't been erased yet. My agent positively identified Lord Vorbataille."

M'lord hissed through his teeth. "He was on my short list, yes. No wonder he was trying so hard to get off planet."

"He was up to his eyebrows in the plan, but he wasn't its originator. Do you remember how you said to me three weeks ago that while there had to be brains behind this operation, you'd swear they weren't in Vorbataille's head?"

"Yes," said m'lord. "I had him pegged for a front man, suborned for his connections. And his yacht, of course."

"You were right. We picked up his Jacksonian crime consultant about three hours ago."

"You have him!"

"We have him. He'll keep, now." Allegre gave m'lord a grim nod. "Although he had the wit to *not* bring attention to himself by trying to get off planet, one of my analysts, who came in last night to look over the new evidence that came in with the necklace, was able to run a back-trace and cross-connect, and so identify him. Well, actually he fingered three suspects, but fast-penta cleared two of them. The source for the toxin was a fellow by the name of Luca Tarpan."

M'lord mouthed the syllables; his face screwed up. "Damn. Are you sure? I've never heard of him."

"Quite sure. He appears to have ties with the Bharaputra syndicate on Jackson's Whole."

"Well, that would give him access to quite a lot of somewhat scrambled two-year-old information about me and Quinn, yes. Both mes, in fact. And it accounts for the superior forgery. But why such a heinous attack? It's almost *more* disturbing to think that some total stranger would— Have we crossed paths before?"

Allegre shrugged. "It seems not. The preliminary interrogation suggests it was a purely professional ploy— although he clearly had no love left for you by the time you were about half done ripping open this case. Your talent for making interesting new enemies has evidently not deserted you. The plan was to create distracting chaos in your investigation just after the group made its getaway—Vorbataille was preselected to be thrown to us for a goat, it turns out—but we shut them down about eight days early. The necklace had only just been slipped into the delivery service's records and dispatched at that point."

M'lord's teeth set. "You've had Vorbataille in your hands for two days. And fast-penta didn't turn this up?"

Allegre grimaced. "I just reviewed the transcripts before I drove over here. It came very close to surfacing. But to get an answer, even—especially—under fast-penta, as useful a truth drug as it is, you must first know enough to ask the question. My interrogators were concentrating on the *Princess Olivia*. It *was* Vorbataille's yacht that was used to insert the hijacking team, by the way."

"Knew it had to be," grunted m'lord.

"We'd have caught up with this necklace scheme in a few more days on our own, I think," said Allegre.

M'lord glanced at his chrono and said rather thickly, "You'd have caught up with it in about one more hour, actually. On your own."

Allegre tilted his head in frank acknowledgment. "Yes, unfortunately. Madame Vorsoisson"—he touched his brow in a considerably more formal gesture than the usual ImpSec salute—"on behalf of myself and my organization, I wish to offer you my most abject apologies. My Lord Auditor. Count. Countess." He looked up at Roic and Taura, sitting side by side on the sofa opposite. "Fortunately, ImpSec was not your last line of defense."

"Indeed," rumbled the count, who had seated himself on a straight chair turned backward, arms comfortably crossed over its back, listening intently but without comment till now. Countess Vorkosigan stood by his side; her hand touched his shoulder, and he caught it under his own thicker one.

Allegre said, "Illyan once told me that half the secret of House Vorkosigan's preeminence in Barrayaran history was the quality of the people it drew to its service. I'm glad to see this continues to hold true. Armsman Roic, Sergeant Taura—ImpSec salutes you with more gratitude than I can rightly express." He did so, in a sober gesture altogether free of his sporadic irony.

Roic blinked, ducking his head in lieu of the return

salute he wasn't sure he was supposed to make. He wondered if he was expected to say something. He hoped to hell no one would want him to make a speech, like after that incident in Hassadar. That had been more horrifying than the needler fire. He glanced up to find Taura glancing down at him, eyes bright. He wanted to ask her—he wanted to ask her a thousand things, but not here. Would they ever get a private moment again? Not for the next several hours, that was certain.

"Well, love,"—m'lord blew out his breath, staring down at the plastic bag—"I think that's your final warning. Travel with me and you travel into hazard. I don't want it to be so. But it's going to go on being so, as long as I serve . . . what I serve."

M'lady-to-be glanced at the countess, whose return smile was decidedly twisted. "I never imagined it would be otherwise for a Lady Vorkosigan."

"I'll have these destroyed," m'lord said, reaching for the pearls.

"No," said m'lady-to-be, her eyes narrowing. "Wait."

He paused, raising his eyebrows at her.

"They were sent to me. They're *my* souvenir. I shall keep them. I'd have worn them as a courtesy to your friend." She reached past him and scooped up the bag, tossed it up and caught it again out of the air, her long fingers closing tightly around it. Her edged smile took Roic aback. "I'll wear them now as a defiance to our enemies."

M'lord's eyes blazed back at her.

The countess seized the moment—possibly, Roic thought, to cut off her son from further blithering—and tapped her chrono. "Speaking of wearing things, it's time to get dressed."

M'lord went a shade paler. "Yes, of course." He kissed m'lady-to-be's hand as she rose, looking as if he never wanted to let it go again. Countess Vorkosigan herded everyone except m'lord and his cousin into the hallway, shutting the door to the suite firmly behind her.

"He looks much better now," said Roic to her, glancing back. "I think your sleeptimer was just t' thing."

"Yes, plus the tranquilizers I had Aral give him when he went in to wake him up a while ago. The double dose seems to have been just about right." She hooked her arm through her husband's.

"Still think it should have been a triple," he murmured.

"Now, now. Calm, not comatose, is the goal for our groom." She escorted Madame Vorsoisson toward the stairs; the count went off with Allegre, taking advantage of the chance to discuss details, or perhaps drinks, in private.

Taura stared after them, her smile askew. "You know, I wasn't sure about that woman for Miles at first, but I think she'll do him very well. That Vor thing of his always baffled Elli. Ekaterin has it in her bones same as he does. God help them both."

Roic had been about to say that he thought m'lady-to-be *better* than m'lord deserved, but Taura's last remark brought him up short. "Huh. Yeah. She's true Vor, all right. It's no easy thing."

Taura started down the corridor but stopped at the corner and half turned back to ask, "So, what are you doing after the party?"

"Night guard duty." *All bloody week,* Roic realized in dismay. And Taura only had ten days left on-planet.

"Ah."

She whisked away; Roic glanced at his chrono and gulped. The generous time he'd allotted to dress and report for wedding duty was almost gone. He ran for the stairs.

The guests were already starting to arrive, spilling from the entry hall through the succession of flower-graced public rooms, when Roic scuffed quickly down the staircase to take up his allotted place as backup to Armsman Pym, in turn backing up Count and Countess Vorkosigan. Some on-site guests were already in place: Lady Alys Vorpatril, acting as assistant hostess and general expediter, and her benevolently absentminded escort, Simon Illyan; the Bothari-Jeseks; Mayhew, in apparent permanent tow of Nikki; an assortment of Vorvaynes who had overflowed from Lord Auditor Vorthys's packed house to Vorkosigan House guest rooms. M'lord's friend Commodore Galeni, Chief of ImpSec Komarran Affairs, and his wife were early arrivals, along with m'lord's special Progressive Party colleagues, the Vorbrettens and the Vorrutyers.

Commodore Koudelka and his spouse, known universally as Kou and Drou, arrived with their daughter Martya. Martya was standing in as Madame Vorsoisson's Second in place of m'lady-to-be's closest friend—yet another Koudelka daughter, Kareen, still at school on Beta Colony. Kareen and m'lord's brother, Lord Mark, were much missed (albeit, in remembrance of the bug butter incident, not by Roic) but the interstellar travel time had proved too tight for their schedules. Lord Mark's wedding present was a gift certificate for the bridal couple for a week at an exclusive and very expensive Betan resort, however, so perhaps m'lord and his lady would soon be visiting his brother and their friend, not to mention m'lord's Betan relatives. As gifts went, it at least had the advantage of shifting all the security challenges inherent in the trip to some *later time*.

Martya was sped upstairs by a maid detailed to that purpose. Martya's escort and Lord Mark's business partner, Dr. Borgos, was quietly taken aside by Pym for an unscheduled frisking for any surprise gift insects he might have been harboring, but this time the scientist proved clean. Martya returned unexpectedly soon, her brow wrinkled thoughtfully, and repossessed him to stroll off in search of drinks and company.

Lord Auditor and Professora Vorthys arrived with the rest of the Vorvaynes, altogether a goodly company: four brothers, three wives, ten children, and m'lady-to-be's father and stepmother, in addition to her beloved aunt and uncle. Roic glimpsed Nikki showing off Arde to his mob of awed young Vorvayne cousins, pressing the jump pilot to decant galactic war stories to this enthralled audience. Nikki didn't, Roic noted, seem to have to press very hard. The Betan pilot grew downright expansive in the warm glow of these attentions.

The Vorvayne side stood up bravely to the glittering company that was Vorkosigan House's norm—well, Lord Auditor Vorthys was notoriously oblivious to any status not backed by proven engineering expertise. But even the bride's most buoyant older brother grew subdued and thoughtful when Count Gregor and Countess Laisa Vorbarra were announced. The emperor and empress had cho-

sen to attend the supposedly informal afternoon affair as
social equals to the Vorkosigans, which saved a world of
protocol hassles for everyone, not least themselves. Not in
any other uniform but that of his Count's House could the
emperor have publicly embraced his little foster brother
Miles, who ran downstairs to greet him, nor been so sin-
cerely embraced in return.

In all, m'lord's "little" wedding numbered one hundred
twenty guests. Vorkosigan House absorbed them all.

At last, the moment arrived; the hall and antechambers
became brief, crowded chaos as wraps were redonned and
the guests all streamed out the gate and around the corner
to the garden. The air was cold but not bitter, and thank-
fully windless, the sky a deepening clear blue, the slanting
afternoon sun liquid gold. It turned the snowy garden into
as gilded, glittering, spectacular and utterly unique a show-
place as m'lord's heart could ever have desired. The flowers and ribbons were concentrated around the central
place where the vows were to be, complementing the wild
brilliance of the ice and snow and light.

Although Roic was fairly sure that the two realistically
detailed ice rabbits humping under a discreet bush were
not part of the decorations m'lord had ordered. They did
not pass unnoticed, as the first person to observe them
immediately pointed them out to everyone within
earshot. Ivan Vorpatril averted his gaze from the cheer-
fully obscene artwork—the rabbits were grinning—a look
of innocence on his face. The count's menacing glower at
him was, alas, undercut by an escaping snicker, which became a guffaw when the countess whispered something in
his ear.

The groom's party took up their positions. In the center
of the garden, the walkways, swept clear of snow, met at a
wide circle of paving brick, with the Vorkosigan crest of
mountains and maple leaves picked out in contrasting
brick. In this obvious spot, the small circle of colored
groats was laid out on the ground for the oath-making couple, surrounded by a multipointed star for the principal
witnesses. Another circle of groats crowned a temporary
pathway of tanbark flung wide around the first two rings,
providing dry footing for the rest of the guests.

Roic, wearing a sword for the first time since he'd taken his liegeman's oath, took his place in the formal lineup of armsmen making an aisle on either side of the main pathway. He looked around in worry, for Taura did not loom up among the groom's guests sorting themselves out along the outer circle. M'lord, his hand clutching his cousin Ivan's blue sleeve, gazed up at the entrance in almost painful anticipation. M'lord had, with difficulty, been talked out of hauling his horse in to town to fetch the bride from the house in the old Vor style, though Roic personally had no doubt that the placid, elderly steed would have proved much less nervous and difficult to handle than its master. So the Vorvayne party made their entrance on foot.

Lady Alys, as Coach, led the way like some silken banner carrier. The bride followed on her blinking father's arm, shimmering in a jacket and skirt of beige velvet embroidered with shining silver, her booted feet striding out fearlessly, her eyes seeking only one other face in the mob. The triple stand of pearls gracing her throat glimmered their secret message of bravado to only a few persons here. A few extraordinary persons. By his narrowed eyes and wryly pursed lips, it was clear that Emperor Gregor was one of them.

Roic's might have been the sole gaze not to linger on the bride, for following beside her stepmother, in the place of—no, *as*—the bride's Second, walked Sergeant Taura. Roic's eyes shifted, though he kept his rigid posture—yes, there was Martya Koudelka with Dr. Borgos on the outer circle, apparently demoted to the status of mere guest but not looking in the least put out. In fact, she seemed to be watching Taura with smug approval. Taura's dress was everything that Lady Alys had promised. Champagne-colored velvet exactly matched her eyes, which seemed to spring to a brilliant prominence in her face. The jacket sleeves and long swinging skirt were decorated on their margins with black cord shaped into winding patterns. Champagne-colored orchids coiled in her bound-back hair. Roic thought he'd never seen anything so stunningly sophisticated in his life.

Everyone took their places. M'lord and m'lady-to-be

stepped into the inner circle, hands gripping hands like two lovers drowning. The bride looked not so much radiant as incandescent; the groom looked gobsmacked. Lord Ivan and Taura were handed the two little bags of groats with which to close the circle, then stood back to their star points between Count and Countess Vorkosigan and Vorvayne and his wife. Lady Alys read out the vows, and m'lord and m'lady-to—*m'lady* repeated their responses, her voice clear, his only cracking once. The kiss was managed with remarkable grace, m'lady somehow bending her knee in a curtsylike motion so m'lord didn't have to stretch unduly. It suggested thought and practice. Lots of practice.

With immense panache, Lord Ivan then swept the groat circle wide with one booted foot, triumphantly collecting his kiss from the bride as she exited. Lord and Lady Vorkosigan passed out of the dazzling ice garden between the lines of Vorkosigan armsmen; swords, drawn and lowered at their feet, rose in salute as they passed. When Pym led the Armsmen's Shout, the sound of twenty enthusiastic male voices bounced and echoed off the garden walls and thundered to the sky. M'lord grinned over his shoulder and blushed with pleasure at this deafening endorsement.

As Seconds, Taura followed next on Lord Ivan's arm, bending her head to hear something he said, laughing. The row of armsmen remained to rigid attention while all the principals streamed past them, then formed up and marched smartly in their wake, followed by the guests, back around and into Vorkosigan House. It had all gone off *perfectly*. Pym looked as though he wanted to pass out there and then from sheer relief.

Vorkosigan House's main state dining room boasted seating for ninety-six when both tables were brought out in parallel; the overflow fit in the chamber immediately beyond, through a wide archway, so that the whole company could sit down at once essentially together. Serving was not Roic's responsibility tonight, but in his role as arbiter of emergencies and general assistant for any guest needing anything, he kept to his feet and moving. Taura was seated at the head table with the principals and the most honored guests—the *other* most honored guests. Between tall, dark, handsome Lord Ivan and tall, dark, lean Emperor Gregor, she looked *really* happy. Roic could not wish her anywhere else, but he found himself mentally erasing Ivan and replacing him with himself ... yet Ivan and the emperor were the very pattern of debonair wit. They made Taura laugh, fangs flashing without constraint. Roic would probably just sit there in inarticulate silence and gawp at her ...

Martya Koudelka passed him in the entryway, where he'd temporarily taken up guard stance, and smiled cheerily at him. "Hi, Roic."

He nodded. "Miss Martya."

She followed his glance to the head table. "Taura looks wonderful, doesn't she?"

"Sure does." He hesitated. "How come you're not up there?"

Her voice lowered. "I heard the story about last night from Ekaterin. She asked me if I'd mind trading. I said, *God, no*. Gets me out of having to sit there and make small talk with Ivan, for one thing." She wrinkled her nose.

"It was well thought of, of m'lady."

She hitched up one shoulder. "It was the one honor here that was wholly hers to bestow. The Vorkosigans are amazing, but you have to admit, they do eat you up. They give you a wild ride in return, though." She stood on tiptoe and planted an unexpected kiss on Roic's cheek.

He touched the spot in surprise. "What's that for?"

"For your half of last night. For saving us all from having to live with a *really* insane Miles Vorkosigan. As long as he lasted." A brief quaver shook her flippant voice. She tossed her blond hair and bounced off.

The toasts were made with the count's very best wines, including a few historical bottles, reserved for the head table, that had been laid down before the end of the Time of Isolation. Afterward the party moved to the brilliant ballroom, seeming another garden, heady with the scent of a sudden spring. Lord and Lady Vorkosigan opened the dancing. Those who could still move after the dinner followed them onto the polished marquetry floor.

Roic found himself, all too briefly, passing by Taura as she watched the dancers sway and twirl.

"Do you dance, Roic?" she asked him.

"Can't. I'm on duty. You?"

"I'm afraid I don't know any of these dances. Although I'm sure Miles would have foisted an instructor on me if he'd thought of it."

"Actually," he admitted in a lower voice, "I don't know how either."

Her lips curled up. "Well, don't let Miles know if you want it to stay that way. He'd have you out there thumping around before you knew what hit you."

He tried not to snicker. He hardly knew what to say to this, but his parting half-salute did not betoken disagreement.

On the sixth number, m'lady danced past Roic with her eldest brother, Hugo.

"Splendid necklace, Kat. From your spouse, is it?"

"No, actually. From one of his . . . business associates."

"Expensive!"

"Yes." M'lady's faint smile made the hairs stir on Roic's arms. "I expect it to cost him everything he has."

They spun away.

Taura nailed it. She'll do for m'lord, all right. And God help their enemies.

Promptly on schedule, the aircar was brought round for the bridal couple's getaway. The night was still fairly young, but it was more than an hour's flight to Vorkosigan Surleau and the lakeside estate that was to be the honeymoon refuge. The place would be quiet this time of year, blanketed with snow and peace. Roic could not imagine two people more in need of a little peace.

The guests in residence were to be left behind under the care of the count and countess for a few days, although the galactic guests would travel down to the lake later. Among other things, Roic was given to understand, Madame Bothari-Jesek wished to visit her father's grave there with her husband and new daughter and burn a death offering.

Roic had thought Pym would be doing the flying, but to his surprise, Armsman Jankowski took the controls as the newlyweds ran the gauntlet of raucous family and friends and made it to the rear compartment.

"I've shuffled some assignments," Pym murmured to Roic as they both stood smiling in the porte cochere to watch and salute. M'lord and m'lady seemed to melt into each other's arms in an equal mix of love and exhaustion as the silvered canopy finally closed over them. "I'm taking night watch in Vorkosigan House for the next week. *You* have the week off with double holiday pay. With m'lady's own thanks."

"Oh," said Roic. He blinked. Pym had been quite frustrated by the fact that no one, from the count down, had seen fit to censure him for the slipup with the necklace. He could only conclude that Pym had given up and decided to supply his own penance. Well, if the senior armsman looked to be carrying it too far, the countess could be relied upon to step in. "Thanks!"

"You can consider yourself free from whenever Count and Countess Vorbarra leave." Pym nodded and stepped back as the aircar eased out from under the overhang and began to rise into the cold night air as if buoyed up by the yells and cheers of the well-wishers.

A splendid and prolonged burst of fireworks made the send-off a thing of beauty and a joy to Barrayaran hearts. Taura applauded and hooted, too, and, along with Arde Mayhew, joined Nikki's cohort for some added, unscheduled crackers and sparklers in the back garden. Powder smoke perfumed the air in clouds as the children ran around Taura, urging her to throw the lights *higher*. Security and an assortment of mothers might have quashed the game, except for the fact that the large bag of most remarkable incendiary goodies had been slipped to Nikki by Count Vorkosigan.

The party wound down. Sleepy, protesting children were carried past Roic to their cars or to their beds. The emperor and empress were seen out fondly by the count and countess; soon after their departure, a score of unobtrusive, efficient servants, on loan from ImpSec, vanished quietly and without fanfare. The remaining energetic young people hijacked the ballroom to dance to music more to their taste. Their tired elders sought quieter corners in the succession of public rooms in which to converse and sample more of the count's very best wines.

Roic found Taura sitting alone in one of the small side rooms on a sturdy-looking sofa of the style she favored, reflectively working her way through a platter of Ma Kosti's dainties on a low table before her. She looked drowsy and contented, and yet a little apart from it all. As if she were a guest in her own life . . .

Roic gave her a smile, a nod, a semisalute. He wished he'd thought to provide himself with roses or something. What could a fellow give to a woman like this? The finest chocolate, maybe, yeah, although that was redundant at the moment. Tomorrow for sure. "Um . . . have you had a good time?"

"Oh, yes. Wonderful."

She sat back and smiled almost up at him—an unusual angle of view. She looked good from this direction, too. M'lord's comment about horizontal height differentials drifted through his memory. She patted the sofa beside her; Roic glanced around, overcame his guard-stance habits, and sat down. His feet hurt, he realized.

The silence that fell was companionable, not strained, but after a time he broke it. "You like Barrayar, then?"

"It's been a great visit. Better than my best dreams."

Ten more days. Ten days was an eyeblink. Ten days was just not enough for all he had to say, to give, to do. Ten years might be a start. "You, uh, have you ever thought of staying? Here? It could be done, y'know. Find a place you could fit. Or make one." M'lord would figure out how, if anyone could. With great daring, he let his hand curl over hers on the seat between them.

Her brows rose. "I already have a place I fit."

"Yeah, but . . . forever? Your mercs seem like a chancy sort of thing to me. No solid ground under them. And nothing lasts forever, not even organizations."

"*Nobody* lives long enough to have *all* their choices." She was silent for a moment, then added, "The people who bioengineered me to be a super-soldier didn't consider a long life span to be a necessity. Miles has a few biting remarks about that, but oh well. The fleet medics give me about a year yet."

"Oh." It took him a minute to work through this; his stomach felt suddenly tight and cold. A dozen obscure remarks from the past few days fell into place. He wished they hadn't. *No, oh, no . . . !*

"Hey, don't look so bludgeoned." Her hand curled around to clasp his in return. "The bastards have been giving me a year yet for the past four years running. I've seen other soldiers have their whole careers and die in the time the medics have been screwing around with me. I've stopped worrying about it."

He had no idea what to say to this. Screaming was right out. He shifted a bit closer to her instead.

She eyed him thoughtfully. "Some fellows, when I tell them this, get spooked and veer off. It's not contagious."

Roic swallowed hard. "I'm not running away."

"I see that." She rubbed her neck with her free hand; an orchid petal parted from her hair and caught upon her velvet-clad shoulder. "Part of me wishes the medics would get it settled. Part of me says, the hell with it. Every day is a gift. Me, I rip open the package and wolf it down on the spot."

He looked up at her in wonder. His grip tightened, as though she might be pulled from him as they sat, right now, if he didn't hold hard enough. He leaned over, reached across and picked off the fragile petal, touched it to his lips. He took a deep, scared breath. "Can you teach me how to do that?"

Her fantastic gold eyes widened. "Why, Roic! I think that's the most delicately worded proposition I've ever received. S' beautiful." An uncertain pause. "Um, that *was* a proposition, wasn't it? I'm not always sure I parlay Barrayaran."

Desperately terrified now, he blurted in what he imagined to be merc-speak, "Ma'am, yes, *ma'am!*"

This won an immense fanged smile—*not* in a version he'd ever seen before. It made him, too, want to fall over backward, though preferably not into a snowbank. He glanced around. The softly lit room was littered with abandoned plates and wineglasses, detritus of pleasure and good company. Low voices chatted idly in the next chamber. Somewhere in another room, softened by the distance, a clock was chiming the hour. Roic declined to count the beats.

They floated in a bubble of fleeting time, live heat in the heart of a bitter winter. He leaned forward, raised his face, slid his hand around her warm neck, drew her face down to his. It wasn't hard. Their lips brushed, locked.

Several minutes later, in a shaken, hushed voice, he breathed, *"Wow."*

Several minutes after *that,* they went upstairs, hand in hand.

The Alchemical Marriage

by Mary Jo Putney

1

The Tower of London, July 1588

Though the chambers were spacious and furnished as
befitted a prisoner of rank, the cold stone walls were
saturated with pain and death. Sir Adam Macrae paced his
prison, shackles rattling, wondering if he would be granted
the formality of a trial before he was executed. Or would
he be kept here forever, quietly rotting as his spirit and
body withered away?

The heavy door squealed open. He turned warily, knowing it was not time for food to be delivered. His expression
hardened at the entrance of two men in dark cowled
cloaks. So the Virgin Queen and her counselors had chosen
to silence him by assassination rather than risk beheading
a prominent Scot.

Well, by God, he'd not be taken down without a fight. He
gripped the length of chain that connected his manacles.
Though the damnable iron curbed his power, the heavy
links would make a fair weapon.

The taller of the men pushed back his hood, revealing a
long white beard and piercing eyes. It was John Dee, the
queen's own sorcerer.

Macrae caught his breath. Dee had true power as well
as influence with the queen, but he would not be sent here
to perform a simple assassination. "I thought you were liv-

ing on the Continent, Master Dee. 'Tis said that you might end your days in Bohemia, where your work is so much valued."

Dee gave a dry little smile. "Officially, I am in Bohemia still, but my queen has need of me, for a great crisis looms."

"England is threatened? Splendid." Macrae applauded, the manacles jangling. "I pray strength to her enemies."

"Don't be so swift to invoke destruction. There are worse fates than Elizabeth, no matter how little you like her."

"She murdered the Queen of Scots," Macrae said flatly. "She deserves everything I said, and more."

"No one regretted Mary Stuart's death more than Elizabeth. She stayed her hand for years—decades—despite all the evidence that your queen was involved in treasonous plots. The necessity of executing her own cousin and fellow sovereign drove Elizabeth half mad with grief."

"Nonetheless, murder her cousin she did."

"Couldn't you have waited until you returned to Scotland before cursing Elizabeth's name and predicting that the wrath of God would strike her? She had no choice but to imprison you." The old sorcerer shook his head dourly. "You supported Mary at the risk of your own life, even though she was Catholic and you a Protestant. Though your loyalty is commendable, one must wonder about your sense."

As a stubborn Scot, sense had never been Macrae's strong point. "What is a man without loyalty? She was my queen, and Elizabeth had no right to execute her. Did you come here to taunt me for my foolish tongue?"

"No, Sir Adam." Dee's gaze was steady. "I've come to ask if you would like to earn your freedom."

Freedom? A vision of Glen Rath washed over Macrae. The most beautiful place on God's green earth, with wild clear air where a man could breathe . . .

He clamped down on his longing, knowing it would weaken him. "Of course I want to be free, but it's possible for freedom to come at too high a price."

" 'Tis said you are the finest weather mage in Britain, Sir Adam." The shrewd eyes glinted. "I want you to conjure me a tempest."

So Dee knew of his powers. That would explain why

Macrae's jailers had known to keep him bound with the iron that curbed his magic. He had wondered about that, since rarely were prisoners of rank manacled. The fact that the queen's soldiers had burst into his lodgings at night and slapped irons on him before he could fight back had made him wonder if he had been betrayed by another Guardian, but apparently not. The formidable Dee had his own ways of learning. "Perhaps I could, but why should I?"

"To save Britain from a great evil." Dee moved stiffly to one of the chairs, shadowed by his attendant. "Do you mind if I sit, Sir Adam? My old bones ache from the journey across Europe."

Reminded of his duties as host, Macrae took wine from a well-stocked cabinet and filled three goblets. Dee accepted readily, but his companion hesitated before taking a goblet and withdrawing to the darkest corner of the room. He moved with the suppleness of youth. An apprentice sorcerer or a body servant? Whichever, he had Dee's trust. Macrae must hope the boy also had discretion.

Macrae took the chair opposite Dee, stretching his long legs out before him, a portrait of ease despite his chains. "You say you want a tempest."

"Spain and England have been at each other's throats since the death of Mary Tudor. Now Spain is gathering an Armada, the greatest fleet ever seen—more than one hundred thirty ships and thirty thousand men. Far more than England can muster." Dee stared into his wine. "I want you to call up a storm that will destroy the Spanish ships and save England from invasion."

Macrae gasped. "Have you any idea what you're asking? The greatest weather mage who ever lived could not conjure such a storm. Particularly not at this season. Magic must build on what exists in nature, and the light airs of summer offer little of the power I would need to spin a small storm into a great one."

"I know it will not be easy, but if any man can, it is you."

Macrae let the metal links slide between his fingers, the weight of the chain crushing his mind. "After more than a year of cold iron, I don't know if I still have power. Even if I do, I'll fry in hell before using it on Elizabeth's behalf."

"This is not about Elizabeth, but about Britain. That

means Scotland as well as England. Do you really want the harsh hand of Spain to fall over this island?"

Macrae shrugged. "They may plunder London, but I doubt they'll touch my people in the wilds of Scotland. Let them come. It matters not to me whether English Elizabeth or Spanish Philip rules here."

"Not even if refusing my offer costs your life?"

His mouth twisted. "I've lived in daily expectation of my death for fifteen long months, Master Dee. How is this day any different?"

With a muffled oath, Dee's hooded companion swirled from the shadowed corner. "If you think a Spanish invasion doesn't matter, you are as ignorant as you are foolish, Macrae. Put aside your prejudices and *think*."

The whiskey-rich voice was female. Sweeping back her hood, the woman revealed blazing black eyes in a narrow, Byzantine face of fearsome intelligence. In her late twenties, she was not pretty. Instead, she was beautiful in the manner of a glittering, deadly sword.

"Sir Adam, meet my associate, Isabel de Cortes," Dee said dryly. "If you need persuasion or assistance, she can provide it."

Macrae studied the woman. Even his iron-crippled inner vision could see that she burned with a mage's power now that she was no longer masking her abilities. "Isabel de Cortes," he said musingly. "A Spanish name, and a Spanish face. Do you hate your own country so much, Mistress?"

"Spain birthed my ancestors, but it is not my country. England has my loyalty." Isabel's dark eyes narrowed. "You think a Spanish invasion will not affect Scotland, but you are wrong. When Mary Tudor reigned, Philip of Spain was her husband, and the burning flesh of Protestant martyrs fouled the air of Smithfield. That was nothing compared to what will happen if the Inquisition comes to Britain."

"That will never happen."

"You think not? Your Queen of Scots bequeathed Philip her claims to the English throne, and his soldiers are coming to seize that bequest by fire and steel. Even your northern wilderness will not be distant enough to protect you."

"You do not know Scotland or the Scots."

She made a sound that reminded him of a wildcat. "As a mage, you must have some scrying ability. Take a long, true look into this, and then tell me it doesn't matter if the Spanish come." Delving into a pocket of her robe, she brought out a disk of polished obsidian perhaps four inches in diameter.

He refused to take the scrying glass. "You forget that iron chains bind me."

"The touch of iron curbs *all* your powers, even the smallest?" Isabel looked shocked. Worse, pitying. "Most mages are not so sensitive."

"I am." His voice was flat. For fifteen endless months, his inner senses had been blind and deaf and dumb, leaving aching emptiness that might never be filled again.

"Master Dee, you have the key to the shackles," Isabel said. "Give it to me so I can free Macrae."

Dee produced the key. "Sir Adam must swear not to use his power to harm."

"If you know anything of the Guardians, you must know that we are pledged to protect, not destroy." To be free of the chains . . . Macrae eyed the key longingly. The conjuror was old, and it would be easy to take the key from him— no. He had not yet fallen so far as to attack an old man.

Deciding that Macrae had tacitly agreed to Dee's condition, Isabel collected the key and came to unlock the shackles. Heart pounding with impatience, he held out his wrists, trying to keep his hands from trembling. She bent her head over the chains as she wrestled with the crude locks, which had not been opened in more than a year. Her fingertips brushed his wrists, searing the chaffed, tender flesh with her mage's energy.

One hand released. He had to exert all his control to hold steady while she twisted the key in the other lock. Her hair had the dark glossiness of a raven's wing.

The lock opened, and the shackles fell across his lap. He lifted the murderous chain that had imprisoned his mind even more thoroughly than his body—then hurled it into the cold fireplace with crashing rage. As he rubbed his wrists, he was painfully aware that his numbed mind felt no different. Had fifteen months of paralysis hammered his power to uselessness?

He stalked to his single barred window and stared out at the sky. Through his long captivity, he had envied the gulls that soared over the Thames. If he were a shape-shifter, he would have transformed himself and flown home to Scotland. But he had no such power, so he had remained earthbound, deprived of his deepest self.

Invoking the discipline of his training, he visualized light pouring through his body, burning away poisons of fear and frustration. Deep within stirred a small flex of power, like a firefly sparking in the night. Torn between wanting to seize and wanting to savor, he nurtured that spark, delicately reviving what had been frozen so long.

Like the spring ice break in a Highland burn, power surged through him. Giddy with the rush of magic, he threw the rage of his captivity into a cloud drifting across the sun. Swiftly it grew and darkened until a storm struck the Tower of London with a fury that rattled the rooftops. Slanting rain swept between the bars, cold and refreshing. He laughed aloud at the heady joy of once again shaping the wind.

"A good use of anger," Isabel remarked. "Now you must learn to hate the Spanish fleet."

Macrae had half forgotten his visitors, who had been waiting in silence. Releasing the cloud, he turned back to the room. The rain began to diminish. In five minutes, the squall would be gone.

"Look now." Once more Isabel offered her scrying glass. She had removed her cloak, revealing a strong, sensual body. He had not been in the same room with a woman since his imprisonment, and he found himself shamefully aware of her femaleness. Her scent sparked thoughts of starlight and desert spices.

He accepted the glass with reluctance. A gifted scryer could see in any reflective surface—water, wine, glass, a gemstone—but this smoky obsidian pulsed with its owner's energy as if it were a living creature.

During his captivity he had been darkly glad the iron had blocked his vision, for surely scrying would show his doom. But even though he feared it would reveal more than he wanted to see, the time had come to look beyond his cell. He closed his eyes, clearing his mind as he formulated a question.

What might a Spanish invasion bring? Then he gazed through the glass with unfocused eyes so images might appear.

Dunrath was burning. His fingers spasmed around the disk. Dear God, his mother was leaping from the tower window, choosing a swift death to the slow horror of burning alive! Why would Spaniards attack his home?

The answer formed in his mind as easily as the image had formed in the obsidian: because his younger brother was another stubborn Macrae who would refuse to foreswear his faith or bend his knee to foreigners. Dunrath would be razed as a lesson to other clans.

Macrae had accepted the imminence of his own death, but he had believed his home was safe. His brother would become laird, the girl Macrae was to wed would find another husband, and his family would continue in health and prosperity. But this . . .

Could Isabel de Cortes have planted false images in the glass? He rejected the idea instantly. True as the blade she resembled, she would not spin lies to make her case even if such a thing were possible.

Temples throbbing, he looked at the scrying glass again, hoping to see some mitigation of the horror of his first vision.

Sweet Jesus, *no!* The image that formed was of Edinburgh Castle looming majestically over the city—a city that looked as if the wrath of God had struck. No, not God, but men of hatred who would force others into their own mold and destroy when they could not persuade. Smoke began pouring from the castle itself. The pride and history of Scotland were being put to the torch while Spanish soldiers ran wild, raping and pillaging.

He didn't need Dee or Isabel de Cortes to tell him that scrying was not Truth, but rather Possibility. Grimly, he forced himself to watch as other horrors shimmered before his eyes. A group of martyrs singing to God as flames consumed them. The Virgin Queen on the scaffold, going to her death with steely courage. Armed soldiers breaking in on Protestants who worshipped in secret, the flash of blades contrasting with gouts of crimson blood.

How long Macrae watched the glass he did not know, but when he looked up his body was chilled and the room was darkening. Isabel rose to light candles against the approaching night. "It is not a good future," she said quietly.

"No." Though he disliked the idea of working with these Sassenach, he could not stand by while wolves prepared to ravage Britain. "I'll do what I can to thwart the Armada, but I warn you that conjuring such a tempest may be beyond my abilities." His lips thinned as he returned the scrying glass. "It will be bitter to harm so many men when I am oath-sworn to protect."

"I have no more desire to take life than you, Sir Adam." Dee looked old and very tired. "The intent is to disperse the ships, destroy their fighting effectiveness, not to kill. A storm in the Narrow Seas would drive the ships onto the Flemish coast, and God willing, most of the sailors and soldiers will survive."

It was a lawyer's quibble—even if the intent wasn't to kill, a tempest powerful enough to scatter so many ships would surely cause the weakest to founder. Men would die—Macrae could not delude himself otherwise. But if he saw true, action on his part might save many more lives than it endangered.

Power was a chancy, dangerous gift. Guardians were trained in ethics and morality from childhood, but no teacher could anticipate all possibilities. When a situation was critical, the Guardian involved must decide what would be best—and may God send wisdom to choose the right. "I shall do what I can, but I will need help."

"Whatever you wish, Sir Adam," Dee said. "What are your requirements?"

"First, get me released from this poxy prison. I want a letter signed by Elizabeth herself saying that all charges against me have been dropped and I am a free man. Explain to her that on my oath I will do my best, but I cannot guarantee that I will be able to conjure a storm great enough to destroy the Armada."

Dee nodded. "Understood. I am authorized to grant that. What else?"

Macrae rubbed his throbbing head, trying to imagine what he would need for an undertaking of this magnitude. "I must have a location within sight of the Channel, preferably in a place of power."

Isabel said, "My family has a small manor in Kent that fits that requirement. What else?"

"I haven't enough power to create such a tempest alone, so I will need your assistance in the working, Master Dee. If I can draw on your magic, there is a chance I may succeed."

The old man exchanged a glance with the woman. "Isabel will be your assistant."

Macrae's gaze swung to her with dismay. He was to work with this dangerously alluring wildcat with her obsidian eyes? Keeping his voice level, he said, "I prefer to work with you. Our energies will blend better."

The old man shook his head. "I am a noteworthy scholar, an astrologer, and a student of ancient wisdom, but my magical power is only moderate. Isabel is the best scryer and most powerful mage I've ever met— except for you, perhaps. She can contribute far more than I."

Macrae wanted to protest but couldn't. His inner senses told him that Dee spoke the truth: For a great magical working, Isabel de Cortes would be a far better partner. More powerful, and more dangerous.

He closed his eyes with weariness and once more saw Dunrath burn.

2

Kent, August 1588

It was midafternoon when the dusty party of travelers arrived at Leighton Manor. The sea wasn't visible, but the scent of it was borne on the wind.

As soon as the half dozen horses pulled up by the Leighton stables, the Scotsman vaulted from his mount, tossed his reins to one of the servants who accompanied them, and strode off toward the shoreline. As his long legs carried him swiftly away, Isabel dismounted and crossed to Master Dee. "Do you think he'll try to escape?"

The old man came off his horse with a groan of fatigue.

"No, he's given his word, and Guardians never break their word. They believe it compromises their powers."

"I would like to know more of the Guardians."

Dee gestured in the direction Macrae had vanished. "There's the man who can tell you."

"He could, but he won't," she said dryly. "Macrae has done his best to avoid talking or looking at me ever since we started this journey."

"He is not comfortable knowing how closely he must work with you. Sharing power is a very intimate process, and you are a stranger."

"And like to remain so."

"Go after him."

"Perhaps I shall, after you are properly settled." She beckoned to the housekeeper, Mistress Heath, who had emerged from the house to greet the guests.

Dee smiled a little. "Don't worry about your hostess duties—the servants will see to my comfort. It is more important that you weave a bond with our weather mage."

Isabel let herself be persuaded because she wanted to follow Macrae. The man intrigued her. He moved like a panther, barely tamed. And though he might dislike her, he was a mage himself so didn't fear her as most men did. She could learn much from him.

Lifting her skirts clear of the tangled wildflowers, she left the cluster of buildings and followed the lane Macrae had taken. The manor house was set in a fold of hills to shelter it from the scouring winds, but the sea was only a short walk away.

She located her quarry in the ancient stone circle set on a bluff that rose a hundred feet above the crashing waves. Local legend said the circle had been built by Druids. For those with the vision to see, three faintly glowing ley lines crossed at the site, creating a starburst of earth energy. As Isabel had promised, it was a place of great power.

Sunlight glowing on his dark red hair, the Scotsman walked the circle, touching each of the irregularly shaped stones in turn. "It didn't take you long to find me, Mistress de Cortes."

"I knew the circle would draw you. It burns with power."

She had spent endless hours in this place, meditating, studying, experimenting to find the shape and limits of her talent. Though it was disturbing to see her sanctuary invaded by such restless male energy, the circle was the logical place to hold the ritual. She could cleanse it of his presence when their work was done.

"You said your family owns this manor?" While his tone was brusque, at least he was speaking to her.

"Yes, but I'm the only one who comes here." Leighton was her home, far more than the grand London house where her parents and brothers resided. Here she could be her prickly, stubborn self. "What does it mean to be a Guardian? Is it a secret society?"

He hesitated, then shrugged, as if deciding that her abilities gave her a right to know. "We are not so organized— merely a collection of families in which power runs strongly. We know one another and often intermarry, but usually we go our separate ways. Our homes are in the fringes of Britain, where the ancient magic is strongest. Scotland, Wales, Cornwall, the Isle of Man, Ireland—you will find us in all those places. We are sworn not only to protect but to keep our powers hidden for safety's sake."

"Are you all weather mages?"

"Power comes in many forms, and weather mastery is rare." He smiled wryly. "Specific abilities don't manifest until a child approaches maturity. My first sign of weather work was blowing the roof off a cowshed. My father was not pleased."

She hadn't seen him smile before and was surprised at how attractive his craggy, bearded face was when he wasn't scowling. "How long have the Guardians existed?"

"No one really knows—certainly since before the Romans came to Britain. In ancient times the great mages engaged in a struggle for power that nearly destroyed us all. The survivors met in council and agreed that we must use our abilities for peace and protection." He gazed out to sea, his expression haunted. "We do our best, but the struggle is unending."

So the name Guardian was literal. How strange and beautiful that these people of power pledged themselves to serve and protect. What would it be like to come from such a family? "You must all be saints if you can agree on what is best."

"I didn't say we always agreed, but we try to do the right thing. We ... don't always succeed." He bent to pick a wild-flower. "I wish my mother was here so I could discuss this undertaking with her. She has the clearest mind of any mage I know."

"Women are accepted as equals in your councils?" she said, startled.

"Of course—some of the most powerful mages in Britain are female."

"What a wonder!"

"Your family is not like that?"

"A few of my de Cortes ancestors had minor gifts, but there has never been one like me." Her parents despaired of her. They had wanted a pleasant, submissive daughter who would marry within their circle. Instead they had birthed a child too strange, too independent, for normal life. "When I began showing signs of unusual power, my father engaged Master Dee to be my teacher so I would learn to control my abilities. He has been my salvation. I never once heard of your Guardians."

"Master Dee has suffered because of his public reputation as a conjuror and astrologer. The abuse heaped on him illustrates why we prefer to stay in the background." He raised his head and gazed out to sea, as if scenting the wind. "The fleets are skirmishing near the Dutch shore. Men are dying just out of sight and sound."

The reminder of their mission destroyed her pleasure in the perfect summer day. "You can see that without scrying?"

"I hear their cries on the wind."

She pulled out her scrying glass, which was always with her. In the smoky depths, she watched the vicious recoil of cannon as two ships blasted silently away at each other, sending smoke and flames billowing. It was a scene from hell. "The English squadron is well-commanded and sea-worthy but vastly outnumbered. The danger is great. We must act quickly."

"No doubt you are right, yet it is hard to undertake a working that will cost so many lives if I am successful."

Her lips thinned. "You do not seem wholly committed to

our cause, Macrae. Has your detestation for the English blinded you to the probability that the Spanish will murder your own mother?"

His head whipped around, his eyes sparking dangerously. "How do you know what I saw in your glass?"

"As your gift is weather, mine is clear-seeing. After you looked into your future, I was able to see the images you had invoked." She shook her head. "Passion fuels power. You need more anger, Macrae. This is not a game, but a life and death struggle. What will make you truly wish to destroy our enemies?"

"If I have too little anger, you have too much, Mistress. Your loathing of the Spanish is like a burning brand. Surely Master Dee taught you that hatred is dangerous for those with power. You run the risk of destroying not only your enemies but yourself. In this case you are hating those of your own blood."

"These Spaniards are not my blood!" Her anger flared, not only at the Spanish but at Macrae for reading her so easily. "It has been almost a hundred years since my people left Spain. We were tortured, murdered, robbed, and exiled forever from the land that we had served loyally. They called us *marranos,* swine. I care nothing for what happens to me, as long as we prevent those Spanish beasts from invading England."

He studied her face, his hazel eyes golden in the afternoon sun. "So you are a Jew. I have heard that a few Jewish families took refuge in England after they were expelled from Spain and Portugal. Did your family forswear the Catholicism they were forced to embrace and return to the faith of their fathers?"

"We are good Protestants now, but our memories are long." And if some Jewish practices lingered still in the privacy of their homes, well, that was no one else's business. They did what was necessary to survive, and to keep the Covenant in their hearts. "You accuse me of hating, yet you hate Elizabeth. Why? She is a just and fair-minded ruler. Her wisdom in balancing Catholics and Protestants has kept Englishmen from spilling one another's blood. Why do you despise her?"

"She executed my queen. For that, I cannot forgive her."

"Mary Stuart, a Scot raised at the French court, who spun plots from her prison and sought to have Elizabeth assassinated," Isabel snapped. "Even a Scotsman as loyal as you cannot deny Mary's treachery."

His jaw tightened. Stubborn man. Knowing they would never agree about politics, she said, "Master Dee tells me you have given your word to conjure a tempest, so let us begin. There is no time to waste." She started to turn back to the house.

He caught her wrist. They both froze as energy surged between them. She felt as if all her breath had been blasted from her body. So this was passion—uncomfortable, inappropriate, undeniable. He felt the same—she could see it in his eyes.

He released her wrist, his breath roughened. "The preparations are complex, and Dee must cast a chart for the best time to proceed. If we don't harness every available wisp of power, there will be no chance of success."

She retreated a step, not wanting to meet his gaze. "Very well, do what you must, but be quick about it, before it's too late."

"As you wish, Mistress Witch," he said with heavy irony. "Perhaps I can conjure a swift squall to end the fighting for the moment, so the English will be able to regroup."

"If you can do that, why haven't you?" she asked with exasperation.

"Because I fear the cost to my soul. But you're right. I cannot hold back any longer, no matter how much I dislike this task." He turned and rested his hands on the largest stone, the one closest to the sea. As he concentrated his energies on the task, he became absolutely still except for the movement of his lips chanting soundlessly.

Keeping her distance from the vortex of power swirling around him, Isabel used her glass to monitor the battle. Skies darkened, vicious rain swept through the warring fleets, and the fighting broke up. The Spanish fell back, and one of their damaged warships foundered and sank.

While Isabel whispered a soft prayer of thanks, Macrae expelled a long, rattling breath and released his spell. His face was gaunt, drained of its usual vitality.

Knowing how demanding weather work was, she silently

asked the obsidian what would become of Macrae. The battle images dissolved into swirling fog.

What about her fate? She cleared her mind and tried to draw her own image from the glass.

Still nothing.

She felt chilled, even though the inability to scry could mean many things. Most likely she couldn't see because she was too closely involved in what was about to happen to have the necessary clarity. But it was also possible that the demands of stopping the Armada would be so great that neither of them would survive.

Concealing her foreboding, Isabel said, "Well done. You succeeded in ending the battle before the English fleet could be badly damaged. I begin to believe you can produce the great storm we need."

His eyes opened, and he turned to lean against the stone, folding his arms across his chest. "I was fortunate. There was the beginning of a summer squall near the ships, so all I had to do was strengthen it. The spell required for that was to a great tempest as a barn cat is to a tiger." His mouth twisted. "Surely you know that magic always has a price, and the one I pay will be high. Are you also willing to pay the cost of this conjuring?"

She thought of the clouded obsidian. "I am willing."

Even if the price demanded all that she had.

3

Calling the winds . . .

The air tingled with power as Macrae and Mistress de Cortes took their places in the ancient stone circle. Man and woman, ever opposite but complementary. Dee was not present, since he would be unable to help and he feared his presence would be a distraction. The old man had cast a chart for the best time, but his face had been somber when he studied the planetary positions. It hadn't been necessary for him to say that the chart did not guarantee success.

But it was the best time available without waiting for

days, so Macrae must make of it what he could. Despite his initial reluctance to undertake this task, the images of Dunrath and Edinburgh haunted him. Now he was as determined as the woman who faced him across the circle.

He inclined his head to his companion. "Mistress, let us begin."

"As you will, Macrae." Her demeanor was reserved, though nothing could diminish the snap of her black eyes or the allure of her lush female figure.

He began by casting a circle of protection, using the familiar ritual to focus his mind. As his concentration increased, his inner vision recognized the essences around him. Isabel de Cortes was the most vivid. Deep and intense, she was a beacon of power.

He reached out and touched her energy. Silently, she acknowledged his presence and granted him access. Another time he would have been tempted to explore the riches of her mind and spirit, at least until she clamped down her shields and expelled him, but now he had more important work.

Widening his perception, he felt Dee's energy in the manor house. The old man's pattern was a structure of immense complexity with a blazing mind at the core. The servants were sparks of light, each unique if one chose to study it closely. He did not so choose, not tonight.

He tuned himself to the earth and the ancient force that resided there. Isabel was right, this was a place of great magic. When he was fully oriented, he flung his consciousness high into the sky, soaring toward the sun like a giant hawk. The circle, the two human figures, the coast, and the rolling seas—all dropped away below at a dizzying speed. With Isabel's power to fuel his flight, he soared higher and higher until his awareness stretched east across the Channel, north to Scotland, south to France, west as far as Ireland.

The day before, Isabel had scryed the English sending fire ships into the Armada. Little damage was done, but only because the Spanish ships had cut their anchors to escape swiftly. Though doing so had saved them from burning, without good anchors the ships were vulnerable when close to shore.

Yes, that was the answer. The Armada was now boxed

between the harrying English and the sandbanks off the Dutch province of Zeeland. If he could force the ships onto the shoals, many would break up, but the shallow waters and nearby mainland would minimize the cost in lives. He would find no better location to fulfill his mission.

He cast the net of his mind outward to gather the winds and discovered why Dee's chart had been equivocal about this time. Throughout the British Isles and the Narrow Seas the airs were light, giving him little to work with.

But there was always weather, even when times were mild. He narrowed his vision to identify wind patterns strong enough to shape to his purpose. Over Holland he found a choppy, gusting breeze. He gathered it in and added a series of light winds from Scotland and northern England. Then he captured an energetic sea breeze from the coast of Cornwall. On the edge of his awareness he sensed a storm over Bavaria, but it was too distant for summoning.

Each of the elements had its own essence, qualities that made him think of rainbows and musical notes, though in his mind there was neither sound nor color. Meticulously, he wove the winds together into a single powerful chord. Then he shaped them into a northwest wind that hammered inexorably against the ships of the Armada.

As he drove the ships eastward, he sensed sailors frantically trying to beat against the wind while priests knelt to invoke God's help in avoiding the waiting shoals. The water beneath the hulls changed color, and the waves turned choppy as the seas became shallower and shallower.

He dimly recognized pounding pain in his temples and trembling in his limbs. The first ships were minutes from striking, but could he maintain his control over the increasingly rebellious winds he had assembled? He reached for Isabel again. Maddeningly, he could channel only a small part of her power. But surely he was strong enough to finish the job he had begun.

The Cornish gust, the strongest and most rebellious element of his coalition, cracked its way loose, weakening the whole. Savagely, he worked to force it back into his pattern. He almost succeeded.

Then the Scottish winds, notoriously chancy, broke away. His painstakingly constructed northwest wind disintegrated like splintered glass. Desperately, he reached again for Isabel, but he couldn't find the key to unlock the deepest reservoirs of her power. It stayed tantalizingly beyond his grasp.

Gasping for breath, he tried again to exert his mastery over the winds bucking against his grasp. As he stretched his mind to keep them in line, his power thinned to the snapping point. Only a few moments more, only a few . . .

Clashing like silent thunder, the spell shattered with a violence that pulsed through his skull. He cried out in agony and fell to his knees.

The last thing he saw before falling into blackness was Spanish ships turning sharply to port as they sought the safety of deeper water.

Macrae's collapse slashed Isabel's mind as viciously as a sword lacerated flesh. After an instant of paralysis, she reached out mentally to steady his convulsing spirit even as she raced across the circle to his sprawling body.

She dropped on her knees beside him. His face was corpse-white, and he wasn't breathing. Moved by sheer instinct, she inhaled deeply and bent over to share her breath with him. Placing her mouth on his, she forced air into his lungs. He was a master of wind and air, surely all he needed was more breath.

Once, twice, thrice . . . She was growing dizzy with exertion when he coughed and twisted under her hands. Finally he was drawing great ragged breaths on his own, God be thanked.

Dee joined her, panting. "I felt the spell go awry. How is he?"

"Breathing now. Beyond that . . ." She shrugged helplessly.

Dee frowned as he rested his hand on Macrae's forehead. "He's burning with fever. Pray God he has not destroyed himself with his exertions."

Getting to his feet with effort, the old man signaled to the pair of male servants who had followed him from the house. Carefully, the servants lifted Macrae onto the battered pine door they had brought, struggling with the Scotsman's deadweight. Then they set off toward the house.

Isabel started to follow, but Dee stayed her with a gesture. When the servants were out of earshot, he asked quietly, "What happened, child? Why didn't you save him from such a disaster?"

"I tried!" Tried desperately, and had been seared by the backlash when his power and concentration failed. "He tried also, but we could not fully connect. Our energies are too unlike. Too clashing."

"That clashing can be a source of strength, not conflict."

She rubbed her temples, too drained to understand. "What do you mean?"

"Think of your astrological studies—opposite signs are both natural enemies and natural complements. Men and women are opposites, and sometimes conflict between them is attraction that will not admit itself. Yet if opposites find balance in each other, they can create a whole greater than the sum of their individual powers."

She thought back to Dee's lessons, when he had poured rivers of information into her eager mind. "Is this the alchemical marriage you once spoke of?"

"The alchemical marriage is a philosophical principle, and it can be seen on many levels. One is male and female." He eyed her speculatively, then shook his head. "The point is moot. Macrae may be out of his senses for days. Or . . . worse. Do you know what has happened with the Armada?"

She had been too upset to even wonder. Wearily, she drew out her scrying glass and conjured the scene. "The Spanish ships are escaping the Zeeland shoals and heading north. The English pursue, but they are still outnumbered. Once the Spaniards regroup, they will be able to resume their plans for invasion."

Dee's face tightened, adding ten years to his age. "I must go to London and report to the queen."

"Perhaps Macrae will recover and try again," she suggested without much hope.

"He will be lucky to escape with his life and his sanity," Dee said bluntly. "Even if he survives, today's work may have destroyed his magic forever."

Having felt the cataclysmic collapse of Macrae's power, she knew that Dee spoke no less than the truth. "I will stay here and care for him. My housekeeper is experienced at nursing. God willing, we will save at least his life."

"He may not thank you for it if he survives deprived of his deepest self." Dee raised his gaze to the restless sea, where Spanish ships were sailing north around Britain. "I once had great power. Not so much as you, but enough to make me a true sorcerer. In my arrogance and lust for knowledge, I pushed my abilities too far and nearly died of it. Since then, I have had to content myself with small magics and scholarship."

The naked longing in his face made Isabel look away uneasily. What would it be like to lose her power? Though her abilities made a normal woman's life impossible for her, the exercise of magic was also the purest delight and satisfaction she had ever known. To be deprived of it would be like losing her limbs. Macrae had been bound in iron for more than a year. Now, after only a few days restored to his full self, he had risked his life and his power to stave off the Spaniards.

Though she had scarcely noticed at the time, she had a sharp flash of memory of how his lips had felt under hers when she had breathed for him. Embarrassed, she said, "If the body is saved, perhaps the spirit will also heal. We will do what we can." The world needed Adam Macrae.

And she needed to know that somewhere he would be living under the same sun as she.

4

He had been lost for so long among the cinders of his mind that at first he didn't recognize returning awareness. All he knew was cool darkness, a soft night breeze redolent of country flowers, a gentle hand on his forehead.

A woman's hand? He forced his eyes open. He was in his bedroom at Leighton Manor, the canopy above him barely visible in the dim light. Isabel de Cortes was perched on a stool beside him, her eyes narrow with concern.

"So . . . I did not die," he said in a rasping voice.

"Not for lack of trying." Despite her acerbic words, she

gave him a smile that softened the austere beauty of her narrow face.

He closed his eyes again. "How long has it been since I conjured the winds?"

"Eight days. Master Dee has returned to London to confer with the queen."

Seeing her expression brought back the last disastrous memories that preceded his collapse. He exhaled roughly. "I failed."

"Perhaps not." Her gaze slid away. "Your efforts have given more time to improve the coastal defenses. Surely that will help if—when—the Spanish invade."

Absurd. Britain's coastline was far too long for defenses to be adequate everywhere, and they both knew it. As his vision cleared, he realized that she looked different tonight. Defeated. Unbowed, but preparing for the worst. "Give me your scrying glass."

She looked doubtful. Guessing she thought him too weak, he repeated, "Give it to me! I must know."

She reluctantly produced the obsidian disk and laid it on his right palm. He was so weak he could barely raise the glass high enough to see the surface, and he couldn't sense the glow of her energy as he had before. As the surface remained blank, he recognized that the center of his spirit was numb, devoid of power.

Sweating, he closed his eyes and tried to shape the slight breeze that fitfully stirred the curtains. It pulsed, then faded. Had he done that, or was the movement only the normal volatility of the night airs?

He tried again. This time he was almost sure that he had briefly strengthened the wind. His power was only strained, not dead. He refused to believe otherwise.

Opening his eyes, he tried the scrying glass again. *What might the Spanish bring?* This time he saw a flickering image of Edinburgh Castle—burning. May God help Scotland, for the Spaniards would come with torch and steel.

Grimly, he tried to conjure a vision of Dunrath, but the glass would show him no more. Trembling, he let his head fall back against the pillows.

"I won't tell you not to overexert yourself, for it would be a waste of breath," Mistress de Cortes said dryly. "But you might consider the fact that you have been out of your head with fever for days. It is normal to be weak as a newborn kitten."

"I have no time for weakness. We must act before it is too late." He struggled for more breath.

"You think it still possible to change the course of events?"

"Aye. Not easy, but . . . possible." Throwing back the covers, he swung his legs over the side of the bed. He was garbed in a coarse nightgown, borrowed from a servant perhaps. He leaned forward to stand—and his knees buckled beneath him.

She swiftly moved forward and caught him around the waist. For an instant they were pressed together as she struggled to prevent his sagging body from falling to the floor. Her breasts were soft and womanly against his chest. Desire blazed through him like storm lightning, and with it came a shadow of renewed energy.

Before he could gather his wits, she managed to shift him back onto the edge of the bed. "You're a damned fool, Macrae," she said a little breathlessly. "Content yourself with talking for tonight."

She expertly lifted his legs onto the bed, which pushed him back against the pillows. His brief energy faded again, but not his memory of it. Angels above, she was enticing. An embrace with her would make a stone saint dance. "We must learn to work together on all levels, Isabel. You must be able to use my gifts as a weather mage, and I must be able to draw fully on your strength." It was the first time he had used her Christian name when speaking to her.

Acknowledging the intimacy, she said, "Does that mean I should call you Adam?"

He smiled a little. "I like the way you growl 'Macrae.'"

"I'm gifted at growling. How are we to accomplish such closeness?"

If she had been raised a Guardian, she would know such things. Groping for the right words, he said, "To share energy fully, there must be absolute trust and a willingness to reveal oneself with naked honesty, flaws as well as virtues. Earlier, time was short and neither of us wished to drop all our defenses, so we did not delve so deeply. If we had"—

his mouth twisted—"perhaps I could have maintained the wind long enough to force the Spanish fleet onto the Zeeland shoals. I was so close . . ."

The silence was long and painful before she said, "I have never done what you are describing. Is it even possible? We have little in common."

"We are both disciplined and know how to wield power." He caught her gaze. "And we will both pay any price to stop the Spanish. That should be enough."

She bit her lip. "The prospect of completely lowering my shields is . . . troubling, but it seems we have no choice but to try."

"This will be hard for you, since you have had little contact with other mages," he admitted. "Even among Guardians, complete openness is rare." Most often it was seen between husband and wife, but sometimes between mages who worked together closely.

"Master Dee spoke of the alchemical marriage, the mating of opposites to create strength and harmony," she said. "Is that what you are speaking of?"

"I am no alchemist, but, yes, that is the sort of closeness we must forge. Usually it takes a long time to develop, but we don't have time, so we must do the best we can."

"Let me try this, and tell me if you experience anything." She closed her eyes, and for the space of a hundred heartbeats there was silence. She gave a quick, frustrated shake of her head, then laid her hand on his.

Immediately, he felt a feather-light stroke of her energy. It gently flowed through him, sliding behind his weakened defenses and soothing scorched places in his spirit. He had felt nothing comparable since his training with his grandfather when he was a boy.

But his grandfather was stern and male, while Isabel was profoundly female. An object of desire whose touch sparked reactions that fizzed through his body. He moved involuntarily, for the effect was as alarming as it was exciting.

Masking his reaction, he said, "You reached very deeply. It is a good beginning."

She sighed. "So little time."

Feeling stronger than when he first woke, he asked, "Are you a healer?"

"Only in a small way." She rested her palm on his forehead again. "Sleep, Macrae. Tomorrow we will begin our second campaign."

He slipped into deep slumber, dimly aware that she had begun to heal the source of his power.

Since Macrae's fever had broken and his wits were well on the way to mending, Isabel left him alone to sleep. He needed the rest, and so did she.

Nonetheless, her night was troubled. Macrae was disturbing at the best of times, like a barely leashed lion. To allow him access to the darkest secrets of her soul—she shuddered at the thought.

The prospect of knowing his darkest secrets was even worse. Raised by protective, baffled parents, her life had been a sheltered one despite her studies. With Dee's guidance she had learned the disciplines of power, and her scrying ability had given her rare access to the workings of her society. But that knowledge was of the mind; Macrae was of the earth, intensely physical and experienced in matters beyond her imagination. The depths of his mind would not be . . . safe.

She should think of their joint endeavor as an opportunity to broaden her knowledge and understanding. Certainly the work was vital, for the Armada was a sword poised over Britain. Nonetheless, she felt like a mouse about to be seized by a hawk.

Reminding herself that she was a mouse armed with powerful fangs, she rolled over and forced herself to relax, one muscle at a time. She must hope that a hawk and a fanged mouse could between them stop the Spanish.

She was rising after a night of restless dreams when her housekeeper entered the bedroom in a rush. "Sir Adam is gone!"

Isabel muttered an oath under her breath. "I think I know where he might be. Don't worry—his fever broke last night, and he's as sensible now as he's capable of. Pack food in a basket while I dress."

Reassured, Mistress Heath left to do her mistress's bidding. After donning a plain country gown of cream-colored linen and dressing her hair in a simple knot, Isabel collected the basket and walked down to the stone circle at a leisurely pace.

As she expected, Macrae was there, sitting on a stone as he looked out to sea. His beard needed trimming—he looked more pirate than gentleman.

Her relaxation vanished when she saw his despair. "What has happened?"

"There is even less time than I thought."

She settled on the stone beside his. "Tell me."

"If events are not changed, the Spanish will sail into the Firth of Forth to provision and regroup, and end by razing Edinburgh."

Isabel frowned, wishing she had spent more time scrying Edinburgh. "Surely Scots and Spaniards are allies—both hate the English enough."

"The intent will not be war, but tempers will clash. The Spanish commander, Medina, will infuriate my countrymen, and soldiers will become drunk and riot. The city will be left a ruin of blood and bones and ashes."

She shuddered at the images he conjured in her mind. "When will this happen?"

"In two days, the first Spanish ships will moor at Leith. No more than two days more before trouble breaks out."

Less than four days for them to change the course of a great Armada. "I did not know you had such skill in seeing the future."

"Usually I don't, but Scotland is bound to my blood." He drew a rough breath. "I'm glad I seldom see the future. It's a terrible gift. My attempt to drive the Armada onto the Zeeland shoals might have increased the danger for my countrymen."

"Don't think about that!" They could not afford for him to become weakened by guilt. "You already had fears for Edinburgh. Perhaps what you foresee now will be less terrible than what might have happened. We cannot be sure."

His mouth twisted. "How arrogant we mages are, to think we can make the world better by wielding our powers. Perhaps Britain would be better off without Guardians."

"It is human nature to seek and use power. At least you Guardians do your best to serve the greater good." She drew her knees up and looped her arms around them as she had in childhood, her gaze unfocused as she watched the waves roll into chalk cliffs. "I envy you for being raised with others of your kind."

"It would be difficult to be as alone as you, Isabel. Yet it has made you strong."

She felt him in her mind, closer than was comfortable. She wanted to slam the doors and hurl him out. Instead, she forced herself to accept his demanding male presence, proud that she could say calmly, "Though the hours are few, there is time enough to eat, and you'll be stronger for it."

She investigated the basket. Fresh bread and cheese and ale, all made on her estate. Pulling out her knife, she sliced the bread and cheese, then poured ale into the pewter tankards.

His expression eased as he accepted the food. "You're a practical woman. That is no bad thing."

"Someone has to be practical, and usually it will be a woman," she said tartly.

Macrae's amusement reverberated within her mind, a surprisingly pleasant effect. As they ate, she cautiously experimented with this unwonted closeness. She could not read his thoughts, and for that she was grateful, but she could sense his emotions with increasing accuracy. As they spoke, his mind shadowed his words with extra richness.

She also could enjoy his ravenous hunger. His startlingly sensual enjoyment of the simple food was so intense that it distracted her from her own meal. As he swallowed the last of his ale, he said, "Sunshine, a fresh breeze, and plain country food. When I was in the Tower, I never thought I would know such simple pleasures again. A pity that my freedom was granted for such a dire reason."

She stopped herself from saying that he might as well enjoy while he could, only to have him say, "You're thinking I might as well take pleasure while I can, since my next attempt at weather working might send me to an early grave."

She flushed and glanced away. "Can you read my thoughts?"

"Only your emotions, but they are clear enough." He set

his empty tankard in the basket. "Now it is time for work. Do you see that dark cloud in the middle distance?"

She shaded her eyes against the bright sky. "Yes."

"We are going to make it rain." He laid his large hand over hers. "The thought intrigues and alarms you. Well enough. You will enjoy this, I think."

And she did. Though his mental powers had not fully recovered from his collapse, his instinctive understanding of wind and cloud was glorious. If he was a hawk, she was now his companion, swooping through the air, feeling the cool damp of the cloud, then disintegrating into a swift shower of raindrops.

She laughed aloud when he drew her back to normal awareness, delighting in the new sensations. "Wonderful! I felt this much more clearly than when we worked together before." Catching a sense of his sadness, she said more soberly, "But it's a very small achievement compared to what will be needed."

Though his face was controlled, she sensed that he was trying to shield her from his doubts. "It is much more than I could have done on my own," he said. "We are blending our energies well, so far."

Her pleasure in what they had accomplished faded in the knowledge of how much further they had to go—and that they had only another day to prepare.

They spent the rest of the long day delving into ever deeper levels of intimacy and sharing. The power of Isabel's mind and spirit amazed Macrae. Her commitment was also profound, but the deeper he probed, the more she resisted.

The last exercise of the day took him for an instant to an area of her emotions he had not yet explored. Raw passion exploded like the devil's own fire, triggering his own passions—and then she hurled him from her mind with numbing power.

Gasping, he bent and buried his throbbing head in her hands. "You have a kick that would do a stallion proud, Isabel."

He could feel her distress when she laid her palm on his brow. "I'm sorry, I—I could not control my reaction."

He closed his eyes, welcoming her soothing touch. "I am trying to teach you in a day what a Guardian learns over years. You are progressing remarkably well."

"But not well enough."

He wasn't sure if her soft words were thought or spoken aloud. "Perhaps tomorrow we will find a good summer storm to work with." He tried to project confidence. "That will do most of the work for us."

She didn't believe that any more than he did, but she didn't argue the point. The two were joined in fatalism. They had no choice but to try another major spell in the morning, this time at a much greater distance than the Zeeland attempt and with no major storm available to build on.

Isabel knew the dangers—after all, she had nursed him through near-lethal brain fever when his first attempt failed. She had accepted the fact that they might die trying. In fact, she accepted it better than he.

When he fell into his bed, exhausted, he uttered a silent prayer. May God grant them success for the sake of Scotland—and if a life must be forfeit in the process, let it be his.

5

Macrae jerked to wakefulness, heart pounding as he picked up a distant note of changing weather. Clouds, rain, and wind were sweeping in from the Atlantic.

How long had he been asleep? Only a few hours, he guessed, since there was no sign of dawn. He lit a candle and scrambled into his clothing, then made his way through the silent house to Isabel's room. As he opened the door, he said, "Isabel, rough weather is approaching quickly from the west. Not a major storm, but enough to give us a better chance if we start work immediately."

He swept back the bed curtains. His candle revealed Isabel blinking sleepily as she pushed herself to a sitting position. Her dark hair fell over her shoulder in a thick braid, and she looked younger and more vulnerable than her daytime self.

He froze as he realized that she was dressed only in her night rail, and the lightweight fabric did little to disguise her softly curving body. Knees weakening, he stepped back, putting the heavy carved bedpost between them. Damn the successful effort to lower barriers between them, for now it was impossible to conceal his desire. Isabel would justly see him as a great randy brute.

She flushed scarlet as she read his reaction. Emotions reverberated between them like images in opposing mirrors, and the hair prickled on his arms at the sheer erotic tension in the room.

Recovering first, she yanked the blankets to her shoulders. "Very well, we shall begin. I will meet you in the stone circle."

Grateful for the excuse to retreat, he ignited one of her candles with his, then bolted. He was a fool for allowing attraction to muddy the waters when all their attention must be fixed on their mutual goal.

He was bleakly aware that, even with the changing weather, the odds did not favor them. Though he was recovering well from his earlier collapse, he was still far below his normal strength. Despite Isabel's enormous power, she hadn't an inborn talent for weather working. If he was unable to weave the spells well enough, they would fail.

Worse, though they had lowered the barriers between them enough for embarrassment, they were still woefully short of being fully capable of sharing energy. If he needed more than Isabel was ready to give, she might lash out at him instinctively, with disastrous results.

But try they must. The Armada was critically near Edinburgh, and if they didn't act right away, it would be too late.

His mind still chasing itself, he stopped in the kitchen for a quick meal of bread and cheese, then picked his way down to the stone circle. It was a night fit for witches, the ley lines that intersected at the circle a glowing spiderweb of power. The wind was rising in fitful gusts, shaping and tearing clouds so that footing on the lane was uncertain. The sea beyond the bluff was lighter than the land, and he could hear the harsh beat of waves against the shore.

He felt a curious fatalism as he cleared his mind and began to lay the foundations of his spell. He would do his best; no man could do more. If he did not survive this last great working, may God defend Scotland and those he loved.

Silent as the wind, Isabel joined him, almost invisible in a dark cloak. She handed him a similar cloak. "Wear this. The night is chill, and fair weather will not return soon."

He accepted the cloak but said mildly, "A sorcerer should be able to rise above heat and cold."

"Why waste energy suppressing discomfort when it can be used on your weather working?"

He smiled into the darkness. A practical sorceress. The contours of her face were barely discernible. He had thought her austerely beautiful from their first meeting, and the intimate knowledge he had gained during their work together had multiplied her beauty a thousandfold. "Are you ready?"

"As ready as I can be."

Knowing he might not survive the night's work, he made a formal courtier's bow to her, the cloak flaring around him. "It has been a pleasure working with you, Isabel de Cortes." Then he buried personal thoughts, grounded himself in the circle's earth energy, and reached for the winds.

As his awareness spiraled upward, he saw that the North Atlantic was blanketed with a vast patchwork of choppy clouds and gusty rain. The Spanish ships were strewn along the Narrow Seas, the leading wave already approaching the Firth of Forth, the gateway to Edinburgh.

He started by sharpening the winds across Scotland, making it difficult for the Armada to sail up the estuary. But that was only a temporary measure to delay them while he constructed a tempest.

Piece by meticulous piece, he began to weave vicious winds, drowning rain, and lightning that could rip the sky and blaze through rigging. It must be so powerful, so well-wrought, that it would continue onward even after his own strength failed. The storm must rage for days, sinking ships, driving others onto rocky shores and into the grip of deadly North Sea currents. The Armada must be destroyed to the point where it offered no threat—and may heaven have mercy on the souls of the sailors.

Already he was drawing heavily on Isabel's deep reserves of power. Her bright awareness followed him as he

spun the winds into a pattern that fed on itself. She helped
him concentrate the rain from many thousands of square
miles into a smaller, more lethal storm. And she soared
with him when he forged the lightning.

A dark, sullen dawn was breaking, the sun only a dim
glow on the horizon. The overall spell was complete, but
the structure was fragile. He needed a massive infusion of
energy to set the pattern so that the tempest could become
a force in its own right.

A gust of rain knocked him to his knees. Gasping, he
reached for his partner, but for the first time he was unable
to tap her strength. Though she had reserves still, they were
beyond his reach.

"Isabel . . ." He tried to call, but his voice was a thin
whisper lost in the rising wind. He was on all fours, most of
his strength and awareness devoted to stabilizing the tempest with none left for holding him upright.

Her arms came around his shoulders. Though her touch
stirred a wisp of energy, it was nowhere near enough to
seal the spell. He tried harder to connect with the silvery
pool of her power. She was struggling equally, he sensed
her frantic effort, but there might have been a glass wall
between them. Impenetrable. Impossible . . .

"Macrae." Her husky voice whispered in his ear. "The alchemical marriage—the mating of opposites to form a
greater whole. It is the only solution left."

With shock, he realized that she meant a physical mating.
His dazed mind tried to evaluate whether her proposal had
a chance to work. There had been strong attraction from the
beginning. In another time and place he would have courted
her, or perhaps swept her onto his horse and carried her off
to the Highlands, but he had buried such thoughts as inappropriate to the work they were doing together.

She might be right that passion could forge their spirits
into a single invincible blade, but the cool voice of his conscience pointed out that he wanted desperately to believe
that surrendering to lust was the key to victory. Was he a
Guardian, a man of honor, or a randy male who would lie
to gain what he desired?

Her lips touched his in a hesitant kiss. Her scent was of
rain-washed roses.

His numb body began tingling to life. Sensing the change, Isabel's kiss became fierce, a demand laced with power.

Primal passion exploded through him, bringing every fiber of his body to blazing life. Be damned to his doubts—he wanted and needed Isabel more than reason, more than conscience, more than honor.

As he kissed her back, the shields he had borne from the cradle dissolved, allowing her access to the depths of his soul. Her fierce determination to conquer entered into his own soul, making them the invincible sword he had imagined. The gentle rain intensified into a downpour, fluid and fertile as it mated with the earth.

"Isabel, my enchantress . . ." He rolled above her, pressing her long body into the wet grass as he kissed her hungrily, blending his essence with hers.

Their lovemaking shattered the skies as the last barriers collapsed. Power was abundant, limitless, flowing through them and into the tempest, stabilizing the intricate structure of the spell. Lightning blazed until he was unsure if they were in Kent or soaring high over the North Sea in the heart of the storm.

As their spirits melded, he discovered that at the heart of her power was a lonely child who was an outsider among those she loved, convinced she was too strange, too unattractive, to ever find the closeness she craved. Even John Dee, greatest alchemist of the age, had found his student disconcerting.

Tenderly, Macrae showed her his vision of her unique, bewitching beauty. How she was a paragon among women, a mistress of mages. In return, she mirrored him back to himself. Was he really so darkly intimidating? Yet she was drawn to his strength, intrigued by his contradictions, so he gloried in his darkness.

He was distantly aware of Spanish ships foundering, sails shredding and masts snapping. Without the anchors they had shed near the Low Countries to escape the English fire ships, they were helpless before the tempest.

With a last paroxysm of power, the hurricane crystallized into a living entity, no longer dependent on its creator. They had succeeded. Against all the odds, they had *won*.

Drained of every shred of strength and passion, he fell once more into darkness.

Exhausted to ashy numbness, Isabel cradled her lover to her breast as the rain drummed into their panting bodies. She had not known the cosmos held such pleasure, or such pain, as she had discovered with Macrae.

Part of her would have been content to lie there and drown, but now that passion had burned out she was aware that the soggy ground and cold wind were wickedly uncomfortable. She managed to pull herself out from under his dead weight.

Dead? Alarmed, she laid her fingers to his throat. His pulse was strong. With effort she invoked subtler senses to look more deeply and decided that he was not profoundly injured as he had been by his earlier attempt on the Armada. Only . . . expended. He would sleep at least a day, perhaps longer.

She tugged his cloak over him, shielding his face from the rain, then stumbled her way up the long lane to the house. Luckily, the torrent disguised her dishevelment. Her household was used to odd activities from her; they would not suspect her of anything so plebian as coupling with a handsome stranger.

A stranger? Her mouth twisted. She knew Sir Adam Macrae to the depths of his stormy, impatient, generous soul.

As her numb fingers fumbled with the kitchen door, it swung open, and Mistress Heath pulled her into the warmth of the kitchen. "Thank the Lord you be all right, m'lady!" the housekeeper exclaimed. " 'Tis worried I've been."

Terrified, more likely, but all Isabel's servants knew better than to disturb her when she was working. "All is well, Mistress Heath, but send the men to the stone circle to bring Sir Adam to the house. He . . . he has not fully recovered from his illness and has been overcome by . . . his exertions."

The sodden cloak was swept from her shoulders and a mug of warm beef broth pressed into her hands. "Drink this, m'lady," Mistress Heath said briskly. "By the time you're finished, a hot bath will be waiting. Then it's to bed with you. I'll see to your Scottish savage."

Grateful to be cared for as a child, Isabel drank her broth, then allowed herself to be led to her room. Macrae was being carried in as she left the kitchen, water pouring off him and the servants who had collected him. When she cast a glance back, Mistress Heath firmly tugged her onward.

The hot bath was spiked with lavender, the healing herb soothing her frayed spirit. Isabel closed her eyes and willed herself to tranquility. What mattered was that they had succeeded. They had forged an alchemical marriage that generated the power they needed, and England would never again be threatened by Spain. Even without her scrying glass, she knew that with absolute certainty. She uttered a prayer for the souls of the Spanish sailors.

Wearily, she rested her head against the edge of the wooden tub. She had sworn she would pay any price, and her virginity was small enough as costs went. Much harder was losing half of her soul—it would have been easier to give up her life. But that loss was not something that could, or should, be undone.

She had found pleasure almost beyond bearing in their joining. Now she must face the anguish of knowing they must separate. Deep in Macrae's mind she had seen his distaste at the prospect of being fettered by marriage. But Guardians were subject to great pressure to wed, preferably to other Guardians so the blood and the power would remain strong. He had accepted marriage as his fate.

Before his intemperance had landed him in the Tower of London, he had been ready to offer for a gentle Guardian maiden called Anne, a blonde as sweet-natured as she was beautiful. Best of all in Macrae's eyes was that Anne was a Scot when most Guardian daughters were English. He could not have tolerated an English wife—his disgust at the prospect had been achingly clear.

Isabel clambered from the tub and began toweling herself dry. Her body was warm now, though her soul was chilled. She had a sudden yearning for her mother, who had never truly understood her strange daughter, but who loved her anyhow.

As she donned her night rail and crawled into her bed, Isabel forced herself to accept that Macrae was intended for another woman. Even if he was not, his taste did not run to black-haired harridans, especially English ones. So be it.

They had won a great victory today. It was enough.
It *must* be enough.

The sun was shining when Macrae awoke. Outside the
diamond-shaped windowpanes, two larks perched on a
branch and warbled to each other. He listened in lazy
peace, scarcely able to believe that they had triumphed,
and survived. Of Isabel's survival he had no doubt; for the
rest of his life, he would be aware of every breath she drew.

He was climbing cautiously from the bed when the
housekeeper entered. Eager to see Isabel, he said, "Tell
Mistress de Cortes that I wish to speak to her."

The housekeeper's brows arched. "You'll have a wait,
then. My lady left for London yesterday."

He stared, unable to believe that she was gone. "Why the
devil did she do that?"

Mistress Heath shrugged. " 'Tis not my place to say."

She would surely go to her father's house. "Where does
the de Cortes family live?"

Ignoring the question, Mistress Heath turned to leave.
"One of the men will bring you hot water and food." The
door closed hard behind her.

Isabel had left him. The damned Englishwoman had
bloody left him! How *dare* she!

Swearing, he opened the wardrobe and yanked out his
cleaned and folded garments. This could have been settled
easily, but nothing about Isabel de Cortes was easy. She
would pay for this insult.

Aye, she would pay.

6

As soon as her mother left the room, Isabel poured the latest tisane into the window box that hung from her sill.
Though her flowers had been tattered by the great storm,
already they were recovering. Perhaps the herbal brews
were good for them.

In her mother's arms she had found the warmth and

comfort she craved, but the maternal fussing was in a fair way to driving her mad, as were the incessant questions about what had happened. Perhaps someday Isabel would be able to speak of it. But probably not.

Master Dee had visited and given her a magnificent ruby ring from the queen's own hand in gratitude for what she and Macrae had achieved. But the visit was brief, for the royal conjuror was anxious to return to his family in Bohemia.

Isabel drifted to the window, wondering what more her life might hold. Her usual studies had no interest for her, and even her scrying glass was cloudy when she tried to see her future. She had been part of a great work that changed the course of nations, so perhaps it was greedy of her to want something beyond a long, desiccated spinsterhood. Though unlike the queen, she was no longer virgin . . .

She heard a distant pounding, as if soldiers were banging on the front door. Then an uproar broke out downstairs. Her blood froze under an onslaught of horrified ancestral memories of the Inquisition coming to take members of the de Cortes family away to torture and death. Surely not here in London, not again!

Heart racing, she darted from her room and to the stairs. She halted in shock when she looked down into the entry hall. Magnificently dressed and fierce as a wolf, Adam Macrae was holding two of her father's menservants at bay with a sword.

Her parents stormed into the hall. Seeing the sword, her father threw a protective arm in front of his wife as he barked, "What is the meaning of this, you insolent devil?"

"You should be grateful, Master de Cortes," Macrae replied in a voice of thunder. "I've come to take your stubborn spinster daughter off your hands."

Her mother gasped. "You'll not touch her, you great brute! My husband is a friend of the Lord Mayor of London, and you'll be hanged, drawn, and quartered if you assault a virtuous maiden."

"A virtuous maiden?" Macrae laughed out loud. "That is not the Isabel I know."

Her shock dissolved by fury, Isabel swept down the steps as if she were one of Macrae's own tempests. "How dare you force your way in and terrorize my father's household!

Take yourself back to Scotland and marry that sweet bland blonde of yours."

His gaze snapped upward. "Isabel!"

With a smile like the sun at high noon, he sheathed his sword and galloped up the steps three at a time. Meeting her on the landing, he swept her into an embrace that bruised her lips. Thunder and lightning, a storm in the blood. Her desire to shove him down the stairs dissolved, and she kissed him back. The damnable man!

He murmured into her ear, "Did you think you could walk away from an alchemical marriage, my beautiful witch?"

"But . . . but Anne, the woman you are contracted to . . ."

"Likely wed to another by now." His long, clever fingers began stroking the small of her back. "Anne had no shortage of suitors, and she found me alarming, which is why the contracts had not yet been signed."

A man cleared his throat heavily. Face beet red, Isabel looked down the steps to find that she and Macrae were the object of fascinated gazes by half the members of the household. Her father said sternly, "You know this rogue?"

"H-his name is Sir Adam Macrae, and he is a well-born Scot," she stammered.

"A Scot?" Her father snorted. "No wonder he behaves like a savage."

"Accustom yourself." Macrae raised his hand, revealing a sapphire ring in a setting that matched Isabel's. "Your queen herself has ordered Isabel to marry me, in return for my services to England."

"You called on Queen Elizabeth?" Isabel's eyes widened with shock.

"I wanted to make sure I held the high ground if you were so foolish as to try to refuse me." He wrapped one arm around her waist and gazed down at Isabel's parents. "I am wealthy enough to gladden any parent's heart, and brave enough to take on your hellcat. As it happens, she and I share certain . . . unusual talents and interests. Now, if you will excuse us, I wish to speak to my affianced bride in private."

Her father's eyes narrowed, showing the formidable merchant who had prospered in good times and bad. "I don't care how wealthy you are, or if God Himself has given you permission to wed my daughter. No man will have Isabel unless she agrees to the union, and if you attempt to force her, you'll face the swords of myself and my three sons."

Isabel's mother placed a hand on her husband's arm, a faint, knowing smile playing over her lips. "I doubt that anything is being done against Isabel's will. Give them the chance to settle matters in private, David."

Isabel's father started to protest, then subsided. "Very well, if Isabel is willing to speak with this rogue."

"I am willing. Matters between us must be settled." Although she wasn't sure if she would accept Macrae or cut his heart out.

As he marched Isabel up the steps, she glanced back and saw that her parents were smiling. Smiling! As easily as that, this barbarian Scot had won them over.

He led her unerringly to her bedroom. "How did you know where to find me?" she asked as he bolted the door behind them.

"It would have been hard enough to hide from a mage, but it's impossible to conceal yourself from your bonded mate. For mated we are, Isabel. Accept it."

He spun her around so that her back was to him and began deftly unlacing her gown. With a swiftness truly magical he unbound her rigid leather corset, then cupped her breasts with his warm great hands.

As she gasped with distracted pleasure, his levity dropped away. "I love you, Isabel," he said softly. "Accept the fact that we are joined for life, and quite possibly eternity as well. Will marriage be so very bad? We've been granted a rare gift of passion and closeness, my love."

She pulled away and turned to face him. It wasn't possible to read his thoughts—the white heat that had joined them when they conjured the tempest was only a distant pulse, though it would always be there when summoned. But they were still in resonance with each other, and with dawning wonder she realized that she was no longer alone.

In his eyes, she saw the reflection of her own soul and the mad glory of his desire. Even, to her surprise, a fear that she would continue to resist him.

She had always had faith in her magical abilities, but for the first time, a pleasing sense of feminine power began to flow through her. Despite Macrae's bluster, he was well-aware that a mage of her power couldn't be brought unwilling to the altar. This great brash Scot was humbling himself. Humility was not one of his gifts, which was why he was doing it so badly.

Secure in her power as both sorceress and woman, she asked, "So you have demanded me as a reward from my queen, invaded my home, and terrorized our servants because you want to marry me even though I am neither Scottish nor a Guardian?"

He smiled wryly. "Aye. It doesn't matter that you are English and not of Guardian blood. You are Isabel—the most powerful sorceress in Britain and my bonded mate, and my family will rejoice when I bring you home. Must I terrorize anyone else to gain your consent?"

"My dear, foolish rogue." With a swift cascade of joy, she linked her arms around his neck. She didn't need her scrying glass to know that they would share passion and battles and unshakable love. Macrae was hers as she was his, bonded for eternity in an alchemical marriage. "All you had to do was *ask*!"

AUTHOR'S NOTE

The defeat of the Spanish Armada is one of those historical high points that just about everyone remembers from high school history classes. It was a watershed that established England's ascendancy as a great sea power and was also a signifier of Spain's decline. The expulsion of the Jews from Spain certainly contributed to that decline. It's ironic that the word *marrano,* which meant swine and was highly insulting, became Marranos, the term by which the exiles are now known.

John Dee is a historical figure, famous as the queen's conjuror. A metaphysical scholar, alchemist, writer, and astrologer, he cast a chart to pick the best time for Elizabeth's coronation. Given the success of her reign, he was obviously good at his work! It was said that he put a hex on the Spanish Armada, which is why the weather was unusually bad that summer and the English triumphed. The running battles in the English Channel did only average damage—it was the storms when the Armada tried to sail north around Britain that destroyed most of the Spanish fleet.

Dee was also a founder of the Rosicrucian Order, a Protestant response to the Jesuits. A devout Christian, he was both praised and vilified in his lifetime. It is said that he was the model for Shakespeare's Prospero in *The Tempest*. His library of more than four thousand volumes was the largest in England.

The Guardians are my own invention. Their descendants will appear in some of my future historical romances, starting with *A Kiss of Fate*, coming from Ballantine Books in summer 2004.

Stained Glass Heart

by Catherine Asaro

1
THE GOLDEN SUNS

Vyrl slipped outside the castle, making sure no one saw him escape. Beyond the village, the Dalvador Plains spread out like a silver-green sea of reeds rippling with the breezes. He took off in a loping run, and the grasses rustled around his legs.

Reveling in his freedom, he soon left the village behind. He ran for the joy of being healthy, strong, and full of life. Out here he could be himself, rather than Prince Havyrl Torcellei Valdoria.

In his more introspective moods, Vyrl realized he lived in an idyll, his life marked by golden days. His parents had set it up that way, to shield their children from the harsh life of the Imperial Court in an interstellar empire. The colonists who had settled the world Lyshriol lived a simpler life, one close to the land. They cared more about a good harvest festival than long titles or dynastic lineages. So Vyrl and his many siblings tended crops, pulled weeds, and looked after livestock just like anyone else.

Reed-grasses rippled around him, the translucent tubes sparkling like glass but bending easily, supple and soft. Iridescent spheres no larger than his thumb topped many of the stalks and floated off their moorings when he brushed by. The drifting bubbles marked his path through the plains.

Running hard, throwing his arms wide, he relished the strength of his muscles and broadening shoulders. After a year of gawkiness, when he had seemed to grow visible amounts every day, he had finally stopped feeling gangly and awkward. He was more comfortable now with his new height and strength.

He tilted his head up, letting sunlight bathe his face. Two gold suns hung in a lavender sky, side by side right now, shaped more like eggs than spheres, and speckled with dark spots. The double star destabilized the terraformed planet, but Vyrl earnestly believed that by the time that difficulty threatened this world, well into the future, his people would have figured out how to fix the problem.

Vyrl ignominiously tripped over a rock. Laughing, he staggered through the grass, flailing his arms until he recovered his balance.

Eventually his pent-up energy spent itself and he slowed to a walk. He glanced back at the village. The distant cluster of white buildings and colorful turreted roofs barely showed above the waving grasses. He could just see the topmost level of his home. His family lived in a castle, a small but lovely one, with towers at the corners, each capped by a blue turreted roof. Spires topped the roofs and pennants snapped on them, violet with gold ribbing.

Vyrl let out a contented sigh. Then he flopped on his back in the grass, breathing deeply, his heart beating hard. Swaying stalks bent over him, releasing bubbles that glistened against the sky. Ah, what a day! He grinned, relieved to have escaped his math homework.

A girl giggled.

Vyrl's sense of peace fled. He sat up fast. "Who is that?"

Silence.

Scrambling to his feet, he glared over the plains. The breezes blew his red-gold curls in his face, and he pushed them out of his eyes.

He saw no one. Although a person could easily hide in the grass, she should have left a trail of bubbles floating over whatever path she took here.

Vyrl peered back the way he had come. He had left more than a trail; his wild race had stirred clouds of glimmering spheres. If someone was following him, she could have disguised her approach by keeping to his path. He should have noticed someone skulking after him, but then, he hadn't been paying much attention. None, in fact.

"Who is here?" he called, trying to sound forceful. The words came out more startled than commanding, but at least his voice wasn't breaking anymore. It had finally finished changing and settled into a deep baritone, which pleased him just fine.

No answer came to his question, however. The girl was playing a trick on him. Hah! He wouldn't let her rattle him. He saw no trampled grass nearby, but the reed-grass always sprang back fast. He had flattened a great deal of it when he lay down and already it was rising back into place.

Vyrl continued his search but found no trace of the intruder. He began to feel a bit foolish. Perhaps he had imagined that giggle. Finally he lay down again, stretching out on his back with his hands behind his head.

Another giggle floated on the air like a bubble.

"Who is that?" He *had* heard her. Glowering, he jumped to his feet and stalked around the area, stomping at the grass. "Who's there?"

Two bubbles detached from a nearby stalk and bobbed off over the plain. There! He strode forward, grasses whipping around his legs.

A trill of laughter rippled in the wind. Then a girl jumped out of the grasses, all red-gold curls and blue skirts. With a laughing glance in his direction, she took off and raced away.

"Hey!" he shouted. "Lily, you come back here!"

Instead of running after her, though, he hesitated. Lily was the daughter of a local farmer. She and Vyrl had been friends practically since they had been born, but lately he had avoided her, unable to do more than stutter banalities in her presence. Lily didn't look like Lily anymore. She had changed, become all curves and mystery.

She ran through the grasses, sending sprays of bubbles into the air. Her blue skirt swirled around her legs and parted the high grass, showing glimpses of her thighs, then hiding them again. The top of her dress fit snug around her torso, adorned by a maze of confusing laces. Vyrl had never figured out why girls needed so many ties on their clothes.

She made a beautiful sight, though, her waist-length curls flying in the wind, streaming around her, shiny and red-bronze, touched with gold sun-streaks.

Hah! He wouldn't let her get away with spying on him. He took off in a sprint. In the village, he would have held back, not wanting people to see them playing like children, but out here he felt less constrained. Chasing Lily, making her shriek and laugh, had always entertained him. Now the thought of catching her made his pulse quicken in a way that had never happened when they were younger.

Lily glanced over her shoulder, her gaze flashing with mischief, her large eyes taunting him with an audacious gleam. Her teasing laugh sparkled across the plains. That laugh had been the bane of his existence for as long as he could remember.

With his long legs, Vyrl easily gained on her. Coming alongside her, he grabbed her around the waist with a gleeful shout. They went into a spin, their momentum whirling them around. He almost regained his balance by swinging her in a dance step he didn't usually let anyone know he had learned, given that men weren't supposed to dance. Then they toppled into the grasses in a tangle of limbs and clothes.

"Got you!" Vyrl flipped her onto her back. Still panting from his run, he pinned her upper arms to the ground. "Say 'Give,' " he demanded. "Come on, Lily! I win."

In years past, she would have yanked up a clod of tube-reeds and thrown it at him, then escaped while he yelled and wiped his eyes clear of the sparkling dirt that clung to bulbs on the grass.

Today, though, she wasn't laughing. She stared up at him, breathing hard, her chest rising and falling, her violet eyes huge. Most everyone in the Dalvador province had violet eyes, including Vyrl himself, but until this moment he had never realized the beauty of the color. Her lashes glimmered gold, a thick fringe against her milky skin. The rosy blush of her cheeks made his pulse race. He felt hot, then nervous, lying here, half on top of her, gazing at her face, which was so familiar and so new at the same time.

Her emotions washed over his empath's mind: confusion, surprise, and an uncertain anticipation, sweet and intense. It all mixed with another emotion harder to define, a warmth that spread through her and made him even more aware of her curves. Vyrl flushed, unsettled by his heightened awareness of her. Usually he shared emotions only with members of his family, who were the only empaths in Dalvador. Even then, they had to be near one another to pick up moods, and they had learned to guard their minds, to give one another privacy. Yet with Lily, his mental defenses were drifting away as if they were no more than ephemeral bubbles that floated on the wind.

They lay staring at each other, Vyrl with no idea what to say. Lily's mouth parted slightly, her lips full and soft. So soft. Plump. How would they feel if he touched them?

Then she dimpled like an imp and grabbed a handful of reeds. "You must let me up, O clumsy sir, or I will be forced to shower your head with sod." Although she spoke as always, full of play, she sounded different today—breathless, a little scared.

In the past, Vyrl would have wrestled her for the grass. Today he murmured, "You must first pay a fine for spying on me."

She gave a mock gasp of dismay, her heart-shaped face as expressive as ever. "And what terrible fine would you wrest, you heartless beast, from a poor girl such as myself?"

"Not so terrible," he said softly. Then he bent his head and kissed her.

As often as Vyrl had imagined this moment, his daydreams were nothing compared to the real thing. A jolt went through him as their lips touched. She tasted sweet and felt soft, her breasts against his chest, her body round beneath his. His heart thudded hard, as if he were still running.

Lifting his head, he whispered, "Lily." Then he kissed her again, moving his hands up her sides, caressing, feeling where her hips curved in to her waist.

Her emotions had become a confusing tumult. Ah, no, she wasn't responding. Mortification swept over him. Had he made a fool of himself? If she pushed him away or laughed at him, he was going to die, utterly die.

Instead she slid her arms around his waist, her embrace

tentative, as if she wasn't sure where to put her hands. Her mouth parted under his and she nibbled shyly at his lower lip.

Vyrl sighed, almost giddy with relief. He wanted to untie her laces and pull up her skirts, touch her everywhere, but he held back, afraid he would scare her.

Her emotions flooded past the natural barriers in her mind, the protections all people raised without realizing it. Then he knew; this was her first kiss, as it was his. Despite his good intentions, his hands roamed. Still kissing her, he stroked her sides, down and up, his touch urgent. He folded his palms around her breasts, filling his grip with them—if only this cloth would disappear! He fumbled with the laces on her bodice, baffled by their complexity. Frustrated, he pulled harder, straining to undo them. Pushing up her skirt with his other hand, he reached for her thigh—

"Vyrl, no. Slow down." Lily pushed his hand away from her leg. She was breathing hard now, but she had tensed, no longer pliant under him.

He groaned softly, one hand on her breast, the other intertwined with hers at his side. With her mental barriers fading, he could feel her shy desire, but also her fear.

"I'm sorry," he said. "You're just so soft and pretty." He brushed his lips across her nose. "I could kiss you all day."

Her blush deepened, as pink as a sunrise. He had always thought Lily was lovely, even in their early childhood when crueler children had called her a "fat little sprout." Now the plump little girl had vanished, replaced by this curvaceous beauty. Warmth washed out from her mind and he closed his eyes, letting it flow over him. She felt so very, very right, as if he had always known he would someday hold her like this.

"You've been working on your father's farm a lot," she said. "I've seen you doing your chores."

Vyrl opened his eyes. "They don't seem like chores." He longed to kiss her more, but he held back, not wanting to ruin this moment by pushing too hard. He shifted onto his side next to her, their bodies fitting together like pieces of a puzzle. The grass waved above and bubbles shimmered in the air. One popped, scattering glitter over them. Vyrl laughed, then flicked the powder off Lily's nose.

"I like to work in the fields," he said. He would far rather plow a field than study the physics his tutors persisted in trying to teach him.

Her mouth curved upward, half shy, half teasing. "You look very fine out in those fields with your shirt off."

He flushed. "You watched me like *that*?"

"You know, Vyrl, you used to be skinny, like a stalk of too-tall-weed."

⸰ Hai! He never had liked it when people called him that, even if it had been true these past years, when he shot up like the too-tall-weeds that grew over houses, seeking light from the suns.

"So what weed do I look like now?" He tried to make light of it, though he would really rather not be called a plant.

Her face gentled. "You don't." Touching his cheek, she spoke in her lilting voice. "You look like a man now, so strong and tall."

An emotion swelled in him, one he wasn't sure how to define. He knew only that he was where he belonged. With a tenderness he hadn't known he possessed, he brushed back a curl that had blown in her face. Then he kissed her again, barely able to believe he had her in his arms. He wanted to feel her skin against his, to make love to her out here under the golden suns, just as he had so often loved her in his dreams. But he held back and did no more than kiss her, taking it as slowly as she needed.

When the larger sun touched the horizon and shadows stretched across the plains, Vyrl and Lily headed back to the village of Dalvador, walking hand in hand, smiling and shy with each other. Vyrl was in no hurry. Now that he and Lily had made clear what had always been unspoken between them, they had plenty of time—their entire lives—to explore what they had begun today.

The Hearth Room was empty. The fireplace at the far end of the long hall slumbered, its coals dark, no flames licking its blue stones. No one sat in the armchairs there, and the standing lamps with their rose-glass shades remained unlit.

Lost in daydreams, Vyrl walked across the other end of the long hall, far from the hearth, in the shadows. As he passed the great stone staircase that curved up to the second floor, he glanced around to make sure he was alone. Then he turned in a circle, pretending to dance with Lily. With a flourish, he snapped his foot to his knee and spun fast, three times. He came out of the turn in a leap, jumping high off the ground. Then he landed on bent knees and stopped, checking to make sure no one had seen him. Laughing softly at himself, he resumed his staid walk.

"You're late," a voice said.

Vyrl froze. In response to the speaker, the lamps at the far end of the hall came on, shedding warm light over the hearth. This far from the lamps, shadows filled the hall, but enough light filtered back to show a man standing a few paces away, in the doorway Vyrl had been approaching. He hadn't heard anyone enter, probably because he had been dancing.

Vyrl managed to find his voice. "Father."

Eldrinson Althor Valdoria, who carried the title of Dalvador Bard, looked to Vyrl like the hero of an epic poem. At five feet ten, his father stood half a hand-span taller than the average man of Dalvador. He had a well-built physique, his muscles firm from years of farming. Wine-red hair brushed his shoulders, its healthy sheen visible despite the dim light. Even Vyrl, who understood almost nothing about how women saw such matters, could tell his father had a handsome face, with its straight nose, high cheekbones, large eyes, and classical features. Although Vyrl never knew how to respond when people exclaimed over how he resembled his father, he considered it a compliment, more because he admired his father than because he cared about appearance.

"Where have you been?" Eldrinson asked, frowning.

"Out in the plains." Vyrl tried not to look guilty about his missed schoolwork. His father would never understand. No one could. Vyrl was all brimming confusion and desire. Although his older brothers sometimes saw girls in the village, he was certain none of them had ever felt the way he did about Lily, as if his heart could soar one moment and shatter the next.

Eldrinson came over to him, and Vyrl again had the unsettling experience of looking *down* at him instead of *up*.

He had yet to become used to being taller than his father, and he was still growing.

"And while you were running in the plains," his father inquired, "who was doing your lessons?"

Vyrl imagined a black velvet cloth over his mind, hiding his thoughts about Lily from his father, who was a strong empath. "I'll finish them tonight."

"You shouldn't leave them until so late."

"I can't study all day," Vyrl grumbled. "I'll turn into a mad marauder."

"A marauder?" Eldrinson tried to hold back his smile. "We can't have that."

Although his father had guarded his mind, Vyrl could tell he wasn't angry, either about the missed homework or about Vyrl dancing, which he had probably seen.

"I feel suffocated in here," Vyrl said. "I need to run."

His father tried to look stern. "If you intend to carry through with this idea of yours, to earn a doctorate in agriculture someday, you have to study."

"If I go to the university, I'll have to go off-world." The prospect dismayed Vyrl. "Maybe I could attend through the computer webs instead."

"You mean in a virtual classroom?"

"Yes." Vyrl's mood lightened. "Exactly."

Eldrinson rubbed his chin. "I don't really understand it, these machines and things of your mother's people."

Having grown up with the technology his mother had brought to Lyshriol, Vyrl had never shared his father's unease with it. Eager now, he said, "I've been checking colleges. Many have programs for virtual students. I would never have to leave Lyshriol." He longed to learn the science behind the farming he loved. Lyshriol was more than his home; the plains, the suns, the land itself were part of him at a level so deep he couldn't separate them from his identity.

His father spoke carefully. "Many possibilities exist."

Vyrl could tell something more than unfinished homework was troubling his father. Disquieted, he looked around. "Where is everyone?" Usually the house bustled with life. He had six brothers and three sisters, all at home except for Eldrin, his oldest brother.

"They went to the festival in the village," Eldrinson said. "I've been looking for you."

"For me? Why?"

"To talk." His father's expression had become unreadable. "If you stay here on Lyshriol, your life will have many constraints. You wouldn't have to accept those limitations if you went off-world."

Apprehension brushed Vyrl. "I don't want to leave."

"You may change your mind when you're older."

He pondered his father. Although Eldrinson didn't seem overly upset, he wasn't happy either. Vyrl had tended to avoid his parents lately, but this cautious conversation bothered him. His father was shielding his mind more than usual. It didn't feel right.

Vyrl went to the stairs and sat on the fourth step, stretching out his legs. "What happened?"

Eldrinson came over and leaned against the banister, his elbow resting on its gold curve. "You are familiar with the House of Majda?"

"I guess." Vyrl knew Majda the way he knew the other noble Houses, as institutions he studied in school and otherwise gladly forgot. In this age of elected leaders, the Imperial nobility were an anachronism—including his own family, the Ruby Dynasty, which topped that antiquated hierarchy.

He winced, reminded of the history lessons he had neglected yesterday, earning his tutor's disapproval. His mother's ancestors had ruled the Ruby Empire until that interstellar civilization had fallen, stranding its colony worlds. During the ensuing dark ages, many colonies had lost their technology. Only in recent centuries had his mother's people regained star travel and begun rediscovering the lost colonies, such as this one on Lyshriol. Although Vyrl knew the House of Majda had been a strong ally of the Ruby Dynasty throughout history, he had never met a single member of that venerated line. Majda belonged to off-world politics, like a distant fog.

"Devon Majda heads the House of Majda," his father said. "She inherited the title of Matriarch ten years ago, just after her twenty-eighth birthday."

"Oh." Vyrl leaned back with his elbows on the stair above him.

Eldrinson shifted his weight, then cleared his throat. "As Matriarch, Devon has . . . responsibilities."

"I see." In truth, Vyrl had no idea what his father was talking about. He couldn't pick up anything from Eldrinson's guarded mind. He wondered if he could make it to the festival in time to have dinner with his brothers.

"Do you know what those responsibilities are?" Eldrinson asked.

Was this a test? Maybe his father was more annoyed with him for playing truant than he realized. If he had to stay in tonight while everyone else enjoyed the festival, he wouldn't see Lily.

He tried to sound knowledgeable. "As the head of her House, Devon Majda has a seat in the Assembly." Vyrl scoured his memory. "Most councilors in the Assembly are elected leaders who represent various worlds. Only the noble Houses have hereditary seats. It's left over from the days when the Ruby Dynasty ruled instead of the Assembly." He squinted at Eldrinson. "You and Mother have seats, too, don't you? Mother is the Councilor for Foreign Affairs."

"That's right." His father paused. "Your mother's seat is more than hereditary; she ran for election and won. It gives her more votes."

"Oh. Yes." Although Vyrl admired his mother's work in a theoretical sort of way, right now he had more concern for his growling stomach. Lately he was hungry all the time. He ate twice as much as his younger siblings, but it never seemed to be enough.

"The Ruby Dynasty and Majda must balance their power with that of the Assembly," Eldrin said, still guarded.

Vyrl knew he was missing whatever his father wanted him to see. "I didn't finish my studies on Majda," he admitted.

Eldrinson hesitated, discomfort leaking past his mental barriers. He didn't even admonish Vyrl for his lack of scholarly effort. Instead he said, "As the head of Majda, Devon must ensure that her line continues."

Although Vyrl wasn't sure why his father cared, he could well imagine that the House of Majda was upset, if their matriarch had reached the age of thirty-eight without producing any children. "She needs heirs."

"That's right."

When his father said no more, relief spread through Vyrl. Apparently the lesson was over. He stood up. "Shall we join the others? I'm starving."

"Vyrl, wait." Eldrinson raked his hand through his hair. "We need to discuss this."

Vyrl stopped, then slowly sat again. "Discuss what?"

His father answered quietly. "Your betrothal."

What? The word thudded in on Vyrl. Betrothal? He must have misheard. "I'm not betrothed to anyone." His voice cracked on the last word.

"I realize this is unexpected." His father gave him a look of apology. "Your mother and I had intended to take more time, to let you adjust to the idea. This visit caught us by surprise. We've just received word that Brigadier General Majda—that's Devon—will be here in two days."

A constriction tightened Vyrl's chest, making it hard to breathe. "Brigadier General? At *thirty-eight*?" He was no military expert, but even he knew that however old it might sound to him, that age was young for such a rank.

"She's good at what she does. Very good." His father added dryly, "Her family connections don't hurt either."

Vyrl struggled to mask his turmoil, to hide the chaos of his emotions. Surely an escape existed from this disaster. "This is too fast."

Sympathy washed across his father's face. "I'm sorry it is such a shock. Your mother and I want you to be happy. Vyrl, we spent a great deal of time checking out Devon. She is a good person. And as the Majda consort, you can follow pursuits you could never have here." Awkwardly he added, "Including an, uh, artistic career, if you wish."

Vyrl barely heard him. All he could see was Lily, her lovely face bright in the sunshine, like a lost dream. Betrothals among the noble Houses were political arrangements; his parents and Majda had probably been negotiating for months, even years. These matters carried the weight of governmental decrees. Nineteen-year-old Eldrin, his oldest brother, had married the Ruby Pharaoh three years ago, his own kin, as tradition dictated. But it wasn't fair. He wasn't Eldrin. He wasn't the firstborn. He had three older brothers and three younger ones. His parents had turned down offers for his other brothers, considering the matches unsuitable. Vyrl had never expected they would accept one for him, especially with the highest placed member of the most powerful House.

What made it even worse was that he understood their reasoning. He was more family-oriented than his older brothers, more suitable as a consort. If Majda needed an heir, she had to marry relatively soon, which left out his younger brothers. And more than anything, he understood the gift his parents wanted to give him, the chance to pursue his love of dance, something he could never do here on Lyshriol.

It didn't matter. He couldn't marry a female warrior. He *couldn't* do it. Just as men never danced on Lyshriol, so women never fought in battle. His stomach clenched. If he revealed how he felt about Lily, his parents would have her sent away, to remove a distraction that might interfere with his betrothal. He couldn't bear the thought.

He struggled for calm. "I don't want to marry."

Eldrinson spoke in the kindly voice Vyrl had trusted his entire life, but which gave him no mooring now. "It's all right. You will have time to get to know her, to feel more comfortable with this situation."

"Why can't Althor marry her?" Vyrl thought of his brother; at seventeen, Althor was preparing to go off-world to a military academy. "He wants that life. He would be perfect for her."

"You're the one she offered for."

"But *why*? Althor is older. So is Del-Kurj." In truth, Vyrl couldn't imagine anyone marrying his wild brother, Del-Kurj, but that didn't make this any easier.

Eldrinson's face turned thoughtful. "I can only guess as to Devon's motives in regards to Althor. Majda is a conservative matriarchy. I suspect Devon doesn't want a fighter pilot for a husband. As for Del-Kurj . . ." He made an angry wave with his hand. "Let's just say he has had a few indiscretions."

Few. Vyrl would have laughed if he hadn't been so upset. Del-Kurj already knew more about women than most grown men in Dalvador. He liked girls and they liked him, and he made no secret about it, despite the trouble it caused him. Del hadn't fathered any children yet, but if he kept up in the way he'd begun it would only be a matter of time.

Vyrl spoke in a low voice. "Does the Assembly want this betrothal, too?"

His father nodded. "Stronger ties between Majda and the Ruby Dynasty will cement alliances the Assembly sees as crucial to the stability of our government."

"I don't want to stabilize a government." He couldn't keep the pain out of his voice.

"Ah, Vyrl." Eldrinson's voice held deep regret. "I am terribly sorry this news is unwelcome. If it helps to know, your mother and I truly believe this can be a good match. Devon Majda will treat you well, with respect and honor."

"She's *ancient.*"

His father's expression lightened. "If she is ancient, I fear to ask what that makes your mother and me." His smile faded. "We do have concerns about the age difference. But with modern techniques to delay aging, eventually you won't be so aware of it." Gently, he added, "You may come to love her, in time."

Vyrl could only shake his head. His dreams were slipping away, like the glitter from a ruptured bubble spreading on the wind.

2
THE SILVERED PLAINS

The circular chamber was high in a tower of the castle. Vyrl stood at the window looking out over the countryside. The three figures crossing the Dalvador Plains were too far away to see clearly, but he recognized his mother's streaming gold hair and his father's confident stride.

Beyond them, about a fifteen-minute walk from Dalvador, the starport made a cluster of whitewashed buildings with blue turreted roofs. It resembled a Dalvador hamlet—except for the gold-and-black spacecraft that crouched on the landing field like an intruder. The shuttle had come down from one of the battle cruisers that orbited Lyshriol. Vyrl had never thought much about the ships up there, beyond knowing they provided one of the best orbital defense systems in settled space. If only they could have defended him against the arrival of Brigadier General Devon Majda.

He wished he could fly away, beyond the suns in the lavender sky. The larger orb was eclipsing the smaller, like a great golden coin surrounded by a halo. To the east and south, farms drowsed in the sunlight, uncaring of interstellar politics. Nearer by, his parents and their guest reached the village. He lost sight of them as they walked in among the houses.

Vyrl bit his lip, his heart aching for Lily. He glanced toward her home, a round white house on a hill, surrounded by other houses. He hadn't dared talk to her in the past two days, since their afternoon together. He had never made it to the festival that night, having been grounded for his truancy. He missed her so much, as if someone had taken out his center and left him with a hole only she could fill.

Yesterday he had seen her while he was walking to his father's farm with Althor and Del-Kurj. She and some other girls had been carrying baskets of bubble fruit. Before he could even think, he had started toward her, his heart surging, his pulse racing. He had gone only a few steps when his brothers called him back.

He couldn't confide in them. Given that one of his brothers might have to marry Devon if he didn't, he doubted they would want Lily distracting him, but neither would they want to betray his trust. Rather than put them in that awkward position, he said nothing. They knew he was hiding his moods, but they respected his privacy and never pried, neither with word nor thought.

Disheartened, Vyrl turned from the window and sat on an elegant stone bench against the wall. He came here when he needed to soothe his agitation. His mother had once referred to this chamber as a "balm for his tempestuous soul." He wasn't sure what she meant, but he did like the austere beauty of this room, with its polished bluestone walls, domed ceiling, and a floor tiled in squares of blue and white stone. Designs in bas-relief bordered the ceiling and floor, as if the chamber were a round gift box—with him as the present.

That last thought dispelled his tenuous serenity. With every fiber of his being protesting, he made himself stand up. He crossed to the arched door of the chamber, but he paused without opening it. Such a beautiful door. He could stay here all day admiring it. Really. He loved its vibrant color. Made with layers of blue-stalk from the Stained Glass Forest, it glowed like a mountain lake. His mother had told him about an off-world substance called "wood" that came in brown shades and didn't glow. He found it hard to imagine such dullness.

As much as he would have been happy to appreciate the door for the rest of the day, he could no longer procrastinate. So he left the chamber and descended the bluestone stairs that spiraled down the tower. He had dressed formally today, in blue trousers with a darker belt embossed in silver. Soft boots came to his knees. Gold-leaf designs bordered their top edges and also the cuffs and collar on his white, bell-sleeved shirt. Thongs laced up the front of the shirt.

At the second story of the castle, he exited the tower into a hall of lavender ash-stone. Wall sconces held purple-glass lamps lit with flames. He thought of stopping to turn on the superconducting light rods hidden in the ceiling, but he didn't pause. It would only delay the inevitable by a few moments, and besides, today he wanted no reminders of off-world technology—or off-world technocrats.

Far too soon, he reached the top of the stairs that went down to the Hearth Room. The great staircase curved around, this part hidden from view of the hall below. Vyrl stood on the landing, straining to hear. Voices came from below, his parents and a woman with a husky contralto. He clenched the banister, unable to continue. He couldn't go down. He *couldn't.*

But if he didn't appear soon, his parents would send someone for him. So he fortified his resolve and descended. Halfway down he came around the curve of the staircase; stopping there, he looked out over the Hearth Room. His parents and an unfamiliar woman were standing at the far end, near the hearth, unaware of him, sipping from ruby goblets. A girl with gold curls had just served them, judging by her empty silver tray. As she walked down the hall, she glanced up. Seeing Vyrl, she started, her mouth opening. Then she averted her gaze and hurried on her way, leaving the room.

Vyrl's face burned. He had known her for years. She and Lily were always giggling together, often at him, though he had never understood why they found him so amusing. Now she wouldn't even acknowledge him. After the news about his betrothal had spread in the village, his friends no longer seemed comfortable with him. Did they look away because he had become different, his title made real, the son of a mysterious queen who came from above the sky?

No one else had realized yet he was on the stairs, so he remained still, watching. His mother looked every bit her Ruby Dynasty heredity. Tall and statuesque, in a soft blue jumpsuit, she stood by the fireplace with a posture of quiet confidence. Gold hair curled around her face, cascaded over her shoulders and arms, and poured down her back. His father stood next to her, one elbow on the mantel as he spoke to their guest.

Devon Majda.

Vyrl couldn't stop staring at the general. She wore a trim uniform, green with gold on the cuffs, and polished knee-boots that made her taller than his parents. Her black hair hung glossy and straight to her shoulders, framing a face of austere, aristocratic perfection, from her aquiline nose to her dark, upward-tilted eyes. With her long limbs and athletic build, she projected a sense of energy. An aura of power surrounded her, as if she took her rank and heredity for granted. Indeed, she should; only one other family had more status or wealth than Majda—the Ruby Dynasty.

Vyrl didn't care about ancient empires, modern politics, or wealth. He just wanted his own family and a farm. Unfortunately, that probably had a lot to do with why Devon had chosen him to sire her heirs. Thinking of what went into that siring, he flushed, certain his face was turning bright red. Given the differences in their ages, he hadn't expected to find her so attractive. But she still seemed old to him. He couldn't imagine her as his wife.

Glancing toward the stairs, his mother caught sight of him. With a smile, she raised her hand, beckoning. Devon idly glanced his way, then did a double take, her gaze widening. A surge of appreciation overflowed her mind; she apparently liked what she saw. Acutely aware of them watching, he came down the stairs. He grew even more self-conscious as he crossed the long room to the hearth.

When he reached them, Devon bowed deeply from the waist. As she straightened, Vyrl nodded with the formality his title required. Raising his head, he found himself looking straight into her eyes. It startled him. He was used to the girls in Dalvador, who came only to his shoulder, if that much. He took after his mother's people, with their greater height.

Devon spoke in Iotic, the language of the nobility. "My honor at your presence, Your Highness."

Although here in Dalvador he rarely needed to follow the protocol of the Imperial Court, Vyrl had learned its ways. He answered in flawless Iotic. "And mine at yours, General Majda." He wondered if he sounded as awkward as he felt.

She smiled, her expression formal but not unfriendly. "Devon, please."

"Devon." He tried to smile back, though the expression felt stiff on his face. "Please call me Vyrl."

She repeated his name in her Iotic accent, making it sound like *Vahrialle,* which was, he supposed, the proper pronunciation. All his friends drawled *Verle* in the rural Dalvador dialect.

They talked for a bit, a stilted conversation. He could think of almost nothing to say. Standing with his parents while he met the woman that half the galaxy expected him to impregnate was about the most mortifying experience he could imagine.

His father was watching them closely. To Devon, he said, "Perhaps you would like to take a walk? Vyrl can show you the countryside."

"I would like that," Devon said.

Vyrl's shoulders relaxed. The idea of being alone with her didn't ease his agitation, but at least his parents wouldn't be watching. Although his mother smiled at him, he felt the sadness she tried to hide. Her heart had ached that same way when Eldrin had left home and when Althor had received his acceptance to the off-world military academy.

I never wanted you to look at me that way, Vyrl thought to her. *I've always wanted to stay on Lyshriol.* But he couldn't say it out loud, not in front of General Majda.

Walking with Devon across the plains made Vyrl twitch inside. Just two days ago he had run free here and held Lily in his arms. It tore at him to return to this place with a stranger, but he did his best to hide his sense of loss. He could almost hear his brother Del-Kurj deriding him: *Enough of your melodramatic adolescent angst!* As if what Vyrl felt for Lily couldn't be serious, or as if Del-Kurj was so much more incredibly mature. Vyrl could tell his parents also believed he was too young to fall in love. None of that mattered. *He* knew what he felt for Lily was genuine.

Devon walked at his side, her dark hair ruffled by the wind. She spoke politely. "This is beautiful countryside."

"I've always thought so." Vyrl glanced around at the nodding grasses that brushed their hips and the lavender sky with its blue puffs of cloud. He wanted to add, *I love it with every part of my being. I can't leave.* But he remained silent.

"Two suns." She peered at the sky, shielding her eyes with her hand. "It's an unstable configuration, you know."

"The suns?" He had thought the problem was with the planet. Contradicting her would hardly be tactful though.

She lowered her hand. "I meant this world, Lyshriol. Its orbit is unstable. The binary star system perturbs it."

"Oh. Yes." Vyrl pushed back the curls blowing across his face. "My tutor says astronomical engineers from the Ruby Empire moved Lyshriol here and terraformed it for human colonists. They had technologies we've yet to recover."

"Yes. They did a good job." She smiled, her aristocratic face warmed by the sunlight. "It's very pretty."

Vyrl had never thought of the land that sustained his people and his dreams as "pretty." At a loss for an appropriate response, he remained silent.

They strolled toward a distant herd of lyrine grazing on bubble stalks. He stopped about a hundred meters away, reluctant to disturb them. "Those are my father's livestock."

Devon studied the herd. "They're genetically engineered from horses, aren't they?"

"That's what we think." Biology was one of the few subjects he actually liked. "But if that's true, they've become very different animals."

She laughed softly. "I must admit, I've never seen pastel blue horses before. And those horns of theirs are charming. They act like prisms, yes?"

"Well, yes, I guess so." He had always liked the way sunlight refracted in rainbow flashes through the translucent horns of the lyrine. Their hooves produced the same effect, making it look as if they struck sparks of color from the ground when they ran in sunlight. It had never seemed unusual to him, but perhaps it was more so than he realized. Or maybe she was simply trying to make conversation.

He motioned at several boulders that crested the grass, which spread around them like an ocean of reeds. "Would you like to sit?"

"Yes, thank you."

They settled side by side on the largest boulder, which was shaped like a huge table. Devon continued to gaze over the plains. The wind whipped back her hair, accenting the classic bone structure of her face. To Vyrl, she seemed out of place here, a technocrat with an impeccable pedigree transplanted to a rustic setting that offered her no challenge. He had a hard time reading her mood. When he tried, he ran into the mental wall she used to shield her mind. Nor could he relax his defenses around her. With Lily, his barriers had dissolved without his even realizing it, but now his mind felt as closed as a fortress.

Devon spoke gently. "You're different than I expected."

"Different?" He blinked. "How?"

"Quieter." She considered him. "More polished."

Although he said, "Thank you," her words didn't feel like a compliment. He followed the manners his parents had taught him. That he lived a rural, simple life didn't make him crude.

Devon leaned back on her hand. "What do you like to do, Vyrl, when you aren't in school?"

"Come out here." He motioned at a nearby field of nodding stalks, each weighed down with orbs as large as a fist. "We're going to harvest the bagger-bubbles soon." He smiled, warming to the thought. "I'll work with Althor and Del, razing the stalks."

"Cutting plants, you mean?" She seemed bemused.

Cutting plants seemed a prosaic way to describe the joy of working with the land and the riches it produced. He wasn't sure, though, if Devon would understand his stumbling attempts to explain feelings he couldn't fully describe even to himself, so he only said, "Yes. Cutting plants."

"Ah."

They sat for a while. When the silence became strained, Vyrl asked, "Are you on vacation now?"

"I suppose you could call it that. I've five days leave, measured in Lyshriol time." She sat forward and rested her elbows on her knees. "The dates for the Metropoli summit have been moved up. That's why I had to reschedule this trip. I have to give a presentation there about the ground-based defense systems for Metropoli."

"Oh." Vyrl had no real idea what she meant. "It sounds important."

Devon grimaced. "Committee meetings always sound important. The more elevated the description, the less we get done." She shook her head. "I see no point in stockpiling more weapons on Metropoli. The planet is already as well guarded as we can make it. But its economy will benefit from the industry. Metropoli has a big population, ten billion, so it holds many votes within the Assembly." Wryly, she added, "Hence my presentation."

He tried to look interested. "I hope it works out."

"I'm sure it will." She didn't sound convinced. He was picking up traces of her thoughts now. She didn't expect the summit to achieve anything useful. He wondered why they bothered with meetings if they didn't think it would help.

After another silence, Devon cleared her throat. She wouldn't look at him, just kept staring across the plains. "The Assembly sent me many files about you."

Vyrl stiffened. What was the Assembly doing with files about him? "Where did they get them?"

She glanced at him. "They have dossiers on every member of your family. Surely you knew that."

His face was growing hot. "No."

"Oh." Now she looked embarrassed. "I'm sorry. I didn't mean to sound intrusive."

"You didn't." That wasn't true, but it wasn't her fault he hadn't known the Assembly kept a dossier on him. Although it made sense, it had simply never occurred to him.

"I've also spoken at length to your parents." She stared hard at the lyrine herd again, avoiding his gaze.

Vyrl wondered what she was trying to say. "They didn't tell me much about the negotiations."

She finally turned to him. "They are terribly proud of you, you know."

"They are?" As far as Vyrl could tell, his truancy and procrastination annoyed them no end.

"Yes. Very much." Now she looked self-conscious. "They've made it clear that if I don't treat you well, I will answer to them."

Vyrl winced. *That* sounded like his parents. "I'm sorry. They say things like that sometimes."

To his surprise, Devon gave an affectionate laugh. "I imagine they do." Her smile faded. "They also made assurances, discreetly of course."

Vyrl waited for her to clarify that mystifying statement. When she didn't, he said, "What do you mean?"

Devon cleared her throat. "There are, ah, certain expectations for the consort of Majda." She squinted at him, her cheeks tinged with red now. "Parents may have idealized views of their children that aren't, well, uh . . . realistic."

Vyrl had no idea what she meant, and he didn't think he wanted to know. But he couldn't restrain his curiosity. "What kind of views?"

"They might assume a certain . . . innocence . . ." Her blush deepened as her words trailed off.

"Oh." Now Vyrl understood. He knew exactly what she meant. He spoke stiffly. "My parents know me well." There. Now that he had humiliated himself with his lack of sexual experience, maybe she would leave it alone.

Mercifully, she just went back to watching the lyrine. Apparently his father had been right about at least one reason why Devon hadn't offered for Del-Kurj. Vyrl suspected Del's brash lack of discretion was the problem more than his actual experience; if the noble Houses had truly required male virginity on the wedding night, they probably would have died out by now for lack of mates.

He focused on Devon—and one of her memories jumped into his mind, a scene so vivid that it escaped her barriers. A tall man of about thirty-five, with dark hair and eyes, stood with his hands spread out from his sides, laughing as he pretended confusion about something, as if he were teasing the person watching him. Vyrl felt Devon's rush of love, followed by a sense of loss, the kind that came from separation, a loneliness so deep it made him ache.

Saints almighty. What an insensitive clod his parents had birthed. Here he was bemoaning his own miserable fate, and it had never occurred to him that this arrangement might be ruining her life, too. Why would she want to court a half-grown stranger when she had a lover her own age whom she would probably be far happier to make her consort, if politics, heredity, and duty hadn't interfered?

Devon turned to him with a strained smile. When she touched his cheek, a tingle went through Vyrl, but it only made him think of Lily. Before he could stop himself, he whispered, "It's not fair."

"I know." She didn't even need to ask what he meant. "But this is how it works for those like you and me." Then she slid her hand behind his head and drew him forward.

Vyrl hadn't expected her to kiss him. When her lips touched his, it jolted him, but from surprise rather than desire. The kiss was just, well . . . lips pressing his. No heart. No passion. Nothing.

After a moment she drew back and gave him a rueful smile. "Perhaps it takes the sparks a while, heh?"

He wanted to crawl under the rocks. "My apologies if I disappointed you."

"Ah, Vyrl, no, I didn't mean that." She sounded as if she wanted to hide under a few boulders herself. "I'm sorry. I'm bungling this terribly."

"No. Don't say that." He struggled to smile. "It's all right."

So they sat on their rock, gazing at the plains, trying somehow, someway, to find a common ground.

3
BENEATH THE LAVENDER MOON

Gusts of wind tried to knock Vyrl off the castle wall. In the light of the two moons, which were both in the sky tonight, he climbed down from his window, hanging on to cracks in the stone. Despite the wind, sweat dribbled down his neck. He had on too many clothes, not only those he had worn earlier today when he met Devon but also a sweater and thicker boots. He had rolled up his cloak and tied it onto his pack, which he wore on his back. Altogether it made him hot, heavy, and clumsy. Even worse, it would make it harder to run if anyone saw him.

Finally his feet touched ground. He hunkered by the wall, hiding behind a cluster of bubble stalks in the garden. Then he checked his palmtop. The silvery sheet unrolled in his hand and lit up with holos, showing the house security system. Nothing had changed since he had turned off the alarms that guarded his room. It hadn't been difficult; the system was meant to keep prowlers out, not hold him inside.

Vyrl reset the system to hide his activities, then tucked the palmtop back into his pack and stood up, scanning the area.

He took off at a steady lope, headed for the starport.

Vyrl clung to the windowsill, praying he didn't fall and smash himself on the gravel two stories below. A night-triller sang in the distance, its musical call echoed by another triller farther away.

"Come *on*," he muttered, scraping his fingernails over the recalcitrant window. "Open, you bog-boil."

With a protesting screech, the window abruptly swung

inward. Vyrl froze. Gods, he was going to look stupid if someone caught him hanging here on the wall of a private home in the middle of the night. It had taken him longer than he expected to finish his business at the starport; it meant he hadn't reached here until well after midnight had passed in Lyshriol's twenty-eight hour day.

Mercifully, no one seemed to be out. This late at night, few people wandered these high, twisting lanes of Dalvador. No one came storming out of the house, and no one yelled from any other house to find out what was going on.

When the trillers began singing again, Vyrl breathed out in relief. He nudged the window wide open, grateful it made no more noise, and peered into the shadows beyond.

Moonlight silvered the room below. The cozy chamber looked as he remembered it, though years had passed since he had last been here. The bed was just below him, but even the screeching window hadn't awakened its occupant. Vyrl grinned. Lily had always slept like a rock; he had long suspected it had something to do with her rock-headed stubborn nature.

He let himself down into the room, gripping the sill as he slid lower. Then his feet touched the bed. Exhaling, he knelt next to the slumbering Lily, his head bent while he caught his breath. She murmured, turning restlessly. This time the surge in his pulse had nothing to do with a fear of being caught. He wanted to touch her, but he held back, having no idea how she would react when she discovered him kneeling in her bed.

Lily rolled onto her back and sighed, her eyes slowly opening. For a long moment she simply stared at him, her gaze fogged with sleep. Then she said, "Vyrl?" She sounded as drowsy as she looked, warm and snuggled in her nest of blankets. The embroidered flowers on her white nightgown gleamed in the moonlight.

"It's me," Vyrl said. For some reason the temperature in the room seemed to be rising. How different Lily made him feel, compared to the enigmatic, cool General Majda.

Her lips curved in the teasing smile she always used with him. "You're a terribly misbehaved fellow, to climb in my window. I must yell and make a great fuss."

"Lily!" His whisper came out fierce. "Your father would kill me."

"You better hide, then." Her voice had an unexpected tremor.

With a start, Vyrl realized she *wasn't* her usual teasing self. She was shaking! In all the years he had known Lily, he had seen her laughing, mischievous, glowering, joyous, annoyed, teasing, and earnest, but she had never been afraid of him.

Vyrl lowered his mental barriers, unsure, but trusting that her thoughts wouldn't hurt him. As her mood permeated his mind, he realized she feared he would leave her forever, disappearing from her life, lost to rumors he had to marry an off-world queen. His crawling in her window didn't frighten her; she trusted him the same way he trusted her.

He touched her cheek. "It's been a long time."

She folded her fingers around his with that new, charming shyness of hers. "Too long."

Vyrl sighed, his memories rushing in. When he and Lily had been small children, they had often curled here in a pile on her bed. Then one day her parents and his had told them that they could no longer take naps together. Now Vyrl felt as if he were returning home, but with full knowledge of why their parents hadn't wanted them together this way. They had been right. If he were Lily's father, he would take a sharpened farm implement to any youth climbing in her window late at night.

But he wasn't her father, he was the boy—no, the man—who dreamed of her every day. He stretched out next to her, still wearing his backpack and sweater, and pulled her into his arms. A jolt went through him, ten times stronger than the shiver Devon had evoked. Nor did this fade. It leapt like fire on oil.

"You make me crazy," he whispered, fighting the urge to put his hands everywhere on her. He pressed his lips against her cheek. "You torment my nights."

She slid her arms around him. "But I've done nothing, good sir." Instead of offering sympathy for his travails, she sounded inordinately pleased by his declaration of unrequited passion.

Vyrl caressed her face, pushing aside her disarrayed

curls. He found her lips with his and held her close, losing himself in her tenderness. He savored their kiss all the more for having so painfully labored to accept, these last two days, that he could never hold her again. She parted her lips, her embrace tightening, her body fitted against his, her touch uncertain but so very, very fine.

With reluctance, Vyrl lifted his head. She smiled, her big eyes luminous in the shadows. Ah, but he could lie here forever, lost in her arms. That was the problem, though. If he didn't stop now, his plan would fail because he would end up staying the entire night. He and Lily would be found in the morning, thoroughly shocking her parents and his. Everyone would hush up his scandalous behavior, and his parents would probably lock him up in his tower room until he was safely married to Devon.

As Vyrl drew away, Lily made a low protest. He swallowed, even more aroused by her sweet, guileless desire. Determined to control himself, he sat up. She regarded him, puzzled and hurt, while he took her hands and drew her into a sitting position. The covers fell away from her body, revealing the soft sleep-gown that outlined her figure.

Vyrl's concentration flew out the window. With a valiant effort, he tore his gaze away from her curves and made himself focus on her face. "Lily Opaline, I have an important matter to discuss with you."

"And what might that be?" Although she tried for a mischievous smile, she looked more scared than playful.

He took a deep breath. "I'm running away."

Her tremulous smile vanished. "Vyrl, *no!* Don't go." Softly, she said, "Please don't leave. Even if you have to marry that—that person, at least we can be friends."

Vyrl couldn't imagine being "friends" with Lily. It would cut out his heart. Nor did Lily understand; to marry Devon, he would leave Lyshriol and go live in some palace with a staff of hundreds, which he would be expected to manage while his wife attended her military duties.

"Lily, we can't be friends," he said firmly. He forced out the words. "General Majda, the woman who came from the sky—the leaders of my mother's people say I must marry her. My parents agree."

A tear ran down her cheek. "Don't say good-bye this way." Her mischief had vanished. "I can't bear it."

"Don't cry." He wiped his knuckles across her cheek, smearing her tears. Then he went deep in himself, calling up his courage, and spoke the words he had come to say. "I want you to run away with me."

For a long moment she didn't react, not in her face, her posture, or even her mood. Then her emotions flooded over him. He couldn't sort it all out, but two responses came through strong and clear: She both feared and hoped he meant what he said.

"It's true." He could hardly believe that he had actually asked her. "Come with me."

"But we can't." She drew his hands together and held them as if they were a treasure. "Your parents will bring us home. With their magics, they will easily find us."

Vyrl had long ago given up trying to convince his friends that technology had nothing to do with magic. "I know they can find us. But I have a . . . well, a—a solution."

"Solution?" Her emotions were clearer now: apprehension that she would lose him; uncertainty in how he felt about her compared to the mysterious adult who had trespassed in their midst; a desire for him that she didn't fully understand; and the shyness that came with that desire, a self-conscious recognition of Vyrl's masculinity, an awareness she had hidden this past year by tormenting him with mischief.

Emboldened, he plunged ahead before he lost his courage. "By the time they find us, we will be married." Then he stopped, terrified. What if she refused him? He would die of shame, curl up into a ball the size of a bubble pod and blow away on the wind, never to be heard of again.

Lily stared at him. Then she gave an uneasy laugh. "You're teasing me."

"I'm not." Vyrl raised her hands and pressed his lips against her knuckles. He spoke with all the persuasion he could muster. "Be my wife, Lily. You're the only one I've ever wanted, the only one I ever will. Say yes." He had gone too far to turn back now. "Tell me you will marry me. Tonight."

She let go of his hands and covered her cheeks with her own. When she said nothing, he added, "I would court you, but we haven't time, I'm afraid. You have to decide now."

Instead of accepting or refusing him, she just lowered her hands. He could no longer catch individual emotions in the tumult of her thoughts. Why wouldn't she speak? Had he offended her? Maybe he had been a fool, presuming where he had no place. Chagrined, he felt his face heating.

"You're always so impatient," she chided, her voice quavering behind her bravado. "This is worse than the time you pushed me into the lake."

"You would have taken the entire summer to jump if I hadn't pushed you." His voice softened. "Be brave now, Lily. Say yes. We may never have another chance. Everyone is busy arranging my marriage. General Majda needs heirs and she's thirty-eight, so she can't wait much longer."

Lily's face changed slowly, her expression unlike any she had shown him before. No imp this, no child. This Lily looked ... older. When she spoke, her voice caught. "Then, Havyrl Valdoria, I—I would be honored to marry you."

Yes! She had said yes! He wanted to shout her answer to the sky, and he would have if it hadn't meant her father would come thundering in here, threatening to skewer him for invading his daughter's bedroom. He took her hands again and spoke in a low, intense voice. "I will make you a good husband, I swear it."

Despite her best intentions to look somber, naughtiness crept into her voice. "But how do I know? You must give me a sample." She put her arms around his neck and tilted her pretty face to his. "Unless you're afraid to kiss me ..."

He grinned, rubbing his hands along her back. "I'm not afraid, you rascal. But we have to leave. We need to cross the Backbone Mountains tonight and find a Bard in Rillia to marry us. If we ask one in the Dalvador Plains, he will probably recognize me and refuse to do the ceremony without talking to our parents. But I look at least two years older than I am, Lily, and that's old enough for us to marry without parental consent. If we go to the Rillian Vales, we can have it done." Vyrl didn't care that in the interstellar culture of his mother's people, he was many, many years away from the age of majority. On Lyshriol, he was almost an adult.

Lily nodded, her eyes glimmering. "Then let us go."

The war-lyrine raced across the plains, thrilling in its speed, releasing its pent-up energy much as Vyrl did when he ran through the endless grasses. Unlike the graceful, slender lyrine he had shown Devon yesterday, this powerful animal had a massive build and a violet coat, almost black in the moonlight. Its muscles rippled as it ran. The Dalvador Plains spread everywhere, an ocean of translucent reeds blued by the moonlight, as if enchanted. Behind them, the village of Dalvador dwindled in the plains; ahead, still a ride of a few hours, the Backbone Mountains speared into the sky.

Vyrl sat astride the lyrine with Lily in front of him, his arms around her waist, his hands gripped on the reins. The Lavender Moon rode high in the sky, bathing them in violet radiance and drawing glints of light from the lyrine's horns. The crescent of the Blue Moon hung above the horizon.

Moonglaze had the full liquid gait of a well-bred lyrine, his muscles bioengineered to even out his motions, making his run so smooth that Vyrl and Lily could speak in full sentences even with their mount racing across the plains. Vyrl's mother had expressed surprise to his father at the poetic names his people gave their war mounts but it made sense to Vyrl, who had been raised on Lyshriol. His mother's people seemed overly pragmatic to him.

Leaning against Vyrl, Lily pulled her cloak tight. "I've never ridden on such a glorious animal before."

"I'm not surprised. The great stallions like Moonglaze let few people touch them." Vyrl didn't want to think what his father would do when he found out his son had absconded with his best war-lyrine. But Moonglaze had always taken to Vyrl, and tonight he needed the animal's strength.

Moonglaze had gone to "war" only a few times; conflicts on Lyshriol were minor, more like arguments than combat. But beyond this simple world, an interstellar civilization teemed with life and violence, caught in a world-slagging war that most people here could never comprehend. Vyrl knew that to survive, his mother's people needed military leaders much as Devon and Althor.

Vyrl had no wish to fight; he wanted only to raise crops and babies with Lily. Although his father had trained him in the use of a sword and bow, he seemed content with Vyrl's preference for farming, certainly the most prevalent lifestyle in Dalvador. However, Vyrl was the only farmer here who wanted a doctorate in agriculture. He could do it without leaving home, as a virtual student, if he could just buckle down to his studies. Lily would help in that; she always seemed to settle him.

As Devon's consort, he could earn as many doctorates as he wanted. And then? Skolian nobility didn't farm. He might like research; he didn't really know. But it wasn't his dream. He had no grievance with Devon; she seemed an honorable person. Even so, he could never imagine life in the Imperial Court. She wanted the innocent farm boy, but if she took him away from the land and life he loved, it would destroy him.

If he hadn't loved another woman, perhaps he could have accepted the arranged marriage. It would have given him a great gift, freeing him to pursue a life he had never dared imagine could be his. He loved to dance and had trained all his life, but only in private where no one except his family and off-world teachers knew. It wasn't accepted among people here that men dance, not under any circumstances, not even at festivals.

It didn't matter. Without this woman in his arms, his life would be infinitely poorer. By the time their parents learned what he and Lily had done, it would be too late; they would have consummated their marriage. Their wedding would be public knowledge. Devon could no longer wed him even if his parents annulled his union.

Vyrl pulled Lily close, and she settled against him. He knew he had made the right choice in asking her to marry him.

He just hoped it didn't cause an interstellar crisis.

Snow pummeled Vyrl and Lily as they rode through the mountain storm, an unexpected tempest after the clear weather down in the plains. He kept his arms and cloak protectively around Lily. His backpack, their most valuable possession right now, was securely lashed in the travel bags Moonglaze carried.

"—there!" The wind caught Lily's voice and tore it away from his ears.

He leaned his head over hers. "What?"

"Need shelter . . . we could be . . ." Gales stole the rest of her words.

"Be what?"

"Hurt," Lily said.

Vyrl clenched the reins. Inside his gloves, his fingers had gone numb. Had he brought his love out here only to lose her to the fury of a blue storm? No! He would never let it happen. He would die first—yes, he would—before he allowed anything to hurt Lily. Not that he was sure how his dying would help matters, but that was how he felt.

Lily was right, though; if they didn't locate shelter, they could find themselves in serious trouble. He couldn't see much of anything. Moonglaze's head was barely more than a shadow in the swirling flurries. The lyrine had slowed to a walk, stepping carefully along the trail.

"—down," Lily was saying. "We're probably safer on foot."

"Yes, I think so." Vyrl reined in the lyrine and dismounted, then steadied Lily as she slid down next to him. Clutching the reins, he put his arm around her shoulders. Darkness whirled around them and wind ripped at their cloaks. His teeth chattered with cold.

Their best hope was probably to take refuge within the clumps of boulders that dotted the meadows on either side of the trail, if they could find some. He took a cautious step, drawing Lily through the swirling storm, almost blind in the darkness. Moonglaze followed, crowding them, his body too close.

"Don't do that," Vyrl muttered at the lyrine.

"He wants to protect us," Lily said.

Vyrl swallowed, recognizing she spoke the truth. What if his rash decision to run away ended in tragedy? Steeling his resolve, he took another step into the icy dark. "I can't see a blasted thing."

She spoke with reassurance. "We'll manage. We've been through worse."

"That's true." He said it to comfort her. Although he had experienced bad weather up here before, he had been part of a well-equipped caravan then. They had simply set up enviro-tents and sat out the weather in comfort. Right now he had nothing but his palmtop; his already stuffed pack hadn't had room for much else. The palmtop could do little more than tell him they were in trouble, which wasn't exactly a great revelation.

Lily tugged on his arm. "Over here!"

He squinted into the darkness. "You see something?"

She pulled his hand forward until it hit rock. "This."

Vyrl frowned. The trail had no outcroppings this close to the road. "It shouldn't be here."

"I think we're farther along than we realized."

His hope surged. "The cliffs above the meadows have caves."

"Little ones, but that's enough."

He groped along the wall with one hand, drawing Lily and Moonglaze with him, all of them faltering through the storm, their progress slow. Snow dusted Vyrl's eyelashes, making it hard to see, and he shivered constantly despite his heavy cloak. He had checked the forecast twice that afternoon. It had predicted chill weather in the mountains, yes, but it had also claimed the night would be calm, with only a dusting of snow.

Suddenly he stumbled into an open space. He regained his balance with ease, never losing hold of Lily or the reins. Mercifully, the storm had quit tearing at them. He drew in a ragged breath, his first full one since they had dismounted.

"You did it!" Lily hugged him hard, as if he had just performed a great feat instead of lurching about in the dark like a dolt. He smiled, his heart warming even if his body felt half-frozen.

When he pulled her close, he felt her shaking. "It's all right," he said. "I think I know this place." He drew her farther into the cave, waving his hand in front of them. The lyrine moved at his side, a large presence in the dark.

His knuckles hit a wall with painful force. "Ah!" Grimacing, he shook his hand. "I found the back."

Lily's cloak rustled as she felt the wall. "We can wait out the storm here."

"Yes." Vyrl reached around for the lyrine, with no success. Dropping his hand, he brushed its back. "Hey! Moonglaze is lying down." Although it wasn't unheard of for a lyrine, it was unusual enough to startle Vyrl.

Lily turned in the small space. "Are you well, Moon?" The lyrine nickered to her.

"He made a wall for us," she said. "He's going to sleep that way, I think."

"He's warming the cave." Although Vyrl still felt cold, he was no longer shivering. He scratched the base of Moonglaze's horn. Although lyrine would let people ride them, the animals rarely showed much affinity for humans, especially the great beasts like Moonglaze. In rare instances, a war-lyrine would decide it liked a particular human, though Vyrl had never figured out what made them choose a person. He wondered if the Ruby Empire biologists had tried to breed loyalty into them, but it either hadn't fully taken or else millennia of genetic drift had changed its manifestation. Whatever the reason, he was glad Moonglaze accepted his company and seemed to approve of Lily.

Lily put her palms against Vyrl's chest. In the darkness he could just make out the pale oval of her face. "Do you think the snow will trap us here?" Her voice quavered.

"Don't be afraid." He curled his gloved fingers around hers. "If this is the place I think, it's under a shelf sticking out from the cliff. It would be almost impossible for snow to block our way out."

"It will be an adventure."

He bent his head and brushed his lips over hers. "I do so love you."

Complete silence.

"Lily?" When she remained silent, alarm surged in Vyrl. She couldn't have been hurt, not in the few moments—

"Hai, Vyrl," she murmured. "And I do love you, too."

He gulped, comprehending what he had done. Caught up in their predicament, he had spoken his love aloud for the first time. Embarrassed, he started to stutter, but she put her finger against his lips, rescuing him from the need to answer.

Vyrl tugged her close, and they sank down onto the rocky ground, wedged between Moonglaze and the wall. He wrapped his cloak around them both, drawing her inside the warmth. But when he tried to kiss her, she ducked her head.

"Lily, let me," he coaxed. "We'll be married tomorrow."

"Goodness, be patient." She stroked his cheek. "Would you have us grapple in a cold, hard blizzard instead of having a proper wedding night?"

Grappling with Lily anywhere sounded just fine to Vyrl, but he could tell this wouldn't be right for her. So he made himself say, "I guess not." He still held her close, though, settling her body against his.

For a while they just sat, listening to the storm. Vyrl imagined how the snow must look, drifted in great blue swells. Eventually he said, "Do you know, snow isn't blue on other worlds."

Lily stirred. "What color is it?"

"White."

"White? How dull."

He laughed. "Their clouds are white, too, or gray."

"People must like coming here to have good water."

"Actually, the water makes them sick."

"But why? It tastes so good."

He kissed her temple. "We have nanomeds in our bodies, little biological machines to deal with the impurities that turn our water blue. Our ancestors were engineered that way. Most people don't have them. My mother had to receive treatments before she could live here."

"It must be strange and wonderful, to live above the sky." Her voice had an odd sound now, as if she feared her own questions. "Don't you ever want to go there?"

"Not really."

"Not at all?"

"Not at all." Lowering his head, he slipped back the hood of her cloak and nibbled at her ear. "Everything I want is here."

"Even if you could marry a great off-world queen?"

Ah. Now he understood. "Even then."

Her relief flowed over him. "She does seem awfully old."

He laughed. "I must seem awfully young to her."

Mischief danced in Lily's voice. "But you are so very

fine, especially when you are falling over after running in the plains."

Vyrl glowered. "I'm not clumsy."

She snuggled closer. "If I tell you a secret, you must promise to tell no one."

His interest picked up. "All right."

"You aren't clumsy." With shyness, she added, "The way you move is, well . . . sexy."

Heat spread through Vyrl. "Ah, Lily," he murmured, trying to kiss her again, his hands searching for a way under her clothes.

"Now you stop that." She thumped him on the head. "Behave yourself."

He groaned. "You torment me."

"You can't tell anyone what I said."

"All right," he promised. "I won't let anyone know that you like me. Certainly they will never guess. We're only getting married, after all."

"Even so."

His good spirits faded as guilt gnawed at him. He owed it to Lily to tell her the truth about himself.

"Lily Opaline." He spoke in his serious voice, but then paused, unsure how to continue. What if his secret disgusted her? She might not marry him. But she had a right to know before they took such an important step.

She leaned her head against his shoulder. "You're so warm."

"I have to tell you. You should know—about me . . ."

"Have you misbehaved?" Her laugh chimed. "Do tell."

"I'm serious." He wanted to tease her, to lose his worries in familiar banter, but he couldn't. If he didn't tell her now, he wasn't sure he would have the courage later.

"You sound somber," she said.

He forced out the words. "I'm not normal."

She snorted. "Well, I know you're not normal. I mean, really, I have never seen any boy eat as much as you do."

Exasperated, he said, "Lily, I'm extremely serious here."

"You sound terribly serious," she said amiably.

There was nothing for it but to reveal the dreadful truth. "I dance."

Silence.

"Lily?"

"You do what?"

"Dance." He waved his arms around. "You know. I spin and kick and jump around to music."

"But you can't dance. Men don't do that."

"I know. But I do. Every morning I have at least three hours of class with my instructors. Often more."

"Oh, that." She laughed, relief in her mood. "Everyone knows you exercise a lot. It makes you strong, good with a sword."

"Yes, well, 'everyone' doesn't know all of it. Lily, I *dance*. Classical, mostly, but some modern and jazz."

"What is jazz?"

"An art form from the world Earth."

"You are making fun of me."

"No. It's true." He stopped, unable to voice his next question. *Will you still marry me?* What if he repulsed her now?

She spoke uneasily. "I don't like this game."

"It isn't a game."

"Men don't dance. Only women." In a matter-of-fact voice, she added, "And, Vyrl, you are definitely not a woman."

"No, I'm not. But I dance." He shifted her in his arms. "Before my mother ran for election to the Assembly, she was a ballet dancer. Men among her people perform, too. No one thinks them strange."

Lily was silent again. Apparently he had appalled her beyond speech. She kept her mind well guarded, shielding the worst of her revulsion. He hadn't realized she could raise mental barriers that strong.

Finally she said, "I've never heard of such a thing."

"Do you hate me now?"

"Hate you? Saints above, what a thing to ask."

"Will you answer?"

"I could never hate you." She sighed. "Although sometimes you do truly drive me crazy."

He squinted at her. "You think I'm crazy?"

"Broadie Candleson told us once that he saw you spinning around, like you were dancing. We laughed at him."

"I *was* dancing." Vyrl felt as if he were poised at a chasm. "You haven't answered me."

Silence.

He couldn't believe his stupidity. Why had he opened his fool mouth? If he had never said anything, and never danced again, she would have never known. Now he had lost her because he had to make his blasted declaration.

Lily spoke slowly. "You must have to hide it all the time, always watching everything you say and do."

"Always."

"Do your parents know?"

"Yes. Also my brothers and sisters."

"But they never talk about it?"

"Not outside the family." His brother Del-Kurj gave him a hard time, but only in private. In a family of empaths, it was too obvious to everyone how much it meant to Vyrl; they knew how deeply it would hurt him if they ruined his joy in dancing by letting people outside the family ridicule him.

He could sense her pondering, but the unusually strong guards around her mind made it impossible to judge how much his confession had repulsed her.

"Will you show me?" she asked.

He blinked, confused. "Show you what?"

"Your dancing." She relaxed against him. "If you have trained so much, for so many years, you must be very good."

"Saints above." Lily wasn't hiding her revulsion. She didn't feel it. That couldn't be true. It *couldn't* be. Could it? In a voice tight with his fear of rejection, he asked, "Does that mean you will still marry me?"

She pressed her lips against his cheek. "I would marry you if you were a beggar in Tyrole, if we had to sit in the market pleading for food."

He tried to answer, but his voice caught. So instead he held her tight, unable to speak.

"Uh . . . Vyrl." Her words came out strained. "I can't— breathe."

Mortified, he loosened his grip. "Hai, what an idiot you fell in love with."

Her laugh trilled, rippling over him like water. "You are a force of nature, Vyrl, sometimes stormy and sometimes sunny, your moods changing as fast as the wind, but you are most certainly never an idiot."

Moisture threatened his eyes. Incredibly, she had learned his darkest secret and still chose him.

A nicker came out of the dark. Something nudged Vyrl, and he realized the lyrine was nuzzling him, its horn poking his arm. He scratched its head again. "She still wants me," he told Moonglaze.

That night, huddled against the wall of a cliff, wrapped in a cloak, he slept for the first time in the arms of the woman he loved. He prayed it wouldn't be the last. The storm had delayed their trip and tomorrow their parents would realize they had run away.

Then the search would start.

4
BARD OF EMERALDS

Moonglaze loped through the meadows at the foothills of the Backbone Mountains. The gray cliffs behind them wore cloaks of snow, but down here only a few patches of melting blue remained. Swaying reeds sparkled in the sun, topped with bubbles. Larger spheres dotted the meadows, vibrant in blue, red, purple, green, and gold, some floating off their stalks and drifting in the breeze. Every now and then one would pop, showering the ground with glimmering rainbow dust.

The lyrine raced out of the hills and into the Rillian Vales, stretching his long legs as if he would leave the ground and fly. Lily and Vyrl held on, exhilarated as fresh morning air rushed past their faces. His cloak whipped back from his shoulders and rippled behind them, a swath of blue in the sunshine that streamed across the land.

They thundered past the first villages. Unlike the Dalvador Plains, where houses were whitewashed and had colored roofs, here the entire structures were glowing hues: blue, green, ruby, or gold-stalk. Although Vyrl could have sought out the Bard in any village, he headed for Rillia itself, the largest city in the settled lands. The Bard in a small town might wonder why an unfamiliar young couple went to him rather than their own Bard, but in a large town with many visitors, it would be more natural.

However, going to Rillia also carried risk; Lord Rillia, who ruled both the Dalvador Plains and Rillian Vales, knew Vyrl's father. As the Dalvador Bard, Vyrl's father was the highest authority in the Plains, or at least as much an authority as their people accepted. He not only served Dalvador; he also presided over the Bards in the other Plains villages. But Lord Rillia held authority over all the Bards, including Vyrl's father.

The Bards acted as judges and mediators, performed marriages, officiated at naming ceremonies, and recorded the history of their people in ballads. Vyrl's father had a glorious baritone, a voice Vyrl loved to hear. Every village also had a Memory. She recorded current events in her mind, performed rites of celebration at festivals, and served as a scholar in the women's temple, where acolytes learned and stored knowledge. Together, the Memory and Bard formed the government of a village.

This morning, Vyrl watched the skies constantly, fearing to see a flash of gold-and-black metal. He had "neglected" to tell Lily that before he had shown up at her house last night, he had gone to the starport—and sabotaged the shuttle. Lily would chide him when she found out, but even so, it had needed doing. His tampering wouldn't hold off pursuit for long, only until the port staff repaired the shuttle or the military sent down another from the ships in orbit, but Vyrl and Lily didn't need long. Only today.

They reached the city of Rillia in late morning. It was large enough to need several Bards, none of whom Vyrl had met. He chose one who lived on the city outskirts in a greenstalk house that glowed like an emerald. As Moonglaze trotted into the courtyard, Lily twisted around to look up at Vyrl, her eyes as huge as a colt startled by a loud noise.

He cupped his hand around her cheek. "Shall we go in?"

She gave him a tremulous smile. "Yes. Let's."

He swung off Moonglaze, his cloak swirling, his booted feet landing with a thump on the ground. Then he helped Lily off the powerful lyrine. A towheaded boy came into the yard and waited to take Moonglaze back to the glass-house, to be tended and fed. Vyrl gave the boy two turquoise stones for his trouble. Although the youth was only a few years younger than Vyrl and Lily, he treated them as if they were adults.

Moonglaze, however, nickered when the boy tried to lead him away. Then the lyrine nudged Vyrl's shoulder, pushing him toward Lily.

"See?" Vyrl grinned at her. "He knows."

She patted the animal's head. "You're a good lyrine, Moon. You go ahead. We will be fine."

Moonglaze snorted, then shook his head and turned away. He walked regally past the boy, his horns held high, his violet coat glossy in the sunlight. The youth hurried after him and grabbed his reins, trying to look as if he were leading the great lyrine instead of the other way around.

Vyrl held his hand out to Lily, and she put her small one in his large grip. Together, they walked to the Bard's door.

Flames flickered within jade lamps, and candles burned around the chamber, filling it with radiance. Vyrl, Lily, the Bard, and the Bard's wife had crowded into the circular room. The Memory stood by the curving emerald wall, her green robe brushing the floor; with her holographic memory, she was recording the ceremony, every word and promise, and images as well.

Vyrl stood facing Lily, holding her hands and gazing down at her face. She filled his sight, her pretty face tilted up to him, a wreath of silvery-green fronds and gold bubbles braided into her hair.

The Bard continued in his mellow voice. "May the love you share fill your lives, and that of your children, grandchildren, and more, keeping alive the line of your heart."

Guided by his words, Vyrl and Lily promised their lives to each other. Then the Bard sang for them, his lustrous tenor filling the chamber, his words graceful in their evocation of love under the Blue and Lavender Moons.

Vyrl's thoughts overflowed with Lily. No matter where their life took them after today, he had found his home, not in a place but in the heart of this girl he had loved his entire life.

The Bard and his wife accompanied Lily and Vyrl into the courtyard. While they waited for the boy to bring Moonglaze, Vyrl scanned the heavens and was relieved to see nothing unusual, no metallic glints, just the normal lavender sky and blue clouds.

The Bard pointed out a half-finished tower that rose above the roofs of the town. "The metal-works needs laborers for the new building they are raising." He glanced kindly at Vyrl. "A big, strong fellow like yourself could earn a place to live, meals for your family, and stones for trade."

His wife smiled at Lily, the lines around her eyes crinkling. "They're needing counters, too. Always looking for a girl with a sharp mind to keep records. It could be a fine start for a young couple."

Their good-natured concern touched Vyrl. "We thank you, kind lady and sir." Lily murmured similar sentiments. Vyrl wished they could lead the simple life these fine people envisioned for them, setting up a home with no worries beyond food, shelter, and children. "Perhaps when we return, we will visit the metal-works boss."

The Bard chuckled. "Ah, I am too old. What newlyweds want to start work the day of their marriage, eh?" He paused as the boy came around the house leading Moonglaze. Then he asked, "Where be you off to now?"

"We aren't sure," Lily admitted. "We're traveling."

Moonglaze walked grandly up to them, watching Vyrl first with one large eye, then the other, turning his head to give himself a good view. The lyrine growled deep in his throat.

"What ho?" Vyrl scratched him behind his horn. "Are you angry with me?"

Moonglaze nickered, mollified by the attention. He butted Lily's arm, pushing her against Vyrl.

The Bard laughed. Then he slapped Vyrl on the back. "Off with you, eh? You two go have your time together."

"My thanks, good sir." Vyrl was pleased to find Moonglaze had been well tended and the backpack was still secure in the travel bags. Excellent! He swung up onto the animal, relishing the motion, his body thrumming with energy. Reaching down, he helped Lily up in front of him. Then he hugged her hard, leaning his head around to kiss her cheek.

"A safe journey to you," the Bard called up to them.

The Bard's wife started to speak, then paused. Although Vyrl couldn't pick up emotions from other people as well as he did from his family, he sensed her turning over ideas much as he might glimpse a wisp of mist curling through glass-stalk trees.

She spoke thoughtfully to her husband. "I have some concerns about our cabin. With no one to look after it, the place lies empty and unattended. Who knows what might happen?"

"Ah, so, this is true." The Bard considered Lily and Vyrl up on Moonglaze. "Then again," he continued, as if speaking to his wife even though he was looking at his guests, "perhaps we may convince some nice young couple to spend a few days looking after the place."

Vyrl hesitated. His first impulse was to decline; the future was too uncertain for them to take on new responsibilities. But his empath's mind felt their intent, like a meadow creek burbling with goodwill. They were offering their secluded cabin so he and Lily could spend their wedding night in safety and warmth instead of sleeping in the forest.

"Lily?" Vyrl asked in a barely audible voice.

"Yes," she murmured, understanding his unspoken question.

Vyrl nodded to the Bard and his wife, letting his gratitude show. "We would be honored, gentle lady and sir, to look after your cabin for a few days."

The woman beamed at him. "Such good manners."

The Bard tilted his head, studying first Vyrl, then Moonglaze. A shiver of unease ran up Vyrl's back as he caught the man's mood; the Bard wondered at his visitor's accomplished style and magnificent lyrine. At home, as a farmer's son, Vyrl tended to forget he was the son of the Dalvador Bard and the queen of an Imperial dynasty. His background probably showed more than he realized.

Whatever the Bard thought, he didn't say. Instead, he

gave Vyrl directions to a cabin in the Blue Mountain Dales, deep within a wild forest of stained glass trees that spread their gem-bubbles over the hills. Vyrl thanked him and gave the couple a gold chain for the marriage service.

Then he and Lily rode into the hills, headed for the cabin, where they could complete the marriage that would sunder the plans of an interstellar empire.

Flames crackled in the hearth. Vyrl leaned his arm against the stone mantel and stared into the shifting play of orange and red. With only fire lighting the cabin, shadows filled the corners. Handmade furniture covered with cushions warmed the room, and a four-poster bed with a blue-and-gold quilt stood against one wall.

The door opened behind him, and he felt more than heard Lily enter, her mood bathing him like sunshine. He turned as she closed the door. She stood watching him, twisting her hands in her skirts, smiling shyly, a pretty girl with red-gold curls tumbling around her body to her waist and tendrils curling around her face. Her lavender dress molded to her torso and swirled around her knees, adorned with laces and slits in tempting places. In the flickering light, her face seemed to glow, so beautiful to him that it almost hurt to see. He didn't know what the morning would bring, but tonight he had everything he had ever wanted.

Lily spoke softly. "Are you hungry?"

"Saints, I'm famished." Belatedly, Vyrl realized that wasn't the most romantic declaration. An inspiration came to him. "For you."

Lily laughed, her melodic voice a delight. "Hah! You don't fool me. You want dinner."

He grinned. "I need my strength."

Her expression turned sultry, yet with innocence; he could tell she didn't realize her anticipation showed in her gaze or that it would arouse him. "Well, then," she murmured. "Let us build up your strength."

Vyrl swallowed, suddenly wondering if he wanted dinner after all. He watched Lily walk to the finely engraved table where he had left his pack. Her hips swayed with each step. Taking a deep breath, he picked up a poker from beside the hearth and stirred the flames. This high in the

Blue Mountain Dales, the nights were cold. It had taken the entire day to reach this cabin; stars had been sparkling in an icy sky by the time they arrived.

"Hai, Vyrl!" Lily admonished. "What did you put in this pack? Rocks?"

He turned with a start to see her digging out the last of the trail rations. She held up his pack in one hand and the food in the other, her expression baffled.

Reddening, he strode over and hoisted away the pack. "It's nothing."

"It is so. Look! It sparkles." Reaching past him, she tugged the pack farther open. "See." She brushed her fingers over the apparatus inside, making yellow lights twinkle on its edges. Holos scrolled across its glossy black surface.

"Oh, Vyrl! It's lovely." She beamed at him. "Are those magic lights from your mother's people?"

He winced, knowing that when she found out what he had done, she would scold him. But he had to tell her the truth. "The symbols are from a language of my mother's people. They're warning you to stop banging the jammer."

"Jammer?" She took the pack away from him and peered inside. "Whatever have you stuffed in here?"

"It hides us," he explained. "It can trick radar, sonar, infrared, UV, visual, even neutrino probes."

She regarded him dubiously. "You are making up these words."

"I'm not. Really. It means my parents will have trouble finding us."

Lily took a moment to absorb his words. "I think you are very clever, to hide us. But are you supposed to have this? It sounds—" She hesitated. "Arcane."

"Arcane?" He tried to laugh, but it came out scared rather than amused. "It's military equipment you need a security clearance to use. I'm not supposed to touch it."

Her gaze widened. "Are we in trouble?"

"Not you. But me, yes." Although stealing equipment from Imperial Space Command wasn't as bad as admitting to her that he danced, it came close. Add to that the damage he had done to ISC property at the starport and he was in it deep.

"Ah, Vyrl." Instead of rebuking him, she did something

even harder to deal with. She came over and laid her palms on his shoulders, looking up at him with trust. "We are together now. If they take you away, they must take me, too." Resolve showed on her face. "Where you go, so do I."

Vyrl sighed, putting his arms around her. "I don't deserve you."

"Well, that's true." Impudence filled her voice. "But nevertheless, you have me."

He glared at her. "I swear, you can sorely bedevil a boy."

Her face and voice, even her posture, softened. "But you are no longer a boy, my husband."

His chagrin vanished, replaced by a more primal emotion. Holding her, he let his mind melt into hers. He could relax his defenses with her in a way he could do with no one else. Her mischief was a disguise; behind it, a nervous young woman faced her wedding night with uncertainty as well as anticipation. He drew her closer, forgetting the trail rations. Stroking her hair, he savored its silky texture against his calloused palms. No prince's hands, these, but those of a farmer.

Tentative, she laid her palm on his cheek. As her eyes closed, he bent his head and let his lips touch hers. She held a curl of his hair as she kissed him, more confident in her response, or so he thought, until she began to pull his hair without realizing it. He folded his large hand around her small one, loosening her grip.

Lily made a small sound, half a sigh, half a moan. He kissed her deeply, wishing he could lift her up and carry her to the bed.

A thought nudged his mind, like Moonglaze pushing him; he *could* carry her off exactly the way he wished. He slowly pulled away, one hand splayed on her back. Bending, he slid his arm under her legs and hefted her into his arms.

"Oh!" Lily flushed. "Goodness, Vyrl."

Once he would have grinned, maybe pulled her hair. No longer. He felt only tenderness tonight, and a desire that he wondered how he would hold in check, or if he should. He carried her to the bed and laid her on the downy quilt. She watched him, her lips parted, a rosy flush on her face, the firelight dimly golden around them.

Kneeling next to her, Vyrl pulled his sweater over his

head. As he dropped it on the ground, Lily reached for him, her arms outstretched, her expression trusting. He lay next to her and his pulse jumped, tingling through him. It was so good finally to have her to himself. As they nestled together, he felt her heartbeat against his chest. When he pressed his lips on the creamy skin of her neck, her pulse beat there as well, strong and vibrant.

She helped him with the laces on her dress. For all that they had resisted his efforts, they unraveled for her at the slightest pull. He and Lily explored each other while they undressed, their touches sweet with the newness of discovery as they joined in the dim light from the embers of the fire. Together they moved in a rhythm more ancient than the Ruby Empire. His heart overflowed; he felt as if it were an airy hall filled with stained glass windows. His love for Lily poured like light through the windows, turning many colors, each window a symbol of another way he knew her. The stained glass was so beautiful it hurt to imagine—for he knew it could shatter under the reality of life.

But in this miraculous night, the colors glowed within him.

5
BLUE-CRYSTAL SHARDS

The pounding dragged Vyrl awake. A booming noise bombarded his head.

"Hai!" He sat up groggily, covers falling away from his body, his eyes bleary. Morning light slanted through a window he hadn't even noticed last night. Across the room, the door shook under the force of someone's hammering fists.

Lily rolled against him, pulling the quilt around her shoulders. Seeing her that way, warm and cozy in a nest of covers, Vyrl wanted nothing more than to stay in bed with her.

"*Valdoria!*" The bellow could have shaken a stone wall. "Open this door, you scum of a mush-bog slime, or I'll break it down."

Lily opened her eyes, wincing. "That is, without doubt, my father."

With a groan, Vyrl grabbed his trousers off the floor and yanked them on. He pulled on his shirt as he scrambled out of bed. With the shirt laces untied, its tails untucked, and his feet bare, he stumbled across the room. He shot a glance at Lily, to urge her to cover up, but she had already pulled on her dress.

At the door, Vyrl shoved out the bar that locked it—and he barely had time to jump back as the door crashed open. Lily's burly father, Caul, stood framed in the entrance. Vyrl had one instant to see Lily's mother hurry by them before Caul grabbed him, hurled him around, and slammed him against the inside wall.

"No slime-mold dishonors my daughter," he roared, swinging his meaty fist.

Vyrl dodged in time to keep his face from being smashed, but the blow caught his shoulder and pain shot through him. Although Caul had neither Vyrl's height nor agility, years of toiling on his farm had muscled the man's already husky build. Vyrl raised his arm up in time to block Caul's next blow, but then Caul used his other fist to sock him heartily in the stomach.

Vyrl grunted and doubled up with pain, wrapping his arms over his abdomen. Lily was crying out and other voices filled the air; from seemingly nowhere, people crammed the small room. His ears rang with the commotion.

Suddenly Caul was no longer pummeling him. Vyrl gasped, but it was several moments before he could straighten up. When he did, he saw his older brothers, Althor and Del-Kurj, holding back the enraged farmer. As hard as Caul struggled, he couldn't free himself. Althor was six feet six, with a massive physique. Del-Kurj had a lankier build, lean rather than bulky, but he was still a good half-head taller than Vyrl and had plenty of strength. Caul finally gave up fighting them and glowered at Vyrl as if his stare could incinerate his new son-in-law.

Vyrl swallowed, regarding his brothers. "Thank you."

"I wouldn't be so grateful," Althor said dryly. "You're in a load of trouble."

Del-Kurj smirked at Vyrl. "Who would have guessed it. I didn't think you even knew what to do with a girl."

Vyrl scowled at him. "Go blow, Del."

Caul jerked his arms away from Althor and Del-Kurj, and this time they let him go, sensing his calmer state. To Vyrl, he growled, "I'll deal with you later."

Behind the men, Lily's mother was holding her daughter. She was an older, plumper version of Lily, maternal rather than nubile, still as pretty as Lily. Seeing her, Vyrl could imagine his wife in twenty years, and it made him love her all the more. Right now tears streaked Lily's face, making his heart ache. As much as he wanted to go to her, his brothers and Caul had him penned in the corner. From the look of Lily's mother, he doubted she would let him near her daughter anyway. Vyrl knew where Lily had inherited her stubborn side.

Althor had unhooked a palmtop from his belt and was talking into its com. "The house is about half a klick from where we landed."

The voice of Eldrinson, Vyrl's father, came out of the com. "We'll be there right away."

Caul fixed Vyrl with a baleful stare. "If I were your father, I would thrash you from here to the Tyrole plains."

Vyrl used his most respectful voice. "Good sir, I would never dishonor your daughter. Lily and I were married yesterday by a Bard in Rillia."

"Don't you give me excuses," Caul bellowed. "I'll make you sorry—" He stopped, blinking. "Married? You, a prince, marry the daughter of a farmer? You expect me to believe that?"

Vyrl didn't think this was the best time to point out that Caul was hardly treating him like a prince.

"Father, it's true." Lily was still trying to escape her mother. "Just ask the Emerald Bard."

A deep voice spoke from the doorway. "Apparently my Emerald Bard is conveniently off on a trip."

Vyrl almost groaned. As if the situation wasn't bad enough already. The last person he wanted to face right now was Lord Rillia. No, make that the second-to-last person. Facing his father was going to be even harder.

Hard or not, however, he had no choice; both his father

and Lord Rillia had entered the cabin. The two men were well matched in build and coloring, though Lord Rillia had darker hair and more height. Rillia was also older, more austere, with silver streaks in his hair and an aloof dignity that had always intimidated Vyrl.

But when Vyrl saw his father's face, he felt even worse. Dark circles rimmed Eldrinson's eyes, and lines showed that hadn't been there two days before. His exhaustion seeped into the cabin. Sensing his father's mind, Vyrl realized Eldrinson had barely slept for the past two days.

"Thank the saints," a woman said, her voice catching.

Vyrl turned with a start. His mother, Roca Skolia, stood in the doorway, her usual brightness dimmed. Like his father, she looked as if she had been awake for much too long.

Vyrl made himself speak. "I am truly sorry."

His mother considered him, then answered gently. "For frightening us, yes, but not for running away."

Vyrl winced. Living in a family of empaths had its drawbacks. He couldn't deny her words; as much as he regretted causing them pain, he would run away again given the chance.

"It's not his fault," Lily said. "It was my idea."

Everyone turned to her. "Yours?" Her father snorted. "I hardly think so." He waved his hand at Vyrl. "You've always had far too much sense for this boy. This is his kind of fool stunt."

"It's true," Lily said earnestly. "I told Vyrl I couldn't bear the thought of his marrying the queen from the sky. I begged him to come with her." She watched them with a wide-eyed gaze. "Really."

Her mother sighed. "Oh, honey."

Caul fixed Vyrl with a hard look. "As if you hadn't caused enough trouble, now you have my daughter lying."

Vyrl met his gaze. "I love your daughter for trying to defend me, sir, but the truth is that I'm the one who urged her to come with me. The idea was mine."

If a stare could have skewered a person, Caul's would have pierced Vyrl straight through. "You better be telling the truth about marrying her."

Lord Rillia spoke. "The marriage is easily checked." He considered Vyrl. "Did a Memory record the ceremony?"

"Yes, sir." Vyrl realized the Bard who married them must not have been the person who had revealed they were at the cabin. Odd that the fellow had chosen now to take a trip. Remembering the man's thoughtful consideration, Vyrl wondered if he and his wife had left deliberately, to avoid having to reveal what they would rather not say.

"Your Lordship," Vyrl began. "If I may ask . . . ?"

"Go ahead," Lord Rillia said.

"How did you know we were here?"

Althor started to speak, then glanced at Rillia. The sovereign nodded, giving Althor leave to continue. In the balance of interstellar hierarchies, Vyrl's family had far more power than Lord Rillia, but here on Lyshriol, Rillia held sway, and Vyrl's parents treated him with the respect due that position.

Althor turned to Vyrl. "The *Ascendant* finally broke through the jamming fields you set up."

Vyrl blinked. "The who?"

"The *Ascendant*. A battle cruiser in the ODS." Sensing Vyrl's confusion, Althor added, "In the Orbital Defense System."

Roca frowned at her wayward son. "As opposed, Vyrl, to the planetary defenses—which includes the equipment you stole and the shuttle you damaged."

Vyrl wondered if the military officers on the *Ascendant* would feed him after they threw him into the brig. He did his best to look repentant. "My apology for any difficulty I caused."

"Please," Lily said. "Don't let anyone hurt him."

Roca glanced at her new daughter-in-law, her expression softening. "I am so sorry, Lily, that Vyrl involved you in this."

"But why?" Warmth radiated from Lily's mind. "It is the most wonderful thing that could have happened."

Sadness came from Vyrl's mother. "Then I am truly sorry."

Lily turned to Vyrl, her gaze questioning and uncertain. Even more uneasy now, Vyrl looked from his mother to his father.

Eldrinson spoke quietly, but in a voice that brooked no argument. "We have the shuttle outside. We will leave now."

"Now?" Vyrl tensed. "You mean Lily and me?"

"No." His father's voice was firm. "Not Lily."

Vyrl went rigid, but before he could protest, Lord Rillia addressed Caul. "I would be pleased if you, your wife, and your daughter would be my guests for a few days. I regret that this affair took place in my city. I hope you will allow me to compensate you for your troubles."

Caul bowed to him. "We would be muchly honored to stay with you, Your Lordship."

"Wait!" Vyrl cried. Everything was moving too fast. "I can't leave Lily here."

His father crossed his arms. "You will do as we say. I want no more argument."

Vyrl protested anyway, but it did no good. His father and brothers marched him to the shuttle, and try as he might, he couldn't get past them. Lily strained to reach him, but both of her parents were holding her back now. With tears streaming down her face, she called to him. Vyrl went wild then, pounding at Althor with his fists. It was like hitting an immovable barrier. Neither his brothers nor father fought him, they just held him back. He felt everyone's dismay; no one liked tearing him and Lily apart. But it didn't stop them from loading him into the shuttle.

As the craft lifted off, Vyrl pressed his palms against the view screen. It showed Lily on the ground below, her face turned up as she watched the ship rise into the sky.

Sitting on the floor, wedged in a corner, Vyrl pulled his legs to his chest and folded his arms on them. Then he dropped his forehead onto his arms and sat in silence. He had come to this studio in the basement of the castle to work out, but he couldn't muster the energy. Since his parents had taken him from the cabin this morning, he hadn't even felt like speaking, let alone moving. He would have run into the plains, but they wouldn't even let him outside.

The footsteps were so quiet Vyrl didn't hear them until cloth rustled nearby. Raising his head, he saw his mother a few paces away. Dressed in a simple jumpsuit with her hair pulled back, she looked more like a farmer's wife than an interstellar potentate.

He spoke in a low voice. "Is Devon Majda still upstairs?"

She nodded, sitting gracefully on the gold-stalk floor near him. "But the colonel who came down from the *Ascendant* has left."

Vyrl tried not to hide his fear. "Will ISC send me to prison?"

"No." She spoke firmly. "But you will be expected to work at the starport until you pay off the damages you caused."

Vyrl exhaled. As much as he disliked working at the port, his penalty could have been a lot worse. He forced out the harder question. "And Majda?" Although he hadn't seen Devon yet, he felt the tension filling his home.

Her voice quieted. "We may be able to mend the fracture between Majda and the Ruby Dynasty. But you and Lily did great insult to Majda."

Vyrl had no excuses. So he said nothing.

Roca pushed her hand over her hair, pulling tendrils out of the clip. Compared to her usual elegant demeanor, now she seemed drained. "A split between our family and Majda could destabilize the government."

"Why? The Ruby Dynasty no longer reigns. We're just a bunch of farmers."

"Do you really believe that?"

He met her gaze squarely. "Yes."

His mother paused. "It is true that the Ruby Dynasty no longer rules the Imperialate. But we still wield a great deal of power. With that comes responsibilities. Our actions, policies, and alliances have great impact on the Assembly. We and they are inextricably linked. So is Majda, to us and to the Assembly." She brushed back the tendrils of hair curling around her face. "When we suffer discord, it weakens the Assembly, and so weakens the Imperialate."

Vyrl thought of his father upstairs with Devon. "So now we have discord with Majda." He knew that, on an interstellar scale, the union of Majda and the Ruby Dynasty was far more important than the happiness of two young lovers. But that knowledge didn't lessen the pain in his heart.

His mother lifted her hand as if to lay it on his arm as she had often done in his younger years, offering comfort. When he stiffened, unable to accept her solace, she lowered her arm. Gently, she said, "Devon is still willing to take you as consort, after we annul your marriage."

No! Vyrl felt as if a cage were closing around him. "Doesn't she know how you found me this morning?"

Roca nodded. "Yes. Despite that, she is willing to accept the arrangement."

He clenched his fists on his knees. "You can't annul my marriage."

His mother frowned. "Young man, we most certainly can. You and Lily are both underage, even for Lyshriol."

He scowled at her. "Then I can't marry Devon either."

"You can with parental consent."

"What, my consent doesn't matter?"

Her anger disintegrated. "Hai, Vyrl. I am so sorry."

He blinked. It was easier to be angry with his parents when they were angry with him. Sympathy and compassion were harder to handle. In a quieter voice, he said, "I'm not a political arrangement. I'm a human being."

"Yes. You are. A special, remarkable human being." She indicated the room around them. "What do you see here?"

Her question baffled him, and he couldn't tell from her mind what she was about. The room looked the same as always: large, longer than wide, and mirrors along one wall with a bar at waist height. His athletic bag hung on the bar. The ceiling shed uniform light, leaving no shadows; the floor was gold-stalk, polished by years of use.

"It's just the dance studio," he said.

She smiled. "When you children were small, I practiced here everyday. For some reason it affected you more than the others." She indicated an area by one wall. "When you were a baby, you would sit in your carrier there and watch me, laughing and kicking your legs with the music."

Vyrl had no idea why she was telling him this, but it brought back wonderful memories. He had taken his first steps in this room, trying to mimic his mother's dancing, which had seemed magic to him. From that day on, she had taught him what she knew, until seven years ago when she had brought in off-world instructors, including Rahkil Mariov.

He couldn't help but smile. "I'm glad you didn't tell me to stop following you around."

"I was delighted." She gave him a rueful look. "Your father was less pleased, to put it mildly. But we could feel how much you loved it, and he couldn't bear to deny you that."

Suddenly he saw, or thought he saw, why she brought this up. "Lily knows I dance. She has accepted it."

A blend of emotions came from her mind, relief at his news, but also sadness. "I'm glad. I can imagine how much that means to you. But I wasn't thinking of Lily." She sighed. "You're a bright young man, Vyrl, but in most things you have so little focus. Convincing you to do schoolwork is like trying to extract a tooth without benefit of modern dentistry."

He grimaced at the apt image. "School is boring. I can't put my heart into it."

Her voice softened. "Three times in your life, I've seen you pour your heart into something. The results have been incredible."

Although he felt her sincerity, empathy could only tell him so much; her specific meaning eluded him. He indicated the studio. "Do you mean this?"

"Yes. This." She regarded him with a respect that startled him, particularly now, when he was in so much trouble. "I wonder if you fully realize what you do. I know of few if any other dancers who have trained like you."

He spoke dryly. "Given that I'm probably the only man on the entire planet who dances, that doesn't say much."

"I wasn't speaking of Lyshriol."

Puzzled, he said, "But I thought you danced with the Parthonia Royal Ballet."

Her gaze remained steady. "I did."

Her comments made no sense. Parthonia was a ballet company of interstellar renown. "Didn't they train?"

"Yes. Of course." With that unrelenting compassion of hers, she said, "But no one in their youth did what you've done. A minimum of three hours a day all your life, almost since you could walk. And now what is it? Four hours? Five? I've seen you spend the entire day dancing, when you have nothing else to do. It's incredible."

He shrugged. "It's fun." In truth, it was a great deal more, so much a part of his life that to stop would be like trying to quit breathing. But he didn't know how to put that into words.

Roca regarded him steadily. "Vyrl, you are more than a 'good' dancer. Rahkil Mariov tells me you are the best he has ever worked with."

Vyrl thought of his instructor. "If he only takes one student at a time, he can't have worked with that many." It surprised him; he considered Rahkil a truly gifted teacher.

"Before he came here, he trained hundreds of dancers. Prodigies. He was one of the most sought-after masters." His mother motioned skyward, as if to encompass all settled space. "In his prime, Rahkil was also considered among the greatest male dancers in modern history."

Vyrl could see why. He had watched holos of Rahkil performing. He was magnificent. And despite Rahkil's constant curmudgeonly disapproval, Vyrl thoroughly enjoyed his classes. Sometimes Rahkil even forgot himself and complimented his young student.

But his mother's comments perplexed him. "If Rahkil is so in demand, why would he come here to teach one boy who will probably never make dance his career?" As soon as he spoke, he saw the answer. Stiffening, he said, "Because I'm a Ruby prince."

"We didn't tell him who you were when we sent holos of you dancing."

Vyrl's anger fizzled. "But—then why did he come?"

She spoke with kindness. "Because you have an incredible gift. You could walk out of here today and win a place in any major dance company. Rahkil says you will someday surpass what he achieved in his prime."

Vyrl gaped at her. "That's crazy."

"Ah, Vyrl." Her voice held a mother's pain. "Shall you spend your life hiding this spectacular gift? Will you live ashamed of a talent and dedication that together could make you a legend in a profession you love more than almost anything else?"

Vyrl couldn't answer. Yes, it hurt, having to hide what he loved, but Lyshriol was his life, all he had ever known. He couldn't imagine anything else.

He spoke in a low voice. "You said you had seen me put my heart into three things. Dance is only one."

"Farming, too."

"I can't farm as the Majda consort."

"You could become an agriculturist. A research scientist."

"I don't want to do research. I want to make my living from the land." Despite the betraying moisture in his eyes, he found himself smiling. "Working in the fields, caring for livestock, making a life out of golden days—that's *magic*, Mother, real magic." Softly, he said, "And you've still only mentioned two things."

Regret washed out from her mind. They both knew the third dream that inspired his heart. "She's a lovely girl," Roca said. "In a different universe, I think you and Lily could have been very happy."

"Not could have been," he whispered. "Will be."

Her voice caught. "I am so, so very sorry." With the grace he had always admired, she held up her hand as if to offer him the studio. "We can't have all our dreams. But we can have some of them."

Vyrl struggled against the heat in his eyes. He wouldn't cry, not now, not in front of his mother.

What made it so hard was that, deep inside, he yearned for the gift she offered, the chance to follow his most secret dream.

Even expecting it, Vyrl jumped when the knock came at the door. He suddenly wished he hadn't chosen this chamber, the circular room high in the tower. When his father had asked where he would like the meeting to take place, he had thought he would be calmer here, but instead it felt as if his sanctuary was being invaded.

Clenching his blue-glass goblet, he swirled its liquid, inhaling the tangy fragrance. Normally his parents didn't let their children drink wine, but today his father had made an exception, treating him as an adult instead of a child. Although Vyrl appreciated the gesture, it didn't help. He had never liked the taste of wine.

The knock came again.

Taking a deep breath, Vyrl stood and walked across the blue chamber. Then he mentally steadied himself and opened the door.

Devon stood on the landing outside.

Instead of a uniform, today she wore suede trousers and a gold shirt. She even had on a gold necklace with a hawk design, the emblem of Majda. She seemed subdued, her face drawn and her eyes dark with fatigue.

She bowed from the waist. "My greetings, Prince Havyrl."

So they were back to titles. He nodded. "My greetings, General Majda." Moving aside, he invited her to enter.

Devon entered the chamber. "This is beautiful."

"It's . . . calm." He couldn't say more. To tell her what this place meant to him would be a betrayal of a trust, somehow, though he wasn't sure to whom. Himself, perhaps.

She waited until he sat on his bench, then settled on another one nearby that curved against the wall.

With stiff formality, Vyrl spoke the words he had been practicing all day. "Please accept my apology for my offense to Majda. I deeply regret any insult my actions gave your line. I hope our House and yours may remain allies."

Devon answered without delay. "Majda accepts your apology. We look forward to a fruitful alliance with the Ruby Dynasty."

Vyrl exhaled. There. It was done.

So they sat.

When the silence grew strained, Devon said, "Vyrl, I—" in the same instant that Vyrl said, "My father—" They both stopped and gave awkward laughs. Then Devon said, "Please. Go ahead."

"My father told me what you and he discussed."

Devon gave a tired nod. "Perhaps it is best to do this soon instead of waiting. As long as you live on Lyshriol, you will be . . ." She hesitated.

"Distracted?" He heard his bitterness. "By memories of my former wife?"

Devon said, simply, "Yes."

Vyrl tightened his grip on his goblet. "So let's just marry off the recalcitrant groom now and get the whole business over with."

She shifted on the bench. "I am sorry you see it that way."

"Everyone is sorry." He looked out the window, trying to hide the pain he knew showed on his face. "Lady Devon, you should marry the man you love. Not me."

Startled tension snapped in her voice. "What are you talking about?"

Vyrl turned to see her sitting rigidly, gripping the edge of the bench. He said, "The handsome man with the dark hair and eyes."

She seemed to close up. "I have no idea what you mean."

"I saw him. In your mind."

For a long moment she remained silent. Just when he thought he had made a fool of himself with his assumption, she spoke quietly. "If the Matriarch of Majda were to marry a commoner, it would be a great scandal. An outrage. She would be stripped of her title and her authority. Nor would the children of any such union be considered Majda heirs."

Gods. What could he say? He and Devon each had their duty, and love had no place in it. What did it matter if they died inside a little more every day, as long as the pillars of the Imperialate remained strong?

Devon gentled her voice. "Vyrl, I won't ask for anything you aren't ready to give. We can live at whichever of my estates you prefer. And you will have advisors, people to help you learn your new role. No one expects a youth your age to manage a palace with a staff of many hundreds. You will have time to adjust."

"Adjust." Vyrl felt as if he were caught in a nightmare that kept going. He would never wake up.

She spoke carefully. "It is true that Majda has certain expectations for your behavior. But this isn't the Ruby Empire. Those days are long in our past. I don't expect you to stay in seclusion or cover yourself in robes. You are free to pursue your interests."

If that was meant to reassure him, it had the opposite effect. "What do you mean, expectations for my behavior?"

"You will be a highly placed member of the Imperial Court. Certain protocols are required."

Vyrl finished his wine with a long swallow, trying to wash away the bitter images. Yes, he knew court protocol. He couldn't imagine living that constrained lifestyle, always under scrutiny by the noble Houses, caught in their webs of intrigue. And regardless of what Devon promised about modern-day freedoms, he knew he would be viewed and treated as her possession.

He stared at his empty goblet. Then he lifted it and let the glass drop. It shattered on the tiles, blue-crystal shards scattering everywhere. "That is what you will do to me if you make me leave here."

When Devon stiffened, he feared he had gone too far and destroyed the long hours of conciliation his parents had spent, repairing the rift he had created. What was wrong with him? He had nothing to accomplish by antagonizing the person he would spend the rest of his life with. But if this was any sample of their future, he didn't see how he could bear it.

Devon stared at the broken glass strewn across the floor. Then she braced her hands against her knees. "I can't do this. I feel like a monster."

Do what? "I don't understand."

She turned to him. "The betrothal."

It was his turn to go rigid. Surely he misunderstood, his heart hearing what his brain knew was false. "What do you mean?"

She took a long breath. "I can't force a child to become my consort against his will." Although she watched him with a guarded expression, there was no mistaking the pain that came from her mind. "If you choose to end this arrangement, I will accept your decision without rancor to your family."

Vyrl's heart lurched. "You mean, I could stay married to Lily?"

Devon exhaled. "Yes."

Yes. Yes! He almost shouted it, but he managed to hold back his exuberance, aware of the insult it would add to the injury he had already done Majda.

Devon continued in her throaty voice. "But, Vyrl— before you decide, consider this: If you choose to stay here, you will never realize your dreams."

His joy crashed down again. He told himself it was only his fear that she would withdraw her offer. That was true— in part. But he longed for the freedom to dance, to perform, to explore the limits of his ability, and to do it without shame or guilt, admired instead of scorned.

The dream tempted him like a siren call.

A small cleaning droid whirred through the doorway. It

nosed around the shards of glass, then began to vacuum them into its interior.

"I've seen holos of your dancing," Devon said.

Vyrl froze. "Who showed you?"

"Your teacher. Rahkil Mariov."

He wanted to sink into the floor and let the droid vacuum him up, too. "I hope it didn't offend you."

"Offend me?" Incredulity washed across her face. "You really have no idea how you look, do you?"

"Yes, I do. I work out facing the mirror." It showed every mistake, again and again, until he fixed the problem.

She spoke slowly. "I have often wondered what it does to a person to stare for hours into a mirror for the sole purpose of finding flaws. Your dancing seems a cruel art."

"But it isn't." He didn't know how to describe what was intuition for him. "It can be frustrating, but when you see improvement, it's magic."

"Magic, yes." For the first time since she had entered the room, her face warmed with a smile. "When you dance, it is extraordinary. Mesmerizing. With your gifts and your spectacular looks, you could have an empire at your feet." In her throaty, compelling voice, she added, "I can give that to you."

Vyrl stared at her, unable to respond. He could barely imagine people tolerating his dancing, yet Devon promised him an empire. Of all the inducements Majda could have offered, she had chosen the single one that made a difference.

Devon stood up. "I'll wait downstairs. Take as long as you need to decide."

After she left, Vyrl pulled up his knee, rested his elbow on it, and gazed out at the rippling plains. Today his tower chamber offered no serenity. He could have what he wanted—Lily and a farm—but it would weaken crucial alliances built on the expectation of his marriage to Devon. Nor could he perform. If he accepted the marriage, he would lose Lily and Lyshriol, but he wouldn't have to give up farming completely, and he could have the dance career he craved, one almost beyond his imaginings.

The droid whirred around his feet, cleaning up the last shards, hiding the broken pieces inside itself. Once again, the chamber was spotless and smooth, like a polished box.

A tear gathered in Vyrl's eye and slid down his cheek. He knew the decision he had to make. He went to the door and descended the stairs, headed toward Majda.

Maybe he could never escape the pain—but he could hide it inside.

6
DREAMS

Vyrl tried the combination of steps again, studying his technique in the mirror as he skimmed across the floor. His reflection showed a young man with long legs and red-gold curls, in black pants and a black pullover, all soaked with sweat. Frowning, he tried the steps yet another time. Pah. No wonder he kept stumbling on the last jump. He was leaning to the side, almost imperceptibly, but enough to throw off his balance.

"Are you going to glare at yourself all day?" a voice drawled from the doorway.

Vyrl refocused on the mirror, looking at the reflection of the doorway. His brother Del-Kurj stood there, resting his lanky self against the frame, his arms crossed. Vyrl glowered at him via the mirror, but he decided to be civil. For all that Del-Kurj could be a bog-boil, he had been remarkably decent lately, even showing sympathy for his younger brother's melancholy.

Vyrl turned to him. "Has the broadcast started yet?"

Del nodded. "In the Hearth Room."

Vyrl felt as if a lump was lodged in his throat. The meditative calm of his dancing vanished. He cleaned up and changed into trousers and a white shirt, then followed Del upstairs.

His siblings were already gathered around the hearth: Althor in an armchair, his large size and self-assurance dominating the room; Chaniece, fraternal twin to Del-Kurj, poised and regal, gold hair spilling over her arms; thirteen-year-old Soz, with wild, dark curls, busily taking apart Althor's laser carbine, trying to figure out how it worked;

twelve-year-old Denric, smaller than his brothers, with a mop of yellow curls and violet eyes; eight-year-old Aniece, also dark-haired, small and pretty, curled on a sofa by their mother; and four-year-old Kelric, a strapping toddler with gold curls, gold eyes, and the kind of heartbreakingly angelic face that only beautiful young children could have. Their father was sitting in a large armchair, his booted legs stretched across the carpet. Only ten-year-old Shannon was missing.

Seeing his family together, knowing this would soon all change for him, Vyrl wanted to hold this moment close, like a treasure within a box. He would miss them more than he knew how to say.

Del-Kurj dropped onto the sofa next to Chaniece and sprawled out his long legs. On the other couch, Soz eyed Vyrl dubiously, as if she hadn't decided yet whether or not brothers qualified as human. But then she moved over, making room for him.

Vyrl sat down, with Soz on one side and Althor on the other. As he settled in, the room lights dimmed.

"Got dark," Kelric stated.

"So it did." Roca picked up the small boy and put him in her lap.

A news-holo formed around the hearth, encompassing the entire area. It unsettled Vyrl; he suddenly seemed to be sitting in a balcony of the Assembly Hall on the planet Parthonia. Hundreds of men and women packed the amphitheater, rank upon rank of interstellar leaders, dignitaries, diplomats, military officers, and newscasters.

In the past, Vyrl had never had much interest in such broadcasts. Nor had he paid enough attention to his physics to understand how this transmission came to Lyshriol, many light-years away, except that the technology bypassed spacetime, making light speed limitations irrelevant.

After a moment, Vyrl located Devon. She was standing on a dais in the center of the amphitheater by a podium. Seeing her, he felt the proverbial shimmerflies in his stomach. She made an impressive sight, resplendent in her dress uniform, tall and strong, like an ancient warrior queen from the Ruby Empire.

People surrounded her, aides and dignitaries. More were

seated at consoles below the dais, probably minor clerks recording the Assembly session. An unfamiliar woman was speaking at the podium, and many people in the amphitheater were talking as well. It seemed like bedlam to Vyrl, but perhaps the meeting had an organization he didn't see.

Finally the speaker finished and moved aside, glancing at Devon. The general nodded to her, then stepped up to the podium. As Devon tapped the com, the newscasters zoomed in, so that instead of being in a balcony, Vyrl abruptly found his virtual self only a few meters from Devon. It gave him vertigo.

Suddenly Vyrl froze. At a console across the dais, a dark-haired man was talking into a com. Heat spread in Vyrl's face. He knew that man. He had seen him in Devon's mind.

Vyrl leaned toward Althor and spoke in low tones, trying to sound nonchalant. "Do you know who that man is? The one with the gray sweater and dark hair?"

"I haven't a clue," Althor said. "Why?"

"I just wondered."

Althor pulled off his palmtop and flipped it open. While Althor worked, Vyrl watched people argue and yell in the Assembly session.

After a moment Althor spoke discreetly. "His name is Ty Collier." When Vyrl turned to him, Althor added, "He's a recorder for the Imperial Library."

"That's it?" Devon was in love with a clerk? Vyrl had expected more. But perhaps that wasn't fair to Collier.

Althor gave him an odd look. "Do you know him?"

Vyrl avoided his gaze. "I thought he looked familiar, but I was wrong." He could tell Althor didn't believe him, but his brother didn't push. Vyrl wondered how he would feel if he met Collier. Right now, Devon showed no sign she even knew Ty sat a few meters from where she stood.

When Devon began to speak, the amphitheater went silent. Vyrl could almost feel people leaning forward. Her throaty voice rolled over the audience.

"A great deal of speculation has occurred in regard to my marital state." She stopped while more newscasters zoomed in. Ty Collier had stopped working and was watching her with poorly disguised pain.

"Rather than let rumors proliferate," Devon continued, "I have prepared a statement." She paused. "It is true that I plan to marry."

"What the hell?" Vyrl's father said.

"The Ruby Dynasty and House of Majda have long been allies," Devon continued. "Strengthening ties between our Houses offers many advantages to the Assembly and its governing bodies." She raised her head, surveying the amphitheater. "The House of Majda honors the Ruby Dynasty. We esteem the Imperial line and welcome the idea of joining our Houses through the Majda Matriarch and a Ruby prince."

Vyrl felt blood drain from his face. No. No! This couldn't be happening. "She told me she would accept my decision! She gave me her word."

His father spoke tightly. "She certainly did. We all heard her."

Lights glittered as newscasters recorded Devon's next words. "And it may be that someday such a joining will grace our House—if my sister Corejida Majda so wills."

"Corey?" Vyrl's mother said. "What the blazes?"

Voices rumbled in the Assembly Hall, and Devon paused, waiting for them to quiet.

Eldrinson gave his wife a puzzled look. "Have we spoken to Corey Majda?"

"Not that I know of." Roca spread her hands in a shrug, then quickly brought them back to keep Kelric from falling off her lap. "I've no idea what Devon is about."

"Devon has a sister?" Vyrl asked.

His mother nodded. "Two sisters. Corey and Naaj. Corey is next in line. She's ten years younger than Devon."

"Maybe she's making Corey her heir," Althor said. "She has to do something, or she will lose power within her House."

Devon was speaking again. "A young man once told me something I found true, words with a wisdom well beyond his age: 'For all that our dreams bring meaning to our lives, we cannot have them all. What we give up may cause regret, even grief, but we must find a balance we can bear. Otherwise our hearts will shatter.'"

Vyrl gaped at her. She had just repeated the words he had spoken when he told her that he couldn't become the Majda consort.

Devon had an odd look now, as if she were about to jump off a precipice. "In this matter of balance, I, too, must choose." Her voice carried throughout the amphitheater. "For that reason, I am abdicating my position as the Majda Matriarch."

"Gods al-flaming-mighty," Vyrl's mother said.

"Has she gone mad?" Eldrinson demanded.

The newscasters exploded with questions. Vyrl couldn't sort them out, the session had turned into such a tumult. Devon stood calmly, waiting for the clamor to subside.

"Why would she *abdicate*?" Roca said.

"Corey is next in line," Eldrinson said. "Saints, Roca, she's making Corey the Matriarch. That's what she meant."

"Corey," said Kelric, snuggled against his mother.

Vyrl absorbed Devon's words. Abdication. It would create a far bigger furor than his refusing the marriage. Had he caused this? When he had spoken with Devon, it had seemed everything would be all right. Had her House demanded she abdicate because her betrothal fell through? That made no sense. Devon was a force to reckon with. They couldn't just make her abdicate, besides which, she could arrange another marriage, if not with the Ruby Dynasty, then with a man from another noble House.

As the amphitheater quieted, Devon resumed her speech. "I do not make this decision lightly. I have considered it for years." Then she held out her hand—to Ty Collier. In front of an audience spread across interstellar space, she asked him, "Will you join me?"

Ty stared at her with undisguised astonishment. Apparently the news had surprised him as much as everyone else. When Devon gave him an encouraging smile, he visibly shook himself. Then he rose to his feet, his movements uncertain, as if he wasn't sure what to do. But he didn't hesitate; he climbed the dais and went to Devon. Taking her hand, he stood side by side with the general at the podium.

Devon spoke into the com. "Marriages of nobles and commoners are not unheard of among the Houses, but such has never been permitted for the Matriarch." Dryly, she added, "Especially not Majda." Still holding Ty's hand, she said, "I cannot marry a commoner and retain my title. So I release the title, abdicating to my sister, Corejida Majda."

Exclamations burst out in the hall, cries, people calling out questions. A rare serenity lightened Devon's face, and Ty stood with her, looking dazed but happy. Vyrl had never heard of such a powerful sovereign giving up her title for love. No doubt holobooks would be written about Devon and Ty, scholarly treatises published, holomovies produced.

Beneath the din, Althor spoke to Vyrl in a low voice. "You knew, didn't you?"

Vyrl shook his head. "Not that she intended this. Just about the man. She thought about him a lot."

The lights suddenly came up in the Hearth Room, jarring and bright. Blinking, Vyrl looked around. His ten-year-old brother, Shannon, had wandered into the room.

"I'm hungry," Shannon announced.

Roca made an exasperated noise. "Shannon, where have you been?"

"With Moonglaze. I missed him."

Vyrl sat up straighter. "Moonglaze is back?" Lily's family had agreed to bring the lyrine home with them after their stay with Lord Rillia. If Moonglaze had returned . . .

He realized everyone was watching him.

His father smiled. "Go on, son."

Vyrl jumped up, knocking Althor's arm off the chair. He mumbled an apology, then strode from the room.

Within moments he was outside, running through the winding streets of Dalvador. His feet pounded the blue cobblestones as he sped along the familiar route. When he was halfway up the last hill, someone came out of a house at the top and ran down toward him, her red-gold hair flying about her body and her blue dress whipping around her legs.

They collided in the middle of the street. Vyrl threw his arms around her, hugging as hard as he could, until she gasped for breath. He pulled her into a kiss, uncaring of the pedestrians around them. Lily was crying and laughing, trying to talk and kiss him at the same time.

Eventually they calmed down enough just to hold each other. Vyrl stroked her curls off her tear-stained cheeks. "It's so good to see you."

She took his face in her hands. "Your father's runner reached us in Rillia. He told us you weren't going with the sky queen."

"I'll never go away. Never, Lily." For all that he would always wonder what he had given up, he could live with that loss. He couldn't live without Lily.

He touched her cheek. "My parents say that if we want, we can live with them until we are ready to run our own farm. But they will help us no matter what we decide."

She ran her hand over his arm as if marveling that he was real. "I don't think I would like to live with parents."

"I neither." He spoke earnestly. "But even with their help, setting up the farm will be a lot of work. And I must finish my schooling. That was the only way they would let me stay married to you."

"We can manage." Her mood shone with optimism. "Lord Rillia gave my father three lyrine and many crop cuttings as compensation. My father says you and I can have it all to help us start out."

Vyrl blinked. "Your father said that?"

She laughed softly. "Actually, what he said was 'If you intend to stay with the damn fool boy, you better take this, because you'll need as much help as you can get.' "

Dryly, Vyrl said, "That sounds more like your father."

"He likes you. Really. He's just worried about us."

Vyrl pulled her close. "I'll make you a good husband, Lily, I swear." He finally became aware that other pedestrians were watching them. His parents were a few houses farther along the road, talking with Lily's parents. Taking Lily's hand, Vyrl drew her off the lane into an alley between two houses, where a bubble tree hid them from view. As they brushed the tree, one of its bubbles detached and floated into the air.

Then Vyrl took his wife into his arms.

EPILOGUE

Light sifted from the hall into the darkened bedroom. Vyrl stood with Lily in the doorway, watching their two youngest children, toddlers of two and three, sleeping on the downy bed.

"They're so sweet when they're asleep," Lily whispered.

Vyrl laughed, quietly so he didn't wake the boys. "And terrors when they're awake."

"They're angels," she admonished. When he didn't look suitably chastised, she tickled him. Vyrl picked her up and swung her away from the door, with Lily struggling not to laugh or make noise. It amazed him how light she felt. He had kept growing after their marriage and his shoulders had broadened even more. Now, at nineteen, he had reached his full height of six feet two.

He set her down outside their daughter's bedroom, and they peered in at their toddler snuggled under her quilt. Then, as quiet as mumble-mice, they walked into the living room of the farmhouse their families had helped them build. Rugs warmed the floor, hangings brightened the walls, and bubble plants in pots added touches of color.

Lily tugged Vyrl toward their bedroom, but he shook his head. "I need to study." He suddenly felt heavy. Sometimes the weight of his responsibilities seemed to sink into him. He was so often tired, working the farm, raising the children, and keeping up his studies. Even having delayed his entrance into Parthonia University until this year, he didn't feel ready. If their families hadn't helped so much, he didn't know how he and Lily would have managed.

She laid her hand on his arm. "Don't worry. Everything will be fine."

Vyrl smiled at her. *Don't worry.* "How often you've said that to me. And how often you've been right." She made him want to dance.

He had less time to work out now, but he managed to keep up his training with Rahkil. That he and Lily had two sets of parents happy to spend time with their grandchildren meant more than he knew how to say. It gave Lily time to learn more about the farm while Vyrl studied. It astonished him that Lily was so good at running the farm. She could do sums faster in her head than he could on his palmtop. But as much as he worried about his university work, he liked the challenge. Lily settled him, and now that he could pursue his own interests in agriculture and biology, it was easier to concentrate on the subjects he dreaded. And no matter how much the children exhausted him, he loved them so much that sometimes he thought he would burst with it. Perhaps someday, many years down the road, he could think of dancing beyond Lyshriol, but until then this was more than enough.

Vyrl pulled Lily into his arms. "Dance with me."

"Always," she murmured.

They twirled around the living room, moving to music they heard in their minds, and Vyrl's heart filled with the stained glass colors of joy.

Skin Deep

by Deb Stover

1

After two years, Nick Riley still wasn't used to the clean, white, fluffy kingdom. Sure, the Pearly Gates and golden thrones were nice, but he was a third-class resident, stuck on the lower levels of Heaven until he proved himself.

"How the hell am I supposed to prove myself?"

"Your language is more like a trucker's than a lawyer's—though I'd rather deal with a trucker than a lawyer any day."

Nick looked around for his ever-vigilant watchdog, Séamus—a former New York City cop, overblown with self-importance as Chief of the Mortal Watch Division.

Séamus crossed his arms over his chest and wore a stern expression on his not-so-angelic face. "Two years and still can't mind your tongue?"

"My father was a marine before he was a real estate tycoon. I probably learned to cuss before I learned to walk." Nick shrugged and pointed at the monitor. "I saw Margo again. She doesn't look any happier."

Séamus sighed dramatically. "Of course she isn't."

Nick didn't argue. How could he? "She didn't love me, but I made her think she did."

"You were too busy trying to win at everything," Séamus said, his tone filled with disapproval. "Well, you won Margo."

"Yeah."

"And now she's alone down there and you're up here,

though I still can't figure out how you slipped through the Gate."

"I wish I could go back and fix things for her." Nick meant every word. He regretted his selfish, shortsighted lifestyle. And short-lived.

"Maybe you can."

He glowered at his superior. "Chief, don't . . ."

"Believe me, it wasn't my idea." Séamus looked upward for emphasis. "A higher authority wants you to go back and help Margo get on with her life."

Nick's thoughts exploded with possibilities. Return to fast cars, expensive vacations, and—

Séamus cleared his throat.

"I keep forgetting you can read my mind," Nick said sheepishly and glanced at the monitor again. "Tell me more. When?"

"Now, but only to help Margo."

"What will she think? I mean . . . seeing me?"

Séamus grinned. A mischievous twinkle glittered in his eyes. "She won't see *you*. You'll have a different appearance."

Now *that* had possibilities. He'd always wanted to be taller. "I'm ready. What are we waiting for?"

"Close your eyes."

Nick obeyed, but he saw images anyway, similar to when he'd died. First there'd been the car crashing into the brick retaining wall . . . pain . . . blackness. Then bright lights, a tunnel, and images of people and places he'd known. After the pain, it had all been rather pleasant until he saw Margo's misery.

Soon he'd see her in person, could tell her he was sorry . . .

A chorus of male voices greeted Nick's arrival in the sauna at his favorite health club. At least Séamus had seen fit to send him somewhere he'd enjoyed when he was alive. But he didn't feel right. Something was different. Missing. And . . . new.

Nick glanced down at what he thought was his body, but it couldn't be. Séamus wouldn't have . . .

"Did you catch the playoffs last week?" A gruff male voice interrupted Nick's thoughts.

Blinking in the steamy environment, Nick tried to discern the identity of the other occupants. The last thing he needed was for someone to recognize Nick Riley with boobs.

Nick pulled the towel up from his waist to cover his chest, an area of his anatomy he'd never seen a need to conceal before. "Séamus, if you weren't already dead, I'd kill you myself," he muttered. *Is that my voice?* That silken drawl couldn't be his.

"Who—what?" A familiar voice sliced through the steam. "Hey, this is the *men's* sauna."

Nick tried to make out the face through the steam. That had to be his former law partner's voice. "Warren, is that you?" *There's that weird voice again.*

Whistling filled the small tiled area. "Hey, Warren," one man yelled, "does your wife know about her?"

"Don't be ridiculous," Warren growled. "Lady, you should go to the women's sauna before you cause any more trouble."

"Uh, right," Nick agreed in his new timbre. A woman—Séamus had sent him back as a woman. What a sick sense of humor.

He clutched the towel across his voluptuous chest and beat a hasty retreat, knowing his lower extremeties—such as they were and weren't—were uncovered. Feeling more exposed and vulnerable than he had in all his life, Nick jogged through the blessedly vacant men's locker room, down the corridor, and into the ladies' facility.

Stunned, he stood frozen in the center of the once forbidden sanctuary. Women of all assorted shapes and sizes walked around in various stages of undress.

Now this *is Heaven.*

Then he caught sight of the most gorgeous redhead he'd ever seen—a *natural* redhead. She was built like a tall Marilyn Monroe, with shapely legs he would've given almost anything to feel wrapped around his body in a clinch of—

"Whoa!" Perspiring, he lifted his hand to touch the reflection. *His* reflection.

Nick Riley was a drop-dead, brick shit-house babe.

"I can't believe I let you talk me into this." Margo Riley sank even lower in her chair at center stage. Any moment now the runway in front of her would fill with nearly naked, sweaty men. What in the world had possessed her?

Steph giggled and drained the contents of her glass. "Admit it, sis," she said. "You've always wanted to do this. Now you have an excuse."

Unconvinced, Margo shook her head and took another sip of club soda. Maybe she should have ordered something stronger. Anything to take her mind off where she was and what was about to happen. "This is so crude."

Steph ordered two more drinks from the passing waiter. "Hey, c'mon, Margo. It's a story. This is work. Your *job*? Remember?"

Simultaneously nodding and grimacing, Margo looked up at the still empty stage. "I always wondered what men saw in watching naked women undulate their bodies in places like this." She shrugged. "Now I guess I'll find out—sort of."

Steph paid the waiter and pushed a drink that looked suspiciously unlike club soda toward her sister. Maybe it was the fruit and little umbrella that gave it away.

"Just imagine what Mom'll think," Steph whispered with a wink.

Margo sucked in her breath. "You wouldn't dare."

Steph arched her delicate blond eyebrows and pursed her full lips in a feigned pout. The innocent look vanished as quickly as it had appeared. "Maybe. Maybe not."

Wrinkling her nose at her sister, Margo took a tentative sip of the tropical drink. After removing the paper umbrella, she took a second taste and nodded in satisfaction. "Not bad. What is it?"

"Something yummy." Steph flashed her a grin. "So, what made that old prude boss of yours give you such a sweet assignment?"

" 'Sweet' is a matter of opinion, I suppose." Margo sighed and leaned back in her chair. "I know what *he* wants for this story, but I'd rather tackle a more important issue."

Steph covered her face. "Not the First Amendment. Why not write about the guys, especially if that's what your editor wants? And the reason women like to come here?" She looked around the nightclub. "In case you haven't noticed, the place is packed."

Margo glanced around, amazed to discover that every table in the club was taken. "I had no idea."

"That's my point, and I'll bet it was your editor's, too," Steph said in her sarcastic, get-a-life voice. She leaned forward, elbows on the table. A shock of blond curls fell across her forehead. "Women come here for one reason— to look at hunks. Take notes, journalist."

Stunned, Margo studied her sister's expression. "What makes you such an expert?"

Steph reddened, laughing. "I've been here lots of times."

"No."

"Yeah, it's fun."

"It's embarrassing," Margo whispered, looking around again. Why *were* so many women here? She bristled, hating to admit her sister was right. "Okay, so there's a story here, but that's all it is to me."

Shrugging, Steph pointed to the stage. "Showtime."

Margo moaned in self-chastisement. How had she gotten herself into this mess? She should have suggested that her new editor take the assignment himself, though looking like Ernest Borgnine might have been a liability in the Studfinder.

"Here we go." Steph whooped and cheered with the other insane women while Margo groaned again. Music with a heavy disco beat reverberated through the small club. Varicolored lights rotated and flashed as the emcee announced the first performer.

"Good evening, ladies, and welcome to the Studfinder," he said dramatically. "And I guarantee you will find more than a few studs." The women roared with laughter and applause. A few wolf whistles rose above the din. "Now get ready for Tarzan."

Tarzan? The ultimate male domination fantasy. Margo suppressed a shudder of revulsion. *It's a story. Get a grip.*

Removing a notepad from her purse, she leaned back and started writing down everything she saw, heard, felt in the dim room. This was freedom of speech and expression in action. She had to remain focused. If people wanted to watch exotic dancers of either gender, that was their business. Government had no business dictating morals. Satisfied she'd found the proper mind-set for this assignment, Margo glanced up at the stage. "Oh. My. God."

A man—an almost naked one—stood directly in front of her. Smiling. Very slowly, his hips undulated to the music, displaying his well-endowed physique in intricate detail. He wore only an exotic leopard print breechcloth. "Oh, my God."

"You said that already. You'll be all right, sis." Steph squeezed Margo's hand in reassurance. "Him Tarzan. You Jane. Chill."

Margo averted her gaze from the grinning god and jerked the umbrella and fruit from another drink. She drained the contents in one smooth gulp, refusing to look again at the wriggling, pulsating male in front of her. "Why'd we have to sit so close, Steph?"

"For your story, of course."

Ignoring her sister's laughter, Margo turned her attention back to her notepad. She made more notations about the subject in the breechcloth, leaving out certain details regarding his anatomy. Her editor wouldn't consider that newsworthy, though Margo couldn't help wondering if perhaps *The Guinness Book of Records* might be interested.

The dancer released what could only be described as a Tarzan yell—one that would have had Cheetah, Jane, and Boy running to the rescue.

"Whoa, baby."

Her sister's reaction made Margo look up. God, how she wished she hadn't. The man chose that particular moment to shed most of his skimpy attire, leaving only a G-string between the ogling women and his family jewels. The crowd went wild.

Margo went into shock.

"I'm out of here. This is disgusting." She stood, and the contents of her open purse rolled onto the floor. "Damn."

The dancer seemed to think her upright position had other implications. He moved closer to their table, lowering himself in front of her until his pelvis was within reach.

Steph, obviously far more astute than Margo in such situations, rose to the occasion. She held a folded bill toward the man and deftly tucked it into his G-string.

Still staring in horror, Margo tried to swallow, but her throat was too dry.

"You need another drink, sis," Steph calmly suggested as

the music faded and Tarzan returned to his jungle. The waiter made rounds during the brief intermission.

Uncertain how or when, Margo found her spilled belongings back in her purse and herself back in her chair with another drink. Immediately removing the fruit, she sipped steadily. Some of her tension vanished beneath the heady power of demon rum. Her limbs felt warm and heavy. This was better. Much better.

When the music again increased in volume, Margo was still uncertain why women paid money to be embarrassed like this, but she was considerably more willing now to investigate the possibilities. The alcohol had numbed her somewhat and loosened her inhibitions, which was probably why she rarely imbibed. Steph had always accused her of being a control freak.

"This is the show with the Eroticops. It's great. I heard they have fresh meat—er, dancers." Steph sighed dramatically. "If all cops looked like these guys, I'd run stop signs on a regular basis."

Eroticops? Steph seemed awfully familiar with the Studfinder's performers. Just how often *did* she come here? Margo cast her sister a cursory frown just as the lights dimmed again. The announcer, along with police sirens and flashing red and blue lights, signaled the beginning of the next set. Pencil and paper readied, she looked across the table at her sister.

"Where'd they find *him*?" Steph asked in undeniable awe.

Curious, Margo sought the catalyst for her sister's reaction and spotted him instantly. Her pencil fell from her grasp and rolled impotently across the table. Her notepad dangled unproductively from the fingertips of her left hand.

This man was built even better than his predecessor, and at the moment he was still fully clothed. A blue policeman's uniform hugged every bulge and hollow of his body to perfection. The bill of his hat shadowed part of his face and eyes. Dark hair curled at his temples and neckline. For some imprudent reason, she wanted to know what color his eyes were.

She felt her sister's gaze on her and jerked her attention away from the man on the stage, but only for a moment. A very brief moment.

"Nice, huh?" Steph asked in that infuriating way she had

of knowing what someone else was thinking. Four other "police officers" joined the first, flanking him in pairs to mimic his seductive movements.

Margo could only nod. Despite her best intentions, she turned her gaze back to the stage, discovering that the lead dancer had moved to the front of the runway and seemed to be dancing just for her. *In your dreams, silly.* His stare never left her as he gyrated his hips and bent his knees, lowering himself for her inspection.

Her face was hot—and the rest of her body wasn't exactly cool, come to think of it. The man still hadn't removed any of his costume, even though he'd been on stage for several minutes. Some members of the audience were suggesting—loudly—that he should proceed as expected. After all, the other four men in uniform had already shed most of their attire.

For some unexplainable reason, Margo wanted to see what this beefcake looked like unwrapped. Flustered, she reached for her glass and drained the contents. Her head swam as he tossed his hat into her lap in one smooth motion. The smile he broadcasted was deadly.

And familiar.

Margo couldn't speak. It couldn't be . . .

He peeled away his shirt and now wore nothing but his trousers. She swallowed hard, unable—unwilling—to drag her gaze from the mesmerizing specimen on the stage. She had to know.

Much to her dismay, he blew her a kiss. It headed straight for her as if it had DNA and free will, planting itself right on her lips. She felt it—really, she did. A strange, fluttering sensation commenced in her belly and spread.

She stole a peek at Steph. Her sister was riveted, as were the other women in the audience. Margo glanced quickly around the room, but her gaze was lured back to the dancing figure as if her optic nerves had a homing device. A blue spotlight suddenly bathed him, illuminating his features clearly.

Realization hit home. With trembling fingers, she retrieved her pencil and made notes, though she knew her scribbles wouldn't make any sense later.

Jared. Why now, after all this time?

She felt his gaze boring into her as he danced and swayed on the stage. He must have recognized her, too.

Commanding herself not to look, she bent her head over the tablet, scratching away as his shadow passed to and fro across the table amid the flashing lights.

Oh, but she wanted to look.

The hammering in her chest was almost as distracting as the heat inside her body. She'd gone two years without even wanting a man, let alone acting on it. A trickle of guilt filtered through her, but her natural instincts overshadowed it.

Had Jared removed anything else? She had to know. Just one little peek ...

Garbed in nothing but a light blue metallic loincloth, he thrust his hips toward her in a timeless movement that never went out of style and never would. Heat suffused her, but she couldn't tear her attention from his gorgeous glistening and—God help her—achingly familiar body.

Dark hair fell across his forehead in disarray. His jaw was square and strong. Of course, she didn't have to see his eyes to know they were blue.

See, Margo, this is what happens when you're celibate for two years. Of course, her reaction was reserved for this man, and only this man.

She drew a deep breath, trying to ignore the twisting, squirming, dazzling male displayed for her simultaneous pleasure and torture. But she couldn't. Lifting her gaze, she found him staring. He gave her a slow, sexy smile when their gazes met.

Oh, yeah, he definitely recognized her.

It was magic.

Just like in the movies.

"This is a raid!"

2

Vaguely aware of chaos erupting all around her, Margo watched Jared retrieve his discarded clothing much more quickly than he'd jettisoned the garments. "Oh, this must be part of the show," she whispered, suddenly wishing she'd skipped the third tropical drink. She giggled at the absurdity of her situation, but Jared appeared at her side and gripped her elbow, turning her knees to rubber. After all this time and everything that had happened, here he was. Touching her.

"You don't know me," he whispered through clenched teeth.

"Wha—"

He tightened his grip and leaned closer. "No matter what happens, you don't know me."

She met his gaze, searching for answers to questions left unasked since college. "For now."

"Thanks, I owe you."

And Margo knew exactly how she would exact payment. Her boss wanted an interview with a male stripper. Well, now there was no doubt in her mind who would grant her that interview. "Yes, you do."

Another uniformed man—definitely lacking a stripper's physique—approached them. "You'll both have to come downtown with—"

"Downtown?" Margo blinked when they started toward the front entrance. "Are we under arrest? I thought this was just part of the show."

"Not hardly," the officer said, shaking his head.

Margo glanced at her sister, who was being politely but firmly escorted to the door by a pair of uniformed officers.

With a sigh, the apparently legitimate police officer gripped Margo and Jared by the elbows and escorted them through the door. "Outside with both of you."

"Suits me. I seem to have worked up a little sweat." Jared shot Margo a lethal smile—one that rivaled the wattage of the parking lot lights.

"Yeah, I'll say." Margo's gaze dipped to the open vee of his unbuttoned shirt. If he expected her to act like she didn't know him, then she would treat him the same way any other patron at the Studfinder might—as a side of meat. Prime, of course.

Swaying slightly when the officer stepped from between them and released her arm, Margo clutched Jared's muscular forearm for support. He was, without a doubt, the most well-constructed male she'd ever encountered. Of course, he always had been. Despite his incredible physique, she still had trouble believing he'd chosen exotic dancing as his career. Not Jared Carson. Even so, she remembered that he'd studied Broadway jazz in college. Apparently, he'd found a use for that talent.

The chilly evening air was like a bucket of ice water on her rum-blurred senses. She squinted, looking around for Steph in the parking lot menagerie. Suspicion nudged its way into the foggy, semidrunken fringes of her mind.

"Are you really arresting me?" Margo asked, her mouth dry and sticky.

"Not unless you give me a good reason." The policeman pushed his hat back on his head, then nodded toward her companion. "The dogs are going in."

Dogs? Drugs. Maybe there was another angle to this story after all. She fished through her purse until she found her wayward pencil and opened her steno pad to make a few notes. "What reason do you have for believing there are drugs at the Studfinder, Officer?"

The man released an exasperated sigh. "A reporter. I should've known." He shook his head and aimed his thumb over his shoulder. "You're all going downtown until we finish searching the place, then there may be some questions. That's all I know."

Margo shot Jared a questioning look, but he was staring beyond her. His expression intense, a muscle twitching in his jaw, just the way she remembered. When his gaze met hers, a mask dropped neatly into place and another dark curl fell across his forehead. He smiled, but it didn't reach his eyes. A stage smile, but why now?

More important . . . why for her?

Still, his grin waged a full-scale attack against her composure and almost won. Why couldn't he be a little less handsome and a lot less memorable?

"I'm sure you'll be out so fast you'll hardly have time to read the graffiti in your cell," the policeman said in a mocking tone. "We usually don't hold you yuppies long."

Pencil poised in midair, Margo swallowed hard. "Cell?"

"Just kidding. Lighten up."

"Hey, Margo, you got the cute one. Way to go, sis."

Groaning as her sister was escorted away, Margo rubbed

her eyes with thumb and forefinger. "Mom's going to kill me when she hears about this."

The policeman chuckled. "She looks old enough to drink."

Shaking her head in self-loathing, Margo released a sigh of surrender. "Arrest me, Officer. Let's get this over with."

Chuckling again, he led her and Jared to a car, passing two women singing "I Am Woman" at the top of their lungs.

They were being dragged down to the police station, and there was more to this than a night of exotic dancing. She could use this situation to her advantage.

Margo tried to stay close to the door as the car rolled out of the parking lot, though knowing Jared sat mere inches away made it difficult to concentrate. Until she found out exactly what was going on, it might be better if she maintained a safe distance.

She turned her attention to scratching a few more notes about the atmosphere, the way it felt to be incarcerated in the back of a squad car, though not under arrest . . .

And trying to ignore the heat of Jared's gaze as he sat staring at her through the darkness.

Heaven, help me.

Not a moment too soon, the officer parked behind the police station. They climbed out of the car and went through the rear entrance. In better times, Margo had used the front entrance. She was mortified, though she reminded herself they weren't being arrested. It could be worse. Much worse.

In the bright squad room light, she couldn't help noticing that the other women from the Studfinder looked quite ordinary. They looked like . . . mothers.

"I want to call my attorney," she said quietly, the rum's numbing effect abandoning her.

"I already did that," Steph said from across the room.

"There you are." Margo breathed a sigh of relief. "You and your bright ideas about how to do my job. Thanks a lot."

Steph flashed her a sheepish grin as Margo slumped into a chair beside her. With difficulty, she ignored Jared's eyes on her from across the room. None of this made sense. The Jared she'd once known and loved would never have put on the show she'd witnessed this evening. And what a show. Her face heated at the memory of his bare skin rippling beneath the flashing lights.

With a sigh, she planted her chin in her hands and peeked at Steph from the corner of her eye, grateful her family had never met Jared in person. "You called Warren, then?"

Steph nodded. "Yeah, but he's out of town."

"Of course he's out of town." Margo straightened and allowed her head to hit the wall with a soft thud. "The perfect finale to a perfect day."

"I wish Nick . . ."

Margo smiled sadly when her sister left her comment unfinished. If Nick were alive, he'd have had them out of here by now. "I know. Me, too."

"They're sending a new junior partner to spring us."

"Oh, that figures." Margo sighed again, physically, mentally, and emotionally drained.

"Who's in charge here?" a feminine voice demanded from the doorway.

Glancing up at the redheaded woman, Margo noted she was well-dressed and built like Marilyn Monroe.

"I am." The officer at the desk looked up at the newcomer. "May I help you, ma'am?"

The woman grimaced slightly, then smiled. "I'm Raquel Eastwood from Riley and Gray—I mean, Warren Grayson's office."

"Oh, thank goodness you're here." Steph stood and grabbed the woman's hands in both her own. "Can you get us out of here?"

"Done."

The woman's smile took Margo aback, and there was something about her eyes . . . "So we're free to go?" Margo asked, rising to stand beside Steph.

Ms. Eastwood nodded and snapped her fingers. "You bet. I have a couple of forms to sign, then we're out of here."

"There were others," Margo began, her gaze inexorably drawn to Jared's slouched figure against the other wall. His expression was so intense it stole her breath. She needed to talk to him, to learn why he was here and why he'd been at the Studfinder. Somehow, she sensed he wouldn't welcome her questions now, and she needed a hot bath and a couple of aspirin. Maybe more than a couple.

But there was a story here—more of one than she'd originally thought. Jared knew something.

Frowning, she dragged her gaze from Jared to ask the attorney something, but Ms. Eastwood was staring at Jared, too. Of course she was. Jared was the kind of man any woman would ogle, and he wasn't Margo's anymore. She had no right to feel jealous. But she did.

"I guess you've all had enough excitement for one night," Jared said with a chuckle, gaining Margo's immediate attention. The expression in his eyes was no longer intense, nor was it for her alone. Again, the mask was in place.

What was his game? Narrowing her eyes, she reminded herself that no one else here knew who he was. He'd shushed her back at the Studfinder. For now she would play along. However, she reserved the right to collect payment later for keeping his secret.

"Excitement?" Her voice dripped sarcasm, and she mentally patted herself on the back when his eyebrow arched ever so slightly. "The only exciting thing that happened this evening was watching *you* parade around in front of a bunch of screaming women. Half-naked. More than half."

"I'll say," Steph said.

Ms. Eastwood shook her head slowly, her gaze riveted to Jared. "Another surprise." She cast a sidelong glance at Margo.

After Margo and Steph finished answering a few questions about the Studfinder and signing some papers, the attorney offered to drive them home. They walked by Jared, who stood and flashed them his stage smile again. "Nice meeting you, ladies."

"*Very* nice." Steph giggled.

"Shake it, don't break it, man," Ms. Eastwood said in a sultry tone.

Margo couldn't prevent herself from giggling along with Steph, though her reasons were far different from her sister's. She'd only known one person who would've had the guts to say something like that to Jared Carson, and he was dead.

Jared's eyes sparked and one corner of his mouth quirked upward. "Lawyers. Who needs 'em?" He turned his gaze on Margo. "Reporters, lawyers . . . and women."

"Hey, watch it, buster." Raquel placed one hand on her curvy hip. "Margo's a reporter."

"Anything for a story?" The expression on Jared's face now could only be called a smirk.

Margo elevated her chin and took a deep breath, sensing this was part of his secretive role. "You bet." She noted a wink of approval from Ms. Eastwood. Just how had Warren's new partner known she was a reporter? Well, it didn't really matter. This nightmare was almost over, except for dealing with Jared.

Later.

3

Nick stripped off his dress and infernal high heels the minute his apartment door closed behind him. Thank goodness he and Grayson had seen the wisdom of opening their offices in an old Victorian. The upstairs was a furnished apartment—the perfect place for the new junior partner to hang out for a while.

The perfect halfway house for a halfway angel.

He had no idea how Séamus had managed to create a position for Raquel Eastwood in the firm, but it was like magic. From the moment Raquel had walked through the door, everyone treated her as if she'd gone through a normal hiring process and they'd been expecting her. Amazing. Even Mrs. Brown, the old bat receptionist, hadn't suspected a thing. This divine intervention stuff had its merits.

Raquel had a driver's license, a Social Security card, a diploma hanging on her office wall, and she was a member of the bar. She was as real as anyone else walking down the street.

"Yeah, and she looks a lot like a streetwalker, for that matter," Nick muttered.

Trying unsuccessfully to unhook his bra—aka torture band—he gave up and yanked it over his head. He used to be able to do it with one hand. Of course, it hadn't been behind *his* back then.

He grimaced as his breasts were freed from the confining garment. It was bad enough being in a woman's body, but why had Séamus felt compelled to make Nick so well-endowed? Raquel was at least a ten and a half. He glanced down at the lush breasts attached to his once flat, once hairy chest. *Okay, maybe a twelve.*

After pulling on an oversized T-shirt, he flopped into a chair in front of the television's blank screen. "Séamus, I don't know what got into you."

"Oh, stop your bellyachin', Nick."

It was hard to get used to hearing voices in his head. Especially when that voice belonged to a former New York City cop who sounded far less than angelic. "I saw Margo," Nick whispered on a sigh.

"Margo's a good person, and she deserves better than you."

Scowling upward, Nick scratched in a manner a lady wouldn't be caught dead doing. But then . . . he was already dead, and he sure as hell wasn't a lady.

"Where'd this body come from?" Nick asked. "Is this an *Invasion of the Body Snatchers* deal?"

"Don't worry about it. The body's owner lived and died in another time and place."

"Okay. So how do I go about finding Margo a new husband?" He chewed a long, manicured nail. It was damned strange, trying to find his own wife another man.

"But you're not a man anymore."

"Yeah, thanks for reminding me."

"And she's already found the right man."

"Already found him?" Nick rubbed his chin, still amazed at how smooth his skin was now. "When do I get to meet him?"

"You know exactly who he is."

"No, I—" Realization smacked Nick between the eyes. Oh, he'd considered the possibility earlier in the evening but had denied it. Repeatedly. Even Séamus couldn't be that cruel. Then again, what about this Raquel gig?

Nick swallowed hard, remembering all those years of lurking in Jared Carson's shadow. All his life, Nick had struggled to stay one step ahead of Jared. And failed.

Until Margo.

"So I'm being punished." Nick sighed, rubbing dried mascara from his eyes and pondering the merits of the entire pint of dark fudge ice cream lurking in the freezer.

"No, you're being given the opportunity to fix your mistakes." Séamus made a tsking sound in Nick's head. *"An opportunity most would welcome."*

Nick closed his eyes and let his head fall back against the chair. "I guess pride is something we aren't allowed to have even after we die."

"Depends."

"Why him?" A shudder crawled through Nick from the top of his stylish, tousled hairdo to the tip of his perfect pedicure. "Jared Carson has always kicked my ass." His new voice dripped sarcasm like battery acid. "Star in baseball, football, basketball, track and field, class president, and I'll bet you already know who ran against him. Gee, thanks, Séamus. Thanks a lot."

Bitterness tasted vile on his tongue. The ice cream would help. Nick kept his eyes closed, but that couldn't block the memory of his father's lectures. Fred Riley's kid was never the best at anything. Sure, Nick had been close many times, but second place was never good enough for his old man. Especially not second to Jared . . .

"Winning isn't everything. In fact, it really isn't important at all in the big scheme of things."

"Easy for you to say." Nick opened his eyes and looked up at the ceiling, half expecting to find a certain angel's ugly mug smirking from the plaster. "Besides, he's a male stripper. Get a grip."

"Think real hard, Nicholas. Does that ring true?"

"No." Nick sat up straight, remembering football hero Jared from college. "Not a bit."

"So use your brain, Red."

"But if he isn't a stripper, then—" Nick covered his face and sucked air between his fingers. "He's a cop. I should've known. He's a frigging *cop*. Why? Huh? Why not a nice stockbroker, a banker, or even another lawyer?"

"She tried that once."

"You have to remind me every chance you get, don't you?" Nick closed his eyes and groaned. "A cop who happens to have been a lifelong pain in my ass? Shouldn't dying get me a reprieve from that guy? No way. I'll find her someone else."

"Nick—"

"You said this is my job."

"What are we going to do with you?"

"Beats the he—" Nick bit the inside of his cheek. "Sorry. I can't—I won't—let Margo take up with a cop. Especially not *that* cop."

"I see."

"Yeah, I'm sure you do."

"Are you forgetting I was one of New York's finest?"

Nick slumped lower in his chair.

"The guilt you've carried around about how you won Margo is only one of the reasons you're here now."

Nick stiffened—his gut twisted into a violent knot. "Séamus, is that why you picked Carson? To punish me?"

"I didn't pick him. He's Margo's destiny. You interfered."

"If it's going to happen anyway, then why do I have to be around to witness it?"

"They need a catalyst. You and Jared were rivals. Besides, you know secrets that will explain the past."

"Secrets? What secrets?"

"You must remember what your father—"

"No way, buster. We aren't going there." Nick punched the arm of his chair and clenched his teeth, determined to change the subject. "So I'm supposed to help her get over me? How sweet." His voice grew hoarse and tears—*tears?*—pricked his eyelids. "This is perfect. Now I'm going to cry just like a woman, too. Thanks a lot, Séamus."

"Crying might do you some good."

"That's a matter of opinion." Nick dabbed at his eyes with the hem of his T-shirt, visualizing himself with the chocolate ice cream and a spoon. "But I'm telling you right here and now, I can find Margo a better man."

Séamus sighed in Nick's head—not a pleasant experience by any means.

"Will you stop that?" Nick rubbed his temples with both thumbs. "You're giving me a headache."

"Jared is the right ma—"

"Over my dead body."

"No problem."

Jared Carson stared at his reflection in the appropriately warped bathroom mirror. A neon sign flashed VACANCY outside the window, less than ten feet away. This hole away from home left a lot to be desired, but it served his purpose.

After popping two aspirin into his mouth, he washed them down with tepid tap water, then raked his fingers through his hair. Tonight had brought a few surprises. That drug raid, for starters. Why had the locals raided the Studfinder? How much did they know?

Bracing himself on the sink's edge, he stared at his reflection as if the answers were hidden in the glass. Fat chance. He had to face the possibility of a leak. His cover seemed intact, though. So far. But if the local boys interfered again, Jared's investigation would fall apart too soon. Way too soon.

And, as if he didn't have enough complications, there was Margo. Why now?

He'd known Lakeview was her hometown, but he figured Riley would have moved his bride to the big city for a life of wealth and glamour. So why was she back here working for a small newspaper? Married to a successful attorney, Margo would shine at the country club, and she'd never *have* to hold down a paying job.

A far different life than he could have offered.

He slammed his fist against the edge of the sink, immediately regretting it. "Damn." Hard porcelain couldn't take the place of a good punching bag for working out his frustrations. A human jaw, on the other hand . . .

Flexing his bruised hand, he padded barefoot to the window and stared out at the night. If he'd known Margo and Nick Riley had settled in Lakeview, he never would have accepted this assignment.

But it was too late to back out now. His cover was in place and he'd just have to explain that to Margo. And her husband. God, the last person in the world he wanted to face right now was Nick Riley.

The man who'd stolen the only woman Jared had ever loved.

Two weeks before graduation, Nick had arranged for Margo to catch Jared in the arms of another sorority sister. Somehow, the girl had managed to get into his room and his bed without him knowing it. In retrospect, he realized Nick must have paid her to set Jared up for a fall.

Nick hadn't let a moment pass before he'd moved in on a vulnerable Margo. She'd refused to listen to Jared's explanations, which angered him enough to allow his pride to get in the way. Big mistake.

"Easy enough to say now." With a sigh, he shook his head in disgust.

Swallowing the bitter bile frying his throat, he trudged to the lumpy full-sized bed and flopped down on top of the tattered bedspread. He had a job to do—an important one. Margo would keep his secret once he explained why he was here. But Nick . . .

Jared rolled to his side and stared at the flashing sign, hypnotized by its rhythmic display.

When he'd seen Margo sitting in the audience tonight, his initial reaction had been embarrassment, then joy. He'd never forgotten her gray eyes, her honey-brown hair, her lithe young body, or the passion she'd shown so openly during their college years. No other woman had insinuated herself into his heart since Margo, and he wasn't sure if it was because he wouldn't allow it or because no other woman *could* take her place.

Or both.

And how could he forget Nick? The rich kid whose real estate tycoon father had owned or held the mortgage on everything and everybody in his small town. Except for Carson's Garage. Jared's uncle and guardian had been an independent cuss who never borrowed or loaned a dime his entire life. Everything they'd ever owned had been paid for with hard-earned cash.

A cold draft seeped in around the cheap, aluminum-framed window, and he shivered. Taking refuge under the blankets, he continued to stare at the flashing sign. What a sorry excuse for a bed. The floor would probably be more comfortable, but colder, too.

And no amount of physical discomfort could blot out his memories. Not tonight.

If Nick had gone to some posh private college instead of the state university, so many things would be different. By now, Jared would be married to Margo. He knew that without a doubt. They'd probably have a baby, or one on the way.

And he definitely wouldn't have taken this cruddy job—not a chance. He would have gone home and worked as a deputy until Sheriff Bob was ready to retire, then he would've run for the office himself.

But Fred and Nick Riley's obsession with winning and Jared's own stupid sense of pride had ruined it all.

Ah, Margo. He squeezed his eyes shut and remembered that night in the woods behind her sorority house, when she'd given herself to him completely. The night they'd both declared their love for each other . . .

No other woman had ever touched him or drained him so completely—physically or emotionally. Sure, he'd had sex with more than a few women in his life, but he'd only made love with one. Margo. Sweet Margo.

Forget it, chump. She was a married woman, and the last person she needed messing up her life was the likes of Jared Carson. He'd had his chance. It was over.

He punched his pillow and sat up in bed. Between worrying about this case and strolling down memory lane, he'd be up all night. Since he couldn't sleep, maybe he'd get some answers instead.

Grumbling, he reached for the phone and dialed his contact's number. Jared's body tensed, thoughts of Margo pushed aside by duty.

"This better be important," a sleep-roughened voice said after one ring.

"What the hell's going on? Is there a leak?"

"Beats the hell outta me." Charlie sighed into the phone.

"And my cover?" Silence. That did nothing to bolster Jared's confidence. "Charlie, is my cover blown?"

"Nah, I'm sure it's fine."

Jared stood and paced. "We'll continue as planned for now, but you let me know *in advance* if anything else crops up. Got it? I don't like surprises."

"Sure. Get some shut-eye."

Jared disconnected the call and dropped the receiver into its cradle. No, he didn't like surprises one iota.

Like seeing Margo again.

4

Margo winced as her alarm clock blasted through her brain. No, not her alarm clock—the phone. What had she done to deserve a wake-up call this morning?

Steph is a dead woman.

Without opening her eyes, she fumbled for the receiver. Anything to keep it from ringing again. Some party animal. Three—four?—tropical drinks had given her a hangover.

"Meet me for breakfast," a woman—definitely not Steph—said before Margo uttered a syllable.

"What? Who is this?" She shoved a pillow behind her head and opened one eye. Her tongue was glued to the roof of her mouth with something resembling wallpaper paste. "Breakfast?" Her stomach threatened immediate mutiny.

"Yeah, how about the Little Diner?"

She and Nick had eaten dozens of breakfasts in that downtown restaurant during their marriage. "Who is this?"

"Raquel. Raquel Eastwood."

No longer groggy, Margo opened the other eye and scooted herself into a partial sitting position. "Why?" Suspicion slithered through her. Was there a complication from last night's trip to the police station? "Am I in some kind of trouble?"

A nervous laugh sounded through the phone. "No, I just thought we'd chat over breakfast. How about it?"

Margo rubbed her forehead and nodded, then remembered that wasn't terribly effective over the phone. "Sure, I suppose." She swallowed and grimaced. "It'll take me at least an hour to get my act together."

"Too much Silver Oaks?"

The mere thought of anything alcoholic made Margo's stomach lurch. "No, I wish that was—" She swung her legs over the edge of the bed. "Wait a minute. How did you know my favorite wine?"

"Uh, you must have told me last night." Another nervous laugh. "Tell you what, bring Steph, too. I'll meet you there in about an hour. Later."

She had *not* mentioned Silver Oaks last night. Margo

shook her head, immediately regretting the sudden movement. Someone at the law firm must have mentioned Margo to Raquel. How else could the woman know so much?

Dismissing it, for now, she called Steph and tried to sound semicoherent. Her sister was disgustingly alert and cheerful. Fortunately, the call lasted only a minute or two, and she dropped the phone.

"Shower," she muttered, pushing to her feet while holding her aching head. "Coffee."

She froze in midstep, suddenly remembering what—rather, who—had plagued her dreams. *Jared.* She would find him today, interview him, then forget him.

Forget him? The lie of the century.

Exactly seventy minutes later, she slid into an old-fashioned booth at the Little Diner. Amazing what hot water, hot coffee, and aspirin could accomplish in so little time.

Steph looked as if she hadn't been out last night at all, and Raquel Eastwood still had bombshell written all over her. Not only did she boast a mane of curls Nicole Kidman would've envied, but she had a body that wouldn't quit. Margo's short-cropped light brown hair and small breasts suddenly seemed more inadequate than usual.

She'd had more than her share of coffee already this morning, so she ordered tea and toast. "So, you're Warren's new law partner." *And why the chummy breakfast invitation?*

"Uh, yeah." Raquel took a sip of coffee and looked from Margo to Steph. "Warren's out of town."

"I know." Steph shuddered dramatically. "When the answering service told me, I was afraid we'd be stuck in jail all night. But, you know, it was all kind of fun until we got to the police station."

A strange expression entered the attorney's blue eyes as she turned her gaze on Margo, then looked quickly back to Steph. "It could've been a lot worse," Raquel said.

Steph giggled and winked at her sister. "Did you see the gorgeous dancer Margo got?"

"I didn't *get* anyone." Margo grimaced. She'd *had* him, once upon a time—definitely past tense. Her memory of last night was like a scene from a bad soap opera. She'd stayed out almost all night, gone to a male strip show, and been arrested—er, taken in for questioning. To punctuate the event, her college flame had barged into her life and her dreams.

"Mmm, the way he was looking at you, sis . . ."

"Oh?" Raquel tugged on her bra as if it was uncomfortable, and her face reddened. "You mean the guy at the station?"

When the attorney peered over the rim of her coffee cup, Margo was struck again by how much Raquel reminded her of someone. For some reason she just couldn't determine why. *Déjà vu?*

"He was dancing at the club before the real police came." Steph wrinkled her nose at Margo. "If you ask me, he was dancing for my sister."

"Stephanie." Margo's face flooded with heat beneath Raquel's stunned expression. "It was really nothing like that. I just happened to be sitting right in front, and—"

"Dancing?" Raquel asked quietly. "So, tell me what he was . . . like."

What was he like? Hot fudge sundaes, my most erotic dreams, and the world's fastest roller coaster. Flustered, Margo stared at Raquel. The woman was awfully nosy. "Well, you saw him, too."

"Uh, yeah. Right." Raquel laughed nervously as she added non-dairy creamer to her coffee even though there was real cream on the table. "I guess I really didn't get a very good look at him."

"That's funny." Steph smiled at Margo. "I thought Nick was the only person who preferred that powdered junk to the real thing."

"Me, too." Margo tried to smile but found a lump in her throat she couldn't swallow. "Must be a prerequisite for the law firm."

"Oh, really?" Raquel shrugged. "That must be the real reason Warren hired me."

"Oh, I doubt that." Steph grinned, tilting her head to the side. "I imagine it had a little something to do with your legs, and a couple of other things."

Raquel coughed into her napkin as Steph dissolved into laughter, but Margo didn't join her sister. There was something really strange about Raquel. Then again, maybe it had a little something to do with Margo's lack of sleep and her hangover.

"Hey, sis, look." Steph leaned forward, pointing toward the door. "Is that who I think it is?"

Dragging her attention from Raquel, Margo looked toward the door. And froze. Larger than life, Jared Carson's impressive physique filled the doorway. This couldn't be a coincidence. She'd called in and told her editor where she was having breakfast, in case anyone needed to reach her. Jared must have called to track her down.

Like a fist, her stomach pressed upward against her heart. Her throat clenched. Well, this would save her the trouble of looking for him later. After all, she still had an article to write, and he owed her a favor.

The thought of Jared repaying a favor sent tendrils of desire stretching through her veins. Seeing him again was dangerous, but by seeking her out he'd left her no choice.

Steph reached out and grabbed Margo's wrist. "Oh, it *is* him, and he's coming this way."

"Great. Not again."

Raquel's reaction made Margo glance in her direction. The attorney's eyes glittered dangerously. She looked angry. Why?

"Good morning, ladies."

Margo jerked her head toward the sound of Jared's unforgettable voice. Though it seemed impossible, he looked even better this morning wearing jeans and a soft gray T-shirt. Muscles rippled in his tanned arms and coarse dark hair accentuated every bulge and hollow.

"Hey, look who's here." Steph feigned surprise. Badly. "I don't think we caught your name last night. I'm Steph Knutsen." She thrust out her hand.

Jared shot her a crooked grin and took her hand in his. "Jared Carter," he said. "Pleased to meet you." Releasing her hand, he looked expectantly around the table.

Carter. Carson. Very smooth. Jared was lucky she'd attended college away from home so her family had never met him. Margo tried to avoid his gaze and turned her attention to Raquel. The woman's nostrils flared slightly, and her lips looked as if they'd been glued together. No doubt about it—Raquel Eastwood had some pretty strong feelings about Jared.

When no one else made an effort to introduce themselves, Steph took it upon herself to do so. Margo sighed, wondering how two sisters could be so different.

"This is Raquel Eastwood, our attorney," Steph said.

Raquel looked up and nodded, but made no effort to extend her hand.

"And this is my sister, Margo Riley."

"Margo. Nice name."

Margo mumbled something polite and allowed him to take her hand. The feel of his warm, rough skin against hers sent a jolt of awareness through her, flooding her mind with memories. Vivid memories. The things he'd done to her with those hands . . .

The interview, Margo. She had to remain focused on her assignment. Jared meant nothing to her—not anymore. She couldn't let him mean anything to her now. She was too vulnerable after losing Nick, though it had been two years. Two centuries probably wouldn't be enough. Besides, everything she and Jared shared had been destroyed forever. Even acknowledging that simple truth seemed disloyal to her dead husband. Guilt pressed down on her, hard and fast.

Jared released her hand and stiffened slightly. "Riley and Knutsen." He kept smiling, but the familiar twitch in his jaw revealed his internal struggle to hold his feelings tightly in check. "Guess one of you sisters must be married then."

"Margo's a widow," Steph supplied, earning a groan from Raquel.

Surprise registered in Jared's eyes. The expression he turned toward Margo was a blend of sympathy and astonishment, without a trace of the malice he'd once held for Nick.

"I'm sorry," he said, sounding sincere.

Tears scalded her eyes, but Margo blinked them into retreat. Sympathy from Jared was more than her raw emotions could take right now. Part of her wanted nothing more than to have a long talk with him, while another part of her wanted to run fast and hard. Facing Jared alone would resurrect it all—the pain, the joy, the hunger. And now, here he was expressing genuine sympathy about Nick's death.

Too much. She couldn't breathe. They were all staring at

her expectantly. Waiting. Somehow, she had to get away. She'd find another stripper to interview. Jared was too dangerous, too memorable.

Too desirable.

"Uh, I really have to get to the office. I have a million things to do today." Resisting the urge to sniffle, she pulled some bills from her blazer pocket and thrust them toward her sister. "This should cover my check. You all have a nice day, and thanks for inviting us to breakfast, Raquel."

Without looking at anyone or responding to Steph's objection, Margo slid from the booth and headed toward the back of the diner. The room was nothing but a blur of moving colors and shadows as she made her way toward the rest room. She was running away.

Damn straight.

And she would hide in the bathroom all day if she had to.

Whatever it takes.

The bathroom was blissfully empty, and Margo leaned her flushed cheek against the closed door. Sanctuary. Her breathing gradually calmed, and the tears ceased to threaten her composure. She blew her nose and splashed her face with cool water, then reapplied her powder and lipstick.

After running a comb through her hair, she stared at her reflection. Shame ebbed through her. Margo Knutsen Riley was not a coward.

Oh, yes I am.

No. No I'm not.

She drew a deep, fortifying breath. *Damn it, I am* not *a coward.* Later today, just before the Studfinder opened, she'd go find Jared and conduct the interview.

And face all her ghosts—past and present.

5

Nick Riley was dead. Jared jogged out to the Studfinder, trying to digest that shocking information. Unbelievable. He'd had no idea.

Margo was available.

He paused across the street from the nightclub, his breath catching. Talk about tacky. He didn't even know how long Nick had been gone, and here he was thinking about—

Past tense. Why would Margo want anything to do with someone in his insane career field—either his current fake one or his real one—not to mention someone her late husband had hated and that she believed had been unfaithful to her? With a sigh, Jared crossed the street.

He had to put Margo out of his mind, though he still needed to talk to her again to ensure she would keep his cover. The Margo he'd known would never break a promise, but they'd both changed a lot since college.

Knowing the other dancers wouldn't be there yet, Jared slipped into the dressing room and ran his usual search, coming up empty-handed—again. So far, he'd seen no proof of drugs coming into or out of this establishment, though he needed to get back into the office again and check out the computer. The muckety-mucks had been sure enough to set up this crazy assignment. All Jared could do was keep his eyes open for anything unusual.

Besides local police interference.

He shook his head, still pondering Charlie's words of assurance last night. They'd sounded weak. Uncertain. If the Studfinder really was a front for a drug cartel, and Jared's cover was blown, his ass was toast.

The door behind him squeaked open, and Jared slid between two lockers, waiting to identify the intruder. None of the dancers had a reason to be here this early. The only other living thing around this time of day was the resident cat. If the owner caught him, he'd come up with some kind of excuse, but not being discovered at all was an even better idea.

He held his breath as the person emerged from the dark hall. *Margo.* Alone, she stood peering around, waiting. She was looking for him—why else would she be here?

Jared stepped from his hiding place and just stared. All the feelings he'd carried in his heart for so many years punched him in the solar plexus. It was a miracle he could remain standing at all. For a few miserable moments, he couldn't even draw a decent breath.

She started toward him, and he dragged in a shaky breath, preparing himself. Seeing Margo again was amazing. And agonizing. *Damn.* There'd never been anyone else for him—never would be.

"We need to talk," she said quietly.

She'd been crying. Over Nick. Jared gritted his teeth and nodded. "Not here."

"Fine." She cleared her throat. "My office is only—"

"Not there. Too public." He gripped her elbow and steered her toward the side entrance. "Do you have your car?"

"Yes, but—"

"Let's just get out of here first." He struggled against the urge to stop and pull her into his arms, to murmur words of love and comfort, to kiss her until they both forgot everything that had happened since the last time they'd kissed. "Then we'll talk."

She remained silent but managed to free her arm. Without looking over her shoulder, she marched toward a red BMW with a vanity plate that read LOVENICK.

Perfect. Just frigging perfect. She punched her remote and the locks clicked. Jared reached in front of her and opened her door. She glanced back at him, her eyes wide and filled with questions, her lips slightly parted and beckoning.

He cleared his throat and pressed his hand to the small of her back, urging her to enter the car before he did something stupid, like kiss her. Besides, the sooner they were away from the Studfinder, the safer he'd feel. Having Margo here, where she could be in danger if his cover was blown, made Jared nervous.

A nervous cop is a dangerous cop.

Remembering those words from his training didn't help put him at ease. Once she slid into the driver's seat, he slammed her door and hurried to the other side. Within seconds, he was in the posh leather interior, buckling his seat belt.

Margo locked the doors and started the engine, backed the car out of the parking space, and pulled toward the exit. The engine purred, the ride like skating on butter.

"Where are we going?" she asked.

"Your place."

"I don't think that's wise."

He looked at her. Big mistake. Trying to ignore the lick of lust that damned near made him groan aloud, he said, "You have questions for me, and my answers aren't for public consumption."

She set her lips in a thin line. "Very well, but this is just business."

"Whatever you say." He flashed her a grin, enjoying the leap of her pulse in the side of her neck and the color creeping upward from the neckline of her blouse. "Nice car." *Except for the license plate.*

"Nick bought it for me." She sighed.

And the vanity plate. Jared didn't want to talk about Nick, but they had to. Dead or not, Nick still lurked between them. He always would.

"I—I'm sorry, Margo." He waited a beat and bit his lower lip. "About Nick. I didn't know."

"You must not go back to Riley's Crossing very often." She turned the corner, keeping her gaze on the traffic, sparing Jared those devastating gray eyes of hers. "The whole town was in mourning."

Because Fred Riley still owns the place. "No, not once since college. My uncle moved to Florida—no reason to go back."

"That's right. You didn't have any other family."

You were the only family I wanted.

Margo stopped at a wrought iron gate and inserted a card. The gates swung open for her, and she drove into the complex. Posh condos sat in a parklike setting among immaculate gardens, fountains, and trails.

Jared kept expecting to see Nick Riley's gloating expression, and every time the thought struck, guilt answered.

Margo punched a button and a garage door opened. She steered the car inside, killed the engine, and lowered the door. Only a small light overhead dispelled the darkness. She punched yet another button on her handy remote and a brighter light filled the garage.

So, this is the good life. Nick had always known how to appreciate the finer things. "Nice place."

"It's all right." She opened her door and Jared unfolded himself from the passenger side.

"Just all right?" he asked over the roof of the car.

She lifted a shoulder. "Nick wanted this, but I wanted a little Victorian fixer-upper across town."

He met and held her gaze. "So move."

She looked nervous as she slammed the door. "No. Not yet anyway. This is fine."

She's not over Nick. Remembering the way she'd left the breakfast table this morning, why did that surprise him? Because he wanted her to be over Nick. *Damn.*

Jared followed her up a flight of stairs, where she keyed some numbers into a control panel and opened the door. They emerged into a huge kitchen where everything gleamed a blinding white, from the ceramic tile beneath their feet to the cabinets and appliances. The place was so contemporary it almost made his eyes ache. There was nothing homey about this kitchen.

Nothing Margo.

Surprised, he wondered what kind of kitchen would suit her. The Victorian she'd mentioned, of course. He could picture her surrounded by wood, some of it a bit scarred or distressed. Ruffled curtains, old-fashioned copper pots hanging from hooks, and friendly pottery sitting all over the place.

And if that wasn't the most unmanly thought Jared Carson had experienced in his adult life, he didn't know what was. He shook himself, banishing the image. DEA agents didn't think about kitchen decor. A smile curved his lips. Damned good thing no one could read his mind.

Margo turned on the flame beneath a white kettle. "Tea?" she asked over her shoulder.

"Sure." Jared never drank tea, but for Margo he'd have said yes to battery acid. She arranged white cups on a white tray with a white carafe. The white thing was really getting ridiculous.

A few minutes later, they were sitting at a small table off the kitchen that overlooked the fancy gardens below. Jared felt uncomfortable as hell. The tabletop was glass, and the base was wrought iron. White wrought iron . . .

He had to ask. "Is the whole place white?"

Margo smiled, and a distant expression flickered in her eyes. "Pretty much. Nick liked the sleek, modern look. He almost fainted when I mentioned painting one wall in the den red."

"I'll bet." The last thing in the world Jared wanted to discuss was anything about Nick, but he didn't want to rush Margo. He still had hours before he was due at the club. "Red, huh?" He managed a smile, just for her.

"Good *chi*." She laughed at herself and poured tea into both their cups. "Milk? White?"

"Uh . . . no. Just sugar. White." Not that Jared knew enough about tea to be sure of his answer. He liked black coffee with sugar, so tea was probably the same.

She leaned back in her chair and took a sip. "Well, I suppose we've delayed this long enough."

Jared met her gaze, hoping his eyes didn't reflect his churning emotions. "I suppose."

She set her cup down with a clatter, reaching out to steady it with both hands. They trembled, making the china clatter even more. Finally, she bit her lip and clutched her hands together on the glass surface. "I'm sorry."

"Nothing for you to be sorry about." He took a sip of tea and remembered immediately why he was a coffee drinker. He set the cup aside, congratulating himself for not shuddering.

Until he saw Margo's hands on the table. Unable to stop himself, he reached over and covered her hand with his own. She flinched slightly, and her eyes widened. A moment later, she blinked and turned her palm upward, into his.

"It really is good to see you again." Her voice trembled a little. "You look well."

"You look ravishing." He followed the comment with a smile, hoping he wouldn't scare her away. This Margo seemed uncertain and frightened, very unlike the self-assured, loving young woman she had been in his arms.

Had Nick done this to her? No. He shoved the thought aside. Nick Riley had been selfish and competitive, but he never would have harmed Margo—at least, not physically.

It felt good to hold her hand. He wanted to do a lot more but sensed that Margo wasn't ready. Meeting her gaze, he had to wonder if she'd ever be ready.

"I really am sorry about Nick." He gave her hand a

squeeze. "There wasn't any love lost between us, but he sure didn't deserve to die so damn young."

She released a breath as if she'd been holding it. "Thanks for that. I wasn't sure . . ."

"How I would react to the news?" He shook his head. "You know me better than that, Margo."

She lowered her gaze for a moment, then looked right at him. "Yes, I do. And last night's performance was definitely out of character." A gleam entered her eyes, and she pulled her hand out from under his. "Do you mind if I tape our interview?"

"Our what?"

She rose and grabbed a leather briefcase beneath the breakfast bar. "Interview," she repeated. "Did you forget?" She withdrew a small recorder and a notebook, then returned to her seat. "You owe me. Remember?"

So much for her being frightened and uncertain, Carson. "Is this a defense mechanism?" he asked, quirking one corner of his mouth upward.

"Is what a defense mechanism?" She gave him a confused look.

"The Lois Lane treatment."

"Ha-ha." Margo grimaced and arranged the tools of her trade. "So can I record the inter—"

"No." His answer came out harsher than he'd intended. "Sorry, but . . ." Hell, now he was the nervous one. He raked his fingers through his hair and released a breath in a whoosh. "Margo, this has to be off the record. I promised you an explanation, but I have to make sure you won't blow my cover first."

"Cover?"

He saw reporter instincts flashing behind her baby grays. "*Off* the record, Margo."

She held his gaze for a few moments, then popped the cassette out of the recorder. "All right, off the record for now, as long as you give me something for my article."

"What's your topic?"

She rolled her eyes and sighed. "My editor's brilliant idea for a human interest piece."

"Uh, okay." He lifted one shoulder. "What human interest piece?"

Margo's eyes danced with mischief, and she waggled her brows. "What would make an intelligent man resort to bump and grind as a career? Basically."

Heat flooded Jared's face. "Not by choice."

"If we aren't taping this, we might as well talk in the den."

With her notepad and pencil in hand, she led him into a room with white walls, white pleated shades, gleaming white-and-glass tables, and white leather furniture. *Weird.*

She sat on the couch, and he sat beside her. All right, so he probably should've taken the chair across from her, but the urge to sit beside her had stolen his common sense. "What do you want to know?"

Clearing her throat, she set her notepad and pencil on the glass-topped coffee table, then half turned to face him. "Before we get to my interview, I want to cover the off-the-record stuff. Why are you pretending to be an erotic dancer?"

A grin tugged at his lips. "Pretending? Does that mean I'm not any good at it?" He pressed the flat of his palm against his chest. "I'm wounded."

"Male ego aside . . ." Her expression was serious. "Why, Jared?"

"It stays between us?"

She crossed her heart, right between her lovely breasts. Jared's gaze followed her movement, riveted to the outline of her nipples showing through her thin sweater. The heat that had filled his face earlier now did an about-face and settled one hell of a lot lower.

"Why?" she repeated, her voice low but intense.

"I work for DEA." He held her gaze, watching for any sign of a reaction. "I'm undercover."

"The cover was pretty skimpy from what I saw last night."

He held his head in his hands. "If I'd realized anyone would recognize me, I can guarantee you I wouldn't have taken this assignment."

"I'm sure. But you had a background in Broadway jazz from college, and the, uh, body to pull it off, so . . ."

Margo's giggle crawled into a special corner of Jared's heart—one that had missed her more than any person in his life. He still cared about her.

No, he still loved her.

Admitting that to himself left him breathless for a few miserable moments. Logic intervened, reminding him that it didn't matter how he felt—she'd married Nick and still mourned him. *End of fantasy.*

"I always knew you wanted to go into law enforcement, but DEA?"

He lifted a shoulder. "Just gullible, I guess."

"Very funny." Her expression grew serious again. "So . . . DEA thinks someone at the Studfinder is dealing drugs?"

"We're still off the record?" Jared directed his most solemn gaze toward her. "If my cover is blown, I could be in danger. I don't think you want that."

Fear flickered in her eyes. "No. Of course not."

The sight of her tongue sweeping across her lower lip sent Jared's blood supply down and dirty in record time. She still turned him on, but that was the least of his problems. The fact that he still loved her was considerably more dangerous than his libido.

"Yes, we have reason to believe the Studfinder might be a front for distribution. I lost the toss." He smiled, hoping to ease the fear he'd planted in her eyes.

"It sounds dangerous."

"Not if I'm careful." He struggled against the urge to pull her into his arms. "And I intend to be careful."

"All right." She released a shaky breath. "I'll keep your identity and your role a secret, if you'll give me the dancer interview my boss wants."

"But I'm not really a dancer." Jared flashed her a grin, enjoying the crimson flush that crept up her neck and bloomed in her cheeks.

"You looked like one last night." Her answering grin almost drove him to his knees. "I don't think you'd get any argument from the rest of your admirers in the audience."

"All right, now you've done it." He chuckled and shook his head. "I'm embarrassed. Are you happy?"

She grew sober and reached for her notepad with trembling fingers, but she knocked it to the floor instead. He reached for it at the same time she did, and they bumped foreheads.

Before he could draw his next breath, he pulled Margo

to her feet and covered her lips with his. A tremor trickled through her body, and he feared she might pull away, but instead she molded herself against him, parting her lips for his.

Oh, God. He never should've let this happen, because he'd forgotten how sweet she tasted. Memories swirled through him of the first time they'd made love, augmenting his desire even further. He pressed his hand to the small of her back and laced the other through the silky hair at the nape of her neck.

This was Margo—not a dream. Hungry for her, he deepened their kiss, swallowing her moan with an answering growl that came from a place he'd believed no longer existed. When he'd lost Margo, he'd buried a part of himself. Now that neglected part of him clamored for release.

The vault where he'd locked these feelings away cracked open a tiny bit. Even that small portion of emotions long denied were potent enough to make him crazy.

He wanted her. Needed her. Loved her.

This was so right. The years fell away. He kissed the corner of her mouth, her cheek, her jaw.

"Jared," she whispered, and he kissed her mouth again.

"Hey, sis, what—"

Margo jerked herself free of Jared's embrace, her face flushed, her breathing labored. "Steph, what are—"

A tall redhead stepped from behind Margo's sister. Jared met Raquel Eastwood's gaze.

And saw murder in her eyes.

6

Margo straightened her skirt and drew a desperate breath. When had she stopped breathing? And why? She was single. So what if her sister and a virtual stranger had just caught her kissing an equally single man? Big deal. Nothing wrong with that picture.

Then why did she feel like crawling under the nearest rock? *Nick is dead.* She struggled for another breath, and though logic demanded she accept her husband's death and his rivalry with Jared, she couldn't. *Traitor.*

Steph extended the key card that had belonged to Nick toward her. "Want this back?" She flashed her a sheepish grin. "Sorry."

"Don't be silly." Margo cleared her throat and noticed the fury glittering in Raquel Eastwood's eyes. Why would she be angry about this? It made no sense at all. Of course, Raquel's early morning breakfast invitation hadn't either.

"Looks like we arrived just in time," Raquel said, her voice sounding deeper than it had before.

"That's a matter of opinion," Jared said quietly.

Raquel took a step toward him. "Yeah. Mine."

"What the—" Steph looked from Raquel to Jared, then back again. "You may be tall, but I think Jared could take you with one hand. Besides, what's it to you?" As usual, Steph had the courage to voice Margo's thoughts.

"I'm interviewing Jared for an article." Margo retrieved her notepad and pencil, as if she needed proof. *Ridiculous.*

"Sorry for interrupting." Raquel's apology came through gritted teeth and was clearly not genuine. However, at least she'd unclenched her fists.

"Interview, huh?" Steph's eyes twinkled, and she waggled her eyebrows suggestively. "Raquel needed a ride to the office, and I remembered I need to borrow your purple dress, so . . ." She shrugged, still smiling.

Margo would never hear the end of this one.

"I'll get the dress."

"I'll help you."

Margo hurried into the bedroom she'd shared with Nick, which augmented her guilt. She hadn't kissed a man since his death, and the first one had to be the one who would have hurt him the most.

Steph came in behind her and put her hand on her shoulder. "Don't you dare feel bad about kissing that sexy hunk of man. It's about time you—"

"Don't, Steph." Margo drew a shaky breath, reeling in her emotions. She turned and faced her sister. "There's—a lot more to this, and I can't go into it with you right now."

"Oooookay." Steph gave her a quick hug, then flung open Margo's closet. "I'm starting to wonder about Raquel."

"Starting to?" Margo shook her head. "She's very strange."

Steph retrieved the purple dress in question and draped it over her shoulder. "She was the one who mentioned we were passing right by your place."

"How . . ." Margo paused to contemplate that. "She probably saw my address at the office or something. Or maybe from the police station last night."

"Maybe."

Why didn't it seem that simple to Margo? Because Raquel had shown an inordinately strong interest in *her*. That made it personal.

"You thinking what I'm thinking?" Steph tilted her head, her expression contemplative. "I'm sure she'll take no for an answer."

Margo would've bought her sister's sincerity, if not for the gleam in Steph's eye as she grabbed the doorknob.

"You're rotten," she muttered to her sister's retreating back.

"I love you, too, sis." Steph giggled all the way back to the den.

Raquel and Jared were still in neutral corners. At least that was something.

"C'mon, Raquel, let's give these two some privacy."

"I'm not sure that's wise," Raquel said, her murderous gaze still on Jared. "After all, Margo is still in mourning."

Steph coughed and grabbed Raquel by the elbow. "Hon, Nick was a really cool guy, but it's been two years. Life goes on."

Raquel paused at the door and faced Margo. The glower she'd directed at Jared was gone. Now the expression in the redhead's mascara'd eyes could only be described as sad. Rejected? *Get a grip, Margo.*

"I see you kept the painting," Raquel said quietly as she shifted her gaze from Margo to the painting in the entryway.

Before Margo could ask the woman how she knew about the painting Nick had purchased while on their honeymoon, Steph had dragged Raquel Eastwood out the front door.

"That was . . . interesting," Jared said.

"More than you can possibly imagine." Margo turned slowly to find that he looked as bewildered as she felt.

"Yes, interesting is one way of putting it." Crazy would've been more accurate. Had Raquel been here before? Ridiculous. After giving herself a mental shake, she grabbed her notebook and pencil again. "Now, where were we?"

Jared touched her shoulder, gently turning her to face him. "Don't you remember?" He took a step nearer, his warmth closing the short distance between them as he cupped her face in both hands and brushed his lips across hers.

Her knees quaked, and her heart pressed upward against her throat. She still wanted this man with the same intensity she had in college. He had the ability to reduce her to little more than crazed hormones with no effort at all. Problem was he seemed hell-bent on exerting a *lot* of effort.

She was in serious trouble.

"Jared . . ." A simple whisper shouldn't have ignited the flame in his eyes she saw now. He obviously knew her resistance to his charms was practically nonexistent. "I . . . we can't do this."

"Oh, I definitely *can*." He exhaled very slowly, resting his forehead against hers. "But I'm a gentleman. Remember?"

"Yes." Margo swallowed hard, and wished more than a little that Jared Carson would forget he was a gentleman, and that she could stop feeling as if she were betraying her dead husband. "Back to our interview."

Margo sat in a chair across the room from Jared this time, and he took the couch. Alone. *Better this way. Really.*

"I can't tell you much about the life of an exotic dancer, since I'm really not one." He held his hands palms up.

"Looks like a duck . . ."

"Cute."

"I thought so." She scribbled down a few comments.

"What are you writing? I haven't said anything yet."

"Just that the subject seems ashamed of his chosen profession. Embarrassed."

"You can say that again."

"Once will suffice." Warmed to her subject, Margo scribbled more notes.

"Just a thought . . ."

She looked up, trying to ignore how delicious he looked sitting on her couch. "What?"

"Aren't you doing the real dancers a disservice?"

"How?"

"By putting my embarrassment in the article. Maybe some of these guys *like* this job."

"Oh." What had she been thinking? Very unprofessional—and very unlike her. "You're right. I can't do it this way. I'll have to go back to the Studfinder and—"

"No." Jared stood, shoving his hands into his pockets. "Please?"

"Don't want me to see you wiggle up there again?" She grinned but could tell he was serious. "Jared, I have a job to do here."

"Tell me what you want to know from the other dancers, and I'll ask them."

She studied his expression, the worry in his intensely blue eyes, and almost surrendered. "Look, as you pointed out, I've already almost blown this assignment." She stood, tossing her notepad onto the coffee table. "If I'm going to write this story, I'm going to do it right. That means interviewing a real dancer. Lakeview only has one Studfinder."

He rolled his eyes heavenward and sighed. "The real Margo Knutsen has returned."

Stunned, she waited for him to meet her gaze again. "What's that supposed to mean?"

His eyes softened. "I didn't mean to insult you, but you haven't exactly been yourself." One corner of his mouth quirked upward. "Except for when I kissed you."

Her cheeks flamed, and she cleared her throat. "I . . . well . . . It's been hard. Losing Nick and all."

"I know." He sighed and walked around the coffee table. "Come here."

Margo hesitated, but she saw compassion in his eyes instead of lust. Between two beats of her heart, she found her head nestled beneath Jared's chin and his strong arms wrapped comfortably around her shoulders. He made no attempt to kiss her this time.

And that made her want him even more.

*   *   *

"I don't believe this." Nick kicked off his high heels and put his feet on his desk. Who cared if the hem of his skirt slid all the way up to the crotch of his—God save him— panty hose? To make things even worse, this really had been his desk, once upon a time.

"Séamus, I just want to know one thing."

"What is it this time, Nicholas?"

"Were you a sadist when you were still alive?"

"I know you don't mean that. You're just upset."

"Noooooo. What was your first clue?" Nick raked his slut-red fingernails through his hair. "I told you I'd find her someone else."

"Jared is Margo's destiny. It's not your place to—"

"Not my place?" Nick stood, wishing he had pockets to ram his fists into. Wishing his punching bag was still hanging in the corner. He'd draw Séamus's face on it and take out his frustrations.

"How thoughtful."

Nick scowled up at the ceiling, then closed his eyes, resignation coiling through him with all the ease of a rattlesnake. *Margo's destiny, my ass.* He clenched his fists, struggling against the urge to put his fist through the wall.

"Do you have any idea how it felt to—" He bit back what threatened to become a sob. Nick Riley didn't blubber, but as Raquel . . .

"It's hard, Nick. I knew it would be."

"But you sent me here anyway, knowing *he* was the one?"

"Remember, this order came from higher up the chain of command."

Nick barked a derisive laugh. "So God really is that cruel?"

"You have to figure it all out for yourself, Nick. Have you ever really loved anyone but yourself?"

"That's bull. I loved Margo. I married her, didn't I?"

"But you didn't love her the way a man loves the woman he's meant to spend his life with. Did you?"

"I . . . hell." He punched his fist into the palm of his other hand. "Just hell."

"I think you're starting to see the truth, though you don't like it now."

"*Now?* You think I'll ever *like* seeing Jared Carson manhandle my *wife*?"

"Widow. And what I think isn't important, but you will come to accept what must be. And perhaps you shouldn't carry your father's secret to your grave either. Maybe it's time to learn something about sacrifice."

Nick dropped his gaze to the floor, scowling at the runner in the toe of his hose. A soggy tear landed on it, as if to punctuate this entire sordid mess.

"If I accept what you call destiny"—he drew a shaky breath and forced the words—"that means I also have to accept that Margo was never really . . . mine."

Only silence answered him, but he knew. His rivalry with Jared Carson and his marriage to Margo were the reasons he hadn't made it all the way into Heaven. He was dead, dammit. Margo wasn't. His mission was to see her happy for the rest of *her* life. But why the hell did that have to make Jared happy for the rest of *his* life, too?

Sacrifice . . . Nick pulled a sheet of stationery from the drawer and scribbled a short note—words he'd buried deep and sworn he would never reveal. Even so, one of the things he'd regretted after his death was taking this knowledge with him, instead of leaving it here for those it affected.

He stared down at the written words, reached for the sheet, fully intending to rip it to shreds. *Sacrifice. Truth.* Instead of tearing it, he swallowed hard and drew a deep breath. The date he wrote at the top of the page was from the week before his death, two years ago. He signed *Nick* at the bottom.

Seeing his real name in his own hand again gave him pause. He'd made so many mistakes—had so many regrets. Maybe Séamus had a few points. Maybe. This one was easier than Margo. He folded the sheet and sealed it in an envelope. Very neatly, he wrote a name across the front and slid it to the back of his top desk drawer. Someone would find it when Raquel was gone and think it had been missed after Nick's death.

The receptionist's voice scratched over the intercom. "Henry Millman on one, Ms. Eastwood."

"What does that son of a bitch want?"

"Are we having PMS?" the old woman asked, her voice dripping sarcasm.

"Eat sh—" Nick clenched his teeth, rather than complete that remark. "I dunno. Maybe. Fine, thanks. I'll take the call."

Nick blew his nose, dabbed the tears from his eyes, grabbed the phone, and punched line one. After he reiterated his refusal to accept the owner of the Studfinder as a client, Nick hung up the receiver. That snake made the need for sexual harassment laws way too frigging personal.

Someone knocked and simultaneously opened Nick's office door. Mrs. Brown, the firm's loyal receptionist, who'd adored Margo and hated Nick in his natural life, entered with a small brown paper bag. The little, gray-haired woman pulled a gigantic chocolate bar from the bag and slapped it into Nick's hand.

"I ran downstairs to the drugstore. This first, to sweeten your mood," she said. "We've never had a female attorney in the office, and I'm, well, beyond all this."

Nick blinked, staring at the bar and back to Mrs. Brown. "But . . ." She'd never given *him* chocolate.

The woman made an annoying tsking sound with her tongue and removed two more items. "Evening primrose for your PMS." She slapped the pill bottle down on the desk and removed two small boxes—one of tampons and one of maxi pads. "And these for later."

Nick sputtered, unable to contemplate the horror of what she'd just proposed. He stared at the diagram on the side of the tampon box. *No way. Not even Séamus would . . .*

"You'll feel better soon," Mrs. Brown said. "Take the primrose. Start now." She opened the bottle, then pulled a slip of paper out of her pocket. "And a phone message from Steph Knutsen." Mrs. Brown moved to the office door.

"Wait." Nick sniffled and tore open the chocolate. "Thank you. I think."

"You don't know it yet, but you already did, dear."

Dear? He shifted the glob of soothing chocolate to one side of his mouth. "I did?"

"Steph included me in her invitation." Mrs. Brown flashed a wicked grin and left the room.

Nick grabbed the phone message and simultaneously bit off another chunk of chocolate. Maybe there really was some truth to that serotonin business. He felt better already.

Raquel, meet us at the Studfinder around seven. Margo's on assignment and we may need our attorney. Bring Mrs. Brown. A smiley face was drawn at the end.

"Oh, my God." Nick Riley was going to watch male strippers. Revulsion slithered through him, until he remembered that Jared Carson was a main attraction.

He broke off another chunk of chocolate, liking the idea of watching old Jar-O humiliate himself. If only Jared Carson knew who Raquel really was, that could make it all the more satisfying.

"Get serious." He dropped the unopened boxes into the wastebasket and looked at the digital clock on his desk. It was too early to call it a day, but he didn't have any appointments. Besides, he didn't feel like himself. Well, even less than usual since his new appearance. Maybe Mrs. Brown was right about the PMS.

Heaven forbid.

He almost laughed. "I know what I'm gonna do to lift my spirits." He'd have Raquel's long red hair cropped off into something more manageable. And get rid of these manicured claws, too. The more he contemplated it, the more he liked the idea.

He pulled a pair of fingernail clippers from his desk drawer—right where he'd always kept them—and rendered Raquel's red nails into nice, neat stubs. He'd have to ask Mrs. Brown what women used to remove this gunk.

Then he went into the bathroom and scrubbed off the makeup. When he looked in the mirror again, he noticed something for the first time since this journey into never-never land.

Raquel had Nick's eyes. Behind all that eyeliner and mascara, he hadn't noticed. Maybe if he'd actually washed it off at night like the instructions said, he would've realized sooner.

"I'll be damned." Maybe the eyes really were windows to the soul. Séamus might have changed Nick's body, but he hadn't changed his eyes or his handwriting. Even Mrs. Brown had commented how much Raquel's handwriting resembled Nick's. Knowing that part of him was still here made him feel better than he had since his arrival back on Earth.

Well, for a few moments he felt better. After using the facilities, he marched back into his office and retrieved the box of maxi pads from the wastebasket. He slammed the bathroom door behind him, tore open the box and read the directions.

"Thanks a lot, Séamus."

7

Jared had a hunch, and he didn't like hunches. He liked facts. Hard evidence.

A local big shot named Henry Millman owned the Studfinder, along with at least a dozen other small businesses in the county. In the two weeks since Jared had started this assignment, tonight was the first time Millman had put in an appearance. Why tonight? And had last night's futile drug raid been timed accordingly?

The rotund, cigar-smoking owner strutted through the dressing room about half an hour before showtime. He made a few ribald comments about entertaining women, not giving any dancer more than a cursory nod, except one.

Millman directed a glare of suspicion that shot right through Jared. He'd seen that look before. The asshole knew something—or at least suspected it.

Jared forced himself to return to the task of closing all the Velcro tabs on his costume, ignoring his sweaty palms and the alarm bouncing through his brain.

Something big was going down tonight. He felt it. Smelled it.

And Margo would be in the audience.

"Damn."

"What's up?" the dancer with the locker next to Jared's asked. His Tarzan performance opened every night. "Tough day?"

Jared searched his gray matter for Tarzan's real name,

and came up blank. "I was just noticing the fat guy." He slid a glance toward Millman, who was now deep in conversation with his emcee. At least he wasn't watching Jared anymore. "He's the owner. Right?"

"Yep. That's the big man himself." Tarzan tucked something that looked like a rolled sock into his G-string. "Padding the fantasies."

Jared managed a chuckle and patted himself on the back for not cringing. "I was just curious. Haven't seen him here before."

"Oh, he comes in around the first of every month." Tarzan pulled his loincloth on and fastened the Velcro. "He never watches the show, though—spends all his time back here doing something in the office."

"Hmm. Seems like he could hire somebody to do his payroll." Jared lifted a shoulder, feigning disinterest. "Tightwad, eh?"

Tarzan rubbed oil across his shaved chest. "I figure the Studfinder is a tax shelter or something."

Or something. Jared had to find a way to get into that office. Tonight. "Anybody ever meet him here?"

Tarzan didn't seem suspicious of all the questions. He appeared thoughtful for a moment, then nodded. "Yeah, come to think of it, I've seen a tall bald guy with him a few times."

Bald guy? The acid level in Jared's gut hit nuclear. His contact with the local P.D. was tall and bald. "Seems an odd choice for a bookkeeper."

"Or a boyfriend." Tarzan chuckled. "Millman could probably take his pick in here, being the boss and all."

Jared coughed. Well, Millman couldn't have his pick of *every* one.

"That bald guy is one scrawny sumbitch, too."

That did it. Charlie. The tall, scrawny, bald guy had to be Jared's link to the local police. That raid the other night had been arranged to rattle Jared. Charlie was obviously on the take, and Jared was in deep shit.

His blood turned frigid, and his breath caught and held. Fear shot through him. For Margo.

"Break a leg." Tarzan flexed his muscles and headed toward the stage door.

"Yeah." Trying not to stare at the small door at the end

of the dressing room through which Henry Millman had disappeared, Jared headed for the bathroom and made a call on his encrypted cell phone. Within a few moments, he'd notified his boss about his suspicions. By the time he took the stage tonight there would be three more agents on site, and more on the way. Turned out the feds already had Millman under investigation for various financial dealings. This case could be wrapped up a lot faster than anyone had hoped.

A few moments later, he stashed his phone and took his place in line with the other Eroticops. With any luck, this would be his last performance. He was more than ready to hang up his G-string.

Jared Carson had other things on his mind now. He couldn't deny the truth. From the first moment he'd seen Margo sitting in the audience, he'd known. This was destiny or fate or whatever. He would pursue her as he should have before she ever married Nick. He should have swallowed his pride back in college and told her he was sorry, that he loved her and wanted to spend his life with her. Loving her.

Then he would leave his life with the DEA and pursue his original career goal of small-town law enforcement. He wanted to buy Margo her old Victorian fixer-upper and to make babies with her. Lots of babies.

He wouldn't take no for an answer either. Not because he was a jerk, but because he'd felt her response. He'd seen love in her eyes, in her smile, and had tasted it in her kiss. They belonged together, and they always had.

If only Nick . . . Jared released a slow breath. No, he couldn't blame Nick any longer. Losing Margo had been as much Jared's fault as anybody's. Nick was dead, and Jared planned to let him rest in peace. Their old rivalry had been stupid when Nick was alive, and continuing it after his death was doubly stupid.

Margo mattered. The future mattered.

He heard Tarzan's yell and barely suppressed a shudder. *Damn.*

Margo and Steph occupied the same table they had last time—center stage. Except, this time, Margo wasn't a bit reluctant to watch the dancers, knowing that very soon Jared would be there.

She couldn't stop thinking about that kiss. Everything he'd meant to her in the past had come flooding back as if they hadn't been apart all these years. As if Nick . . .

No. She wouldn't think about Nick now.

"I wonder what's keeping Raquel and Mrs. Brown," Steph said as she slid a drink across the table toward Margo.

"I'm still trying to figure out why you invited her here tonight." Margo wasn't looking forward to seeing the unusual woman again so soon.

"I called to invite Mrs. Brown, and she said Raquel had PMS and would probably enjoy it." Steph grinned and waggled her eyebrows.

"Hmm." Margo glanced at her watch again. "Maybe they changed their minds about coming."

"Mrs. Brown said Raquel had a hair appointment. I guess those gorgeous locks take longer."

"What gorgeous locks?" Margo stared past her sister as Mrs. Brown and a very different version of Raquel approached the table between sets.

Steph looked over her shoulder, then turned her wide-eyed stare on Margo. "Yikes! She got scalped."

A more subdued Raquel slid into the empty chair next to Mrs. Brown. Raquel wore jeans, a blue sweater, and very little, if any, makeup. Her flaming hair curled around her face. She didn't look a thing like the fancy woman she'd been this morning.

"Look what she did, just because of a little PMS." Mrs. Brown kept looking at Raquel and shaking her head. "Shame. What a shame. Such beautiful hair."

"I donated it to a charity that makes wigs for kids on chemo." Raquel caught their server and ordered a Glenfiddich single malt scotch. "I don't miss that mop a bit."

Nick's favorite label . . . Margo shook off the memory of Nick and smiled. "I think donating your hair to charity was a very nice thing to do."

Raquel shrugged and her cheeks pinkened. "I hope they put it to good use."

"You missed Tarzan," Steph told Mrs. Brown. "But the Eroticops are next, and they are to die for."

Especially one of them. Margo had to stop mooning around about Jared and concentrate on her job. Tonight, her notes would make sense, and Jared had promised to find a likely dancer for her to interview.

"So, Margo, what did old Fred want when he called earlier?"

"Just letting me know he's passing through town tomorrow and wants to have lunch." Margo drew a deep breath. Her father-in-law had never been particularly fond of her—especially after Nick decided to settle in her hometown instead of returning to Riley's Crossing. "He doesn't have any other family with Nick gone."

Raquel made a choking sound, and Steph patted her on the back. All the color had drained from Raquel's face.

"Are you all right?" Margo asked.

A pained expression crossed the redhead's face. "Yeah, sure. Why wouldn't I be?" The server delivered her drink, and Raquel ordered another before she took her first sip. "I, uh, take it you were talking about your father-in-law?"

"Yes, exactly." But how did Raquel know that? "Nick was his only son, and I think he's lonely. He misses him."

"Will minor miracles never cease?" Raquel downed the scotch with one smooth flick of her wrist.

"Do you know Fred Riley?" Steph asked, not bothering to hide her curiosity.

"I'm not sure I ever really knew him at all." Raquel rested her chin on her fist, her expression wistful. "I, well, never mind. We're here to have fun. Right?"

Talk about avoidance. Did Raquel know Nick's father or not? Margo exchanged glances with her sister, knowing Steph was also confused by the ambiguous answer. And how had Raquel known about the painting, or where Margo lived?

"Did . . . did you know my husband?" she asked, uncertain how or why the question had left her lips.

"I . . ." Raquel's gaze shifted around the table. "Yes, yes, I know—er, knew—Nick."

"I thought you just moved here," Steph said.

"I lived here until two years ago, but now I'm back." Raquel flashed a nervous smile.

Two years ago? Raquel had left town about the time Nick died. She studied the woman's guilty expression, and a sinking sensation struck.

No. She couldn't accept that. Nick had never given her reason to believe he was unfaithful.

The lights and sirens signaled the beginning of the next act, and the crowd went wild, forcing Margo to shove her suspicions aside. Nick was dead, and thinking ill of him was wrong. Still, how did Raquel know so much?

Once the dancers entered the stage, Mrs. Brown leapt to her feet and gave a wolf whistle that would have put the most sexist construction worker to shame.

Steph laughed, and Margo turned her attention to Jared. He was dancing for her again—now she knew that for certain. No one else in the room knew his real identity, or why he meant so much to her. Tears scalded her eyes, but she blinked the liquid traitors away, focusing instead on holding Jared's gaze.

Watching him reminded her again of his kiss. Her body softened and heated, hungry for him. And why shouldn't she indulge her desire? After all, she was single, and it wasn't as if Jared was a stranger. He'd been her first lover. Her first *love*.

Her only love?

Guilt shoved its ugly face to the forefront of her mind again. If any other man had attracted her attention, would she feel this way? The answer came swiftly—a resounding *no*.

Oh, but she had loved him. And . . . she still did. Her heart raced ahead as she gathered that knowledge about her like a protective cloak. She wanted to invite Jared home with her tonight. Could she find the courage? And could she forget the past enough to think of a future with him?

Nothing ventured . . . A smile curved her lips, and she blew Jared a kiss before she lost her resolve.

"Well, isn't that special?" Raquel muttered.

Margo girded herself and faced Raquel. A myriad of emotions danced in the woman's eyes—regret, sadness, and something more.

"He's Margo's," Steph told Mrs. Brown.

"Lucky girl!" Mrs. Brown laughed. "If my hormones were thirty years younger, I'd give you a little competition."

Raquel extended her glass toward Margo, her eyes misty. "I wish you the best in every . . . way." Her voice broke, and she drew a shaky breath.

"Thank you." Margo wasn't sure what else to say. Why did this strange woman's words mean so much? Why was Margo relieved to hear her say them? It was almost as if she needed Raquel's approval to seduce Jared. *Ridiculous.*

Of course, what Margo really wanted with Jared was a lot more than merely a night of sex. Her face flamed, and her heart did a pirouette.

Nick is dead, Margo. She didn't need anyone's permission to do whatever she wanted with Jared or any other man. She'd been a good wife to Nick. Hadn't she? Wouldn't he forgive her now, knowing she was still in love with Jared?

No, probably not. Though she'd loved Nick in her own way, she hadn't been blind to his faults. He'd been pretty self-centered, and competitive to the extreme. She sighed. Especially with Jared.

Somehow, she had to come to terms with all this, because she couldn't let Jared just walk out of her life again. She needed this—needed him—in her life.

Give me strength.

Determined, she turned her attention back to the stage, watching Jared do things with his hips that set her insides ablaze. She bit her lower lip and sighed.

"Ooops."

Margo glanced over to find Steph shoving napkins toward Raquel, who had spilled her drink.

When Margo met Raquel's gaze, a jolt went through her. The woman's eyes had disturbed her before, and now she knew why. Without all the makeup, Raquel's eyes were just like Nick's.

Impossible.

Raquel's expression grew solemn, and she gave Margo a sheepish grin as she pushed to her feet. "Be right back." Raquel left the table to weave her way toward the rest rooms.

"She's wearing *sneakers*," Steph said. "Amazing transformation. Kind of like a butterfly in reverse."

"PMS." Mrs. Brown sipped her tropical beverage, her gaze never leaving the stage. "Can I take one of them home with me?"

Steph laughed. "Now, what would Mr. Brown think of that?"

"He won't care. He's been dead ten years."

He won't care. He's been dead . . . Mrs. Brown's words echoed through Margo's brain. She was alive. She had a right to lead a happy and fulfilled life.

With anyone she pleased.

Would Nick's ghost always lurk between them? Would his memory always create this surge of guilt in Margo's heart and mind? Did Jared feel guilty about Nick?

And who the hell was Raquel Eastwood?

Deciding to focus on the present for now, she looked at the stage again. The set ended, and Jared blew Margo a kiss as he followed the other dancers offstage. Somehow, she would find a way to come to terms with everything.

Right now, though, Margo had to find out why and *how* Raquel Eastwood had looked at her with her late husband's eyes. And how she knew so many things about him.

"Running to the rest room." Without giving her sister a chance to respond, Margo rose and made her way through the crowd on wooden legs. Had she lost her mind? This was crazy—whatever *this* was.

Reincarnation? Margo didn't know much about such things, but it seemed to her that people weren't reincarnated back into the same lifetime they'd left. Were they? Wouldn't that disrupt the space/time continuum? Or something?

Gibberish. She squared her shoulders and turned down the dark hallway leading to the rest rooms. A movement at the end of the hallway caught her attention—another door opening and a redheaded woman slipping through it.

Margo didn't hesitate. She shoved open the same door and realized it was some kind of storage area, with another door leading outside. What was Raquel doing back here?

"Come on, Séamus," Raquel said to the stacks of boxes. "Cut me some slack here. She's on to me."

Was Raquel talking to herself? "Who's Séamus? And who's on to you?"

Raquel slowly turned to face Margo. She drew a deep breath and held her hands out at her sides, palms up. "He's . . . an angel."

Margo looked around the deserted room again, her heart pounding so loudly in her ears she could barely hear anything else. "Your . . . guardian angel?"

"I guess you could say that, with the emphasis on *guard*. Never gives me a moment's peace."

"Who *are* you?"

Raquel stared at Margo for several seconds. "I think you know."

Margo shook her head. "No, I don't." She backed toward the door. This was insane. "You have Nick's eyes, and you know things Nick knew. But he's dead."

Raquel nodded, and resignation filled her expression. "And he's going to stay that way."

"Who are you?" Margo repeated, reaching behind her for the doorknob.

"Séamus, let me be myself now." Raquel glanced toward the ceiling. "Please?"

Margo needed air, and Raquel needed a good psychologist. "I'm going back to watch the show now," she said carefully, not wanting to upset Raquel. "How about you?"

Raquel just stood there, staring at Margo, taunting her with her dead husband's eyes.

"Are you Nick's sister?" she finally asked, though she knew Nick didn't have any siblings.

Raquel shook her head, her smile sad. "I'm—"

The door behind Raquel burst open, admitting a gush of chilly evening air. The door obviously led to the parking lot. Men's hushed voices and lots of grunting and groaning followed. Raquel shoved Margo behind a stack of boxes.

They waited while the men hauled several boxes into the room and piled them beside the door.

"Boss says we can retire on what this shit'll bring," one man said. "I'm ready for that."

The door Margo and Raquel had entered through opened, and two more men entered. "This all of it?" one man asked.

"Yeah, boss."

Margo's reporter antennae twitched. Was this the drug operation Jared was investigating? She peered around the edge of a box. Two of the men wore suits. They could have been doing a Laurel and Hardy imitation—one overweight, one tall and thin.

All she had to do was keep quiet until they left, then she could give Jared at least a partial description. Maybe that would help his investigation.

And then she would deal with Raquel—whoever she was.

Margo swallowed the lump in her throat, remembering those eyes. Nick's eyes. How could it be?

Something soft brushed against Margo's legs. She knew from its purring that it was only a cat, so she forced herself to relax. She'd always had a cat as a child, but with Nick's allergy, she hadn't had one since. Maybe she'd get a cat now.

Raquel, less than a foot away from Margo, glanced down at the friendly furball.

And sneezed.

8

Nick tried to toe the cat away from his shapely leg before he sneezed again, but when someone knocked away the box in front of him, he figured the cat was the least of his problems. The walking allergen scurried away, leaving the scene of his crime.

The man knocked another box aside and made a grab for them, but Nick dodged him, grabbed Margo's hand, and dragged her out of their brief sanctuary and toward the door. "We were looking for the ladies' room. Wrong turn. Sorry."

An iron grip stopped Raquel's hand just shy of the door knob. "Shit," Nick said.

"That ain't very ladylike," the man taunted. He shoved Nick and Margo toward the center of the room. "Got us a couple of problems here, Boss."

Henry Millman had been in Raquel's office just yesterday, and he had called earlier this afternoon. Raquel and Margo were in big trouble here, unless the lecherous old fart didn't recognize the attorney he'd tried unsuccessfully to proposition. Getting rid of Raquel's hair and makeup had been brilliant. Nick had turned down the retainer Millman had offered *and* what he'd called his "magic in bed." *Weasel.*

Millman narrowed his already beady eyes and shoved the omnipresent, unlit cigar into the corner of his mouth. "Don't I know you?"

Nick shrugged, but Millman took a step closer, jabbing his cigar toward Raquel for emphasis. "I've seen you somewhere before." He turned his attention to the two men who'd hauled in the boxes. "Tie 'em up for now. After the place closes, take care of the problem."

Nick was supposed to be here to help Margo—not get her killed. What a mess he'd made of things. Again.

"Waitaminute here," he said, desperate. "All we did was get lost on our way to the bathroom. Is that a crime around here?"

A tall, skinny guy stepped into the light. Nick recognized him immediately. He'd always suspected Charlie Fritz was on the take, and now he knew. He'd had more than a few run-ins with the guy in court as Nick—never as Raquel. At least that was some consolation.

Séamus, get us out of this.

Nothing. Now that they were in really serious trouble, Nick's guardian had pulled a vanishing act. *Just perfect.*

"Sly, you stay here and guard these two," Charlie said, eyeing Margo closely. "Reporter."

Nick should've realized Margo might be familiar to these bastards, too. To her credit, she didn't utter a sound. Nick prayed for a miracle. He'd screwed up Margo's life once, and now he'd put her in danger.

The one called Sly put two chairs back-to-back, and the

others forced Margo and Nick into them. Sly wrapped a nylon rope around them both, securing it under the seat of a chair, completely out of reach.

C'mon, Séamus.

Charlie left the room, and Millman stood back from the dirty work, staring at Nick. His gaze dropped to where Raquel's overblown breasts jutted out between the ropes. *Perfect. Just perfect. Humiliate me all you want, Séamus. Just don't let them hurt Margo.*

Millman shoved the cigar between his flabby lips and said to his goons, "You got a delivery to meet. Come back and take care of these two during the last act. No one will hear them over the music and screaming dames."

"Let us go," Margo said, her voice strong, her worry undeniable. "We'll forget everything that happened here."

"Yeah," Nick added, remembering how and why he'd convinced himself he was in love with Margo Knutsen all those years ago. She was brave, honorable, and beautiful. What wasn't to love? But he hadn't loved her enough. "Let us go."

"In your dreams." Millman's eyes widened suddenly. "I got it now. You're that bitch lawyer who was too good for me."

Nick sighed, not bothering to answer.

"Good for you," Margo whispered.

"Now I don't feel so bad about havin' to shut you up. Sly, you and Harry need to move the truck before somebody gets suspicious." Millman chuckled as he waddled through the door that led into the club.

Sly—obviously the brains of Tweedles Dee and Dumb—pointed upward at the sprinkler in the ceiling. "Gotta move the truck before Millman pisses hisself over it."

They locked the door leading back into the club, then left through the outside door. Nick heard the keys rattle and the dead bolt slide into place.

"Isn't this just perfect?" Nick shook his head and sighed, disgusted with himself.

Margo kept stretching toward the bottom of her chair. "Can you reach the knot?"

"No." As Nick, he might have been able to, but not as Raquel. "C'mon, Séamus."

The music fell silent suddenly. "Help!" Nick even tried

a shrill whistle, and Margo shouted as well. The music resumed within seconds, drowning out their combined efforts.

"We're going to die anyway," Margo said, "so tell me who you really are."

Nick swallowed the lump in his throat. "You aren't going to die. Trust me."

"Why?" They both kept twisting and squirming, trying to work their arms free of the ropes. "Why should I trust you if you won't tell me the truth?"

"Margo . . ." Nick stopped squirming. "I . . . Dammit, Séamus!"

"Tell me." Margo's voice trembled. "I have to know."

Nick squeezed his eyes shut, hoping for some kind of guidance. Hearing nothing but the infernal music and the customers' cheers, he sighed. "I'm sorry for hurting you. Damn, this is killing me." He gave a nervous laugh. "Again."

A tremor rippled through her. "Who *are* you?" Her voice sounded wretched.

Nick hated himself for hurting her, but he had to finish his mission. Séamus had known, and Nick could no longer deny it.

Jared Carson was the right man.

His throat clogged, and he cleared it several times. It hurt, but Margo's happiness came first. Seeing her happy would relieve his guilt, and he'd be able to watch her be happy for the rest of her life. Wouldn't she love him more for that?

He searched his memory for something only Nick could know. "Do you remember your twenty-fourth birthday?"

"Of course. What does that have to do with any—"

"Your husband dressed up in a clown suit and delivered a singing telegram." He cleared his throat and sang the opening lines of "Good Ship Lollipop." At least Raquel wasn't a soprano. That would've been too much.

Margo made a choking sound. "How did you know that? Why do you have Nick's eyes?"

"My eyes—not Nick's. I'm Raquel, remember? So he had blue eyes, too. End of coincidence."

"You . . . know too much. The condo. The painting."

Sacrifice . . . Would sacrificing his widow's memory of him be enough? Would that end this nightmare, so she could get on with her life?

With Jared?

Nick sighed, knowing the answer. It would hurt her at first, but in the long run, it would set her free. *You only loved yourself.* "Okay, if you insist . . ."

"Tell me."

"I was in love with Nick Riley." *The truth. Sorta.* "And he loved me."

Margo was silent for several seconds while sweat trickled down Nick's face. Intimating to his own widow that he'd been unfaithful to her was sickening, especially since it wasn't true. His gut clenched, and his eyes burned. Raquel bawled more than anyone Nick had ever known. Séamus had said Nick never learned to make sacrifices. Destroying his widow's memory of him might make up for all his other failures as a husband. As a man . . .

"So—so you're saying you had an affair with my husband?" Margo's voice sounded surprisingly strong. "And that's how you knew about my condo, the painting, my father-in-law . . . and Nick?"

Nick drew a shaky breath. He was committed to this self-sacrifice shit now—no turning back. What was pride anyway? "An affair . . . if that's what you want to call it." His male ego would never be the same after this. "Besides, Nick always said that you . . . really loved someone else. I don't remember the name now." *Okay, so that's a lie.* "I'm sorry I've hurt you." His voice fell to a whisper.

"I . . ." Margo released her breath in a loud whoosh. "I don't know what to say."

Well, now he'd done it. Margo was crying, and there wasn't a thing he could do about it, but that was the least of their problems right now. First he had to make sure she survived this nightmare.

"Let's stop reliving the past and see if we can get out of this mess," he said with a lot more cheer than he felt. "On three, try to stand and move us toward the door you're facing." It took several attempts, but they finally managed to move their chairs next to the door. Nick tried using his chin to turn the knob, but it didn't budge.

Okay, Jared. Best Nick Riley one more time and save Margo. Please.

Jared slipped into the empty office and hit a key on the computer keyboard. The screensaver of a naked woman in various poses cleared, and he ran a search for a few keywords. Nothing. Of course, that would have been too easy. Millman might be sleazy, but he obviously wasn't stupid.

A thumping sound came through the wall. Jared released the safety on his gun and eased toward the closet door. He heard muffled voices, more thumping. Cautiously, he eased the closet door open and peered inside. He glanced back over his shoulder and flipped the overhead light on to illuminate the inside of the closet.

Several file drawers occupied the closet. He'd need more time to search them. Tomorrow, before the Studfinder opened, he'd be back, unless—

The music fell silent suddenly, and he heard the voices through the wall again. Female?

After closing the closet door behind him, Jared examined the wall between him and the voices. There was a small door about three feet high behind a stack of boxes. He turned off the overhead light in the closet and crouched down to open it just a crack, expecting to find a safe or a cabinet. Instead, the door revealed an adjoining storage room.

Something weird was going on here. A door to the outer office closed, and he heard footsteps over the muffled music from the club. Jared weighed his options. The footsteps came closer to his hideout, and he stopped pondering and slid through the small door, closing it behind him.

A stack of boxes shielded him from the room's occupants. With both hands wrapped around the barrel of his gun, he rose to his knees, edged closer to the nearest corner, and saw Raquel Eastwood. Her eyes grew wide when she saw him, then one corner of her mouth curved upward in a grin that unnerved him.

"It's about time."

"Jared, thank God," the other woman said in her unforgettable voice.

"Margo?" He slid his gun into his shoulder holster and pulled a knife out of his pocket. Within a matter of seconds, he'd freed both women. "What the hell hap—"

"No time for that," Raquel said. "They're coming back to kill us after the last set." She aimed her thumb toward the stack of boxes beside the door. "Drugs. We're the unfortunate witnesses."

Jared pulled out his agency phone and hit one number. His backup should be in place by now. The man who answered eased his mind. Gary was one of the best, and he was in the parking lot, watching a pair of men who'd left by a back entrance. Jared told Gary where they were and what they assumed was stashed there. Knowing the local P.D. wasn't trustworthy, Gary's partner would detain the two thugs in the truck, freeing him to join Jared.

"Very nicely done," Raquel said. "I'm impressed. In fact, I—"

"You two get back to your table. They won't try anything in front of all those witnesses."

"Jared, be careful." Margo kissed him quickly on the mouth.

"She always did love you more." Raquel's voice cracked. "Take good care of her, Jar-O."

"Jar . . ." Jared's blood turned to ice. Only one person had ever called him that. "Later. Get back to the club, *now*. Trust no one—not even the cops."

"Especially not them." Raquel snorted. "Charlie Fritz is in this up to the last hair on his pointed head."

Margo bit her lip and nodded. "Be careful."

"Promise." He unlocked the door and made sure the hallway was vacant.

"Charlie Fritz's pointed head," a man repeated from behind them. "Did you hear that, Charlie?"

"Sure did."

Jared wanted to spin around and unload his clip, but common sense reminded him that the others were probably armed as well. By the time he took one down, another would fire. He couldn't risk it.

"Hands in the air, Mr. DEA, and close that damn door."

Jared complied and met Margo's gaze. He saw her fear, and hated that she was in danger. What the hell had she and Raquel been doing back here in the first place?

"Turn around *real* slow."

He obeyed, hearing Margo's sharp intake of breath. *C'mon, Gary.*

"Let the women go." Jared tried to remember his training, but knowing the woman he loved was right behind him didn't help matters. "They're no threat to you."

"C'mon, Séamus," Raquel whispered, reminding Jared how odd she was.

"No threat?" Millman walked toward Jared. He didn't have a gun—at least not in sight. "Like hell."

Charlie stepped from the shadows. *He,* of course, had a gun. His face was expressionless, his eyes cold. "Always wanted to best one of you fed hotshots. Guess I get my wish."

"Not necessarily." Raquel stepped forward. "The place is crawling with agents. Your asses are toast."

Jared cringed. "Uh, thanks, Raquel, but—"

"Shut up!" Charlie shouted. He waved his gun around, losing every iota of cool he'd shown earlier. The guy was freaked.

And dangerous.

"Music's stopped. Someone will hear you if you fire that thing." Raquel took another step, showing no fear, and no damned sense.

Millman rolled his cigar from one corner of his mouth to the other. He gave his partner in crime a sidelong glance. "She's right. Wait for Sly and Harry."

"Oh, but they aren't coming back." Raquel folded her arms, standing at an angle between Jared and Charlie.

Margo crept up beside Jared, whose hands were still in the air. "Get back," he whispered.

"Whatcha mean they aren't coming back?" Millman asked, narrowing his eyes. "What'd you do to 'em?"

Raquel gave a throaty laugh. "Wouldn't you like to know?"

"She's bluffing." Charlie swallowed so hard his Adam's apple climbed the length of his throat and back.

The door to the outside rattled. Millman glanced at his watch. " 'Bout time. The show's over and the club closes in six minutes. Now we have three mouths to shut up permanently."

The door burst open, but no one was there. Jared managed to shove Margo behind a stack of boxes, then dove in with her. He peered around the corner, readying his aim.

Charlie grabbed Raquel, who didn't put up any fight at all. "Watch the hands, Curly," she said, her tone sultry as ever.

That woman had grit or she was insane. Either way, she was now a hostage, and that presented a brand-new set of problems.

"Come out with your hands up," a voice called from outside.

By now, Gary probably had enough firepower to blow the Studfinder to Mars. All Jared wanted was Margo out of here safely.

"Drop it, Fritz." Jared took aim on Millman and stepped from behind the box. "Tell your partner to let the woman go."

"Oh, let him shoot me, Jar-O," Raquel said.

Jared swallowed hard, resisting the compulsion to look at Raquel just now. He had to watch Millman for any sudden moves.

"Drop your weapon," Gary called from the open doorway, his gun pointed at Charlie and Raquel.

"Dammit, Charlie, they got us. Let the bitch go." Sweat poured down Millman's face, and his cigar hit the floor.

"Don't move or she's dead."

"I'm already dead. Go ahead, make my day."

Something that sounded like a sob erupted from Margo. He couldn't comfort her now, but he understood her concern about Raquel. Jared had seen some agents with death wishes in his day, but Raquel Eastwood was either the bravest person he'd ever met or else certifiable.

The door leading into the club swung open behind them, and Charlie started shooting. Gary took him out in one shot. Jared had Millman pinned against the wall before they even knew who'd opened the door.

And Raquel Eastwood was lying in a pool of her own blood.

Margo bolted out of her hiding place and dropped down beside Raquel. Jared still had his gun on a cowering Millman. Until someone relieved him, he couldn't help Raquel or hold Margo.

"Oh, my God!" an elderly woman wielding a bathroom plunger like a sword said from the open doorway. Steph Knutsen, armed with a mop, stepped in beside her.

"Paramedics are on the way," Gary said. Two other agents entered the storage room and cuffed Millman, then dragged him outside. Gary inclined his head toward Charlie's body. "That one's dead."

The moment Millman was out of there, Jared dropped to his knees beside Margo. *Don't let me be too late.* Raquel had risked her life to save him. He had absolutely no doubts about that. God only knew *why.*

"Don't go yet," Margo said.

Don't go? Jared supposed she meant *don't die.*

Steph stooped on the opposite side of Raquel and helped Margo and Jared apply pressure to the gaping wound in the woman's chest. At such close range, it was a miracle she'd survived this long. It didn't look good.

"Is she . . . going to make it?" the elderly woman asked, parting with her plunger.

"I'm afraid . . ." Raquel opened her eyes. "It isn't PMS now."

"Don't go. Not yet. Please?" Margo left the first aid to the others and grabbed Raquel's limp hand.

"Who all is here?" Raquel's smile was weak.

"Jared, Steph, Mrs. Brown, me."

"That's all?"

Jared looked around. Gary stood right outside the door, talking with other agents. What the hell was taking the paramedics so damned long?

"They won't get here in time, Jar-O." Raquel turned her gaze on him. "I have that on the highest authority."

Margo gasped. "I'm so sorry."

"Don't be." Raquel grinned again. "I'm really not in any pain, you know. This is my Oscar-winning performance. Besides . . . somehow, you know. Don't you?"

Margo nodded, tears streaming down her face. To Jared's amazement, Raquel winked.

"What the hell?"

"Séamus, since she's on to me anyway . . . ?" After a moment, a solemn expression crossed Raquel's face. "Hey, Jar-O, wanna see something *really* scary?"

Jared watched Raquel's flaming red hair fade to blond. Her face changed from soft and feminine to hard and masculine. Blood stopped pumping from her wound, and her breasts became flat.

He jerked his hands away, meeting Steph's gaze for a brief instant as they both realized there was no longer a wound to tend. He looked at Raquel's new face again, and recognition made him sway.

"Nick?"

"In the flesh, so to speak."

Jared couldn't speak. A dead man was talking to him.

"Margo," Nick said, "Mr. Honest-to-a-Fault here didn't cheat on you back at the university. I set him up." He sighed, remorse evident in his eyes. "I'm sorry for that."

Margo remained silent, still holding Nick's hand.

After a moment, Jared realized there was something he needed to say—something Nick needed to hear, though he never would have believed the need was there before this. "I . . . I forgive you. After all, who wouldn't love Margo?"

Nick smiled. For a moment, he reminded Jared of the smart-assed kid who'd given Jared hell most of his life.

"Not much time." Nick patted Margo's hand and looked at her. "I love you, but not the way he does. But if he screws up, I'm going to find a way to come back down here and kick his ass."

Margo nodded. "You know I didn't buy into that affair garbage."

"Ah, well . . ." Nick shrugged. "Thanks for that."

Jared shook himself. *I'm losing my mind.*

Steph took Nick's free hand and kissed the back of his knuckles. "I've missed you."

"Ah, I've missed you, too, but don't be sad." Nick placed Margo's hand in Jared's. "You'll get to break in another brother-in-law. Make him suffer just a little, though. Will ya?"

"You bet I will." Steph sniffled and smiled at the same time.

"How about you, Mrs. Brown?" Nick looked at the older woman. "Have you missed me, too?"

"I . . . I bought you tampons and evening primrose."

Steph leapt to her feet to catch Mrs. Brown, but the woman shook her head and righted herself.

Nick managed a weak smile. "And I'll never forget it either.

"And you . . ." Nick turned his gaze on Jared, his expression solemn. "There's a letter for you in my desk. You won't like it."

"What?"

Nick blinked. "Our father should've told you, but I figure he's living his own kind of hell now."

The air whooshed out of Jared's lungs. "We're . . ."

"Brothers." He took Jared's hand and gave it a firm shake. Their gazes met and held. After a moment, he looked upward. "I hear you, Séamus." Nick looked at Margo again. "Name your first daughter Raquel. Okay? Hey, if it's a boy, name him after his uncle Nick."

Nick's face transformed back into Raquel's. The blood returned, though no longer flowing. Her eyes closed, and she released her final breath.

Jared remained at Raquel's side with Margo until the paramedics arrived. Nick—his *brother*—was already gone. *Back*, he'd said.

"Do dead lawyers really go to Heaven?" Mrs. Brown asked, echoing Jared's thoughts.

Margo smiled. "This one did."

EPILOGUE

"I never thought I'd say this to you, but I'm impressed," Séamus said upon Nick's return.

Still numbed by all his experiences, Nick blinked several times before he realized it was all over. Raquel was dead, and he was back where he belonged. Resignation eased through him, and he gave Séamus a nod. "Thanks."

Séamus patted Nick on the shoulder. "Well done. Your promotion is in the works."

"Good to hear." Nick walked over to the monitor and peered down at the scene he'd left a few moments ago. Seeing Jared and Margo together didn't upset him now. Instead, it made him smile. This was as it should be. Fate. Destiny. More . . .

"Not only did you learn about sacrifice, but also to forgive."

Nick turned to face Séamus again, oddly at peace.

The Trouble with Heroes

by Jo Beverley

1

Refugees.

A dead word from the Earth history books had shockingly come to life. Jenny Hart first heard it at the print shop as she was closing her station ready to go home.

". . . a queue of refugees that goes out of sight and beyond because the gates of Anglia are closed for the first time during the day in living memory."

The office screen ran Angliacom most of the day and Jenny was used to treating it as background noise. It took a moment to register, but then she turned to stare at the wall. The screen was split into max cells, but Sam Witherspoon, the manager, had the volume pegged to the picture of a line of crowded vehicles on the road. Buses, lorries, even farmvees of one sort or another.

"Refugees?" Sam echoed blankly.

"Like from plague, famine, and war?" Jenny asked, and they looked at each other.

She'd asked a question, but she knew. He probably knew, too.

"The blighters," she said.

He turned and picked up his case. "I'd better get home. Lock up, all right?"

"Sure." Jenny was still staring at the screen, but she knew why he was rushing away. He had a family. Children. Probably her mother would be fretting about her.

She picked up a phone and claimed a screen cell for it. Her mother liked to see her children when she was worried. Her younger brother's face came on first. He took one look and yelled, "Mum! Jenny!"

Madge Hart appeared, red hair wild, eyes flashing. "Are you all right?"

"Of course I am, Mum. I'm not outside, you know."

"But isn't it awful? Those poor people. We should take them in. But they say there's more and more, and room elsewhere. But they'll end up out in the dark. I don't know."

"It makes no difference, Mum. Blighters don't care whether it's night or day." All the same, Gaians didn't like to be outside at night.

"It's all panic," her mother said, clearly remembering her maternal duty to reassure her children. "If there was real trouble, we'd know."

"That's right."

"Are you coming home for dinner?"

"Not right now. I want to see if I can find out what's really going on."

"That's a good idea. Ask Dan. He'll know. Bring him home for dinner as long as it's not too late. He's been looking peaky."

"Right, Mum."

Jenny clicked off before she smiled. Her mother had fussed over Dan since he'd been a toddler, long before he'd been spotted as a fixer and sent off to the Gaian Center for Investigation and Control of the Hostile Amorphous Native Entities—generally known as Hellbane U. Now he was back and living on his own in the fixer's flat, she acted as if he might be starving to death. It wasn't as if he didn't have a family of his own here.

She powered down the screen and checked the place over, then went out, coding the lock. Where to go for news? The Merrie England pub?

No. She wanted to go up on the walls to see for herself. God knew why. A camera did a better job than human eyes, but she was sure the walls were crowded with gawkers. The Olde English battlements and turrets had always seemed like a pleasant whimsy, but as Jenny hurried toward the nearest steps, she wished they really could keep an enemy out.

They couldn't. In nearly two hundred years, Anglia had only experienced one blighter attack, but one was enough to show thick walls and drawbridges were no protection at all. Sixty-eight years ago, in the lovely Public Gardens, a blighter had killed a child in front of her horrified mother. Rendered her into a pile of greasy ash amid her pink pantsuit. There were photos.

A statue in the Gardens depicted a beautiful little girl holding a posy of flowers. Quite likely she'd been a pest, but she hadn't deserved to die in terror like that. No one did.

"Hostile amorphic native entities." That was how the exploratory services had labeled the one puzzling problem on an otherwise perfect settlement planet. HANES.

Technically accurate, but it hadn't captured reality. Within a generation they had become known as hell-banes, and some settlements had their own name as well. Anglia, with typical wry humor, called them blighters. No coincidence that back on Earth blight had been a disease that turned plants to slime. But the Frankland *terreurs* was perhaps a better word. Jenny could feel it now, in herself and in the people all around, milling in gossip, heading to the walls, or hurrying home to protect or be protected.

Fear. Deep, formless fear, as if something terrible were blowing on the winds from the south.

An arm snagged around Jenny's waist and she whirled.

"Gyrth!"

Gyrth Fletcher was thin, long-faced, with blond curls and beard that made him look as if he'd stepped out of a medieval manuscript.

"Want to come down a dark passageway with me, pet?" he asked in mock villain voice.

She winked at him. "Depends what you're offering, don't it?"

"A better view. From an arrowslit."

"Lead on!"

He worked for wall maintenance, so he'd know those passageways, but the main appeal was company. That'd blow away her creepy feelings.

She couldn't help stating, "There's no real danger to being outside in the dark."

"Right." He didn't sound any happier than she was about it.

"Perhaps we should go and look for Dan. He'll know what's going on."

"He's probably in a stuffy room with the Witan."

"Oh, I suppose."

Strange to think of Dan as official like that. They'd been born within weeks of each other three houses apart, and according to her mother, been stuck together like toffees until they reached that age when the other sex suddenly seems alien. Before they'd had time to get over that, he'd tested positive for fixing and been sent to Hellbane U.

Bloody fixing. His three fortnights home each year hadn't been enough to keep the closeness over eight years, especially when Jenny had known he'd not come back in the end. Fixers didn't. They went where they were needed, and they always seemed to be needed far away. Anglia's fixer before Dan had been from Cathay.

"You all right, Jenny?"

"Sure. Where's this arrowslit? Perhaps we'll be able to hear what people are saying out there."

They held hands so they wouldn't be pulled apart in the crowd, but Jenny was thinking about Dan. Her childhood friend. Anglia's fixer. The one who'd be expected to deal with any blighters who invaded here. Sure, fixers trained to fight blighters, but there weren't any. Not here, at least, or anywhere far from the equator. So they fixed other things. Broken machines. Broken bones. Broken hearts if the break was physical. Things that didn't fight back.

"If there's trouble in the south, do you think Dan'll have to go to fight blighters there?" she asked.

Gyrth stopped and shook his head at her. "Hellbane U'll deal with it. They're not going to leave the towns without a fixer, are they? Not short of something desperate. And it can't be desperate. Didn't Dan say that blighters are so rare they have to hunt them to find one for the graduates to zap in their final test?"

"Yes, but then why the refugees?"

"You're such a worrier! What did that old Earth politician say? We have nothing to fear but fear itself. Come on."

Jenny went, but asked, "Have you ever thought it's strange that Dan came back here? Fixers don't."

"He said once that he asked. Apparently most don't." He grinned. "You've got to admit that a lot of times the town wishes he hadn't. He's a right change from quiet Miss Lixiao."

That he was. When Dan had left he'd been mischievous and thoughtful, and he'd come back wary and wild. It was a good wild, though, making him the burning heart of a group of lively twenty-somethings. Jenny wasn't sure she fit in with all the group, but she spent time with them because of Dan. She and he weren't toffees anymore, but they were still friends. Friends enough to worry.

They reached High Wall Street and the width of it meant she could let go of Gyrth's hand. Thirty feet wide, it was edged on one side by railings overlooking the lower street, and on the other by shops, pubs, and cafes that backed onto the wall. So how did they get to an arrowslit from here?

Gyrth headed toward the space between Porter's Pies and Castleman's Ironmongery.

"Down there?" Jenny asked dubiously.

"It's safe."

But then he stopped, waved, and shouted. Jenny saw his sister Polly and Polly's husband, Assam, who waved and walked toward them. Or rather, Polly waddled. She was pregnant and bigger every time Jenny saw her. It didn't seem she could swell any more and not burst, but she still had a few weeks to go.

"We're going to get a better view from a slit," Gyrth told them. "Want to come?"

"I'll stick!" Polly protested but let herself be persuaded.

There was no real danger of Polly getting stuck, but it was definitely single file. Rubbish crunched under Jenny's shoes, some of it stinky, and despite the fact that the ginnel was open to the sky two stories above, she began to feel trapped. Or perhaps the faint pulse of panic was because of refugees, blighters, and war. It couldn't be true, but then, why all the people on the road?

She was ready to give up, turn back, when they reached the maintenance passage, wide enough for two or three. As a bonus, it was either cleaned regularly or the rubbish didn't drift this far. Gyrth led them to an arrowslit directly above the gate. From here, the amplified official voice was clear, though the response was indistinct.

Driven by her strange urgency, Jenny wasn't her usual polite self. She climbed first into the embrasure and worked forward to the slit. It was six feet high but only about a foot wide. Even so, she felt as if the world was spread before her, and all the voices outside were clear.

"What's going on?" Gyrth asked.

"Someone's asking distances to Skanda."

Jenny wished she knew how far back the queue stretched, but it wove out of sight between a coppice not far away.

"Didn't they used to keep the space around castles clear?" she asked Polly, a history teacher. "So they could see an enemy coming?"

"Certainly. But it's not as if anyone could see a blighter, or stop it if they did."

"Shame. I see how these work. I could fire out at the enemy, and they wouldn't be able to hit me."

"Seems a bit unsporting to me," Assam said, clearly teasing.

Polly frowned at him. "War was not a sport."

Gyrth jumped up into the space. "Let me have a look, Jenny."

She gave way and climbed back out. There'd been nothing out there to settle whatever was bothering her. "I don't know about that," she said, joining the other two. "Tournaments and things. And didn't they have what they called 'war games' even in recent times?"

"Probably still do," Polly said, rubbing her belly. "They still have war, though mostly robotic. Thank heavens for peaceful Gaia."

Jenny hugged herself, suddenly cold in this dank, shadowy space. "I wish our ancestors had chosen a more peaceful design."

"All part of good old Merrie England," Assam said.

"Merrie? They used to pour boiling oil down on the attackers, didn't they, Polly?"

"Well, probably not. Oil would have been expensive. But boiling water, and sometimes pitch, which would stick."

"Ugh!"

"And the attackers would hurl dead cows back with catapults," said Assam, clearly enjoying himself.

"Ugh, again. Stop it, Assam! It was bad enough learning about all this in school."

"But very necessary," said Polly in her best teacher manner. "Lest we forget."

Then Jenny heard the gates opening beneath her. "Are they letting someone in, Gyrth?"

"Yes. Must be an Anglian in the family. They can't keep native Anglians out, or their families."

"Then I suppose I'll be able to go to Erin if things get bad here."

"Not unless your mother's with you," Polly pointed out. She was always precise about such details. "And would you really want to leave?"

"Of course not. It was just a thought."

Jenny said it lightly. No one else seemed seriously concerned, but something was pressing on her mind. A kind of foreboding that defied words, as a half-remembered dream does.

Assam was still teasing Polly about castles. He was probably trying to amuse her, but Jenny thought she was getting upset.

"Talking of hurling cows," she interjected, "do you still show that film? The grail one. Though I suppose they were hurling cows from inside."

"*Monty Python and the Holy Grail*?" Polly said. "Of course. It's a key work to understanding ancient Earth warfare."

"The words *Fetchez lavache* illuminating the strife that arises out of separate languages and the consequent misunderstandings, and also the instinctive desire for union in the creation of a blended language, franglois. I got an A-plus on that paper—mainly by paraphrasing the textbooks."

"If you got an A-plus, you must have done more than that."

Jenny shrugged. "I liked the film even though I didn't really understand it."

"It is deep. I don't think we've truly grasped the meaning of shrubbery."

"The dark warrior's need for healthy, beautiful plants rather than destruction," Assam stated. That certainly was straight from the textbook.

"I feel there's more," Polly said. "After all, we've only just made the connection that explains Monty."

"Which is?" Jenny was glad for the distraction, even though she felt as if she was back in sixth-form history.

"Someone recently found a film in the archive called *The Full Monty*. Monty," Polly said with the air of one sharing an exciting treat, "turns out to mean naked!"

"Naked snake?"

"No, no! The snake is obvious. It's the serpent in the Garden of Eden—and that connects to shrubbery, of course. And Holy Grail is the ultimate freedom from strife to which all humanity aspires. But nakedness builds powerfully on the concept of Eden, don't you see? Nakedness in Eden—honesty and openness—threatened by the python of deceit."

"Ah," said Assam, "but what about the rabbit?"

Jenny wanted to kick him.

Polly merely gave him a look. "We don't quite understand the rabbit yet. I think it warns that the threat to the grail, to Eden, can trick us by appearing harmless."

"Well, that rules out the blighters. We've known they were bloody nasty since first settlement."

"I don't know," Jenny said. "I think we'd have mostly forgotten about them if they didn't show schoolkids that film of the scout being ashed."

"That's a crucial part of Gaian history," Polly protested.

"Perhaps, but it gave me nightmares for weeks."

Assam moved closer to the embrasure. "Anything new going on there, Gyrth?"

"Not really." Gyrth turned and climbed out. "Let's go to the Merrie. See what people are saying there."

No one argued. They headed out, but Jenny carried gloom with her, remembering the film of the scout's death.

Settlement was always preceded by exploration, and the first wave, the scouts, wore full recording equipment that sent real-time data to the ship. New worlds are unpredictable, after all, and corpses don't tell what killed them.

In this case, the data told the tale but left a mystery. Even though the suit-sys recorded 360 degrees, it had shown nothing, absolutely nothing, of what had attacked. The various sensors had recorded no change in air pressure, temperature, or radiation.

The body system readouts, however, had charted extreme stress—a racing heart, rapid breathing, and sky-high adrenaline and blood pressure. The scout had gasped and expressed terror, but she had screamed only once, at the point of death. The oblivious suit-sys had kept on recording, even when the person inside had become a pile of ash, but it had registered as little after the event as before.

Hostile Amorphic Native Entity.

Jenny could imagine how often that data disk had been viewed and reviewed, but in the end Gaia had been approved for settlement. There'd been no further attacks, and in all other respects it was the best EPP—Earth Potential Planet—ever found. It had the rarest of rare earths to provide an economic base and needed little amendment. It had even been free of anything close to a sentient species that might complicate ownership.

The perfect place, but when they emerged into the light and bustle of High Wall Street, Jenny sucked in a deep breath. She'd not thought she was claustrophobic. "Does anyone smell something funny?" she asked.

"Just the chip shop fat," Gyrth said. "Look, there's Dan."

Jenny turned, suddenly breathing more easily. Dan, and he looked normal. Not worried at all. Everything must be all right.

He was in his fixer uniform of brown shirt and trousers, with assorted badges and braids of significance to those who understood them, but there was nothing special about his looks. Average build, average height. Brown hair and blue eyes in an average face. Like her, really. But not anymore.

Something drew people to Dan Fixer like flies to jam. A fizz in the air, a brighter light, an energy that meant there was never a dull time when Dan was part of a group. Jenny thought she could feel the fizz now, even though he seemed relaxed, as if this were just another evening in Anglia. Work over. Time to play.

"I wondered where everyone was. Poking around down cracks between buildings?"

"Peering out through arrowslits," Jenny said, hooking arms with him as they all turned to go down the circular staircase to ground level. "And reanalyzing Monty Python. Polly, tell Dan about the monty stuff."

That kept things light and away from blighters for a while. Now, with Dan by her side and showing no sign of concern, Jenny wanted to forget about it all.

But it wasn't so easy. Despite the chatter and laughter, that something grated on her like an off note in music. When she and Dan ended up together behind the others, she had to ask, "Are there really more blighter attacks near the equator?"

His look was quick, and perhaps guarded. "Yes, but don't worry. It's all under control."

Leave it. Leave it. But she couldn't. "Then why are people pouring north?"

She thought he wasn't going to answer, but he pulled a face. "You'll hear soon enough. Central has recommended that everyone in the affected areas leave until the hellbanes are stamped out. After all, one person ashed is one person too many."

He declared it as a trite motto, but Assam caught it and turned back. "Damn right. But the problem won't reach here, will it? Polly can't travel now."

Polly and Gyrth stopped to listen.

"Blighters have always been more active near the equator," Dan pointed out. "There are plenty of fixers there, and Hellbane U as well, with the most skilled and experienced of us. They'll deal with it."

Jenny relaxed, and Polly said she was too tired to walk. Assam suggested a tram and Gyrth went with them.

Jenny and Dan strolled along in comfortable silence for a while, but she had questions, and this seemed the time to ask them. "Fixers can feel blighters, can't they? That's how you hunt them."

"I wouldn't exactly call it hunting. Just stand around and they come."

"I thought you had trouble finding them."

"True, but the only way we know is to bait a trap."

"With what?"

"Cow, pig . . ."

"Then you zap it?"

"That's the idea. Ideally before it ashes the poor beast."

"Do fixers ever fail? I mean . . . die?"

"Very rarely."

They paused to let a tram pass, and Jenny thought about that. She'd never imagined that fixing might be dangerous. "What does it feel like?"

He pulled a face. "It can't really be described. It's like a nightmare. It evaporates if we try to describe it."

As they crossed the tracks, she asked, "Can nonfixers sense this? At a distance, I mean?"

His look was quick and sharp. "You're sensing something now?"

"No! Maybe . . . I'm not a fixer, Dan. Don't even think it!"

"I don't, but some people have a trace. What are you picking up?"

She tried to explain, but it was as he'd said. Like trying to tell a dream. She didn't like the fact that it seemed to make sense to him. "So you're feeling the same thing, but much stronger?"

"I assume so."

"So they are coming?" she asked.

"No. Seriously, there's no need to worry, Jen. The action is all in the hotter lands."

She stopped. "*What* action?"

"The blighters, and the fixers dealing with them." He grabbed her hand. "Come on. The others will be there long before us." But three steps later he stopped and put his hand to his ear. He muttered something, but pulled the fine wire from his earring round to his mouth. "Fixer."

After a moment he pushed it back. "Kid fallen off High Wall near Watling. Luckily, only a broken leg. Want to come?"

"Of course!" She rarely got a chance to see him work, and it always delighted her.

Hand in hand they ran across to the nearest tram line and Dan waved one down, his uniform his authority. He seemed to have a map of the lines in his head. They jagged rapidly across town to the west wall, where they found a boy on the ground with two nurses in attendance and a small crowd of gawkers.

The patient was about thirteen, with freckles and ginger hair. A tubby, dark-haired lad hovered, looking more shocked than his injured friend. It turned out that the patient had already had something for the pain.

"Right leg," said the nurse who was kneeling beside him. "Tibia and fibula, I think. Might be spinal, too. Name's Jeff Bowlby."

"Thought you could fly, Jeff?" said Dan, sitting cross-legged beside him.

"Just fell. Will it hurt?"

Dan smiled at him. "Not at all. Relax."

He put his hands on the boy's leg, which was still covered by his jeans. Jenny knew the rules. Everyone did. In case of an accident do nothing except pain relief until the fixer comes, unless it's necessary to prevent death.

The youth tensed anyway, but then his eyes widened. "It tingles."

Dan didn't say anything. There really was nothing to see of what he was doing except a stillness that was very un-Danlike. But this time, Jenny realized, she could feel something.

Tingling? That was one way to put it. What she felt was in the air, or in her mind—or rather, in a part of her mind she hadn't known was there. Oh, she didn't like this. She didn't like it at all. She wasn't a fixer!

A man rushed up. "Jeffy?"

Jenny and the second nurse took an arm each before he could interfere.

"He's fine," said the nurse, his voice steady. "Mr. Bowlby, is it? No great harm done, and it's being fixed. We'll just need some details from you."

The young man led the father away to comfort him with record taking, and sting him with a bill. Copayment for foolishness.

"All right?" Dan said.

Jenny turned back to see a slight shudder pass through him as he raised his hands from the boy's leg.

"That's good as new, but take care of my work, okay, Jeff? Let's see if you've done any other damage." He passed his hands over the boy, pausing for a moment in one spot, then rose easily to his feet. "All clear."

The boy started to sit up but the nurse beside him held him down. "Oh, no you don't. We'll help your father take you home and keep an eye on you until the shock and medicine wear off." She looked up at Dan. "Good job, Fixer."

Dan gave the nurse his tally, and she typed the code in that would authorize his payment from Anglia's health program. Jenny let him guide her toward the tram stop, thinking about fixing. Really thinking about it for the first time.

"Does that take a lot of your power?"

"Not particularly. A string of those, and I'd be wiped for a while. Normally."

She thought about querying that, but he went on. "As it is, I welcome the work. If I don't use the energy, it tends to . . . flare."

"Flaring's bad?"

"It can turn me a bit wild."

"Wild's your greatest charm, Dan Rutherford, and you know it."

He laughed. "I like it when you call me that. I know people like my energy, but there's an edge there."

That put her worry into words. She thought he danced along an edge.

Flaring. Good word for it. Flaring high spirits that led to exciting times, but that threatened a conflagration, perhaps mostly of himself. Though fixers could fix so many problems, they rarely lived to a hundred.

"It's the magic," he said, putting an arm around her.

A shiver rippled up her back at his touch. Not particularly unpleasant, but a shiver, and for a moment she thought that was what he was referring to. But then she realized he meant the flaring. "You mean fixing?"

"Magic's a better word. A more realistic one."

"Realistic? It doesn't exist."

"Who knows? Why so many Earth stories if it never existed? And they show it as dangerous stuff. Magic creatures who lurk in dark places and trick people to their deaths. Or seduce them with gifts and feasts, then keep them prisoner forever. Or make them dance themselves to death for amusement. That fits."

She eased out of his arm. "That's superstition, and it's nothing to do with what you do. With fixing."

"Isn't it?"

She didn't want this, not now, with her stomach queasy and her mind jangled by his touch, and by an illusion of ashes on the wind. But his silence demanded something, and friends should be friends, so in the end she asked, "Well, is it?"

He leaned against the tram shelter. "There's no way to compare, is there? They say it doesn't work on Earth, but I'm not sure when they tried. I've thought of going back to find out, but who can afford it? Someone once said that any sufficiently advanced technology is indistinguishable from magic. That's another way of looking at it."

The tram glided up, and they climbed on. He led the way to the back, where they used to sit as kids, but he talked quietly, even though there was no one close.

"Fixers aren't normal, Jen. You have to see that. They warn us to be solitary, that it's safer. Not to return home. To keep aloof wherever we go."

"Aloof?" It pulled a laugh from her. "Failed that part of the course, didn't you?"

"Abjectly. And I insisted on coming back home." A fleeting grin faded. "But sometimes I think they're right."

"No, they're not. Bad enough that you had to go away for years."

"People marry out. Your mother did. Or in, in that case."

"That's different. That's love. And I wonder how people can love enough to do a thing like that."

"So do I. I didn't like it, Jen."

It was the first time he'd said that, and he'd been back two years.

2

The tram stopped in Market Square then, however, and they got out and crossed to the Merrie England Pub. Gyrth, Polly, and Assam were at an outside table with a bunch of the others. Everyone hailed Dan as if he were rain in midsummer, asking where he'd been. Chairs shuffled. Yas, who looked like a princess from the Arabian Nights, snagged Dan's sleeve and towed him down beside her. Jenny went to a seat at the other end of the table, between Gyrth and Rolo.

She needed space. Things were shifting, and she didn't know what to do.

Magic.

Seduced with gifts and feasts.

Driven to dance to death.

For some reason Dan had wanted to tell her about that, and now it was scarily easy to imagine when she remembered some of the wild times, often here, at the Merrie England. Not tonight, though. Beneath chatter, the mood was definitely not merrie, and it wasn't just her group. The tavern, even the square, seemed subdued. Thoughts of war returned to trouble her. People didn't flee their homes for no reason.

A quarrel started behind them, then Yas complained about "some bitch" who'd stolen a promotion from her, and the means she'd used. Back in the tavern, a crash suggested someone had dropped a whole tray of glasses. Raised voices . . .

But then it changed. Being so aware of Dan, Jenny saw him do it, saw him open his gifts and set everyone alight. Saw him create a wild Dan Fixer night.

Yas laughed and let her complaints drop. The shouting stopped. Someone called for music. Jenny went with Rolo and Tom to fetch the instruments from the back room and started rollicking folk songs. That wasn't unusual. Three nights a week they did it for pay. It went beyond that, though.

Market Square was ringed with taverns and restaurants, all with tables outside on two levels. Soon everyone was joining in, thumping hands and feet with the rhythm. Fiddling into a sweat, Jenny glanced at Dan. There was no way to tell whether he was still making it happen, but she knew he was.

Dancing to death . . .

Other musicians joined them, and the crowd urged the group of them out into the center of the square. Jenny ended up on a precarious spot high on the central statue of the first ship to Gaia leaving Earth. Perched up there, surrounded by singing and stamping, she felt like the heart of a bright-burning bonfire that shone out on hundreds of faces at tables, in windows, and crowding the open space as well.

She realized people were being drawn here from all around.

Like moths to a flame? Or like a firestorm, sucking everything into infernal destruction? And what became of those at the center of such a storm?

Where was Dan? She found him, leaning against the base of the ship, singing along with the rest. This couldn't be bad. Dan wasn't bad. He was just flaring, burning off his whatever, and creating light against the dark at the same time.

But why tonight did Dan the fixer need so much light, laughter, and song? Why did he have so much energy to burn, even after fixing that boy's leg? What did it say about the blighters?

Jenny escaped that by diving back into the music.

Tom called an end to it at midnight.

"We've got to stop. I'll get fired if my mates turn up." He was a policeman. "Last song!" he called in his strong voice.

Despite protests, they huddled, trying to come up with the best piece to wrap this up without a riot.

" 'Gaia,' " Jenny said.

Tom looked at her. "The anthem?"

"You can sing it, can't you? I think it's right."

No one argued, which was strange. They weren't in the habit of singing the planet's syrupy anthem based on a bad poem by one of the first settlers. Each settlement had its own anthem, but "Gaia" was dragged out at any planetary-wide event—usually to groans.

Jenny wondered where the idea had come from and glanced at Dan, but he was sitting now, an adoring woman on each arm. She didn't even know them.

Flies to jam. She'd better watch it. She wasn't going to ruin a friendship by turning stupid over Dan. But if he wanted the anthem, he could have it. She struck up a chord and Tom started to sing in his deep, strong voice.

What a wonder it is
To find a planet like this
In the limitless oceans of space.
Where the air is pristine,
And the oceans are clean.
Oh, Gaia, you sweet, blessed place.
Though hellbanes may ash,
Our dream will not crash.
We will cherish our new home forever!

The crowd was singing along by then, and in the chorus, the thunder of it seemed to rattle the windows all around. With the gates closed and blighters attacking, the words had new meaning. Power crept up Jenny's spine, almost making her hands fumble on her fiddle.

She glanced down at Dan again. He had his head back and his eyes closed as if he was absorbing something from the air.

We come from an Earth
Under burden of birth,
Its beauty long gone and turned rotten.
But here it is new,
A rich gift to the few.
Oh, Gaia, here pain is forgotten.

Though hellbanes may ash,
Our dream will not crash.
We will cherish our new home forever!

With a treasure so grand,
With such beauty to hand,
What can we be but peaceful and giving?

Never strife, never war,
We will spill blood no more.
Oh, Gaia, you were made for blessed living.

Though hellbanes may ash,
Our dream will not crash.
We will cherish our new home forever!

It was the crowd rather than Tom that repeated the chorus one last time, almost softly despite the hundreds of voices.

Though hellbanes may ash,
Our dream will not crash.
We will cherish our new home forever!

Like a lamp turned down, the roaring energy settled to a glow, and everyone began to drift peacefully away.

Jenny sat in the convenient dip between ship and Earth because her legs had turned weak. The others looked pretty shocked.

"The power," Tom said.

The magic, she thought, and she might have a bit of it.

Dan stood waiting to help her down, but she jumped down by herself, then hurried back to the tavern with her fiddle.

The publican, Ozzy Rooke, shook his head. "You're supposed to get the customers drinking, not out there singing the planetary anthem!" He was joking, though, and he gave them all a free round of beer.

Dan sat beside Jenny at the bar. She made a business of picking up her glass because it let her move an inch away. She probed the air around him. Nothing. Nothing more than the usual aura that was Dan. Had he burned it all up in that singing?

By the time Ozzy threw them out and locked up, the city was quiet—a soft quiet that seemed infinitely safe. They set off home together, but Rolo and Tom split off not far from the square. Jenny, Dan, Gyrth, and Yas carried on in a group, singing, teasing, and even tussling sometimes.

Like kids again. Or like teenagers. Dan kept apart a bit, and Jenny remembered that he'd missed most of these nights—the singing, the horseplay, the maneuvering for possible bedmates. She noticed Yas maneuvering for Dan. That'd be nothing new, but she was glad he wasn't responding tonight.

In Chestnut Copse, Yas went into her building alone with a last, hopeful look. Gyrth turned off at the next corner, leaving Jenny and Dan alone for the last little way. Nothing unusual in that, except that, for the first time, she was nervous.

It was just that it had been a strange day, but she hoped he wouldn't touch, wouldn't even want to talk. Perhaps he felt the same, because he walked beside her in silence, and by the time they came to his place, that silence was comforting as a lambswool blanket. It said that everything was all right.

The fixer's flat took up the whole ground floor of a large house. They held parties there sometimes because no one else had such a space to themselves. Jenny still lived at home.

They paused at the bottom of the steps. "Night, then," Jenny said.

"I'll walk you to your place."

She stared at him. "You expect a blighter to leap out of the pavement?"

"You never know." But then he smiled. "I'm just not ready to go to bed."

Tension ricked her shoulders, but she said, "Oh, okay, then. Thanks."

He touched her arm. "You're feeling the effects of the music, aren't you?"

"No. Yes, but it was okay. It was good." She might as well tackle it. "Did you make it happen?"

"I helped." He turned her, and they walked on. "I am the town's fixer, after all."

"What were you fixing?"

"The closing of the gates upset a lot of people."

How often did he do things like that? Could he, did he, fix people's moods? Fix hers? They were on her street now, a tall terrace facing a small park called Surrey Green.

"It's a bright-burning night, and I'm not ready for sleep," he said. "Do you want to walk around the park and talk some more?"

It was the dead hour on a chilly night, and Jenny felt drained, but she couldn't not go. Something important hovered here. They walked through a gap in the hedge, but as soon as they were away from the sparse streetlights, she couldn't see what was in front of her feet.

She stopped. "I'm likely to break a leg."

Dan put an arm around her. "Then you're with the right person. Come on."

"It'll still hurt." It came out light as she'd hoped, but her entire skin was jumping as she let him lead her forward. "Night vision, too?"

"Right."

And what else?

There was talk about fixers and sex. Yas spoke about Dan in a way that suggested things. But this was Dan. They'd played in the sandbox here together. *Say something, Jenny.* Something light and normal.

"The anthem really is terrible, isn't it?"

"Awful. But you know, that used to mean full of awe. And terrible might not be a word to toss around these days."

No talking about terror or awe. "Perhaps we should write a new one."

"I don't think you can do that with an anthem. It has special powers."

No talking about special powers. "Do you think Yas'll resign over not getting that promotion?"

"No, she'll sabotage her rival and get her way in the end."

"Poor rival."

"Some people are forces of nature."

Jenny knew then that he wanted to talk about forces of nature, about powers, about blighters. Was it because she'd admitted to sensing things, revealed that she might have a bit of whatever made up the fixers? She'd rather bury that in the Surrey Green sandbox.

Distant streetlights glinted on bits of the playground, and she grabbed on to the past. "Remember the hours we used to spend on the swings here?"

"And the high slide."

"You certainly kept the fixer busy."

"I sometimes wonder if that caused it. If it's infectious."

She stiffened, on the edge of pulling away. "Really?"

He laughed and snagged her tight. "No. I could always do weird stuff. Mum and Dad tried to get me to hide it, but testing sniffs it out anyway. Remember that time you caught the cricket ball funny and thought you'd broken your finger?"

"Yes."

"You had."

Jenny remembered the horrible pain that had suddenly eased, so that when some adults came running they thought she'd been making a fuss about nothing. They'd been—what?—eight? Dan hadn't even touched her. He'd just stood there saying stupid things like "Are you all right, Jen?"

She knew he didn't glow or anything, but she'd thought he had to touch. She tried to remember whether there'd been a tingle. She'd probably been in too much pain.

"We're lucky, aren't we?" she said.

"You and me?"

She bumped him with her hip. "Gaia! The perfect planet. Healthy, fruitful. Rare earths to pay our way, and fixers to mend almost everything."

"And blighters," he pointed out.

"Perhaps every grail has to have a python."

"I'd rather have the fluffy bunny. But blighters aren't too high a price to pay."

Jenny thought of the refugees. "Still? Could the price become too high?"

"When there's no choice, the price can never be too high, can it? Earth's recovering, but it's still trying to ship people out rather than take them back. Even spread around other colonies we'd be an unbalancing factor."

"So it's Gaia or nothing. That's all right. I can't imagine leaving."

They wove through the playground where the swings, the slides, and the roundabout sat still, as if waiting for ghostly children. A vision swept upon her—of the whole of Gaia like this. The blighters didn't destroy things, only animals and people.

"There's no real danger, is there? From the blighters? I mean to Gaia."

He didn't immediately answer, and chill seeped into her bones. He was going to be honest, and she wished she hadn't asked.

"There's danger," he said at last, grabbing a bar of the roundabout and spinning it as if doing so might whirl something away. "People are being ashed. A lot of people, and even more animals. But the local fixers and teams from Hellbane U should be able to control things, especially now that people are leaving. They've been told to kill all the large animals before they leave so the blighters won't have anything to feed on."

"*Feed* on?" She moved out of his arm, spinning the slowing roundabout as an excuse.

"Where else do the victims go? They're consumed, so it has to be a kind of feeding. Of energy, we assume. The blighters are a form of energy."

Jenny shivered, even though it wasn't really so shocking. It was more that she'd not thought much about blighters before. Why should she? They were nasty, but they hardly ever popped up even near the equator, and if one did, a fixer got rid of it before it could do more damage.

Like pimples—of a lethal sort.

The roundabout had slowed again. She gave it a running spin and jumped on. "So you're going to starve them, and that'll be an end of it?"

"That's the plan." He caught it, spun it again, and joined her, but on the other side for balance. The world whirled, but they were steady inside this circle.

"What are the blighters doing, Dan? What are they? What do they want?"

"We don't know. Despite generations of study, we know grot all. They're not easy to study. Until recently they were hard to even find. There've always been people who thought they were an hallucination, or a neurosis brought on by bad air. Or by planetary contamination of our food."

"Food? We brought in Earth plants."

"But they feed on Gaian soil. As we do."

The roundabout slowed and slowed, and neither of them spun it again.

"Blighters can't be imaginary," Jenny said. "What about the ashes?"

"That's the rub, isn't it? But apparently there's something called spontaneous combustion. It's been recorded on Earth. People suddenly burst into flames and burn up, leaving acrid ash. It doesn't fit because blighters cause no flames or smoke, but we humans hate something we can't measure and explain."

"Like magic," she said, stepping off the still roundabout.

"Like magic," he agreed, joining her on the grass.

The late night and the chill were getting to her, aching in her bones, shivering over her skin, especially now they were apart. "How do you zap a blighter?"

"We sense them coming and instinctively *fix* them. It seems to kill them. It's hard to explain. We don't really understand what we do. We just know it works."

"So the fixers down south are fixing things, but they need help from Hellbane U?"

"There are rather a lot of blighters."

"Why so many now?"

"No one knows."

"No one knows much, do they?"

He laughed, but wryly. "No."

She was suddenly exhausted, as much by a sense of helplessness as by the late hour—and that helplessness came from Dan.

"I have to get to bed," she said. "I have to go to work tomorrow. Music usually invigorates me, but tonight it wiped me out."

Without protest, he turned to cross the soccer pitch toward the houses beyond the hedge, but he put an arm around her, and she found it too comforting to resist.

"I'm sorry," he said. "I don't need much sleep. I sometimes forget that normal people do."

Normal. On the street, beneath the lights, she gently moved away from him, trying to ignore a drag, as if two sticky surfaces were pulling apart. Stuck like two toffees . . .

"You don't sleep much because of your fixer abilities?"

"The energy of it, yes." He took her hand, rubbing the knuckles with his thumb. "There are things that help."

All kinds of interesting muscles contracted, but she knew—perhaps had always known—that her friend Dan Fixer was too strong a drink for her. Spontaneous combustion.

"You should have gone with Yas, then."

The streetlight two doors down showed his smile. "I don't think so." He raised her left hand and kissed the palm—a lover's move, designed to invite without words. "Anytime you'd like, Jen. Sleep tight."

She watched him walk away.

Anytime?

She had only to ask?

She turned and pressed the lock, her exhausted mind staggering around perilous possibilities.

She stumbled up the stairs and fell into bed thinking she'd probably dreamed the whole thing. For that and a bundle of other excellent reasons, she couldn't imagine taking him up on the offer.

3

For a few days everyone spent time on the wall watching the stream of refugees, but then they lost interest. There was nothing new to see, it was depressing, and Anglians were growing more worried about their own security. The town was overcrowded, but that wasn't the problem. It was worry about whether they, too, would end up on the road north.

An occasional group of refugees had a citizen in the family and had to be let in. Those people told tales of whole families ashed. Angliacom showed charts and maps that tracked the hellbane wave, though the announcers assured everyone that the fixers down south had everything under control and that the refugees should be able to go home any day.

However, part of the screen constantly showed the warning that refugees must slaughter large animals before leaving. It was presented as a kindness—the animals would lack care and possibly be victims of a terrifying death—but it was, of course, to starve the blighters.

Jenny wondered how many people recognized that. She also wondered how many saw how the news was sugaring everything and sensed the darker truth. Was she the only one to feel she could taste bitter ashes on the wind, who sensed the peril in the earth, thrumming stronger and stronger, coming, coming, coming . . .

If the starve-them-to-death plan was working, why did the pressure grow day by day?

Attempts to contact settlements near the affected areas either failed or found people frightened and planning to move. Gaia Central was having trouble keeping track of who was where. Just possibly the first settlers had made a mistake when they'd rejected Earth's efficient communication system and strong, centralized government.

Paradise didn't need that, they'd said, but Gaia wasn't paradise anymore.

Tension was making her jumpy and queasy. Drops got her through her workday, but she stayed home at night, watching the screen with her family.

Dan came over once. He checked her out, but said there was nothing he could fix. He looked worried, and she knew then that the way she felt was to do with the blighters. He looked fine, however, and she heard that every night at the Merrie was a wild night.

She decided all that energy might help her and went there after work, but it was nothing like the music night. Dan flared with too much energy, edgy energy that screamed down her nerves and twisted up her spine, giving her a crashing headache. No one else seemed bothered, but she fled for her own salvation, and because she thought Dan might burn himself to ash.

There was nothing she could do.

Or nothing she wanted to do.

She'd caught his eyes on her once. He'd held the moment before looking away. There must be a hundred women ready to have sex with Dan Fixer, especially now, and she couldn't. Not now.

Spontaneous combustion.

Then Polly's baby was born sick. Jenny was at the hospital with some of the others, waiting for the exciting news. She caught a glimpse of the baby being rushed from delivery room to intensive care in a red pod incubator. It looked tired of life already. A word came into her mind. Blight.

A tight-faced nurse came out of Polly's room. Jenny stepped in her way. "Has the fixer been called?"

"It's not a problem that can be fixed." The nurse walked away, and Jenny turned to the others.

"There must be something Dan can do!"

Yas gave her a look. "This isn't a broken bone or a gash, Jenny. You think he walks on water."

The sharpness of it took Jenny aback. "It wouldn't hurt to ask."

"If you want to chase him down . . ."

Jenny controlled an angry retort. "I do."

She strode to a wall phone and punched in his code. Nothing. She left a message, then tried Ozzy. Dan wasn't at the Merrie. She tried three other possible places. Nothing, nothing, nothing. If only she had his buzzer code, but that was for official business.

She'd always thought Gaia's ways right, but on Earth and most other worlds everyone had a buzzer. They could phone and be phoned anywhere, anytime. A horrible thought, but right now she wanted it.

She should give up, but Yas was looking at her with something close to a smirk, so she went out to search. She hopped a tram and rode it around Low Wall, then took another in to Market Square. Where the hell was he?

He might be at the hospital by now! She leapt off the tram at the next stop and ran to a phonepost. He wasn't there, and the baby was fading fast. She turned from the post—and found Dan there. She knew from his face, but asked anyway. "You heard?"

"Yes."

"So what are you going to do?"

"There's nothing I can do."

"What do you mean? You're a fixer."

He looked worn. Not so much tired, but fined down, burned down.

"I can't do anything, Jen. Do you think Assam and Polly want me there to toss out platitudinous comforts?"

"No, they want you there to do something, no matter how small."

"Think!"

She jerked back, feeling for a moment as if he might shake her.

"My father died last year. I'd have fixed that if I could do miracles, wouldn't I?" He sucked in a breath and ran a hand through his hair. "This is why they recommend that fixers don't return to their homes. Too many personal pressures."

His resistance was like a hand pushing her away, but she said, "Since you do live here, can't you at least try? Come on." She took his hand and tugged. After a moment he went with her, but she felt his reluctance like a weight.

She pulled him onto the West Street tram, but stayed standing near the doors. She couldn't bear to sit down. "Are you all right?"

"Of course."

But he looked almost as weary as the sick baby and she was going over his words. He'd said he couldn't do anything. Had he lost his powers? Had he blasted them away?

They got off at the hospital stop, and she steered him toward the main entrance. But then he balked and turned aside.

"Dan!" She hurried after. "Dan, stop. Please!"

He turned down a side street, and she caught him at a small door. "What are you *doing*?"

He pressed a lock. Hand print, not code. He used this door often.

The door opened, and she followed him in, watched as he took a set of hospital grays off a shelf and pulled them on over his uniform. "Jen, think. What happens if Dan Fixer walks around the hospital?"

"Everyone wants you to heal them." Why hadn't she thought of that?

He added a stretchy helmet, one designed for a man with a beard, which left only his eyes uncovered. He looked older, harder. Or perhaps he was.

"Why don't you, then? Heal everything."

"For a start, there's not enough of me to go round. But I can only fix things to make them right, which means mostly injuries. Disease is part of nature, like death. I can't fix nature."

He was angry. At the limits of his powers, or at her?

"I'll look at the baby," he said, "but I doubt it's fixable."
He turned and headed out of the room.

Jenny followed, wincing. How arrogant to drag him here,
as if she knew better than the hospital. She ached for Polly,
for Assam, and for Dan who must want to make their baby
healthy as much as she did.

At the intensive care nursery he said something to a staff
member, and Jenny was given a gray coverall and cap. She
didn't want to go with him, but she'd dragged him here. She
must. They walked through the steriline into the gently lit
room where soft music played with a beat that was surely
that of an adult human heart.

It was so peaceful. Surely it couldn't be a place of death.

At least Gaia accepted the latest technology for problems like this. There were four red-laced incubator pods
and two nurses moving between them, constantly checking
the sheath monitors on their arms.

Dan paused at each incubator, then stopped at one. He
signaled a nurse, and she hurried over. Jenny saw the sudden light in the nurse's eyes, and tears pricked at her own.
Dan had found something he could fix, but the name card
said Smithers. It wasn't Polly's baby.

She went closer and saw a tiny baby under a multicol-
ored mesh. Its chest labored, and its legs and arms seemed
grayish instead of pink. Dan pushed his hand through the
mesh and touched the child.

The baby clutched his finger as babies do, but to Jenny
it looked as if the mite recognized a lifeline. The little
chest still rose and fell, but less desperately, and the fingers and toes began to turn pink. The mesh began to fade
and retract . . .

"Heart," said a nurse, coming up beside Jenny. "Valve,"
she went on. "I was hoping it would be fixable when Dan
came around. I'm glad he's early. It's always special to see
him work."

"He comes every day?"

"Or when we call. We wait if we can. He has to have a life."

Yes, he did. Jenny was ashamed that she didn't know his
real life at all. Some friend she was.

He eased his finger out of the baby's clutch, then

touched the round cheek, smiling a little. But the smile faded as he moved on to the last incubator.

"He won't be able to help there," the nurse said, obviously surprised.

Jenny trailed after to see the flaccid, laboring baby. It already looked ancient and withered. Dan put his hands on the shell and leaned there. She tried to believe that he was doing something, something miraculous, but she knew it was simple grief.

She wanted to say, *Sorry, sorry, sorry . . .*

He turned and walked out. She hurried after.

"Since I'm here I might as well do my rounds. You'll want to be with Polly and Assam." It was a dismissal, but he added, "If they ask, tell them I'm sorry."

Then he was gone, and Jenny fought tears, for him as much as for the baby, as she worked her way out of the hospital gear.

After that, things only got worse. Polly and Assam had been the first of Jenny's friends to choose pregnancy, and the disaster appalled them all. Pregnancy was supposed to lead smoothly to a beautiful, healthy baby. The other babies in the pods had shown that problems happened, that perhaps disaster was natural, but it felt all wrong on top of so many other all wrongs. She couldn't stop thinking that it was blight, carried as spores on the wind.

Polly and Assam didn't blame Dan, but they avoided him. Jenny thought about telling them that he'd visited the nursery, but would it make it better or worse? Two weeks after the birth they decided to visit Assam's family in Araby, even though it was farther south. The good-bye party was subdued. Dan attended, but briefly.

Jenny looked at him and thought his flame was dying. Was it drowning in the blighters' growing power? Or was he as sick as she was of the bitter catch at the back of the throat, the amorphic taste of ashes on the wind?

Or was it simply the dead baby?

She couldn't fight off strange thoughts about that.

Had Dan struggled for a moment over that incubator? He'd talked about hard decisions. He'd used the word "can't." That didn't just mean able to; it could mean allowed to. She cornered him just outside the room.

"Could you have saved little Hal?"

He looked at her, eyes guarded. "Yes."

"What?"

He put fingers over her lips. "Not here."

He grabbed her arm and drew her out of the house, into the street. "There are rules, Jen. We can't fix what shouldn't be fixed."

"Who says? Who says what shouldn't be fixed?"

He shook his head as if it buzzed. "The rules. There's a difference between something broken and something sick. Nature must rule in the end."

She stared at him. "You let your father die because of *rules*?"

He didn't answer, but she knew it was true.

She turned and walked away, walked home to find her parents talking about it being too long since they'd visited cousin Mike in Erin. Obviously the soothing reports of "progress" and "imminent solution" weren't working anymore.

Or the soothing had stopped. When she turned on the Angliacom screen cell, the announcer was talking about the blighters "swarming." It made them sound like maniac bees.

Where, then, was the honey?

"However, we will soon see victory in the Hellbane Wars."

That was the first time she'd heard it officially described as a war.

She knew war. They'd studied it in school. Armies and battles, diplomats and negotiations. One side knew who the other side was, knew what the enemy wanted. If this was war, what did the enemy want? Where were the negotiators with whom they could bargain for mercy?

Then one day a news camera accidentally caught an ashing. The camera was panning a deserted settlement, but then switched to a person in the distance, walking toward the road. The woman, in dusty shirt and trousers, a knapsack over one shoulder, waved and hurried forward, probably hoping for a lift.

Then she looked around as if she'd heard something or caught something out of the corner of her eye. And she became afraid.

Jenny watched, tasting that fear as the woman began to run, calling for help but constantly turning and twisting as if trying to track an enemy. She stumbled, scrambled up, then stopped, frozen, mouth wide in a scream of terror. There was nothing to see of the blighter; not so much as dust stirring in a breeze.

The picture juddered, though, showing the operator's fear. The mike caught his mutters along with the scream. "Can't do anything. Can't help. God help us. Gotta go. Gotta go . . ."

But he stayed, holding the camera as steady as he could, to record the anonymous victim's abrupt translation into empty clothing and that small pile of ash.

No explosion, no fire, no wind.

Just dissolution.

Jenny's mother broke down in tears, then declared that they were all leaving, now.

Jenny protested. "I don't even know cousin Mike."

"That's not the point, and you know it!" Her mother turned to Jenny's ashen fifteen-year-old brother. "Charlie, grab some clothes. Not too many."

"I have work to do," Jenny said.

"Gaia can live without another brochure or handbook. No, you can't take all those books. Bill!" she yelled to Jenny's father. "Pack for Charlie, will you? Jenny, love, please. You saw that film. You want to stay for that?"

"I don't think we can run from it, Mum. If the fixers can't stop them, the blighters are going to eat us all."

"Not my family, they aren't." Her mother dashed around, gathering little things—photographs, documents. "Of course the fixers'll fix it. It'll just take a little more time. And during that time it's stupid to stand in the way!"

Jenny helped stuff the things in a bag. "You're probably right, Mum, but I can't go. I'm sorry."

She realized then that part of the reason was Dan. She was still angry with him, but she couldn't abandon him.

She helped everyone pack, went with them to the station, and bit back tears as she waved them off. She didn't regret her decision, only her mother's tearful despair.

She wandered back home. Because the house was so empty, she started going to the Merrie every night, though it wasn't very merrie. It was never more than half full, and people often asked for melancholy songs. Rolo and Gyrth had left. Yas was still around, perhaps because she seemed to be attached to Tom now, and he couldn't leave, being a policeman.

So who was with Dan these days? From the look of him the odd time he turned up at the pub, perhaps no one. He was Anglia's sole defense when the blighters arrived. Perhaps she should . . .

But she felt too fragile now. She thought she'd break under any pressure beyond even Dan Fixer's ability to mend.

Jenny was playing a Scottish lament when she saw the *Urgent News!* line scrolling across the message section of the silent screen. Ozzy switched the sound up, and she stopped playing.

"In a new move to put an end to the blighters," an announcer said, "all the fixers have been called to the front. Reports from Hellbane U . . ."

"What the heck's 'the front'?" someone asked.

"Old Earth war term," replied Ozzy. "The place where one army meets the other. Don't reckon it can be far from here now."

As if in answer, a map popped up, showing the red tide lapping at Anglia's borders.

"Pap," Ozzy said, muting the sound again, but he added, "Perhaps it's time to close the bloody dismal England."

Jenny could only think that Dan was going to leave. To fight blighters. And Gaia was losing the war.

"Any idea where Dan is, Ozzy?"

"Haven't seen him in a couple of days, luv. Perhaps he's on his way."

"No." Could she sense him, or was it wishful thinking? She left her fiddle there on the bar and went in search. Stupid, stupid, to have kept her distance all these weeks! He was probably right about nature. He'd told her, hoping for understanding, and she'd walked away.

The pubs were quiet, the music somber, and Dan was nowhere to be found. Not in the square, not at his place, not at the hospital. Not at his family's home; his mother and brothers hadn't left but looked as if they already had news of his death.

Jenny stopped outside the house, fighting tears. Weeks ago he'd mentioned the experts from Hellbane U going to help the local fixers in the fight. Since then the blighters had only grown in strength. If the experts had failed, what could simple fixers like Dan do?

Die, that's what.

She remembered another old war term. "Cannon fodder."

Perhaps he was already on his way, but she wandered the streets looking for him, hoping against hope that she'd have a chance to say something, do something to help before he left.

Eventually, she gave up, stopping to lean against some railings. Then she realized they were the ones around the Public Gardens—the place where the one solitary blighter had dared to pop up in Anglia.

The perfume of herbs and flowers played sweetly on the night air, and she thought how strange it was that all of this—all the simulations of Earth they'd created—would survive when the people were ash.

4

She turned in through the wrought iron gates and followed the wandering path toward the lake and the statue of the little victim. And there, near the statue, stood Dan, tossing stones into the lake.

Jenny paused, purpose tangling into uncertainty. Perhaps he wanted to be alone. He'd have no trouble finding company if he needed it.

Then he turned and held out a hand. "Jen."

There was welcome in it, but there was more. After a teetering moment, she went forward and put her hand in his. "Are you going to have to go?"

"I am going."

"You haven't been called?"

"I'm not sure there's anyone left to call me."

"The news . . . ?"

"I gave Angliacom that information."

He slid his hand free and went back to tossing stones into the glassy water. *Plop. Plop. Plop.* Each stone made a mesmerizingly slow arc, as if the air was denser than it should be.

"What do you mean, no one's left to call?"

"They're all gone." *Plop*. "The staff from Hellbane." *Plop*. "The fixers down south." *Plop*.

A chilly emptiness weakened her, and she sat where lawn met the lake's shingled edge.

Dan stopped tossing the stones. "There's just the ones in the northern and southern settlements. We've decided we might as well have a go, as they used to say."

It was like listening to nonsense. "Who used to say?"

He turned to her, and she thought he looked more relaxed than she'd seen him in weeks. But thin. Too thin.

"Men in war stories. It's usually men. I've been checking out books and films about war. *Lawrence of Arabia. The Dam Busters. Reach for the Sky. Sirius V.* Looking for suggestions."

"Did you find any?"

"Be brave, don't give up, and have the right weapons."

Tempting to think him mad, or joking like the old Dan, but he was deadly serious. *Bad adjective, Jenny.*

"What's going to happen, then?"

"I'm going to die. But," he added with an almost Dannish smile, "in the best tradition of English heroism, I'm going to keep a stiff upper lip and take as many with me as I can."

Jenny wanted to say no, to deny reality, but she knew it was the flat truth. "We're all going to die, I suppose. Is there anything the rest of us can do?"

"Give us reason to try, perhaps."

"If you fail, you die. Isn't that reason enough?"

He sat on the grass facing her. "I'm worn out by the waiting. In a way, I want it over."

She shivered, recognizing a reflection of her own state.

"Living and dying don't seem particularly important anymore," he said, "but Gaia is. I mean us, the people who've made Gaia home. I'm going to fight for that as long as I can. Perhaps I can make a difference."

She reached out and touched his hand.

"I know what it'll cost, though, Jen. You probably know, too. Why it seems easier to die now. Get it over with."

It was the ashes in the wind put into words.

Praying she read him right, she moved close and grasped

his tense hands, then raised one for the lover's kiss, as he had done to her, so long ago.

His hand flexed slightly against her jaw. "Are you preparing to sacrifice yourself for the cause?"

"No." If he could face the blighters, she could face honesty. "Just hoping."

He closed his eyes, then drew her hand to his mouth. "I called you. Tonight. Bad form when you'd not taken up my offer, but . . . I need you, Jen. You. Now."

Breathtakingly, she didn't doubt it. There'd been no reason for her wandering search, and in fact she hadn't wandered, but had drifted here like a feather on the wind.

"How. How did you call me?"

He drew her close, and his lips traced her cheek, her ear, her jaw. "I'm practicing rusty skills. If I'm going to fight, I'm going to fight dirty."

"I don't understand."

"You don't need to . . ."

And she didn't. There was nothing rusty about his lovemaking skills, and she sensed the something extra. It was little to do with her, no matter what he said, but everything to do with magic, with death. With more than death.

It sprang from hovering annihilation. Fear of it surrounded them and played in the magic of their minds. Fear of a void, which he fought with fire.

She let him undress her because he wanted to, and because each incidental brush of his hands on her skin was like liquid pleasure. It flowed over her and into her, and she pushed off his shirt to get to his skin, to give back, to draw more.

When she was naked, she stripped him, stroked him, cradled him. Then he was in her, slow, relentless, eternal, building a dizzying power. She might have been afraid of dying if things like that mattered anymore. All that mattered now was the cauterizing conflagration, and the drifting postapocalyptic dream.

She came back to reality to find that she was lying on her back on soft grass with Dan half over her, his head cradled on her breasts. He seemed relaxed, replete, and she felt the same way. What a fool she'd been—they could have been easing each other's bodies, minds, and souls like this all along.

So much wasted time, and now he was going off to die.

"Rusty skills," she said, playing with his shoulder-length hair. Longer than he used to wear it.

"Is that a complaint?"

She heard the smile in it so didn't answer.

She'd rather not think at all, but her mind was coming back to life, protesting fate. "The stones. What were you doing?"

"Controlling matter." He lazily pulled a handful of grass and tossed it in the air. She watched it hang there, then suddenly shower down on them.

"Sorry," he said, brushing it off her. "Still rusty."

The fire was in his touch, though, and brushing led to nibbling, nibbling to kissing, and kissing to another apocalypse. An easy way to mindless pleasure, but reality returned. He couldn't die. She had to save him.

"Someone must have sent for help," she said.

"Weeks ago, but it won't arrive in time. And anyway, what do federal bureaucrats know about blighters?"

But he sat and pulled her up to face him. "Any response might arrive in time to take some survivors off. Go north tomorrow, Jenny, and keep going north. Try to survive."

It was good advice, but Jenny doubted she'd take it. She couldn't imagine fleeing north while Dan went south to die. And she didn't want to leave Gaia. Perhaps it was the scrap of magic in her, that mysterious Gaian part, but she felt she'd wither and die away from here.

"I didn't know you could do things like that—the grass. How's that fixing?"

His grimace showed that he'd noticed her lack of promise, but he didn't pursue it. Perhaps he understood too well. "It isn't."

He collapsed onto his back, hands beneath his head, beautiful enough to distract. Perhaps that was his purpose. It wasn't going to work.

"So what is it?"

His eyes swiveled to hers. "Wild magic."

She knew he was about to tell her something important, but this time she wanted to know. "What's that?"

"The elemental force, I think. Fixers are born with magic. No one knows why. It doesn't go in families. No amount of effort can create it or increase it."

Okay, so she was weak. She leaned up on her elbow to trace the contours of his chest. "What about the training?"

"That's not to teach us how to do things. That's to teach us how not to do things. Here's the truth, Jen. Hellbane U makes such a fuss about finding fixers because they daren't leave a single one unchecked. We can't have wild magic."

"I don't understand."

"Remember when I fixed your finger?"

"But there was nothing bad about that."

"What about the baby?"

She'd pushed that to the back of her mind. "Would it really be so terrible for fixers to heal like that?"

"Yes, yes it would. In that, the training's right. We can't fool with nature. That's what drove Earth to the brink. Death's natural. Without orderly cycling of the parts the whole will rot."

"Then what are you doing with stones and grass?" She couldn't stop a sharp edge in her voice.

"Looking for a weapon. What if wild magic is more useful than tame against the blighters?"

She stared at him. "Tell me."

He rose and pulled her to her feet. "If I'm going to be coherent, we'd better get dressed. I have tea."

He picked up his shirt and found her bra and knickers underneath. With a grin, he tossed them to her. She resisted the urge to make a performance of putting them on. They needed to find a way to survive.

She noticed his small campfire, tucked behind rocks where it wouldn't be easily seen from outside the park. She dressed and went to sit there with him, holding her hands out to the warmth, though the night was not particularly cold. "Now tell me."

"I'm not sure I have my thoughts straight yet." He moved a metal pot onto a trivet over the flames. Steam began to curl out of the spout.

"Talking sometimes helps."

"Yes." He poured the tea into two cups. Had he always planned to draw her here?

"Talk," she said. "How do you suspend something in the air, and what use is it?"

"I don't know." He picked up a stone and released it in midair. It hung there, but then fell. "We don't understand what fixers do any more than we understand the blighters, but I think our . . . energy . . . comes from the same place."

"Negative and positive?"

"Perhaps, but perhaps not." He put his cup aside. "Look, assume that the blighters are not just energy but a species—undetectable to us, but following the same patterns as other species. They are born, they reproduce, they die, and they need to take in nutrients."

"Do they?"

"I have no idea. This is a working hypothesis. It would mean that they ash animals to feed, transforming them into the same kind of undetectable energy that they are."

"Like water transformed into steam by heat?"

"Or like green plants transformed into our ungreen bodies. That's a kind of magic if you don't know how it happens."

"Any sufficiently advanced technology is indistinguishable from magic," she said, remembering his words.

He pulled a face. "I can't see anything about the blighters we could remotely call technology. Perhaps that comment should say that everything we humans don't understand we classify as magic."

"And thus unreal."

"Until the unreal starts to eat us."

Jenny swirled the stewed tea in her cup, swirling what he'd said in her mind. "If the blighters are eating us, they'll have to stop, won't they? Otherwise . . ."

"Otherwise, they'll be like people on Earth and the cod."

"Good point. But they re-created the cod stocks from DNA."

"And the blighters almost certainly can't do that."

"So what are you saying? That they'll eat us all then die of starvation? That's not much comfort."

"I've been reading up on it. There are creatures that eat almost all their food source then go dormant until the supply recovers."

Pieces of the puzzle clicked into place. "That's why Gaia was so perfect for us! Fertile, lush plant life, but no large or sentient animals. The blighters had eaten it down to a nub. How long would they be dormant?"

"Probably as long as it takes."

"But instead," she said, almost breathless, "we arrived . . ."

"Like a delivery dinner."

"But it's been centuries!"

"Perhaps they're not programmed to stir until now. Perhaps their life cycle is naturally measured in centuries. Perhaps it's something to do with base energy stores . . ."

"Or perhaps," she said, "they were waiting for the dinner bell."

He nodded. "My guess is that the occasional blighters have been checking things out."

"Like the drones combing the universe for usable planets. Fair's fair, I suppose."

"And survival is survival." He broke a twig off a nearby bush and began to strip the leaves off it. Something he'd done as a boy when fretting. "Interesting, isn't it? Gaia was the perfect planet, settled with extreme care to ensure infinite harmony and balance. But it all comes back to the jungle in the end."

"Perhaps we had a good run because we developed fixers and learned to zap the blighters."

"Screwed up their system a bit?" He tossed the bare twig into the fire where flames licked at it. "Perhaps, perhaps, perhaps. This is all crazy speculation, you know."

"But it makes sense." Jenny looked from the spluttering twig to the statue of the little girl. "Ashes to ashes . . . Something's told them dinner's ready, and they're rushing to the table. What do we do?"

"That's the question. When we humans find a planet we like, the native life-forms can't stop us from cleaning them out to make things right for settlers. Perhaps we can't stop the blighters from cleaning us out for food. Some small animals will survive, and one day, who knows how far into the future, it'll be dinnertime again."

Jenny pressed her fingers to her head as if that might somehow make her brain sharper. "But you can beat the blighters. The fixers, I mean. So why can't you beat them now?"

"Numbers. A fixer can beat a blighter one-on-one with power to spare. A fixer might be able to beat ten, or even more. It's never been tested, blighters being rather rare." He shook his head. "That sounds so crazy now. We aren't efficient killers—it's a real case of using a hammer to kill an ant, but it hasn't mattered before. Now, if we have to zap one after another we're soon drained—and then they eat us.

"If the fixers had concentrated to begin with, we might have stopped them, but by the time Hellbane U woke up to it, there were too many, too widely spread around the equator. It's been like trying to drain a swamp by standing in it with a bucket. With the swamp eating the bucket."

"How many have you zapped?"

"One, to graduate."

"That's all? No wonder the war's not going well."

He shrugged. "I assume some of the fixers near the equator saw more."

She sipped the tea, then pulled a face at the bitter taste and put it aside. "What was it like?"

"We don't have words for it. *Blighter* is too . . . mundane. Even *hellbane* doesn't capture the sense of the alien that screeches against everything we know to be real and tries to latch on to parts of our brain that shouldn't be there. But are."

Jenny shuddered in recognition.

"Then there's the awareness of ravening hunger, of a blind need to consume. Us. That we are nothing more to it than a food source. Like a cow, or a fish, or a loaf of bread." She saw the shudder shake him. "And that's just a start. You have to be there."

"No," she said. "I know exactly what you mean. I can feel it now."

His look was quick and sober. "Then I'm sorry."

She pushed back the sick feeling. "Let's look at wild magic again. What can it do?"

He reached toward the fire. She saw him hesitate, but then he grabbed a glowing end of wood and held it, flames licking through his fingers. She gaped, but then he hissed and dropped it to blow on his hand. "Good job I'm a fixer."

Jenny wanted to laugh and cry. She wanted to hug him and keep him safe. She wanted someone to hug her and promise her that everything was going to be all right.

"Pathetic," he agreed, "but this is all we have to fight with. I'm sure it's the way. It's at the heart of Gaia."

She turned it around in her mind. "So you're magic and blighters are magic, and when a fixer pushes magic against one of them, it's gone."

"Not quite. The energy comes into us."

"Ah-ha! So you get stronger from stopping them."

"And they feed from eating us."

"Ergo, you need to kill more of them than they kill of you."

"Two problems. One: We get a lot less energy from one zap than we use. Two: I assume it works the other way for them because they're feeding."

"I'm not sure I follow that."

"Imagine I carry ten units of power. I use them to zap a blighter and get five back. With a bit of recovery time, I get back to ten again. These days, fixers are having to fight one hellbane after another. In theory they should be able to use the energy gained from a kill to destroy the next, but it's not working. As best I can tell, we become exhausted, so there must be leakage. When a fixer is drained, a blighter eats."

"But if 'dinner' is exhausted, is there any energy there?"

"There must be since they mostly feed on nonfixers, and even cows and pigs."

Something was teasing at her mind. She caught it. "But you said zapping one didn't take all your energy, so why don't you use less? Half a unit. A quarter. Then you'd be ahead."

He tossed the remains of his tea to hiss on the fire. "Because we don't know what the bloody hell we're doing. We just swing that hammer as hard as we can. If we could gather a bunch of them, we might be able to get a lot with one blow, but they seem to hunt alone."

"What are you going to do?"

"I don't know. Yet. I've suggested that all the fixers left gather to work on it. There has to be something."

"*You* have?"

"No one else seems to be in charge."

She took his hands. "I'm proud of you for doing that."

"I'm groping in the dark, Jen."

"No, you're not. You're finding lights."

He rested his head against hers. "You give me strength, Jen. When things were tough at school I used to think of you, that protecting Gaia meant protecting you."

Tears filled her eyes. "I'm not worthy of that." She unfastened the few buttons he'd done up. "I'm sorry for not doing this sooner. I was scared."

"So was I."

"I mean, of you. Of your magic."

He slid his hand under her top. "Why not? It terrifies me."

They kissed, and love came slowly, gently this time. Not hard, wild, and desperate, but like a secret flower in a winter garden, unexpectedly discovered and to be guarded from a killing frost until it bloomed.

They lay together afterward, talking over their lives. As dawn touched the sky, she said, "Can I come with you?"

"God, no. Go north."

She thought of lying but shook her head. "Win or lose, I'd rather be here."

"You're a stubborn woman, Jenny Hart."

"There's more to life than living, Dan Rutherford. I'll be here to meet you or the blighters, whichever comes first."

They dressed, then sat, holding hands within the glow of the fire.

"I've never been one for the old Earth religions," Jenny said, "but perhaps I'll pray."

"Pray for a bouncing bomb, then."

"What?"

He shook his head. "Just something from an old film."

When the sun rose, she helped him kill his fire and pack, then walked with him hand in hand to the southern gate. She cradled his face and kissed him, determined not to cry. "Come back. That's an order."

He smiled. "Yes, ma'am! I've coded my place to let you in. Keep an eye on it for me."

He hesitated only a second more, then walked up to and through the small, pointlessly guarded postern gate.

5

Jenny watched the gate close, then turned back into the quiet town. She walked to the old building and put her hand to the plate.

The door opened.

Despite the night they'd shared, she felt like an intruder in Dan's flat. Or perhaps she was afraid that people would realize what had happened. She wasn't ashamed of it, but it was delicate, not yet for public attention. He'd left everything neat. Nothing unnecessary out in the kitchen. Nothing in the fridge or the larder that might go off. His bed was made, his clothes all clean and put away.

The meticulous preparations for a future tenant. For death?

She flicked her way along the hangers just to touch things that had touched him, enjoying the hint of him that lingered even after laundry soap. At the left side, almost out of sight, she found some clothes that stirred memories.

She dragged them forward. A yellow shirt, a pair of striped trousers, and a red jacket. Gaudy fashions of ten years ago, now outgrown. Dan's favorite clothes from before he'd left Anglia. Tears escaped then, because the clothes showed how much he hadn't wanted to leave, hadn't wanted to be marked as different.

She pulled out the red jacket and huddled into it.

Wearing it, she wandered into the living room, where she ran her hand over his bookshelves, looking for a way to share his thoughts. Had he left his system open to her, too? She sat on the sofa and switched on his system. He had.

He'd mentioned films. He must have downloaded those from the archives. She pulled up his menu and found them, the war films he'd talked about, but the last thing he'd used was an audio.

Sir Winston Spencer Churchill, the title read. *Speech on Dunkirk, June 4, 1940. (Radio with sim.)*

She clicked on it, and a gravelly voice began. Dan had switched off the sim, and she left it like that, hearing it as it had been heard originally, when radio had been all they had. At first the flat delivery seemed ponderous, but then it began to shiver down her spine.

... we shall fight on the beaches, we shall fight on the landing grounds, we shall fight in the fields and in the streets, we shall fight in the hills; we shall never surrender.

The man spoke as if surrender was not an option and death a strong possibility. Did she hear the tone of one who tastes the ashes on the wind? He'd won his war. Had Dan found hope in that?

When that finished, she scanned the list of films and clicked on one from that war—World War II, a concept that had boggled her until now—*Reach for the Sky*. She watched it, hugging the jacket closer; watched the pilot be victorious; watched him lose his legs, then take to the air to fight again. And without fixing. She understood what Dan had drawn from that. She didn't like it, but she understood.

When the file ended, she clicked on the next. *Lawrence of Arabia.*

She didn't move into Dan's flat—there'd be too many questions—but she spent most of her spare time there. She watched the films, seeking what he'd found in them, using the lessons to keep going as the town emptied around her and the blighters came closer on the wind.

Keep going during the blitz. Don't let the enemy get you down. Keep a song in your heart. We'll meet again. Wave a white feather. She even made herself a red poppy to wear. No one knew what it meant, and she wasn't sure herself.

Red for courage?

Red for blood?

She stopped running the Angliacom cells of the screen because, even though the news was grim, it wasn't nearly as grim as the messages in her mind. She used her drops and went to work for something to do. Paperwork, it seemed, never entirely stopped.

Then one day she awoke to realize that something had changed. A lightening. A lessening of pressure ...

She clicked on Angliacom. There was no reporter—there hadn't been one for more than a week. Instead, the screen showed a still, tourist-style picture of Hellbane U up in the mountains on a perfect, sky-blue day. Across the bottom of the picture ran: *News in from our brave fixers at*

*the front. The spread of hellbanes has been halted. Repeat,
the spread of hellbanes has been halted. The wave has been
turned, and ultimate victory is in sight.*

Jenny watched it five times, joy building, then dashed to
the Merrie to see if anyone knew any details.

They didn't, but they were all close to delirious anyway.
There would have been another wild night if anyone had
been there to spark it. As it was, it was wild enough. Tom
and Yas were still around, and he and Jenny played rollicking songs. They even played the anthem again, and
some people sang it in tears.

Most of these people were packed and ready to flee not
just Anglia, but Gaia. Now they had hope. They drank
round after round of toasts to the fixers, especially to Dan
Fixer, their own hero.

Jenny had not heard from Dan, but he'd not called his
family either. She didn't think the blighters could knock
out com-towers, so there must be some other reason.

He could, of course, be dead. It was a fact she lived with
day by torturous day, consoling herself that no news was
good news. Surely the families would be told, like in the old
movies. Whatever the fixers were doing must make it difficult, perhaps impossible, to send any kind of message, but
that would surely change now.

She slipped away, slipped home, to sit in front of the
screen on max, showing ten different things. Maps on most
tracking where the blighters had been stopped. The
blighted area was still an appallingly huge belt around the
planet, and the closest edge was only fifty miles south of
Anglia.

Talking heads, but when she flipped between them none
had solid information. She muted the system, setting it to
alert her to mention of Dan Fixer, then fell asleep with no
new information. She woke to sunshine and the screen still
on. One section was flashing. Partial match.

An excited woman was mouthing silently, an exhausted
man behind her, sallow-skinned and haggard. A fixer?
Jenny hunted, cursing, for the clicker, finding it down the
side of a cushion, and turned that section onto max and
sound.

"... here at the front, as they call it. My friend here as-sures me I'm safe." The stocky reporter grinned, but she looked tensed to run at a word.

For some reason she was wearing a dull green shirt and trousers that looked vaguely like the army uniforms in the old films. Jenny snorted. Fat lot of good that would do her if a blighter came along. The woman chattered on, not really saying anything because there wasn't anything to say. Behind her lay peaceful, normal countryside.

"So," she said, turning to the man—flabby, middle-aged, grim—"you think this is the turning point of the war, Jit Fixer?"

"We're getting the upper hand."

It was direct, but the flat tone made Jenny's heart pound. No jubilation at all.

"Can you tell Gaia how you've managed to turn the tide, Jit?"

The man's eyes shifted for just a moment. "It's very technical," he said, then went on about concentration of powers, of nodes and impacts and strategic distributions of forces. Was she hearing Dan's theories put into practice?

If so, Jenny couldn't follow it, and by the look of the reporter, she couldn't either. Even so, Jenny sat glued, praying for a mention of Dan, even though she knew it was unlikely. There had been—what?—more than five thousand fixers before the war.

But Dan had said he'd been the one to gather the remaining fixers. He might be important enough to get a mention. No such luck. The reporter, glassy-eyed, brought the technical ramble to an end, wished the fixer success in the fight, and returned the screen to the "your local station."

Jenny slumped back in the chair. That hadn't even been Angliacom. It could have been anywhere around the world.

On sudden impulse she clicked on the directory and found the numbers for Hellbane U, scrolling down to *Information*. She clicked on that. After two rings a message flashed: *We regret that due to the current emergency the Gaian Center for Investigation and Control of the Hostile Amorphic Native Entities is unable to respond to enquiries. Please call back when normal conditions resume.*

Jenny went back to the regular screen and lay there

watching the maps and charts, then a string of interviews with displaced people, community administrators, even artists sharing their thoughts about victory. No mention of Dan.

If he was dead, wouldn't she know it?

She staggered up to go to the loo, grabbed some food, then collapsed again to watch. She'd had to switch the prompt to search for Dan Fixer only, which stopped the constant flashing and replaced it with nothing. A string of fixers gave interviews, and she learned to spot them simply from their debilitated look. All the fixers, young and old, seemed to be exhausted, and it was more than physical. It was as if something vital had been sucked out of them. What a terrible struggle it must be, but now they were winning.

Slowly, Jenny began to hear something in their voices, an echo of the war films. One of them even said, "We will never surrender," in a flat tone almost identical to Winston Churchill.

Was that anything to do with Dan?

Then one of the fixers cried. He was a dark-skinned man, perhaps, by his accent, from one of the African settlements first affected. Partway through his technical description, tears began to well in his large, dark eyes. He blinked and kept going, but then suddenly choked. He covered his face and turned away from the camera.

The reporter—another young black man, but speaking meticulous Earth Standard English—took over, talking about the exhaustion of the noble heroes who were fighting the terrible battle.

Jenny watched, hearing not the reporter but the sobs of the man off screen, shaken by that deep and desolate grief.

Was the talk of victory lies?

Or did the fixer weep for the price the victors had to pay?

In the past weeks she'd become an expert on war. All kinds of war. Now she remembered the words of the Duke of Wellington after the bloody victory at Waterloo: "Nothing except a battle lost can be half so melancholy as a battle won."

If Dan was alive, was he as melancholy, as soul-shocked, as the weeping fixer? Oh, to take him in her arms and comfort him. She'd have walked out of Anglia to find him if she'd had any idea where to start.

All she could do was her bit to keep the home fires burning. She had a shower, went to work, and even suctioned dust out of the idle presses. She kept part of the office screen on to Angliacom as she worked, set to alert her to any mention of Dan Fixer.

The parade of fixers stopped, however, replaced by a middle-aged woman called Helga, with gray hair and a stony, unreadable face. Helga flatly reported daily successes, giving details on areas that were cleared and safe. She did not take questions.

News readers returned. Jenny phoned Angliacom asking for news about Dan. A short time later she heard back. They'd put in a request for a report on him and received no response.

Anglia itself was perking up like a spring flower after a frost. People were pouring back in, and Jenny finally had enough work to distract her, enough that she grew impatient for her coworkers to come back.

Reporters ventured out with cameras, but apparently the fixers had ordered everyone to stay away from the front, so they could only send back pictures of peaceful countryside and occasional close-ups of heaps of clothing and ash. Even they were rare. War hadn't changed the weather, so most remains had been scattered by wind and rain.

Daily, Helga reported progress, and the red tide on the map ebbed. Then she began to announce places that were now safe, inviting people to return. There was never a trace of joy or triumph.

Jenny had learned to distrust the news, but she'd come to believe in Helga. The woman reminded her of jowly Churchill, someone who tamped down emotion and simply got the job done.

Anyway, Jenny knew in other ways that what Helga said was true. The pressure of sick fear in her mind was easing, the bitter taste was less. She actually had some appetite and began to put back the weight she'd lost. Sometimes she had to probe for the unreal parts of her mind instead of fighting them off.

With victory clear, it was like Christmas. She could have gone to ten parties a night, but instead she spent every night in Dan's place. She didn't watch the war films anymore. Instead she wandered through his sys—music, poetry, games, comedies. She saw *Monty Python and the Holy Grail* listed but skipped over it. She didn't think she'd find it funny now.

Then she came across his family album and some film from when they were kids.

A group of them running around screaming in the park under water jets.

A birthday party with Dan wearing a Sirius V helmet, a milkshake mustache, and missing his front teeth. Had they really once played at war?

Dan and her building something out of Robot-Robot, then cheering as their construct poured juice into a glass without spilling any. She thought about Earth, where apparently war was mostly waged by robots.

Lucky Earth.

Helga stopped reporting, and Jenny missed her stony stolidity, but the good news kept coming. The red swath around the equator shrunk thinner and thinner, and Jenny linked it to Dan's return. He was working hard, to his limit, destroying hellbanes. When that shrinking stain disappeared, Dan would come home.

Then one day she realized that her magic had gone. No, no, that wasn't quite it. That strange bit of her brain that shouldn't be there was still there, but it felt . . . alone. As if the rest of the magic had gone.

As if the fixers had gone?

She clicked on the screen, heart pounding. More jubilation. More stupid speeches. Say something about the fixers, you berks!

After an hour or so of nothing, she phoned the station. She managed to talk her way through to the newsroom and asked why there were no interviews with fixers.

"I thought you were offering to set up an interview with a fixer," a woman snapped.

"It's hard?"

The woman cut the connection.

With the screen on mute, Jenny closed her eyes and tried

to sense Dan. She probed for him, hunted him, blanked her mind so something could come on its own. Eventually she opened her eyes, defeated. It was as if the magic didn't exist anymore.

As if Dan didn't exist anymore.

Surely if the fixers were gone someone would say so.

Stomach churning, she watched ten screen-sectors at once. She stilled on one that showed people returning to their homes. The camera was like a predator itself, seeking the moments of horror, the faces of loss. Even while thinking that, Jenny couldn't move on. The continuing scenes of return were made weirder because all the buildings and machinery were intact, simply waiting for the inhabitants to return but often coated with ash.

A camera swooped in on a woman scrubbing, weeping, saying over and over, "Who am I cleaning up here? Who am I cleaning up?"

Soon it was almost as if the Hellbane Wars had never been, and yet, and yet, it seemed to Jenny that people held their breath as she did, not really able to believe that the terrible things were gone for good. And no one mentioned the other terrible thing—that they might have to carry on without fixers.

Eventually Jenny had to return to life. She cleaned Dan's place one last time and moved into her own home. Her family was coming back anyway, so she had to stock the house with basics and restart the energy sys. She went back to work and found that the manager, Sam Witherspoon, was back. Her family returned for a tearful reunion and told her Dan's family was back, too.

Jenny hurried over there, and her last hope died. They'd heard nothing, and they assumed he was dead. A hero, but dead.

Someone designed a poster of Dan Fixer, Hero, and it hung everywhere. Heaven knows where'd they'd found the shot to start with, but it didn't look much like Dan in the end. Square-jawed and rugged, he looked resolutely into the distance against a flaming red sky.

Jenny bought one and kept it, knowing he'd be amused.

Hoping he'd be amused.

Her last hope wasn't really dead.

Then Angliacom announced that in view of the lack of response from the fixers, a team of Mayan reporters was on its way to the Gaian Center for Investigation and Control of the Hostile Amorphic Native Entities. They would carry the thanks of the world and report back on the situation.

Needing privacy, Jenny watched on Dan's screen, watched through the camera's eye as the reporters approached the pale rock walls that looked like part of the Mayan mountain. The gates stood open, but no one waited to welcome them.

With the benefit of top-reality technology, she wandered empty streets and peered into deserted buildings. The mikes picked up only silence broken by breeze-blown dust and rubbish. At least the dust seemed ordinary dust, sandy and dry.

Were any of the houses places where Dan had been? Had he shopped at that bakery, drunk at that tavern? A reporter was droning on about Hellbane U in former days. Jenny made herself listen.

New students had been housed in dormitories in the central buildings ahead. Later, they could board with families in the town. Most of the citizens of Hellbane U were fixers—teachers or researchers—but some had been family and descendants of fixers, without special powers.

Then Jenny realized that the reporter was such a person, that he was a refugee from Hellbane U, returning to his former home and shocked by the desolation. He was a professional, however, and his voice stayed steady as the team progressed through the ghostly town, but she could hear the thickness of tears in it.

Tears were falling down her own cheeks.

Where have all the flowers gone?

Eventually the camera reached the central buildings. It panned lecture halls, libraries, and rooms that defied general descriptions. The tour continued, and Jenny watched it all, but Hellbane U was a dead place, the inhabitants gone. She remembered an old Earth term for it. A ghost town.

Where have all the flowers gone?

She found the song in the system and set it to play.

Another war song.

Damn war.

She listened, and watched, and wept for all the heroes who weren't coming back from the war.

6

They held a parade, renamed Bond Street Dan Fixer Way, and life went on.

Doctors had to learn how to mend broken bones with splints and plaster, but the latest technology was on the way. Apparently they had bugs and bots now to do just about anything the fixers could do. The Minister for Post-Fixer Adjustment moved into the fixer's flat. Dan's things were sent to his parents, who turned most of it over to a committee planning the Dan Fixer Museum. Jenny managed to sneak the red jacket out and take it home.

No one knew what the fixers had done, but they were heroes for sure. Yet it seemed to Jenny that, other than Dan's family and friends, people didn't seem deeply affected by the loss.

Her pain was beyond words or expression, so she hid it, glad that no one knew about that last night.

Then, as she wandered out of work at the end of another meaningless day, a woman in the street bumped into her.

"Did you hear? Dan Fixer's back!"

Jenny stared at her. "They found his body?" But then she answered herself. "No. Blighters leave nothing but ash."

"Alive as you and me! Outside the southern gate, he is."

Alive? Outside? The words didn't make sense.

"They're keeping him out, till they figure out what to do."

The gates would be shut, yes. They were still shut and guarded, though now she thought about it, she didn't know why. "Then it can't be Dan," Jenny said. "He's a citizen."

"*And* a fixer. Citizen of all, citizen of none."

A sort of glee in the woman's voice shattered the blankness in Jenny's mind. "You don't want him back? How can

you not want him back? He's a hero. He saved the world.
We had a parade and named a bloody street after him!
Don't you at least want the fixing back?"

The woman backed away, then turned and hurried off.

Jenny stood frozen. Dan was *back*?

Alive?

She was already running toward the nearest tram stop.
She needed to get to the gate, get to Dan. Then she realized
it would be on screen. If it was true. She stopped, made
herself look calm, and walked into the nearest pub.

One of the big screens faced the door, split between a
cricket game, comedy, and a dim, sunset landscape. She
saw a fire and a figure by it. She moved into that line of
sound, having to squeeze up against two men in business
clothes.

". . . claiming to be Dan Fixer," an announcer was saying.
"The Witan is meeting to discuss this development and as-
sures everyone . . ."

Jenny stepped into the cricket commentary so she could
focus on the picture. The camera must be up on the wall,
looking down at the road. On the grass verge a small fire
burned and a man sat beside it, reaching for a kettle, pouring boiling water into a pot.

Memory staggered her, then hope swept in, as weakening in its own way. She grasped a chair to hold herself up.

"Creepy, if you ask me."

Jenny blinked and looked at the two young men in office
wear drinking pints. One was blond with a sharp face, the
other dark-haired and heavy.

"They've always been a bit strange, haven't they, fixers?"
the blond said.

"No one knows how it works," the heavy one replied.

"No one knows what they did to win, either. One minute
the blighters are all over us, next minute they're gone."

"Fixers were supposed to be gone, too. So it can't really
be him, can it?"

"Or they're playing silly buggers with us."

More faint hostility. Was this a dream? It wouldn't be
surprising to dream that Dan was back, but why would she
dream this? She wanted to ask what the hell they were
thinking. If Dan was back, it was wonderful!

"They had stories on Earth about this sort of thing," the heavy man said.

"About what?" his friend asked.

"About people who come back from the dead. Ghouls. Vampires. Zombies. Ghosts. Monsters."

Jenny couldn't keep quiet. "*Monsters?*"

The man turned to her. "Can't know for sure, can we?"

Perhaps she looked alarmed rather than angry, because the other one said, "It's probably not even him, luv. Some berk thinking he can impersonate a hero, that's all. And not even good at it. I saw Dan Fixer not long before he left, and his hair was no longer than mine. Look at that."

He pointed at the screen, and Jenny looked. The camera wasn't on zoom so details weren't clear, but it did look as if the man had a rope of hair down his back.

She didn't realize how much hope she'd gathered until it drained away.

"Like a Trojan horse."

Jenny looked at the dark-haired man in disbelief. "Bringing what into the town?"

"Who knows. That's the point, isn't it?"

Jenny couldn't entirely fight off the idea. The fixers and the blighters had fed off the same force. What if in the end the remaining blighters had taken over their enemies?

She opened that neglected part of her mind, trying to detect something. Was the faint tingle real, or wishful thinking? Was her churning stomach and throbbing head a sign that the blighters were back, or just shock and nerves?

The screen picture changed to a stocky man. Alderman Higginbottom! She sidled over so she could hear him.

". . . have to take the cautious road here. We were given to understand that all the fixers had died in their gallant victory. We've been in touch with other major centers, and none of them have heard from their fixers. None of them have one on the doorstep, so to speak."

The camera shifted to the reporter, an eager young woman. "But Dan Fixer has explained that some survived, hasn't he?"

"He can explain all he wants, but we can't just take his word."

The message bar on the screen began to scroll: *Alder-*

man Jack Higginbottom talking to Angliacom reporter
Alinda Brown. Subject—arrival at the southern gate of a
person claiming to be Daniel Rutherford Fixer, our hero
of the Hellbane Wars. Gates are currently being kept
closed to everyone while a committee of the Witan reviews
the situation.

Committee. Jenny had to bite back laughter. It was a
standing joke that when anything unusual happened in
Anglia, the response was "Let's form a committee." Now
they were doing it, and as always it was a way of passing
time in the hope that the problem would go away.

"But given the heroic victory," Brown asked, "doesn't it
seem wrong to leave someone outside for the night?"

"Well, now, there's no saying how long it will be. The
committee may come to a rapid decision. As always, all citizens of Anglia are welcome to observe the discussion and
make presentations, either at Parliament Hall or from
screen phones."

"But why not let him in to speak for himself?" Brown
persisted.

Alderman Higginbottom shed his official veneer and
looked older and more strained. "Because we don't know
what's come back from the war, and nor do you! This is a
time for cautious thought, not impulsive action."

The screen abruptly switched to the Angliacom desk.
"We have reporter Nell Raiseby now with Dan Fixer's
mother . . ."

Jenny turned away. She couldn't bear watching that.
Should she go and support Annie Rutherford? Or to the
Witan to speak up for Dan?

But was it Dan? If Dan was alive, wouldn't he have con-
tacted his family? Or her? Especially her. Worse than that,
deep inside, painful as a fatal wound, she, too, had doubts.
If it was Dan, what had come home from the war?

"But he is a hero." When she realized she'd spoken
aloud she glanced around.

No one was paying attention, thank heavens.

She slipped out of the pub. She needed to go up on the
wall but dark was settling. Soon even the zoom camera
wouldn't see much, and she didn't need to see. She needed
to think.

She longed to have Dan back in her life, in her arms, but even if that figure by the fire was Dan, he could be changed. She'd seen that, too, in war films. People who returned not just with physical wounds but with mental ones, driven crazy by the things they'd had to do, destroying those they'd fought to save.

How did she find that out? How did she do the right thing, with her heart yearning to have him back?

She stepped back into the pub to see the screen. Part was covering the committee meeting now. Another section showed the huge basement pub in Parliament Hall with its fully screened wall that made it a popular place to watch official proceedings. An illusion of being close to the action.

As the camera scanned the attentive crowd, Jenny saw Tom, Rolo, Yas—a bunch of Dan's friends—at a table. They would be coming up with some way to help him.

She ran to catch a tram, aware that she'd made one decision. The man by the fire *was* Dan. And that meant she had to help him, no matter what the situation.

She was soon pushing into the crowded room, looking for the others but keeping an eye on the screens. She paused a moment to listen to the committee. Surprise, surprise. They weren't getting anywhere fast.

Where were the others?

Then someone shouted, "Jenny!" and she saw Gyrth standing and waving.

She made her way over, and those on one side wriggled together so she could squeeze in on the end of the bench.

The mood was grim. "It's not going well?" she asked.

Gyrth poured her a beer. "Who knows? At this rate they'll probably talk until the next blighter attack."

"The blighters are gone."

"Whatever."

Jenny took a deep drink. "Are they going to let Dan in?"

"Probably not."

"Then what are we going to do?"

Everyone looked at her blankly.

"What can anyone do?" Rolo asked.

"Argue. Protest! They can't keep a hero out."

"When Sillitoe argued that, Alderman Potts came up with the bright idea that we can't welcome home a hero of the Hellbane Wars without adequate preparation. He wants Dan to go away until we're ready."

Jenny groaned. "Let's form another committee."

No one laughed.

Jenny eyed them all. "We could sneak him in."

Instead of approval, eyes and bodies shifted.

"That wouldn't be right," Gyrth said. "It would be . . . undignified."

"It's not very dignified to leave him sitting out on the grass, is it?" She stared around. "Let's do form a bloody committee."

"Don't take that tone!" Yas leaned forward, poking a long, beringed finger onto the table. "It's not a simple matter, and if you think it is, you're naive. None of us know what Dan is now. Perhaps he is dangerous."

"You know better than that!"

"It's because I know better that I'm wary. There's more to him than the laughing friend, you know."

Jenny was shocked by her own outrage at Yas's claim. But none of them knew what had happened that last night. Perhaps she should tell them, but she couldn't do it. Perhaps they wouldn't even believe her.

"He's bound to be different, Jenny," Tom said gently.

"I suppose."

Then Rolo said something about there being more point watching cricket, and Yas turned it to office politics. In moments three different conversations were going on around the table, none of them about Dan.

If his closest friends didn't care, what could she do, especially when she knew better than any that Dan could be changed, would be changed. Not into a vampire or a ghoul, but in power. He'd begun the shift before he left.

Wild magic.

Then a screen section closed in on the long, severe face of Alice Cotrell. Jenny rolled her eyes. Mrs. Cotrell was a great one for drawing up petitions and addressing committees.

"I speak for more than a hundred citizens of Anglia—the names are here, Alders, if you wish to verify." Mrs. Cotrell waved some sheets of paper. "We wish to make it clear that many Anglians do not wish to see Dan Fixer back within our walls. While duly grateful for the service the fixers have done, we believe that his home, the home of all the fixers, is the Gaian Center for Investigation and Control of the Hostile Amorphic Native Elements."

How interesting that she used the full and formal name.

"It is intact," Mrs. Cotrell went on, "and suitable for habitation. As Dan Fixer claims there are only a small number of fixers left, there is plenty of accommodation ..."

"There are others alive?" Jenny whispered to Gyrth.

"Apparently. It might be best for them to gather there to figure out what to do in the future."

"True," Jenny said. But Dan wanted to come in.

He wanted, she suddenly realized, to come home.

Alice Cotrell was listing the many possible dangers a fixer might now present to normal people.

Normal, thought Jenny. How very interesting.

Alderwoman Sillitoe interrupted. "He seems perfectly normal, Mrs. Rutherford. And he was born and raised here."

Alice Cotrell stood straighter. "We do not understand his sort, any more than we understood the hellbanes. Who is to say that the fixers themselves won't turn wild on us one day?"

A murmur rolled around the room, but Jenny couldn't tell if it was shock or approval. She'd never thought of that. When a predator is eliminated, the prey often takes over as pest. She followed the debate, no longer certain what was right.

In the end, she grabbed on to one thing. "Listen!" she said.

They all stared at her.

"If everyone's afraid of what Dan might be, then someone has to go outside and find out. Yas—"

"Oh, no!" Yas raised a hand. "We weren't that close."

"What?"

"Not when he left. I don't know who he was rumpling with then."

Jenny turned to Tom, hoping the dim lighting hid her blush. "You're a good friend."

He turned his beer glass in his hands. "I don't know, Jenny. It's not that I'm afraid of Dan," he added quickly. "I don't think he'd deliberately hurt any of us."

"Tom!"

"You know better?" Yas demanded. "Why has he pretended to be dead for weeks?"

That was the overwhelming question. "I don't know," Jenny said. "I just know that someone has to go and find out why he's here and what he wants." The resistance around the table dragged her words to a halt. "All right. How many here want Dan back home?"

Eyes shifted. Perhaps some hands twitched, but none went up.

"It depends . . ."

"We can't decide yet . . ."

"I need to know . . ."

"My, my. The committee really is in touch with the mood of the voters, isn't it?"

"If you're so set on this," said Yas, "why don't you go and find out what's come home from the war?"

It was a challenge, one Jenny knew Yas didn't expect her to accept.

She turned her attention to the screen, hoping for something that would save her. No. They were consulting some expert about the place of Hellbane U in Gaian society. She didn't want to do this, but she had to. She'd remembered what she'd said when she'd parted from Dan.

"Come back," she'd said. "That's an order."

And he'd replied, "Yes, ma'am."

She took a deep breath, then looked back around the table. "I will, then, on one condition."

After a stunned moment, Tom said, "You don't have to—"

"If no one else will, I will. But on one condition. I'm your representative. If I come back and say Dan's safe, you all support that."

"What good will it do?" Rolo asked.

"If necessary, we smuggle him in and carry on the fight from here. Once people see he's just Dan, they'll change. Most of them want the fixing back. Medical technology doesn't fix machines and Earth china. Are we agreed?"

She thought for a terrible moment that they'd chorus no, but then Yas, of all people, said, "Yes. Fine. After all, you're such a careful sort. If you think he's safe, he's probably comatose."

It hurt, but Jenny hid it and waited until they'd all agreed. Then she stood. "All right. Let's do it."

The easiest way out was through the storage basement of Gyrth's uncle's grocery. They'd used it as teenagers when sneaking outside had seemed like an adventure. It didn't take long to move the stack of heavy boxes, then work out the loose stones that blocked the tunnel through the thick wall. Wriggling down the rough, dusty hole wasn't Jenny's favorite thing, but right now it seemed a small challenge. She went backward so her feet went out first, hung on with her fingers a second longer than necessary, then dropped the six feet or so to the grass.

She was committed now.

7

Jenny waved at Gyrth, whose blond head was sticking out of the hole to make sure she was all right, then turned toward that glowing fire.

She shivered under the swamp of chill air and dark infinity. Once again she couldn't see the ground beneath her feet, and Dan wasn't guiding her. She made herself step forward. She knew this was smooth grass, but she still felt for each step as if an abrupt crevasse might pitch her into destruction.

Then light shimmered, forming a silvery path across the grass, a path to the fire. To that figure by the fire, even though he hadn't moved.

She froze. He could do this. What else could he do?

Then he turned. "Hello, Jen."

He was still just a shape against the glow, but it was Dan's voice for sure, just the same as before except for the tone. She searched that tone for welcome, for warmth, and found none. Something inside shrank, wanting to run away. What if he didn't even remember the night that was so im-

portant to her? Combat stress caused neural damage that
could show in many ways.

"Don't be afraid. I won't hurt you."

She walked forward, picking that apart. I won't hurt you.
Not, I can't hurt you.

She'd known that—that he was controlled not by what
he could do but by what he allowed himself to do—yet she
was suddenly crushed by the mission she'd so carelessly
chosen. Who was she to decide the fate of a town? Of a
world, even. Who was she to assess Dan's capacity to harm
and destroy?

When she arrived close to the fire and was touched by its
light and warmth, she finally saw him clearly.

Changed. Very.

Dan. Still.

She realized what made him look harsher—his hair was
drawn back in a plait, into that rope of hair hanging down
his back.

Hair didn't grow that much in the time he'd been away.

"Would you like to sit," he said, "or did you just come to
stare?"

She flinched at his tone, but then he added, "I have tea,
and two cups. It's not stewed."

She sat suddenly on the grass, on the opposite side of the
low fire. He remembered. "How are you?" It was a stupid
question, but it had to be asked.

"Better." He poured tea into a cup she remembered so
well and passed it to her.

Better than what? she wanted to ask, but she was
groping through the dark here, afraid of rocks and cre-
vasses.

"Have the governors sent you any message?" she asked,
sipping. It was perfectly made tea, delicate and fresh. It
made her want to laugh and cry.

"I thought perhaps you were it."

"Unlikely."

"Sometimes messages are judiciously indirect."

It was a subtle point, made with a cynicism that was
strange from him.

"So?" he asked. "What's going on?"

"They've formed a committee."

His lips didn't even twitch. He might as well know the truth. "They're afraid of you, Dan. Grateful, mind, but afraid."

"That's fair. I'm afraid of myself."

Well, there was the answer to her question. She put down the cup because her hands had started to shake. "Then why do you want to come back?"

"It's my home."

"A person doesn't bring danger to their home."

"Why are you here, then?"

Truth. "A group of us—Tom, Yas, you know—thought we needed to find out about you. Before doing anything."

"And you drew the short straw?"

She sighed. "I was the only one willing."

He suddenly smiled, a flickering hint of the old Dan. "Ah, Jen. That's part of why I've come back."

"For your doubting friends?"

"For you."

Her heart missed a beat. "Why?"

"Do you have to ask?"

"Yes."

He looked down. "Perhaps because you commanded me to."

Coward that she was, she didn't want that burden. "Really?"

"Partly."

She realized then that he was being as painfully careful of truth as she was.

He looked back up, faced her. "I need you, Jen, to have a chance of survival."

"You have survived! The war's over. Isn't it?"

"I'm not sure wars are ever over. The repercussions rumble on and on."

"You don't need me." She meant it to be cheerful, bracing, but truth tumbled out after it. "I don't want to be needed that way, Dan."

"I don't want to need you that way. Sometimes we run out of choices."

He reached into the fire and grasped a burning brand. He lifted it, flames licking his fingers. She waited for him to drop it, but he didn't.

"I can hold a burning brand, Jen. You can hold me."

She tossed her remaining tea over the flames. They hissed, but then burned on undaunted.

Burning what?

He released the brand in midair, and it hung there as he showed her his unmarked hand. "You'll survive, too. I think."

When he'd left, a small piece of glowing wood had burned his fingers. Sharp as a knife, Jenny knew everyone was right. Dan was more dangerous than she'd ever imagined, too dangerous by far for a peaceful town. Or for her.

"You can't force me, Dan."

"I can, in fact, but I'm trying not to." Abruptly, the brand fell back into the fire, scattering golden sparks. "I've learned many things, Jen, and one is that we do what we have to do to win." Suddenly, he lowered his head, his fingers digging into his bound hair. "I'm sorry. I shouldn't have put it like that. I've not talked to real people for a long time. Rusty skills . . ."

Oh, if he was looking for a weapon, he'd found a good one. It was as if she were back by the lake again, with Dan facing death and the ashes gritty in her mind. She longed to reach out and soothe those anguished hands, but she held back. She had taken on a greater role, had accepted the responsibility of judge. And she was scared. She felt a lick of fear that might be what a hellbane victim felt, and a pull toward him that was almost as bad.

"I need you, yes," he said, with the kind of calm that takes great effort, "but there's more to it than that." He looked up, eyes densely dark in the fire's shadows. "The world needs you. Needs both of us. You say you can't. You don't have that choice. You must."

She blocked that. He was powerful, and he was wounded. He might be very dangerous indeed.

But he needed her, and she knew what she must do. "I'm yours, Dan. Forever, if you want me. I'll come with you to Hellbane U."

A ghost of a smile touched his lips. "Thank you for that, love, but it isn't so easy. I need the town."

The word "love" collided with the rest of it. "The town doesn't need you."

"Same argument as before. They have no choice."

"Then why are you sitting out here instead of going in?" She pointed at the closed gates. "Blow them open!"

The brand rose again without touch and began to whirl, shooting flame into the dark. She glanced at the wall. Was that damned camera still running? "Put that thing back before someone sees it!"

It stopped, then settled with perfect gentleness into the fire bed. "Better?" he asked.

Her heart raced, and tea and ale churned. "Was that demonstration of control designed to reassure me? Because it failed. *What are you doing?*"

He inhaled, and she thought she saw impatience, frustration, anger—an army of dangerous emotions. Every bit of her flinched, but she made herself meet his eyes.

"All right. I hoped if I just turned up, they'd let me in before they thought about it. Once in, I knew it would be a different game. I didn't expect the guard on the gate now it's over."

"It's become a habit."

"A bad one. Once I was stopped, I could only try persuasion. Nothing would work if I stormed my way in. It's like that night in Surrey Green," he said, "and you. I need . . . welcome, Jen."

"The town's not going to fall in love with you." It was an indirect response to his declaration of love, and she saw him note it and put it aside as she had. Their feelings were not the crux of this matter. "What do you mean 'nothing would work'? What are you trying to do?"

He flexed his hands in a gesture of frustration. "I don't know. I know I need the town, and I need you. I can pay my way," he added, almost pathetically. "I'm still a fixer."

"More than a fixer."

"True. But I could do only what a fixer did."

His desperation tormented her. Whatever he'd become, he'd done it for them all—for the town, for Gaia. They should be welcoming him, but a wounded animal is a wounded animal, no matter what the cause.

"If you could pretend to be the old Dan Fixer . . ." She answered herself. "But you can't. We all know, or at least guess. You're a hero of the Hellbane Wars, mighty and to be feared. Do you know they renamed Bond Street Dan Fixer Way?"

"That's ridiculous."

"But you're stuck with it." She eyed him. "Why do I feel comfortable all of a sudden? Is it magic?"

"I don't think so."

The relief only lasted a moment. "Are you saying you don't know? Don't know what you're doing?"

"No, not that. But I can't say there isn't any . . . radiance from it. If there is, I can't do anything about it. Does it matter?"

It was an anxious question, and she didn't know the answer. She raised her knees and rested her weary head on them. "Explain, Dan. Please. Explain what you're trying to do."

He picked up a dead stick, an ordinary one, and poked at the fire. "The remaining fixers are all more or less as I am now. In power. Hellbanes are a powerful potion."

"Is that why you let everyone think you were dead?"

He nodded. "We had to decide what we'd become before we could decide what to do. We could have disappeared, let everyone think us dead. The thing is some of us are . . . out of control. Mad, I suppose. But mad with great power. We're guarding them, but it takes nearly all our resources. Perhaps they'll heal. If not . . ."

"You'll kill them?" She was proud of her calm voice.

"We'll have no choice. We can't spend all our energy on them."

"Why not? We miss fixers, but we can cope."

He shook his head. "Gaia needs fixers. We have to rebuild the system."

"What, with a handful of you? Perhaps Alice Cottrel had the right idea and you should stay at Hellbane U and come when called. For important things only."

"I'm not talking about that kind of fixing."

"What, then?"

"If the blighters come back. We have to be ready, and we have to find a better way."

Blighters back? But her mind fixed on the pain at the end of the sentence.

"What happened, Dan? What did you have to do?"

"You don't want to know."

She gripped her hands together. "Tell me anyway."

He tossed the stick into the fire, and it burst into wild flames, making her flinch away.

"All right. It was my idea, clever lad that I am. Fixers were dying one by one, and the blighters only grew stronger. We all wanted to rush out and fight, but I persuaded everyone to play with their magic like I'd been doing, to find the stuff training had locked up in us."

His eyes brightened for a moment. "It was amazing what some of us could do, Jen, the power we could draw on. It became clear that the presence of so many blighters was making us stronger, day by day. But what to do with it?"

Any light in him died. "Do you remember what I said about power gained and lost? We figured out that we could act in a group and have even greater destructive force, but we still couldn't modulate it. What we needed was blighters bunched in huge numbers, and that doesn't seem to be their way."

Jenny was trying to follow his logic, but mostly she was following something that ran beneath his words. Something terrible.

"So we baited a trap."

Her mouth dried. "With what?"

He leaned back on stiff arms. It might have been a relaxed posture, but it wasn't. "They like people more than animals, but they really love fixers—like I love Walker's spiced meat pies, and you love those big strawberries your father grows. A solitary fixer draws blighters from all around. Perhaps they fight over the prey. I don't know . . ."

She stared at him, but apart from that betraying pause, his tone was flat.

"So we formed troops of the ideal size—about forty, as it happens. We'd form a circle and put the bait in the center. When the blighters rushed in to feed, we cleared the area. We'd get thousands sometimes, and the juice would flood into us, making us stronger still. Then the troop moved along and did it again. And again. And again. Troops had to merge, of course, in time . . ." After a moment he said, "It was mostly my idea, and it worked."

She was still trying to form words when he added, "We drew lots. My name was never drawn."

After three swallows, she managed, "How—how many of you were there in the beginning?"

"More than a thousand—" Like a violently untethered spring, he curled forward, hands over his face. "One thousand two hundred and twenty-three."

And eighteen came home. Day after relentless day, numbers dwindling, lots drawn, good-byes said . . .

"We all wanted to be noble sacrifices, but the fear's too strong. So we used magic to hold the bait. Right in the middle. It's most efficient that way."

She scooted around the fire and gathered his pain tight into her arms.

"You dread being chosen," he whispered. "You dread not being. You dread living—"

"Dan. Dan . . . don't. Don't think about it." Oh, how crushingly stupid.

He turned to her and clung, and she did the only thing she could and held tighter still. She wished he'd cry, but he'd surely drained himself of tears long ago.

"You don't want to be here, where you're not wanted," she murmured, rubbing her face against his hair, stroking him, tears escaping. "If it's me you want, I'll come with you. Anywhere."

He turned his head against hers to brush lips. "It's you I want, Jen. It's you I need. You. I thought of you, dreamed of you. When I wanted to throw myself into the blighters because it would be easier, I thought of coming back to you." He kissed tears from her cheek. "Don't cry, love. Don't cry."

"How can I not? But you're home now, Dan. Home."

Then she realized what she'd said. She drew back, cradled his face, looked into his eyes. "It's important to you? That you come home?"

"I don't think I can carry on without it, but . . . there's more. I'm the only one with a real home to come back to. To heal, I need you. To live, I need you. But I need the town, too. To do what needs to be done, to be what I need to be, I need my family, your family, our family, our friends. Those are the roots of the tree that I am, the tree that magic is, the tree of the future."

She remembered then what he'd said. "When the blighters might return?"

"I don't think we destroyed them, Jen. We zapped a lot of them, millions maybe, but I think in the end they retreated. We were down to eighteen, and though we were each bloated with power we were close to the end. Yet they went. If this is their life cycle, perhaps they retreated with enough energy to reproduce, or whatever they do."

"The last time must have been a thousand years or more ago."

"But that's because they ate this place almost to extinction. We've survived. If we slacken birth control, we could build the population again in a generation. Even without that, it'll probably be back in a century or so. Or Earth might send more settlers."

Jenny pressed her face against his shoulder. Eighteen left, all crippled in some way, yet they had to be teachers for a new generation of fixers who might be needed within decades—needed to sacrifice themselves again? He was right. There had to be a better way.

Dan and the few other sane fixers would have to come up with that better way while training new ones. And they'd have to train them in the wild magic as well as the old sort.

She remembered Polly's baby. She knew now he'd been right. They shouldn't interfere too much with nature, but that meant the world must change so that it could accept that. Accept that, no matter the personal suffering, the magic must be restrained unless the blighters returned to feed again. To lead all this, Dan needed his home, and above all, he needed her.

She turned to touch her lips to his brow. "I am home. I am yours. Always."

Lips joined, and she tasted need and lingering ashes. No, need was too frail a word. Starvation. A gaping hollow in the soul he'd tried so hard to hide from her. She could not deny him the feast, no matter what the cost. Gathering him into her arms, she deepened the kiss, took the ashes, held him close, until she felt the first desperation diminish.

"Come, love, come." She pulled his shirt loose and put her hands to the hot skin of his back, already rolling him out of the fire's low glow into some privacy. They tore at clothes, and he thrust deep within, seeming to burn her in the surging connection with those alien places only he could touch.

She climaxed quickly, but he went on, pounding into her until she wanted to protest, to cry out to him to stop. She braced herself and bore it, knowing he was far away, seeking something deeper and stronger than mere orgasm. Something healing for those invisible, terrible wounds. He drove her through two more mechanical annihilations before he shuddered and stopped, limp as the dead.

She winced as she bore his weight, knowing it symbolized some of what was to come. His need was great, but she would grow strong enough to bear it. His healing would draw on her, but she would be a deep enough well. His thoughts would not always be centered on her, but that was as it should be. He was a hero, and a hero's intent is always on the greater goal.

Dan had become what he was in order to save them all. She could do no less. For his sake and the world's, she'd feed and nurture him.

And, tomorrow, she would bring him home.

They dressed as the sun began to rise and breakfasted on stale bread and stewed tea. They laughed about that, remembering the park and the horrible boiled tea there. They talked of the future, gently. He thought there might be many people like her, with a little fixing ability that could be developed so they could take on some of the load.

"Perhaps everyone on Gaia's that way," she said. "It could explain why it's such a flourishing, stable world."

He met her smile. "Which it is, and will be."

When the sun was up, they extinguished the fire, packed his bag, and walked up to knock on the postern gate. The wide-eyed gatekeeper opened it and put the formal question.

"What business brings you to Anglia?"

Jenny answered. "I'm Jenny Hart, citizen, and this is my chosen partner, Dan Rutherford Fixer. We're returning home."

The rule was ancient and absolute. Any citizen's partner had freedom of the town.

"I'll have to see about this," the gatekeeper said, shutting the door on them.

Jenny looked at Dan, trying to see him as others would see him. She thought he looked as he always had. He'd done something magical to make his hair short again, and he didn't think it would grow so fast anymore. Some of the stress was fading from his features.

They'd made love again with the dawn, that time for her. When she murmured about cameras, he said he'd blocked them. She knew for sure now that she wasn't bringing wildfire into the town, but winter fire, and she would be its hearth.

The gatekeeper returned to open the gate for them. Holding hands, Jenny led Dan through to face the bewildered, hastily assembled alders.

The trouble with heroes is that they want to come home.

But home needs its heroes, and home is also their just reward.

Shadows in the Wood

by Jennifer Roberson

*A*wareness stirred. Then stilled. Stirred again, weakly; was like a weary man struggling to open eyelids grown too heavy for his will. Opened. Closed. Awake, then asleep.

He had lived in darkness so long he did not at first believe such a thing as light existed. But it sparked at the edges of awareness, kindled fitfully into life. A very quiet life it was, timid and halting, but incontrovertibly life. He recognized it as such. And in that recognition, he acknowledged sentience. Victory at last over the enemy.

At last? For all he knew, it had been no more than the day before now, this moment, that he had been defeated. Enspelled. Entrapped. But with sentience and awareness came also understanding that such imprisonment as his had been conjured to last a lifetime, or a hundred lifetimes of men older than he. For time out of mind.

But he was not . . . man. That he knew. The body, the soul, remained imprisoned. Only the mind, the barest flicker of awareness, bestirred itself out of the long, enforced lethargy.

He wondered what had awakened him. Here, there was no scent, no sight, no sound. He tasted nothing, because he had no mouth. He merely was, when before, for time uncounted, he was not.

Was not.

Now, again, all unexpectedly, he was.

Astonishment. Relief. Exultation.

Alive. Not as men marked it, for he, in this place, was nothing approaching human. He had no heart to beat, no mouth

*to speak, no eyes to see; neither ears to hear nor nose to smell.
No body answered his will. No pulse throbbed in his neck.
But for now it did not matter. Something in him sensed,
something in him knew, release after all was possible.*

Someone is coming.

No more than that.

Someone is coming.

*It was his comfort. It was his joy. It was the light against
the darkness, the shield against the spear.*

Someone. Someday.

For now, it was enough.

England, 1202

She felt the morning fog drift down and settle, a cool caress
of dampness upon her face and hair, insinuating itself beneath the peaked hummock of rough-spun blanket draped
across one shoulder. She burrowed closer into the blankets
and hides to the warmth that was male, to the Crusade-
scarred body grown precious years before; beloved before
even they met in carnal congress beneath the roof of the
tiny oratory built onto her father's manor at her mother's
behest.

All dead to her now: father, mother, brother; even the
manor, which now was held by the Crown, embodied by a
man she knew as heartless. John Lackland. John Softsword.
John, King of England. Who refused to return to her the
hall into which she had been born, in which she had found
a worthwhile living even after she knew herself the only
one left of her blood. A man, a king, who listened instead
to another man she named enemy: William deLacey. High
Sheriff of Nottingham.

The warmth, the body beside her, sensed her awakening
and began its own. He turned toward her, drawing her
nearer, wrapping her in his arms and legs. One spread-
fingered hand cradled the back of her skull, tucking her
head beneath his chin.

He stroked the black strands escaped from her braid.
"Cold?"

She felt more than heard the words deep in his chest and
smiled. "Not *now*."

The prickle of unshaven jaw snagged her hair as he shifted closer. " 'Twill be winter soon."

"Too soon," she murmured, twining her limbs more tightly with his.

One hand wound a strand of her hair through his fingers. "I had hoped to offer you more than a rude cave and a bed upon the ground."

Of course he had. And would have: wealth beyond imagining, power, title, castle. But he, as she, was denied that legacy, stripped of all his father had labored to build even as hers had labored, even as hers was stripped, albeit in death. Her father had been a mere knight, his a powerful earl, but it mattered little to sheriff or king. Knight and earl were dead, and the heirs of both, through royal decree, lacked such claim as would put them beneath the roofs their fathers had caused to be raised.

She gazed upward, blinking against moisture. The only roof now they called their own was the canopy of trees arching high overhead; their hall made of living trunks rather than hewn pillars; windows not of glass but built instead of air, where the leaves twined aside and permitted entry to the sun. Such little sky to see, here in the shadows of Sherwood, where their only hope of survival lay in escaping the sheriff's men.

She and Robin—formerly Sir Robert of Locksley, knight and honored Crusader, companion to now-dead Lionheart—took such privacy as they could find in the depths of the woods, laying a bed some distance from the others, friends and fellow outlaws, screened by the lattice-work of limbs and leaves, of bracken and vine. A pile of small boughs, uprooted fern, an armful of hides and blankets spread upon the hummock. Some would call it rude, a peasant's crude nest. But so long as he was in it, she would call it home.

Yet Robin was right. Already autumn's leaves fell, cloaking the ground and everything upon it, including themselves. They would soon have little warmth, and less foliage to hide behind. It was close on time to go to the caves.

But not just yet. His hands were upon her, and hers upon him, finding eager entrance into clothing beneath the blankets of cloth, of hide, of fallen leaves. As dawn broke upon them, sluggish behind the fog, they affirmed yet again beneath the vault of tree and sky what had been obvious to their souls, obvious to their hearts, from even before the beginning that night in the oratory, with illumination banished save for lightning's fitful brilliance.

Robin set his shoulder against the bole of a broad-crowned oak and gazed down the road, one hand wrapped around the grip of a strung bow that stood nearly as tall as he. A leather baldric crossed from left shoulder to right hip; from a quiver behind the shoulder sprouted a spray of goose feathers and a sheaf of straight-hewn shafts a full cloth-yard long. He wore hosen and tunic as any peasant, woven of crude cloth, but also boots upon his feet—once fine, now scuffed and soiled—and a brigandine taken from a man he himself had killed. Once accustomed to weighty armor, he found the shirt of linked rings to be no burden.

In the Holy Land, on Crusade, stealth had not been an issue. He had ridden with an army headed by three sovereigns and many high lords. But Sir Robert of Locksley had returned to England a very different man. And that man, now stripped of his knighthood, his earldom, and his home by the Lionheart's brother, lived among the shadows in the company of outlaws instead of kings and queens.

Robin in the Wood, Robin in the Hood. Robin Hood. Whose entire life, now, was defined by stealth.

He listened for hoofbeats. Then knelt, pressed a palm against the beaten track, and felt for the same. He heard, and felt, nothing. There was no prey upon the road.

Once awake, awareness did not slide again into sleep. The tiny spark he recognized as himself, in spirit if not embodied, continued to glow brightly, slowly gathering strength until he had no fear it might be snuffed out. He remained bound, bodiless, with no recourse to escape, but he was awake, aware, and alive. He understood this, too, was a part of the spell, that to know oneself trapped for uncountable days was as much a torture as a lash upon bare flesh—as if betrayal such as he had known were not torture enough. But he rather thought not. These happenings seemed unplanned, and unforeseen, by the enemy who had enspelled him.

He recognized—something. Nebulous yet, wholly un- formed, but his senses comprehended what his body could not feel.

Someone is coming.

Awareness coalesced, compacted, then spasmed in recog- nition. In comprehension of—opportunity.

He lacked a mouth, but the words, the plea, formed nonetheless. Oh, come. Come soon. Come NOW.

Marian had grown accustomed to living among the trees, naming the forest her hall. She had arrived at a compro- mise with the results of such surroundings: the damp soil that worked its way into her clothing, the stains of vegeta- tion, the litter of crumpled leaves, the occasional thorn punctures and scratches. So long as no true hurt came of such importunities, she could suffer them in silence, except when a broken thorn stuck fast beneath her flesh, in which case someone—usually Robin, or Much with his quick, deft hands—dug it out for her.

She had, three years before, cast off the binding skirts of a lady's embroidered chemises and went now clothed more like a man, in heavy woven hosen, tunic, and boots. Over it all she wore a surcoat belted around her hips, the sleeve- less, open-sided length of cloth invented on Crusade to beat back the blow of the Holy Land's sun on metal armor. But hers was not made of fine cloth with the red cross of Crusade on her breast or shoulder; hers was leather, cut to her size, and offered more maidenly modesty than hosen and tunic alone.

Though, at that, Marian smiled. She was no more a maiden, being too often titled *whore* despite the fact she and Robin had married a few years earlier. And her mod- esty had been shed years before in the oratory.

But the part of living as an outlaw among the trees and deadfall that she most detested was packing to move the camp. They had all taken to heart the lessons learned of keeping safe from the men who would capture them. They claimed no true home except what they made for a day or a night, though occasionally they settled some few days longer in a place deemed safe; no tables, no stools, save for the trunks of fallen trees, a tumble of moss-laden stone. But there were such things as iron pots, a tripod for the fire, bowls, mugs, bedding. Not to mention the swords, the staffs, the knives, and the invaluable bows Robin had taught each of them to use with frightening accuracy, from Much, the simpleton boy, and the giant, Little John, to Will Scarlet and the minstrel Alan of the Dales; even poor Brother Tuck, preferring to trust to God rather than to the bow, learned it nonetheless. An English longbow, Robin had explained, was a more powerful weapon even than a Norman crossbow with its deadly quarrels, for a cloth-yard arrow could punch through armor from long distances, with the archer well-shielded behind trees and brush.

Marian had cause to know. She had herself learned how to use a bow years before, but now knew also how to fletch the shafts with goose feathers, to tie on and seal the deadly iron broadheads with sinew and glue. A few of the sheriff's men had been wounded by her arrows, by the accuracy of her aim that might have, could have, killed them, had she chosen to do so. One day, she knew, she would choose, would be brought to the choice. She did not wish to make it. But so long as such men as the sheriff set upon them desired the lives of men she cared for, Marian would not shirk the task of preserving those lives at the cost of their own.

Now Robin came back from the High Road linking Nottingham to Lincoln, a byway that afforded them opportunity to improve the lot of the poor while inconveniencing the lords and wealthy merchants who protested the loss of coin and ornamentation. He slipped through the trees and foliage as if born to the life, making almost no sound. When he saw what little was left to do before departure, he smiled at her in accord. They knew each other's thoughts. Knew each other's habits.

"Anyone coming?" Will Scarlet asked, picking idly at his teeth with a green twig. "Any rich Norman rabbits for our stewpot?"

Robin shook his head with its cascade of pale hair. "No one."

Little John reached down for his pack. "Gives us time, then, to make some distance."

Alan of the Dales was making certain his lute case rode easily against his shoulders. "We'll have to take a deer once we reach the caves, or go hungry tonight."

"And tomorrow," Tuck put in, patting his ample belly. "No doubt I could go without, but—"

"But we dare not risk it," Scarlet interjected, "or we'll be hearing your complaints all night!"

Tuck was astonished. "I never complain!"

"Your *belly* does," Little John clarified pointedly.

"Oh." The monk's expression was mortified. "Oh, dear."

"Never mind," Robin told him, grinning. "We'll take our deer and feast right well."

Marian swung her own pack up and slid her arms through the straps. It was a matter of less effort now, to arrange pack, bow, and quiver about her person without tangling anything. Outlawry and privation had trained them all.

Much, grown taller than when he had joined them but still thin and hollow-faced, doused the small fire. He could not fully hide its signs or that people had gathered around it, but his job was to make certain none of them could be identified. The sheriff's men might find a deserted clearing, but there would be no tracks to follow, no indication of who had camped there. Sherwood housed innumerable outlaws. Not every fire, nor every campsite, hosted Robin Hood and his band.

Robin's hand fell on Much's shoulder, thanking him in silence. Next he glanced at Marian. She nodded, drawing in a breath. Then they turned as one to the trees and stepped into the shadows, fading away as if their bodies were wrought of air and light, not formed of flesh and bone. In such meager human sorcery lay survival.

He sensed impatience, emotions that had been dead to him for days, years, decades. He sensed urgency and yearning; he tasted the promise of power, the ability once again to make a difference in the world.

Kingmaker. Widowmaker. Reviled, and beloved. But he knew only one path. Impediments upon it were to be overcome.

Hurry, *he wished.*
He wished it very hard.

The outcry echoed in the trees. Robin spun around, gesturing sharply to the others strung out behind him on the deer track. Even as all of them dove into foliage, separating to make more difficult targets, a second cry rang out, a different voice now, followed by shouts in Norman French. He held his breath, listening; now it was possible to also hear the threshing of men running through the forest and the louder crashing of horses in pursuit.

Robin, grimacing as he dropped flat behind a downed tree, swore in silence. Poachers, likely, or even known outlaws, had been spotted by one of the sheriff's patrols. It was sheer bad luck that those pursued were heading straight toward him and his party.

He raised his head slightly and searched over his shoulder. Save for the last fading movement of stilling branches and waving, hip-high fern, there was no hint that a woman and six men were hidden close by. He wished he could see Marian, but if she were invisible to him, neither could the Norman soldiers see her.

More crashing through underbrush. Now he could hear panting, and wheezing, and the blurted, broken prayers of a man who would do better to hoard his breath. Not far away another man cried out, and then a triumphant shout went up from the soldiers.

Underbrush broke apart in front of Robin. The second outlaw was abruptly *there,* his arms outstretched, his batting hands attempting to open an escape route through hanging vines and low, sweeping branches. Robin briefly saw the scratched, agonized face, the staring eyes, the open mouth. And then the man teetered atop the very trunk Locksley took shelter behind.

Growling oaths behind gritted teeth, Robin reared up, grabbed the man's tunic, and yanked him off the tree. The outlaw came down hard and loose, limbs splayed; a knee caught Robin in the side of the head hard enough to double his vision.

"Stay down!" he hissed, as the man lay sprawled belly-down on the ground, sobbing in fear and exhaustion.

A soldier on horseback broke through, blue cloak flapping. He wore the traditional conical Norman helm with its steel nasal bisecting his dark face. Robin ducked as the horse gathered itself and sailed over the tree—sailed, too, over two men seeking protection in its meager shelter.

Robin turned on his knees, shouting a warning to the others. More soldiers were crashing before him now, spreading out. The Norman who had jumped the log was calling to his fellows in French, wheeling his horse even as he raised an already spanned crossbow, quarrel resting in its channel. But Robin had had more time; his own arrow was loosed, flying, and took the soldier through the throat.

Now he focused on another—*how many are there*?—as he deftly nocked a second arrow. *So many*—there was no time to think, to plan. Only to react.

He stood. Pulled the bowstring back to his chin. Sighted and let fly.

The Norman flew backward off his horse as if a trebuchet stone had struck him in the chest.

But others had broken through. They had spotted other game now, shouting positions to one another. Even as Robin nocked a third arrow, someone clutched at him. "Don't let them catch me!" the rescued man cried. "They'll cut me 'and off!"

His aim spoiled, the arrow went wide. Cursing, Robin caught a glimpse of flared equine nostrils, the gape of equine mouth, and the flash of a sword blade swinging down at his head.

"Get *off*—" he blurted, diving for the ground.

But the blade sheared through hair and flesh, and the sharpened tip slid across his skull.

Marian was well-hidden until Robin's arrow took the first soldier through the throat. The Norman tumbled limply off his mount, but one booted foot caught in the stirrup long enough to spook the horse, who responded with great lunging leaps sideways. Marian, directly in the animal's path, attempted to scramble out of the way. But the panicked horse wheeled around, and the body, coming loose at last, was swung out sideways in a wide arc.

The impact of the mailed body colliding with her own knocked Marian off her feet. She was aware of weight, disorientation, her own startled outcry—and then she went down hard against the ground, sprawled on her back, pinned by the weight of the soldier.

She had heard the term "dead weight" before. She had not truly known what it implied. Now she did.

Breath was gone. She gulped air as fear crowded close. She could not *breathe*—

Panicked, she shoved at the body, trying to dislodge it. Her struggles did nothing but waste what little breath remained in her lungs.

A dead man could not kill her.

The thought stilled her, calmed her, permitted her to draw a normal breath again. Air came in with relief, and then she became aware of more than the soldier's weight, of his stench. Bladder and bowels.

Blood. Blood in her mouth, running into her throat. She choked, coughed, felt the spray leave her mouth. She turned her head and spat, not knowing if it were dead man's blood or her own.

The body muffled sound, but she heard shouting. And then abruptly the terrible weight was lifted, dragged aside. Someone was grunting with effort.

"Lady . . . Lady Marian—" Tuck. His hands grasped one of her arms, dragged her up from the ground. "They're distracted—you must go now!"

She was dizzy, blinking at him woozily as she put a hand to her mouth. Blood filled it again.

"You're swifter than I," Tuck wheezed. "You must go on. Take Robin and go!"

That got through. "Robin?"

"Injured." Tuck yanked her to her feet. "Can you stand? Good. Here . . ." He pulled her to a downed tree. She saw Robin then, slumped against the tree as blood sheeted down the side of his face. "Go, both of you." Tuck pushed her. "The others are leading them away. Waste no time. 'Tis Robin they want more than any of us."

She knelt beside Robin. He was conscious but clearly in pain. She put a hand to his face and realized they both bled badly.

"Up," Tuck insisted. He helped Marian back to her feet, then pulled Robin from the ground. "Go on. Get as far as you can."

"Caves," Robin said between gritted teeth, weaving in place.

Tuck nodded. "We shall meet you there when we can."

Marian spat blood again. Hers, she realized, not the dead man's. She had cut her mouth. "Can you walk?" she asked Robin.

Through the blood, he managed a twisted smile. "Given a choice between that or hanging?" He closed her hand in his own. "Say rather I can *run*."

Robin pulled her over the fallen tree, and then both of them were running.

Awareness encompassed more than he had expected ever to sense again, to know, to feel. It was nearly tangible now, coming closer, closer. If hands were his to use, he could nearly touch redemption. Nearly know release.

Come—

Robin's lungs were afire, but even that pain did not match the pounding in his head. His right hand clutched Marian's left; otherwise, he would have pressed it against his temple in a fruitless attempt to dull the pain. To halt the blood.

Head wounds. He had learned on Crusade how badly head wounds bled, even if they were not serious. And he believed his was not; the pain was immense, but no worse than anything he had felt before. He remained conscious and on his feet, albeit those feet were clumsy.

Marian's breathing matched his, ragged and whistling. Together they stumbled through the foliage, attempting to put distance between them and the Normans. Tuck had done them a huge service, Robin knew; it was possible he and the others were captured by now, some of them even killed. But the monk had gotten *them* away from such danger, and if they were careful they might yet be worthy of his sacrifice. He did not know where they went, merely that they ran. They left behind the deer trail and fought to make a new one, raking aside with outstretched hands impediments such as vine and undergrowth.

"Wait—" It was barely the breath of a sound expelled from her bloodied mouth. "Stop—"

He halted, catching a hanging vine to hold himself upright. Marian released his hand and bent over, sucking air noisily. Her long black braid was disheveled, strands pulled loose by branches as they ran. A bruise was rising on her face, blotching one cheekbone. She wiped her mouth free of blood, studied the slick hand dispassionately, then looked at Robin, still panting.

"—head?" she asked.

"Attached." It was all he could manage, clinging to the vine.

Marian nodded vaguely, attempting a smile. She straightened, then turned and staggered toward a great old oak, roots thick as a man's thigh where they broke free of the soil in a tangle akin to Celtic knotwork. She drooped against the trunk, pressing her forehead into bark.

Robin loosed his grip on the vine and made his way across to her, wincing against the renewed pain in his head. With care he avoided tripping over the oak roots, but when he reached the trunk he nearly fell. He caught himself with one outstretched arm, then turned and set his spine against the trunk, sliding down until he sat on the ground, cradled between two twisted roots.

With gentle fingers he explored the side of his head. Fortunately the sword blade's motion had mostly been spent. It had sliced into the flesh above his right ear, but had not cracked the skull beneath. That skull would no doubt house an abominable headache for a day or two, but he was mostly undamaged.

Robin shifted his position to a more comfortable one. Breath came more easily now. Marian's surcoat swung as she turned; then, like him, she sat down amidst the roots. She looked aside, spat blood, then blotted her mouth against her tunic sleeve.

She studied the soiled sleeve critically. "Stopping, I think."

Robin stretched out his arm, slung it wearily across her shoulders, and pulled her close. "I think we are out of danger." He paused. "For now."

Marian didn't answer. She was staring around, frowning. "Where are we?"

Robin glanced into the shadows, noting the trees seemed almost uniform in size, shape, and placement. Mistletoe clustered in branches, foliage crowded the ground, but the huge trees took precedence over the rest of the forest.

He felt at his head again. "When I was a child, my mother told me there were oak groves planted by Druids in Sherwood. That they were the oldest part of the forest, and sacred. But she was always telling me stories. I never knew which were true."

"These are oaks," Marian said. "And—" She broke off sharply. "Robin . . . there are *faces*." Alarm chilled him. He sat bolt upright, preparing to gather his legs under him until she waved him back down. "No, not Normans—at least, not living ones. Look! Do you see?" She gestured. "Look at the trunks."

He looked, and saw nothing.

Marian got to her feet and crunched through fallen leaves to the oak closest to the one Robin leaned against. "Look here." Her blood-smeared hand touched the massive trunk, tracing a shape. "Here are the eyes, the nose— and the mouth. See it?" She looked back at him, waiting expectantly.

He rolled his head in negation. "A trick of light and shadow."

"On *all* of them? Look around, Robin." Marian's outstretched arm encompassed their surroundings. "This is an oak grove, one far older than you or me . . . or even, I daresay, our fathers' fathers. Just as your mother told you." She moved to the next tree, intent. Once again her hand traced a shape. "Eyes, nose, mouth . . . and here is the chin."

He made a noncommittal sound.

Marian's expression was sympathetic, but clearly she was certain of what she saw. He closed his eyes and rested as she walked from tree to tree, murmuring to herself. He was nearly asleep when she reached his tree, circling it. He heard her stop, heard her startled blurt of sound, and then abruptly she was attempting to haul him to his feet.

"Come and see," she ordered.

His remonstration made no headway. She dragged him

around to the back side of the huge old tree, took his hand in hers, and pressed his fingers against the wood.

"Feel it." She moved his hand, tracing something. "Here, see? The brow, the bridge of the nose, the cheekbones—this one is much clearer than the others. Do you see it?"

He did. This time, he did. There in the bark, no longer merely a trick of light and shadow, was the shape of a face. It was more defined than those in the other trunks. Sightless eyes stared.

"It's a man," Marian said quietly.

And then, beneath their bloodied hands, the wood began to move.

The spell attenuated, began to shred, broke. He felt it fail, felt the last minute particles attempt to bind themselves together once more in order to also bind him, but it was too late. Awareness melded with spirit, merged with comprehension, joined with the power that had been held too long in abeyance. He tapped it, called it, welcomed it; felt it bound joyously back to him like a hound to its hearth. One moment it was absent; the next, present.

With a roar of triumph, he ripped himself free of the tree, wood chips flying, banished the clinging aftermath of the long, dreamless sleep and stepped into life again, into the world again, into his body. Flesh, blood, and bone. And power incarnate.

The empty tree screamed.

As the body tore itself free of the massive trunk, shredding strips and chips of wood, Marian blurted a sound of shock and hastily backed away. A root caught her, and she went down hard. Even as Robin bent to help her up, he halted, arrested in midmotion. Both stared at the stranger who had wrenched himself out of living oak.

He was wild-eyed, breathing hard. From the tree he went to his knees as if in supplication, or perhaps weakness. Splayed hands pressed against the layers of leaves, elbows locked to hold himself upright. Shoulder-length hair, dark save where it was frosted with the first touch of gray, tumbled around his face. Marian could not see his expression now as he knelt, but she heard the rapid,

uneven breathing, saw the shuddering in spine and
shoulders.

For all she and Robin were stunned, the stranger seemed
more so.

She let Robin pull her to her feet. They put a cautious
distance between themselves and the man but did not flee.
Instead, they stared at each other in blank astonishment,
then turned as one to the stranger. Robin's sword chimed
as he unsheathed it.

When the man looked up, Marian saw gray eyes clear as
water, black-lashed, and pale, unblemished skin. His beard
was short and well-tended. He wore a blue robe of excellent
cloth, and pinned to his left shoulder was a red-and-gold
enameled brooch, dragon-shaped, of Celtic workmanship.
When he brought his hands out of the loose, powdery
leaves, she saw he wore a gold ring set with a red cabochon
stone she believed might be a ruby.

"Robin." She kept her tone carefully casual. "Is this a
trick of light and shadow?"

Equally casual, he replied, "This appears to be flesh and
blood."

"We are awake, are we not?"

"As far as I can tell, we are awake." He tugged her litter-
strewn braid sharply. "Feel that?"

"Yes," she said crossly, putting a hand to her scalp.

"And I still bleed a little, so this must be real." He
paused. "My mother apparently told me the truth."

Marian was amazed at how calm he sounded. She didn't
feel calm. She felt oddly detached. Somehow distant from
what she had witnessed, and what she was witnessing now.
And yet every noise she heard sounded preternaturally loud.

Should I not be running? Or, if she were a proper
woman, fainting?

But then, she had not been proper since meeting Robin.
Still, Marian wondered why she felt no urge to run. It
wasn't fear that the stranger might harm her if she tried;
she wasn't certain a man who had been trapped in a tree
trunk moments before *could* harm her. But she found herself immensely curious to know what had happened to
him—and to be quite certain she had truly seen him tear
himself out of a living tree.

Still on his knees, the man looked over his shoulder at the tree. Except for a hollowed gouge in the trunk, the oak appeared no different. It was simply a tree. But a glance at other oaks still bearing likenesses of other men emphasized the truth of his own presence.

He turned back to face them. With hands now grown steady, he pushed heavy hair away from his face and bared a narrow circlet of beaten gold. He was, Marian realized, only ten or twelve years older than she.

She wondered what Robin was thinking. A quick glance at his face showed grimness, his skin drawn taut beneath the golden stubble and smeared blood. He seemed at ease; but then he always looked relaxed, wholly unprepared to strike when but a moment later the enemy was down. They had lost their bows along the way as they ran but were not unarmed; they had a meat-knife, quiver, and arrows, and Robin the sword.

Oddly, she wanted to say, *"Do not harm him,"* which made no sense. She knew nothing of the man save he had, to all appearances, been a resident of a tree. A resident *in* a tree.

The stranger's eyes fixed themselves on Robin's sword. A sudden light came into them, an expression of sharpened awareness and understanding. He stood up abruptly. Sharply, he asked something in a language neither of them knew.

Robin said something in fluent Norman French. The stranger frowned, plainly impatient, and tried several different languages in swift succession. In each there were words that sounded vaguely familiar to Marian, but he remained a cipher until a final try.

"Latin!" Marian exclaimed. "Oh, where is Tuck when we need him?"

This time, when the stranger spoke, his words, though twisted, were in an accented English they could understand. "When is it?"

Robin began to ask a question of his own, something to do with a carved man turning into flesh and stepping out of a tree, but the stranger overrode him.

"When is it?"

When. Not where. Perplexed, Marian said, "The Year of Our Lord 1202."

The gray eyes widened. "So long? I had not thought so"—his tone took on bitterness—"when I had mind again to think at all." He looked more closely at Marian, then at Robin, inspecting them.

Marian became aware of her disheveled clothing, her braid half undone, bits of leaf and twigs caught in her hair and the loose weave of her hosen beneath the surcoat. Her chin itched from drying blood, and her face stung from scratches. Then the stranger turned to the tree again and put out a hand, feeling the bark. When he brought it away, smeared streaks of red crossed his palm.

"Blood," he murmured. "Surely she did not foresee this, or she would have prepared for it. But who would have expected the blood of two Sacrifices to commingle in the Holy Grove, let alone upon the walls of my prison?"

"Sacrifices?" Robin demanded. "Are we meant to die here, when somehow all of your companions are let out of *their* trees?"

The stranger ignored the question and looked at Marian. "The Year of Our Lord, you said." She nodded. "You mean the man Christians called the Nazarene?"

Marian blinked. "Of course."

"Of course." He sounded rueful. Then his expression altered. His eyes were once again fixed on Robin's sword. "There is a task before me. It was mine to do before the enchantment, and no less mine to do now that I am free of it, regardless of how long it has been. Will you aid me?"

"Aid you?" Robin echoed. "Perhaps you should aid *us* by explaining what just happened."

The stranger smiled. "I see power is no more understood now—whenever this time may be—than it was then." Absently, he touched the brooch on his left shoulder. "Vortigern meant me to be the Sacrifice when his walls would not stand; instead, I gave him news of the dragons under the water. When the red defeated the white." His pupils had swollen, turning eyes from gray to black. "He is dead. The red dragon of Wales. And so the task lies before me." His eyes cleared, and he looked at them both as if seeing them for the first time. "Forgive me. Perhaps it will all explain itself upon introductions. I am Myrddyn Emrys." He gave it the Welsh pronunciation, tongue-tip against upper teeth. "Men call me Merlin."

"Merlin!" Robin blurted.

The stranger nodded. "The task is to find a sword, and give it back to the lake."

"*Merlin,*" Robin repeated, and this time Marian heard adult disbelief colored by a young boy's burgeoning hope.

Merlin had spent his entire life being—*different*. People feared him for it, distrusted, disbelieved; some of them were convinced he should be killed outright, lest he prove a danger to them. But that life, that time, was done. He faced a new world now, a different world, and far more difficult challenges. In his time, magic at least had been acknowledged if often distrusted; here, clearly, no one believed in it at all. Which somewhat explained the inability of the young man and young woman to accept what had happened.

An enchantment, he had told them as they knelt to wash their bloodied faces at a trickle of a stream, a spell wrought by Nimüe, the great sorceress. He did not tell them his own part in the spell, that he had allowed himself for the first time in his life to be blinded by a woman's beauty and allure, to permit her into his heart. Once she had learned enough of him, enough of his power, she had revealed her true goal: to imprison him for all time and thus remove the impediment he represented to the new power in Britain.

A Britain without Arthur.

He grieved privately, letting no one, not even Nimüe, recognize the depth of his pain. Arthur he had wrought out of the flesh of Britain herself, a man destined to unite a world torn awry against the threat of the Saxon hordes. And so he had for a time; but then other forces took advantage of a childless king and a queen in disrepute, dividing Arthur's attention when it was most needed to settle an uneasy court. By the time the Saxon threat became immediate, Arthur had lost too many supporters among the noblemen—and too many knights. The advent of a bastard got unknowingly on his own sister had sealed his fate. Merlin, in retirement, had done what he could, but Arthur died and Britain was left defenseless.

A Britain without Arthur could not survive as Merlin had meant her to, safeguarded by the one man empowered with the natural ability to keep her whole. Hundreds of years had passed since Arthur's death, and even now Merlin had only to look at the man kneeling at stream's edge, with his fall of white-blond hair and pale greenish-brown eyes, his height, to see that the Saxons had triumphed. And so the man agreed when asked, explaining that Britain's people were now called "English," born of "England," that once had been "Angle-land." The land of Angles and Saxons.

Marian, however, was not. It was clear when Merlin looked upon her. She was small, slight, and black-haired, bearing more resemblance to the people of his time in her features, despite the blue of her eyes. She called herself English, but her blood was older than Robin's.

And now England—Britain—had fallen again. To a people called the Normans, Robin explained, who refused even to learn the language of the people they conquered. A people who had a king whose excess of temper was legendary, along with the greed and turbulence of his reign.

"Then we should waste no more time," Merlin told them. "Arthur is dead, but his legacy may yet be realized."

"By finding the sword," Marian said dubiously, rebraiding her hair.

Robin's smile, even as he felt at the clotted slice in his head, was very nearly fatuous. "Excalibur."

"The sword belongs to the lake," Merlin said, "now that Arthur cannot wield it. Britain's welfare resides in it. Arthur, with Excalibur, drove away the Saxons once, but Mordred and his faction kept him from completing his task. You have told me of other invasions. To keep Britain from ever being invaded again, we must find the sword and return it to the lake."

"That will be enough?" Marian asked. "No one ever again shall invade England?"

"No one."

"You are Merlin the Enchanter," Robin said. "What use would we be to *you*?"

"You will recall it was you who got me out of the tree," he reminded them dryly.

They exchanged glances, still perplexed.

"You are the Sacrifices," Merlin explained gently. "Just as Arthur himself was."

And as he saw the confusion deepening in their eyes, he realized that with the years had disappeared the knowledge that was beginning to die out even in his time.

He gestured back toward the way they had come. "That was a Holy Grove, sacred to the Druids. It was Nimüe's conceit to imprison me there—and, apparently, others as well." His expression reflected regret that he, Marian, and Robin had been unable to free the others. "There are men and women born into the world who are meant to be Sacrifices for their people, for their times, to keep the land strong and whole. They need not be killed upon an altar, though that was done once, but merely die in defense of their land and ideals. To die serving the greater whole."

"We are outlaws," Robin said. "We are fortunate if we can feed ourselves each day; what service can *we* offer England?"

"Hope," Merlin answered. "Have you not told me you give over most of what you take to peasants?"

"Because the king is taxing the poor to death," Marian declared.

Merlin nodded. "And so you steal from those who have wealth to spare, and divide it fairly among those who have none." His eyes were unwavering. "At the risk of your own lives."

He had made them uncomfortable. Neither of them fully understood what they represented to the folk they aided. Perhaps they never would. It was the nature of Sacrifices to do what was required without acknowledging the selflessness of it, because they saw only the need and simply acted. Arthur had not been raised to be a king per se, but to be a decent, honest, fair man of great ability, capable of leading others to the goal he perceived as worthy, because it served the people.

Arthur had come into privilege and kingship because it was the position needed to guide Britain. Robert of Locksley and Marian of Ravenskeep had been stripped of their privilege because that loss led them to the position of aiding the poor, when no one else in England appeared willing to do so.

Who else was worthy of aiding him in his task?

"We had better go," Merlin said.

"Wait." Robin's brows were knit beneath raggedly cut hair. "Do you even know where the sword is?"

Merlin smiled. "Do you expect a quest? To be a knight of the Round Table, searching for the Grail? But the answer is disappointing, I fear: Nimüe *told* me, as my body was turned to wood."

Robert of Locksley, born the son of an earl—albeit last, and thus inconsequential—wanted very much to say he disbelieved the nonsense the stranger told them. He recalled too vividly the beatings meted out by his father, wishing to purge what remained in his sons of anything fanciful, such as stories of Arthur and his enchanter, Merlin. But Robin's mother had told him to believe as he wished, that stories were good for the soul as well as the heart. And so he had learned the stories, and loved them, and believed them, until he grew up and joined a Crusade that took the lives of innocents as well as warriors. He could not say when he had come to understand that there were stories and there were truths, with a vast gulf between the two, but he knew that Merlin, Arthur, and all the others of the legend were not real.

Except that Merlin was—*here*.

The part of him that wished to believe wondered why Merlin did not simply conjure a spell that would move them to wherever it was he wanted to go, without benefit of walking. The rational part of him believed in no such ability, that the stranger was nothing but a madman. But he remembered all too well the sight of the tree disgorging a man. Still, Merlin did not do so; he said he could not.

They slept little, ate less, and followed whatever it was that guided Merlin. The enchanter pronounced himself stunned by the changes that had overtaken England—no, Britain—and yet admitted there was much that had not altered. He seemed unimpressed by the fact that he had been entrapped in a tree for hundreds of years; if anything, he considered it quite natural. Such things as sorcery were expected by Merlin, while Robin found it impossible to accept that fanciful stories, no matter how beautiful, no matter how entrancing, were grounded in fact.

But when at last they walked out of the forest and saw

the wooded hill rising before them, surrounded by a ring of grassy lowlands, and Merlin sank down as if in prayer, murmuring in a language neither he nor Marian understood, Robin knew more was at work than fancy or folly.

From his knees, Merlin said, "Avalon."

Robin started. "No!"

"It was an island," Merlin persisted. "Look, you, and see how it might have been. The shore here, the water there—and the isle beyond."

Robin looked upon it. An expanse of land stretched before him, and a high hill above it, swelling out of turf. There was no water, no shore, nothing to cross save grass.

"It is much changed," said Merlin, "but not so very altered that a man of my begetting may not recognize it."

A man of his begetting. A chill prickled Robin's spine.

Marian gazed upon the hill. "Women ruled there."

"For time out of mind," Merlin agreed. "It was the goddess's place, and that of her servants. Men were occasionally tolerated but never truly welcomed."

"You?" she asked.

His tone was dry. "Tolerated."

"And the sword?" Robin inquired.

Merlin seemed to have drifted away from them. "There is a grave upon the island," he said. "A man sleeps in it. But also an ideal. He and others embodied—and yet embody—it. The sword is there." He looked at Robin. "Come nightfall, you and the goddess's daughter must climb what is now a hill, but once was an island."

Marian's brows rose. "Goddess's daughter?"

"In your blood," he answered. "In your bones. But those who remain will attempt to stop you regardless." He smiled as they exchanged a concerned glance. "Just as the sheriff attempts to stop you from robbing the wealthy and poaching the king's deer."

That put it in perspective. Robin sighed. "What do you want us to do?"

"Find the sword," Merlin answered. "I am known there, even by the stones that outlive us all; I cannot go. It is for you to do."

"I am a man," Robin said. "Will I be—what did you say? Tolerated?"

Merlin inclined his head in Marian's direction. "Because of her, yes."

Marian's tone was implacable. "We go nowhere, and do nothing, without knowing what we may expect."

"Resistance," Merlin told her.

Suspicious, Robin inquired, "What *kind* of resistance?"

The enchanter spread his hands. "That I cannot say. It may take many forms."

Robin remained suspicious. "But you will not accompany us."

Merlin shook his head. "If I go, the task cannot be completed. And it must be, for Arthur's sake and the welfare of Britain."

Robin laughed. "You have a way with words, Myrddyn Emrys. Perhaps that is the secret of your sorcery. You convince others to do the work for you."

Merlin said, "So long as the work is done, it matters not who has the doing of it."

Marian continued to gaze upon the hill. "How will we know to find the sword? Is it standing up from a stone?"

Robin's laughter rang out. The enchanter was mystified, until the story was explained. Merlin frowned. "It was not like that at all. There was no such drama. It was—"

Marian halted him with a raised hand. "Please. Let it remain as we know it. Tales and legends are akin to food when there is little hope in a poor man's life."

Merlin's smile twitched. "This is as much as I know: The grave and the sword are on the isle. Where, I cannot say."

It felt like a challenge. Or even, after all, a quest. Marian looked at Robin. "The moon will be full tonight. Shall we go a-hunting?"

He put out a hand and brushed a strand of hair away from her eyes, smiling. "Let us make a new legend."

Moonlight lay on the land as Marian and Robin crossed the grass Merlin claimed had once been a lake. She wondered if it might possibly be true, as its appearance was so different from that of the forest behind them and the hill before. There were no great oaks, beeches, and alders, no tangle of foliage, no stone outcroppings. Merely grasslands, hollowed out of the earth.

A faint wind blew, teasing at their hair. Robin's was awash with moonlight, nearly silver-white. The metal of his brigandine glowed and sparked. The light was kind to his face, for all his expression was serious; she wanted abruptly to stop him, to kiss him, to vow again how much she loved him, but something in the night suggested such behavior would be unwelcome. She felt urgency well up into a desire to find the sword for Merlin and return to him as soon as possible. Nothing in her wished to tarry.

Beside her, Robin shuddered. He felt her glance and smiled ruefully. "Someone walked over my grave."

Fear sent a frisson through her. "Say no such thing. Not here."

He glanced around, rubbing at the back of his neck. "Perhaps not," he agreed.

Before them lay the first incline of the hill, a ragged seam of stone curving into the darkness, and a terrace of grass above it. Here vegetation began, clumps spreading inward, ascending the hill. The trees stood higher yet, forming a crown around the summit. She and Robin climbed steadily upward, until he stopped short just as they entered the outer fringe of trees.

The look on his face startled her. "What is it?"

"I am not supposed to be here." He worked his shoulders as if they prickled with chill. "Merlin was right—men are not wanted. But—" He broke off, feeling gingerly at the cut on his head.

"But?" she prodded.

"But I in particular am not wanted. Or so it feels." He studied his fingers. "Bleeding again."

"Let me see." She moved around to his other side, turning his head into the moonlight. "A little, yes . . ." She peeled hair away, saw where fresh blood welled. Moment by moment it ran faster, thicker, until even her fingers could not stop it. "Perhaps we should turn back."

Robin's expression was odd. "He said there would be resistance."

Marian frowned as she drew her meat-knife and commenced cutting a strip from her tunic. "You believe you are bleeding again because of that?"

"I believe that on a night such as this, it may be possible." He winced. "And the ache is returning."

"Bend your head." Marian tied the cloth around his head. "Do you believe what he says? That there even *is* a sword, and if we find it, it may guard England?"

Robin sighed, fingering the knot she had tied in the makeshift bandage. "I am not certain what I believe. But if there *is* truth to it . . ." He shrugged. "What harm if we try?"

"An aching head."

"Ah, well, I daresay I can stand that." Robin looked at the vanguard of trees springing up around them. "The stories say Arthur was taken away by nine queens and given secret burial rites. If this *is* Avalon—what remains of it, in any case—it is possible his grave is here. And what else is there to do but bury the king's sword with the king's body?"

"Give it to his son," Marian answered promptly. "Save that no one of Arthur's court would wish to see a bastard, a patricide, carrying it."

"Merlin was not there when Arthur died," Robin went on thoughtfully. "He may have meant to give it back to the lake on Arthur's death, but if the women of Avalon took it away with the body—"

"—they would have brought it here." Marian gazed up the hill to where the trees thickened, choked with undergrowth. "But all of it is merely a story . . ."

"Is it?" Robin asked. "Stories are changed over time, embellished the way Alan embellishes his ballads, but what if the kernel is true? What if that man back there, whom we witnessed come out of a tree no matter how much we wish to deny it, truly is Merlin?"

"Then Arthur's grave is up there."

"And the sword," Robin said. *"Excalibur."* He reached out a hand to her. "Shall we find it?"

Marian put her own in his. "Alan would make a fine ballad of this."

Robin's teeth gleamed in a wide grin. "Oh, that he would! He would have us being beset on all sides by unseen enemies, battling evil spirits, making our way up a hill that crawled with the shades of long-dead men."

"Well," Marian said dryly, "of such fancies are legends born."

With every step he took ascending the hill, Robin felt oppressed. Heavy. As if his body gained the mass and weight of stones, ancient under the sun. Breath ran ragged. His head ached. It took all of his strength to put one foot after the other and continue climbing.

He knew Marian was concerned. He saw it each time she halted a step or two above him, looking back to find him toiling behind her, expending effort merely to keep moving. The bandage around his head stilled most of the blood, but a stubborn trickle dribbled continuously down beside his ear. His shoulder was wet with it, where the blood had fallen.

They were nearly to the crown of the hill when he drew his sword. He could not say why it was necessary, save to know it was. In his years upon Crusade, and more years yet as an outlaw in Sherwood, he had learned to trust his instincts.

Just as they crossed beyond the last line of trees and stepped out onto the rocky summit, Marian stopped short. Her eyes, he saw, were stretched wide, unblinking; trembling hands moved to cover her ears. The sound she made was like nothing he had ever heard from her, a combination of whimper, protest, and astonishment.

He reached out to touch her, to put his hand upon her shoulder, but found such resistance in the air that he could not. His hand stopped short of her body, unable to go farther. "Marian?"

"I hear them," she said.

Robin heard nothing.

She drew in a breath. "Their souls are still here."

"Whose souls?"

"The women—the women who lived here. Those who worshipped the goddess." She closed her eyes then, intent upon something he could neither see nor hear. "They knew peace here, in life and death. Not Christians, but reverent in their own way, following their faith." She removed her hands and looked at him. "Merlin was right: He could not come here. Nor do they wish you to be here."

"And you?" he asked.

Marian smiled crookedly. "I may or may not be descended from women who lived here in Merlin's day. The power has faded, but there is memory here. I will not be chased away." She closed her eyes again. He could see the lids twitching as if she slept; her mouth moved slightly. The words she quoted were nothing he had ever heard, from her or anyone else.

"Marian?"

This time it was she who reached out to him. Resistance snapped. He felt her hand on his, smooth and warm, as she led him to the center of the hilltop.

"He is with *me*," she said, and the world made way.

There were voices in her ears. Nothing she could make out, not words she understood, but voices, women's voices, calling out. Was it her help they desired or her absence? Marian could not tell what it was they wanted, merely that they existed, that they filled her mind with sound and her heart with yearning.

His hand was warm in hers, but she was barely conscious of it. She led him without hesitation to the center of the summit, to the place where stacked stone had tumbled into ruin, from graceful lines into disarray. Most were lichen-clad, moss-grown, buried in soil and ground cover. Some had cracked wide open, broken into bits by frost and sun. Nothing here resembled a place to live, but live they had. She could feel it in her bones, sense it singing in her blood.

"Here," she said.

Robin stopped beside her. "The grave?"

She turned her face up to the moon, squinting at its brilliance. "No. The women worshipped here."

He was silent. Marian sensed his unease. She turned to him, to reassure him that she was welcome here, that so long as he was her consort he would be tolerated—but she forgot the intention as something came down between them. A hissing line of light lanced out of the sky, so cold it burned. They broke apart and fell back, guarding their eyes. In the flash of illumination Marian saw Robin's drawn and hollowed face, the grimness in his mouth. The bared blade of his sword glinted in the darkness.

She was Christian-born and -bred, not a goddess-worshipper. But something within responded to the place. She, a woman, had a right to be here. None of the women of Avalon had ever turned away one of their own, though not all had remained. What remained of them would not turn her away. Still, she was uneasy.

Resistance, Merlin had said. Robin had spoken of unseen enemies and evil beings. Marian sensed neither here, merely the memories of women who had left the world of men to make their own way, to find their own faith. That memory could make itself tangible did not, somehow, strike her as unusual. Not here. Not this night. Nor that the souls of the women, tied to the stone and soil of Avalon, would be present still. They had not known a heaven such as Christians did. They had worshipped another way.

Blasphemy, the priests would say. Heresy. It was not Marian's way, but she could respect that women before her might seek another road. A woman's life was difficult, with or without a man.

Her man stood beside her.

Marian looked into his eyes. Blood yet ran down his jaw to drip upon his shoulder. She reached up, touched his face, felt the warmth of his flesh beneath the beard. Felt the stickiness of blood.

In her heart welled a strange, strong fierceness. *We have come at Merlin's behest,* she said within, *not to disrupt, not to dishonor, but to set to rights what has been perverted. England—Britain—must prevail, but she cannot without your aid. Allow us to be the vessels of this aid. Let us have the sword.*

A moment later, the answer was given.

Marian smiled. "I know the way."

His brows arched. "To the grave?"

She gestured. "Look."

She waited for him to see it, to find it, to remark in satisfaction. But he did none of those things. He looked, but he was blind.

"Here." She took his hand again, led him to the stone. Beneath a scattering of dirt, encroached upon by ground

cover, lay a flat, crude plinth of weathered stone half the
length of Robin's height.

"This?" he asked. "This is—nothing."

The answer was immediate. "If men knew Arthur slept
here, they would come. And if they came, they would un-
doubtedly expect a monument to the king. But that is not
what the women, or Avalon, wished. Only peace. And that
they offered Arthur."

He was dubious. "How can you be certain this is his
grave? Surely others have died here."

She shrugged. "I can give you no explanation. I just—
know." *Because they have told me.*

Robin closed his mouth on his next question and squat-
ted down. He set aside his sword, then leaned forward.
One hand went out to the stone, to touch its surface. He
ran his fingers over the stone and stopped. His expression
abruptly stilled.

"What is it?" Marian asked.

He traced the stone again, feeling more carefully this
time. She saw the pattern: down the length of the stone,
then across.

" 'Tis carved here," Robin said. He motioned her to
kneel down, then took her hand and pressed it across the
stone. "Do you feel it?"

Marian shook her head.

"Wait . . ." He guided her hand up, then down, then
across. "Do you feel it?"

She frowned. "Some kind of carving, I agree. But I cannot make it out."

Robin retrieved his sword from beside the stone and set
it atop the pitted surface. And Marian understood.

She said, "Merlin came out of the tree. Out of wood."

Robin nodded. "And this is stone."

With the touch of our blood. She stared at the sword as it
lay atop the plinth. Then slowly she bent and took it into
her hands. Her right she curled around the leather-
wrapped grip. Her left she closed upon the blade, closed
and closed, then slid it the length of the blade.

"Marian!" His hands were on hers, freeing the sword. He
swore under his breath as he saw the blood flow.

"No," she said as he searched hastily for something to

stop the blood. "Wait." She reached up, touched the side of his head with its soggy strip of cloth, brought her other hand away. Carefully, she pressed both against the stone. In the wake of her touch, she left bloody handprints.

"Marian." He caught her now, trapped her hands, wrapped around the left the cloth he had cut from his own tunic. She allowed it, watched his eyes as he tended her. In this moment he thought only of her, not of what they wrought atop Arthur's grave.

When he was done, she looked at the stone. "There," she told him.

Robin barely glanced at it, more concerned with her welfare. But when he looked again, his eyes widened.

He stood up abruptly, stiff with shock. Of utter disbelief.

Marian smiled through her tears. "Take it up, Robin. Excalibur was never meant for a woman's hands, any more than Avalon was meant for a man."

But for a long time he stood atop the hill, moonlight bleaching his hair, and did not touch it.

Smiling, Marian rose. In her hands she carried the other sword, the blade that knew its home in the sheath at Robin's hip. She began to walk away, back to the trees cloaking the shoulders of Avalon's crown.

"Marian."

She held her silence. When he joined her, when he came down the hill to walk beside her through the trees to the shore on the verge of grass, not water, he carried Arthur's sword.

The enchanter saw it in their faces as they came up out of the grasslands below the hill. He had seen it many times before, hundreds of years before, in those who served Arthur: the acknowledgment that they were a part of something greater than any man might name, though he could not explain it. Goddess-touched, god-touched, God-touched; the name did not matter. What mattered was that they had, this night, become a part of the tapestry others long before Merlin had begun to weave. A tapestry made of living threads, dyed in the blood of the Sacrifice.

He smiled. The Nazarene, too, had been a Sacrifice.

He waited in silence as they came up to him. Marian carried Robin's sword. The other, the one Merlin himself had been given by the Lady, rested in the hands of a man who would have, had he been born in an earlier time, aided Arthur with all the loyalty in his soul.

Well. He aided him now.

Merlin smiled. "It is well done."

Robin's expression was solemn. "What would you have of us now?"

"Your part is finished," Merlin answered. "This is for me to do." He took the great sword from Robin, held it almost reverently. "In the morning, you will go back to Sherwood, to the life you have made. I thank you both for your time, and your aid. I promise you this much in recompense, because I have seen it: You will not die for years and years. No one so petty as the Sheriff of Nottingham will cause your deaths; time will take its toll. But where I go now, I go alone."

"To the lake?" Marian asked.

"We could follow you," Robin threatened mildly.

Merlin laughed. "But you are there already."

He turned then, put his back to them, took three steps away from them. Even as he heard each begin to ask what it was he did, he sent the sword spinning into the air. Moonlight sparked and glinted. Not meant to fly, eventually the weapon came down. It struck the ground soundlessly, too far for them to hear.

"Now," Merlin murmured.

Beneath the sword, the earth opened. From it swelled water, bursting free to spill out onto the grasslands between forest and hill. Satisfied, Merlin watched as it ran and ran, as it filled and filled, more rapidly than a man could clearly see, until at last the water stilled. Lapping at his feet were the wavelets of a lake. Floating upon the waters, shrouded in mist and moonlight, was the isle of Avalon.

"Lady," Merlin said, "I give it back to you. I give *him* back to you. So both may guard Britain."

After a moment he turned to them both. He marked the pallor of their faces, the stillness of their bodies, the blood upon their flesh. Smiling, he stepped close. He set each hand to the backs of their skulls, and, such as it was in him to do, blessed them both even as he healed their hurts.

Robin said, baffled, "It was on Avalon already."

Merlin nodded. "The women safeguarded it, not knowing it was the Lady who entrusted it to me until Arthur came of age. But it was never of earth. It was for no one to keep, not even the well intentioned."

"Why us?" Marian asked. "Why not you?"

"In the old ways, the old days, a woman ruled. But never alone. She had a consort. She made the Great Marriage. And it was sealed with blood." He smiled at them both. "The times have changed. No need for the consort to die, but the blood of the Great Marriage remains sacred. I had none to offer." He saw the frowns in their eyes, the uneasiness with the idea of ancient rituals. "Go home," he said gently. "You have served Britain well. She will not fail for time out of mind."

Tears stood in Marian's eyes. "What about you?"

"The same," he answered. "I go. This is not my time. This is not my place. I belong—elsewhere."

"Where *will* you go?" Robin asked.

Merlin smiled. He indicated a shadow upon the water, stretching out from the island. "They are sending a boat for me."

"But—you said you were not wanted there," Marian said.

"I am tolerated," Merlin answered, "now and again." He looked over their heads at the forest beyond. "Make a bed among the trees. There is an oak grove there that will serve you well—and I promise there are no faces in the trees, nor captive enchanters."

They were reluctant to leave but did as he bade, slowly walking away. He watched the man reach out for the woman's hand; watched the woman reach out for the man's. Their fingers entwined, then locked, and they walked together toward the trees.

The boat bumped quietly against the shore. Dark shapes were in it, shrouded in such a way he could see no faces. He stepped into the boat, found his balance, nodded. The boat began to move.

Merlin looked back at the shore. In the moonlight he saw them, and then they stepped into darkness, became shadows in the wood.

He turned away and took his seat in the boat. He stripped off the circlet, the ring, and the dragon brooch. Without regret, he tossed them over the side into the water. Payment rendered.

For want of conversation, he said to the wraiths of Avalon, "They will be legend themselves one day. Just as Arthur is."

Then the mists came down around him as Avalon disappeared, and the Lady took him home.

About the Authors

Lois McMaster Bujold

Lois McMaster Bujold was born in Columbus, Ohio, in 1949; she now lives in Minneapolis. She began reading science fiction at age nine. Romances came later, when in her early twenties she discovered Georgette Heyer. She started writing for professional publication in 1982, a goal achieved in 1986 with the release of her first three science fiction novels. Bujold went on to write the Nebula-winning *Falling Free* (1988) and many other books featuring her popular character Miles Naismith Vorkosigan, his family, friends, and enemies. The series includes three Hugo Award–winning novels; readers interested in learning more about the far-flung Vorkosigan clan are encouraged to start with the omnibus *Cordelia's Honor*. Bujold's books have been translated into nineteen languages. In 2001 came a new fantasy, *The Curse of Chalion*—which won the Mythopoeic Award for Adult Literature. A sequel in the same world, *Paladin of Souls*, followed in 2003 and won the Hugo, Nebula, and Locus Awards. The series continued in 2005 with *The Hallowed Hunt*. A fan-run Web site devoted to her work, The Bujold Nexus, may be found at www.dendarii.com.

Mary Jo Putney

Mary Jo Putney is a prolific *New York Times* bestselling novelist with too many book credits to list in full here. Her most recent releases—*Twist of Fate, The Bartered Bride, Stolen Magic,* and *A Kiss of Fate*—are all superb reads published to broad commercial success and rave reviews from even the stodgiest of critics. Her rare ability to portray complex, flawed characters with deep emotions makes her one of genre fiction's strongest voices. She's been the recipient of many national awards for her work, including two RITAs, two *Romantic Times* Career Achievement Awards, and five appearances on the *ALA Journal*'s annual list of the year's top five romances. *Booklist* says, "It's no wonder that bestseller Putney is a favorite of romance fans. A master storyteller." Visit her Web site at www.maryjoputney.com.

Catherine Asaro

Catherine Asaro grew up near Berkeley, California. She earned her Ph.D. in chemical physics and A.M. in physics from Harvard. A former dancer, she was artistic director for the Mainly Jazz dancers and Harvard University Ballet. A bestselling and critically acclaimed author, Asaro has written many books, including *Primary Inversion, The Last Hawk, Spherical Harmonic,* and *The Phoenix Code*. She's famous for her outstanding ability to mix hard science with strong, emotional story lines. *The Quantum Rose*, a science fiction retelling of Beauty and the Beast, received the 2001 Nebula Award. Her books and novellas have won numerous awards, including the *Analog* Readers Poll, AnLab the Sapphire, and the *Romantic Times* Reviewers Choice Award, and have been nominated for the Hugo. Catherine says she is a walking definition of "absentminded" and has managed to spill coffee in every room of her house, much to the amusement of her daughter, husband, and cats. Her Web site is at www.sff.net/people/asaro.

Deb Stover

Once Upon a Time, Deb Stover wanted to be Lois Lane, until she discovered that Clark Kent is a fraud and there is no Superman. Since publication of her first novel in 1995, Deb has received the 1997 and 1999 Pikes Peak Romance Writers' Author of the Year Award, three Dorothy

Parker Awards of Excellence, a 1998 Heart of Romance Readers' Choice Award, three Colorado Book Award nominations, ten *Romantic Times BookClub* nominations, and won more than a dozen other Readers' Choice Awards. Many of her novels have earned the *Romantic Times BookClub's* Top Pick rating, and *Publishers Weekly* called her "clever, original, and quick-witted." Also "contorted," but she tries to ignore that part. For more information, visit www.debstover.com.

Jo Beverley

New York Times bestselling author Jo Beverley is one of the most critically acclaimed romance authors writing. She is the author of more than twenty Regency and historical romances and is a member of the Romance Writers of America's Hall of Fame for Regency Romances. Beverley is also on RWA's Honor Roll of best-selling authors, and she has won five RITAs, RWA's premier award. Her science fiction story "The Fruit Picker" was a finalist for the Canadian Casper Award (now the Aurora). Her story in this collection won the Sapphire Award for Best SF Romance, Short Form, of 2004. *Romantic Times* calls her ". . . one of the great names of the genre." *Publishers Weekly* agrees: "Arguably today's most skillful writer of intelligent historical romance . . ." Her Web site is www.jobev.com.

Jennifer Roberson

Jennifer Roberson is an award-winning author who has published twenty-two novels in several different genres, including historical romance and romantic suspense, but she primarily writes fantasy. Her literary agent is on record as saying Jennifer pioneered the romantic fantasy sub-genre beginning in the 1980s with the publication of two critically successful and popular ongoing series, the *Chronicles of the Cheysuli* and the *Sword-Dancer* saga. In 1992 *Lady of the Forest,* the first of two novels featuring Robin Hood and Marian—with an emphasis on Marian's role in the legend—was published to great acclaim. Its equally popular sequel, *Lady of Sherwood,* followed a few years later. And Roberson turned to her Scottish roots with the publication of *Lady of the Glen*, a romantic historical about the documented Massacre of Glencoe in the seventeenth-century Highlands.

In 1996 Jennifer collaborated with two other fantasy authors, Melanie Rawn and Kate Elliott, on *The Golden Key*, a historical fantasy that was a final nominee for 1997's World Fantasy Award. Other awards include *Romantic Times'* Best New Fantasy Author (1984), and, for *Royal Captive* (written as Jennifer O'Green), RT's Best New Historical Romance Author/Lifetime Achievement Award (1988). Roberson has also edited the fantasy anthologies *Out of Avalon*, *Return to Avalon*, and *Highwaymen: Robbers and Rogues*. The short story presented here is a sequel of sorts to her Robin/Marian novels, featuring another legendary individual who has inspired many historical, romance, and fantasy novels. Roberson is currently completing the first volume in a new fantasy series, titled *Karavans*. Her Web site is www.cheysuli.com.

New York Times Bestselling Author

Jo Beverley

MY LADY NOTORIOUS	0-451-20644-4
SOMETHING WICKED	0-451-21378-5
SECRETS OF THE NIGHT	0-451-21158-8
DEVILISH	0-451-19997-9
WINTER FIRE	0-451-21065-4
A MOST UNSUITABLE MAN	0-451-21423-4
THE DRAGON'S BRIDE	0-451-20358-5
THE DEVIL'S HEIRESS	0-451-20254-6
HAZARD	0-451-20580-4
ST. RAVEN	0-451-20807-2
SKYLARK	0-451-21183-9
THE ROGUE'S RETURN	0-451-21788-8
LORD OF MY HEART	0-451-20642-8
DARK CHAMPION	0-451-20766-1
LORD OF MIDNIGHT	0-451-40801-2
FORBIDDEN MAGIC	0-451-20642-8
THREE HEROES	0-451-21200-2